Paper & Ink, Flesh & Blood

Share Your Thoughts

Want to help make *Paper & Ink, Flesh & Blood* a bestselling novel? Consider leaving an honest review of this book on Goodreads, on your personal author website or blog, and anywhere else readers go for recommendations. It's our priority at Hearthstone Press to publish books for readers to enjoy, and our authors appreciate and value your feedback.

Our Southern Fried Guarantee

If you wouldn't enthusiastically recommend one of our books with a 4- or 5-star rating to a friend, then the next story is on us. We believe that much in the stories we're telling. Simply email us at southernfriedkarma@gmail.com.

Paper & Ink, Flesh & Blood

Rita Mace Walston

To Tim, my love, my best friend, my North Star
And to Tante Marel, my own personal Aunt Vieve
And to the books.
Always, to the books.

Part I

One

2019

In retrospect, shooting the horse was probably excessive.

Nowadays there would be repercussions, but thirty years ago, people minded their own business. Drakes Forge was, and still is, a fairly small village. We don't bring the authorities into anything unless absolutely necessary.

Through the thick, wavy glass of the alcove window, I can see snow falling in broad flakes outside, but the electricity, notoriously fickle out here, is still on. I have a good fire going in the fireplace, plenty of wood stacked on the hearth, and an excellent bottle of Bordeaux breathing in the heavy, cut-glass decanter I didn't throw through the window back when I was fighting to hang on to the estate. I can feel the presence of the books on the shelves all around me just as I still feel the absence of my husband in the large leather chair across from me. There's already a foot of snow on the ground outside, and more on the way. I sent my housekeeper home. She lives with her grown daughter and four Corgis down the road in the village, and I know she was nervous about getting stuck here. She left me a pot of Brunswick stew on the stove and a loaf of her bread on the counter. The stew is good, but I may just bring the whole loaf of bread in here to have with the wine. Adele makes the most marvelous bread.

I've decided to use this time to write. I've taken so much from books over the years; it feels time to acknowledge it. I have no intention of actually publishing my memoir, of course. I expect that the statute of limitations has run out and I defy anyone to get me committed at this point of my life, but there's no need to tempt fate. No, no formal publication. But I do want to put to paper, as best I can remember, what happened all those years ago. I feel as though I owe it to the books. When I'm done, I'll tuck the pages away in this library. I doubt anyone will ever find them or, if they stumble across them, take the time to read them. I don't think anyone but me has taken a book from these shelves in nearly twenty years.

I take that back. There is the young man I hired a few years ago to fix up the old cottage. He borrowed *As I Lay Dying* the day I had him for coffee here in the library, and has borrowed other books from time to time. He's a good carpenter and always returns the books without a single dog-eared page or smudge. He likely would read my pages, should he come upon them. I would trust him with my secrets, I think. He has the look of one who can keep secrets. The books sometimes hum when he's here, but they don't speak to me about him. They're helping him keep his own secrets. That's fine. It's as my Great Aunt Genevieve told me all those years ago—books can be fickle. They don't speak on cue nor respond to our desire to have them speak.

But when books do speak, I've learned to pay attention.

Two

1984

It was April 21. The weather was beautiful, which just added to the storm I'd felt building in my chest all day. I would have preferred overcast and gloomy.

I lowered the gun, fairly certain the shot had been heard by the mourners gathered in my home. The stable was large, but not that distant from the house, and the three sets of tall French doors leading from the dining and living rooms onto the bluestone terrace were open to the gentle afternoon breeze.

I stepped over the dead horse and out of the stall, the hem of my black skirt skimming the once-strong neck. I felt the weight of the revolver in my hand, imagined I could still feel the reverberation of the gunshot running up my arm. August had been so proud of that damn horse—all seventeen hands and fourteen hundred pounds of him. Proud that no one could handle him the way he could. That horse had nearly taken a chunk out of my shoulder two years before. Well, this time I'd handled him just fine.

I heard the other horses, agitated in their stalls, though everything sounded muffled since I'd pulled the trigger. The smell of cordite was familiar to them, the explosion of sound that always preceded it, the scent of blood that frequently followed. These were horses ridden to the hunt, trained to stand placid as August and others brought down prey, bearing the carcasses back from the field. It wasn't the sound and smell of death that was causing my mare and the others to whinny and kick against the heavy, scarred wood of the stalls, shifting restlessly over straw that had been changed just earlier that morning. It was because the sound of the gun, the smell of the cordite that mingled in the air with the tang of fresh blood, was here, instead of out in the fields and woods and up the slopes of the ridge where it belonged. I didn't comfort them, didn't pause to stroke the deep brown velvet nose of my mare. I just didn't have it in me to comfort anything or anyone, at the moment. Besides, I had spatters of blood on my hands that might further spook the horses and I wanted to put the gun away. There were still five bullets in it, and shooting the horse that had been an accessory to my husband's death hadn't given me the release I'd expected. I still felt the storm in my chest, held back only by the pain I felt in my sternum, the feeling of bruised bone. But there was no visible mark, nothing to be detected with stethoscope or other medical instrument. And so the doctor had told me, in what I'm sure he thought was a calming voice, that the sternum pain was all in my head. Just recalling his patronizing tone reinforced that it really was best I put the gun away. Our stable manager and horse trainer, Grant Brodigan, was in the house with the rest of the mourners. The horses would calm when he came to investigate the sound of the gunshot.

I took the gun to the tack room, locked it in the metal box that held petty cash, and pocketed the key. I'd clean it later; take it back to my bedroom after everyone was gone. If I walked into the house with it now, likely that fool on the other horse—what was his name? Pritchard? Packard?—would break the furniture or himself in his hurry to exit the premises. The man had been so damn apologetic when he'd approached me after the funeral to say how sorry, how very *very* sorry he was about August's accident. He'd stressed the word accident. Repeated it several times as he noted how awful it was when these things happened, as they did, he'd said, from time to time. I had smiled at him—at least I think it was a smile; it seemed to startle him—and focused on keeping my eyes dry and steady. Idiot. It wasn't his fault my husband was dead. Some might see it that way, but I knew better.

I had seen August fall.

It was during the Owners Race of the first point-to-point of the season, just after the water obstacle on the third turn. I'd had the binoculars up to my eyes, had been watching his black and gold riding helmet every time it had reappeared from behind a stand of trees or crested yet another of the rolling hills. I hadn't been watching his hands. It's unlikely I would have been able to see them anyway, amidst all the riders. So I couldn't say how or why he fell. I just saw his helmet suddenly disappear, his horse continuing without him. And then I saw him on the ground. His body jerked and spasmed when another horse, trailing the pack by a couple of lengths, ran over him.

And in that moment, a flash of light hit my eyes and I felt an unbelievable pressure on my chest. I heard screams around me, and through the light that made everything look gold I saw Grant and a few other men vault the rail to run to where August lay still in the hoof-churned turf. The pressure suddenly lifted, went away, taking the golden light, my breath, and something torn from inside me with it. I realized I was clutching the rail, wooden splinters digging into my hands.

I felt my knees buckle but I clutched the rail tighter and stayed upright. And I knew.

I'd just felt August's soul leave.

He'd taken a piece of my own with it.

The doctor said later that August's neck had broken in the fall; that it was either the fall that had killed him or perhaps a massive heart attack causing the fall, but definitely not the weight of fourteen hundred pounds of horse traveling down one sleek leg into the hoof that had planted squarely on my husband's sternum.

I had declined an autopsy. Dead was dead, I'd said, whether it had come from a heart attack, the fall, or being run over by a horse. An autopsy wouldn't change anything. The coroner had agreed. There had been plenty of witnesses to the accident; the Owners Race always drew a crowd at the rails.

I was told the mortuary had done a fine job, given the circumstances. But don't let anyone ever tell you different: a body drained of its essence and filled with formaldehyde does not look like a person sleeping, I don't care how expertly the airbrushing and makeup are applied. I had taken one look at the mannequin they had said was my husband and told them it would be a closed-casket funeral. Following the graveside service, everyone had come back to Lockeswood. I had stayed with my guests as long as I could stand it before climbing the stairs to fetch the gun from the nightstand on August's side of the bed and going out to the stable.

I watched the blood swirl and sluice away as I washed my hands in the stable's deep work sink. I thought of Lady Macbeth as I washed, but I didn't fear any sort of haunting residue. Lady Macbeth had plotted murder; had spiraled later into madness. I had executed justice. There was a difference. And I knew she wouldn't speak to me from the book in the library anyway. That wasn't how it worked. Which usually disappointed me, but in this case . . . Well, let's just say I didn't want her opinion on the matter.

The water was cold and numbed my fingers. I thought of the day of the horse race. I remembered August had looked tired, but had he rubbed his left arm? Surely I'd recall if he had—would have done something other than kiss him before he mounted Rockefeller, the horse now sprawled with a sizable hole in its head. He'd held my face between his hands and kissed me gently, tenderly. Then he'd mounted the horse and looked down at me. What had that expression on his face been?

Watching him through the binoculars on that third turn, I had been focused on his helmet, hoping to get the right angle to see his face, to see joy on it. The joy of the race, of the competition. Riding—and especially riding in a point-to-point—was his escape from all the other pressures, he'd told me so often.

So of course he hadn't purposely let go of the reins.

Of course not.

I felt a sudden surge in my gut and leaned over the sink, coughing up bile, since there was nothing in my stomach. The strain made my sternum ache and threaten to breach, which would let loose the storm held at bay in my chest. I gripped the metal sides of the sink and clenched my eyes shut. Now was not the time to fall apart. I could do that later, privately. Grant would walk into the stable any minute. One word of solicitude from him, one look of concern, would be my undoing. I needed to focus.

I needed the storm to keep me from dissolving into my grief, but I needed it contained.

I wasn't quite sure yet who or what was to blame for taking August from me, how the blame should be apportioned. The bay Thoroughbred had been a start. Much as it twisted my insides to contemplate, I had to consider that a good part of the blame might rest with August himself. Had it truly been just an accident? Was it hubris August overconfident that he could handle the horse? His father had died in a riding accident, with whispers afterward that maybe it hadn't been an accident. Was history repeating itself? If so, was there anyone else involved?

If Aunt Genevieve were here, she'd already have a mental list of a half dozen books that might have something to say on the matter. She would expect me to do the same.

I turned off the water and, drying my hands on the rough towel that hung next to the sink, glanced across the room at the shelf above the desk where the petty cash box with the gun inside sat center stage. As ever, I could feel the presence of the books I kept there, although with no one in the stable other than me, they were silent. I should have brought some of them to the point-to-point. Maybe one would have spoken a clue that would have let me know not to let August get on the horse. Then again, I was considered eccentric enough without showing up at the rail with a stack of novels. I'd promised August a few years before to limit the "book toting" to events and occasions where it didn't seem entirely out of place. His and my definition of "out of place" had not always matched.

I checked again to make sure the petty cash box was locked, and I left the stable. I heard a hoof bang impatiently against the wall as I shut the door behind me. My hearing was almost back to normal.

GRANT MET ME halfway across the lawn on my way back to the house. He was wearing a dark suit and a relieved expression. It occurred to me that the last time I'd seen him in a suit had been at my wedding; that he was relieved because he hadn't been sure I'd walk out of the stable.

That thought led me to picture the people currently in my house, the groupings and cliques that form when an event draws together those who otherwise are unlikely to ever associate with one another. I imagined Trey Janus and the handful of August's colleagues from the investment firm who'd come to pay their respects. At the sound of the gunshot, would they perhaps have paused in their appreciation of the deceased's finest single malt? Which one of them would have been the first to propose odds? Which would look disappointed, a wager lost, when I crossed over the bluestone terrace and came through the French doors, accompanied by the mild April breeze, the dark velvet of my black sleeves masking the horse's blood?

The two of us stood there a moment, looking at one another.

"I never liked that horse anyway," said Grant.

He walked past me, and I knew he would settle things in the stable. I was grateful for his calm. I didn't say anything; didn't watch him go. I continued on to the house. Grant was my Jake Barnes. *"Isn't it pretty to think so?"* I'd heard *The Sun Also Rises* tell me years ago when August, Grant, and I had sat in the library to toast August's first Owners Race win. It was one of only two times a book ever spoke to me about Grant, and I remember it startled me and I spilled some of my red wine on the rug. I can still find that spot, even though it blends with the pattern. Even after I reread the book, that line the very last, it took me a while to acclimate myself to what that particular passage of Hemingway's meant, what it said about Grant's perception of me.

I walked through the middle set of French doors, the storm still in my chest, feeding me. I kept my head high, my eyes dry. I knew I likely looked cold and unsympathetic and I didn't care. I had my hair pulled back into a tight chignon, and I was wearing little makeup and a Forties-era black dress August and I had found on an antiquing foray. About half of the people in the room had known August before we'd married almost a decade before. He had been nearly twenty years older than me, and more than a few of them thought he'd robbed the cradle, that I'd married him for his money. I felt most of the people in our home were there to honor August, rather than in support of his widow. Maybe that was unfair, a harsh assessment, I chided myself as I looked around the room, picking out familiar, concerned faces. But August had been the engaging, gregarious one. He'd been bigger than life, six foot three with a full head of hair even in his fifties. Blue eyes that had crinkled at the corners when he'd smiled, which he'd done a lot. He'd had a laugh that had often ended on a hiccup, which had startled people who hadn't known him because it hadn't been what they'd expected to come out of such a broad chest. I, by comparison, was considered eccentric. Very pretty, charming in her own way, and a good horsewoman, I'd overhead at one party, "but she is very peculiar when it comes to books . . . "

The tone of the room was different than when I'd left, the conversation more of a buzz than a hum. Looks now darted my way, heads leaned toward one another. Trey Janus was across the room, standing, as he had been when I'd left, with the cluster of colleagues from the investment firm. He saw me, and a hint of a smile touched his lips. He raised his glass slightly, a toast to the widow of his childhood friend and business partner. Wager won or lost? I wondered. I felt the storm swell in my chest, and I pulled my shoulders back to give it more space so it wouldn't force its way out of my body.

I was glad I'd left the Smith & Wesson locked away in the tack room.

Three

1952

When I was four years old, I became convinced I had a magic book.

It was *The Velveteen Rabbit*, and its cover was worn and some of the pages a bit foxed since it had been my mother's favorite book before it had come to be mine. The summer day had been unusually sultry, and shortly before the sun started to sink, the storm clouds that had been gathering in the west billowed out like rising bread dough. Mother ran out to take the laundry off the clothesline. My sundresses jerking and turning in the wind reminded me of marionettes, except these puppets had no heads or legs or arms. It was a little spooky, and I turned my gaze away just in time to see the sheet my mother was unpinning from the line press itself against the length of her, against her face. It seemed like it was trying to suffocate her. The bottom edges flapped around her calves as though looking to further envelop her, encase her in an airless cocoon.

I yelled and ran out of the house, the screen door slamming behind me, past the ghost marionettes and to the sheet that was trying to kill my mother. The whole sky was dark by then, and big splats of rain started to fall, hitting my head as though to distract me. By the time I reached Mother, she had subdued the sheet and was bending to stuff it into the clothesbasket. She took one look at my face, glanced at the sky, then gathered me up in her arms and quick-stepped back to the house, leaving the killer sheet and ghost marionettes to fend for themselves.

It was a loud storm, and when Mother took me upstairs to change into dry clothes, she brought the big camping lantern with us that we kept in the laundry room. It wasn't long before I was curled up next to her in my bed as she read to me, transporting us to a playroom where the wise Skin Horse taught the Velveteen Rabbit about what is real.

"'Does it hurt?' asked Rabbit," my mother read, and I heard another voice, a higher-pitched voice, very quietly asking the same question along with her.

I looked around my bedroom, but it was just the two of us. Mother lounged next to me, long legs crossed at the ankles, waves of damp brunette hair spilling over her shoulders, the book with its worn cloth cover held in one hand, leaving the other free to stroke my towel-dried hair and turn the pages.

"'Sometimes,' said the Skin Horse," she read. "'When you are Real you don't mind being hurt.'"

Again a harmony of voices, this new one lower, slightly gravelly but barely above a whisper, blending this new with my mother's. I looked from the printed page up at her, but she continued reading, not giving any indication that she heard anything other than the melody of her own voice. The other voices didn't scare me. They sounded warm and loving, just like hers.

Outside, the rain continued to beat against the windows of my corner bedroom, hard torrents trying to break the glass. There was still the occasional flash, but the thunder was now a growl rather than a roar. My bedside lamp flickered several times and then went out. Mother leaned over and deftly lit the camping lantern, and my room was once again bathed in a soft glow of light. I felt safe leaning against Mother, the sound of her voice and the feel of her stroking hand shielding me from the storm.

She continued to read the story, but I didn't hear the other voices again that evening. In the morning, I held *The Velveteen Rabbit* on my lap, my finger tracing the gilt letters on the worn cover. It was a magic book, I decided. And if I could just learn to read, I could figure out how to unlock its magic. I didn't know why Mother hadn't heard the book speak, but that was just part of the magic, I concluded. I imagined having conversations with Velveteen Rabbit and Skin Horse. I could tell Skin Horse that I believed he was Real, too.

It seemed very exciting and not at all complicated.

Four

1958

In fifth grade, it became complicated.

I had become a voracious reader. In first grade, I had whipped through the Dick and Jane primers, far outpacing my classmates. I was motivated, certain that as soon as I had the skill to read for myself the many, many books my parents read to me at bedtime and whenever else I could coax them to do it, I would once again hear *The Velveteen Rabbit* speak. Somehow I had decided it was a magic I had to *earn*. The book had spoken to me that stormy night in order to show me a goal—to let me know what was within my reach if I just accomplished my task. It was like so many of the fairy tales (read mostly by Mother) and stories of derring-do and perseverance (read mostly by Papa)— there were obstacles to overcome, feats to accomplish, and a worthiness to be proven before the reward would be bestowed.

I had mimicked my parents and created a small library in my bedroom, categorizing the growing collection according to my own special system. I had dozens of books, at least half of which had been sent to me by Great Aunt Genevieve. This was the 1950s, when people still wrote letters. Long distance tele-phone calls were obscenely expensive, let alone international calls between Virginia and Quebec City, and Papa had written to his favorite aunt about my mania for reading. On one shelf to the left, I had a neat row of Beatrix Potter, the short green spines grouped together. On the right side of that same shelf, I had the cherished books that I had outgrown: *Curious George*, *The*

Story of Ferdinand, Caps for Sale, and *Mike Mulligan and His Steam Shovel,* among others. On another shelf, I kept the books that I read and reread: *The Secret Garden, The Boxcar Children, Charlotte's Web,* and *Half Magic.* On a lower shelf were books that had started out a challenge, but were becoming less so: *The Swiss Family Robinson, The Adventures of Tom Sawyer,* and *Animal Farm.* (Great Aunt Genevieve had included a note in cursive with these that had said I would grow into them.) My parents were reluctant to let me keep *The Velveteen Rabbit* in my room. It was valuable, I was told, not a book to be left outside or spread facedown, putting strain on the spine. So it wasn't officially part of my library, but it did spend quite a bit of time on my bedside table, snuck from its special place on Mother's dresser. I glanced at it frequently while reading other books, waiting for it to again demonstrate its magic—out of jealousy, perhaps.

WE LIVED IN a small town in Virginia, in an old, two-story house a few blocks off Main Street. It had long casement windows of small square panes of glass, tall ceilings, and floors made of wide planks of polished wood. There was even a butler's pantry, where Mother stored the pears, peaches, cucumbers, beans, to-matoes, and other fruits and vegetables she canned every year. The house had belonged to her aunt and uncle and their three sons. She had been close to them growing up, but I'd never met them. One of the sons had been killed by a car while riding his bicycle when he was thirteen. The other two had died in the War. Aunt Trudy had taken to her bed when she'd gotten the news and had never gotten out of it. The doctor had said she'd always had a weak heart—Mother had said it had simply broken when she'd learned her last child had died on an atoll in the Pacific Ocean. Uncle Owen had lived to hear that we had beaten the Japanese, but he'd died suddenly while mowing the lawn on a brutally hot August day a couple of summers later. Mother had inherited the house, and she and Papa had moved in. They had still been newlyweds; they had met at a USO Club where she had been volunteering. I was born in December 1948, the first and last child my parents would have.

It wasn't common to be an only child in those years following the War. The school I attended was new, in fact; built to accommodate all the children born in and around the year I was. By the time I was ten years old in 1958, my place in the pecking order at school and in our neighborhood was pretty much established—and it wasn't high. I was tall and gangly. My hair, the same color as Mother's but not as tame as hers, tended toward frizzy in Virginia's humid air. I'd had books instead of brothers and sisters, so I hadn't adequately learned the social survival skills that seemed to come so easily to my classmates. Plus, I lived in the house where *everybody had died* in a span of six years—and there were a lot of people in my neighborhood who still remembered Aunt Trudy and Uncle Owen and the three boys who had played and laughed and pulled pranks (mostly harmless) and then had grown up to die before ever leaving their teenage years.

BY FIFTH GRADE, lots of books talked to me. But they never spoke when I was alone, which was frustrating, since that was when I would have been able to concentrate on what they were saying instead of having to divide my attention between the book and whoever happened to be in the room with me—frequently a teacher and lots of classmates. My grades were good, but I had a number of notes sent home, starting in first grade, about my propensity to "let my mind wander." I couldn't help it. Around the time midway through first grade that I'd mastered being able to read a "real" book by myself—one with a storyline and no pictures—I'd started to hear voices from the shelves. Often there were four or five voices all talking at the same time, if there were multiple copies of the same book—which is frequently the case in a classroom. It was distracting. My teachers thought I was daydreaming and not paying attention to their instruction. Well, in all honesty, I often wasn't paying attention to them. But I wasn't daydreaming. I was trying to figure out which book was saying what. I tried to answer them, thinking responses at them, like telepathy. But the books ignored me, no matter what I did. It was always a one-sided conversation, them prattling on, a near-constant noise in my head.

I devised a plan that hopefully would break through the veil that kept books from hearing me the way I could hear them. I'd have to do it in school, since the books in my bedroom never spoke to me. A classroom would provide the most privacy, if I timed it right. The school library, though, had more different books, and so increased the chances my plan would work. Finding privacy there would be a bit more challenging. I was convinced I was on the right track and determined to try both locations, if necessary.

My plan turned out to be a very bad idea.

"Margaux? Who are you taking to?"

Breath left my body, and I felt my face redden at the voice, even before I lifted it to see Mrs. Harrington standing in the doorway of her classroom, Georgia Pillard just to the left and behind her.

It was lunchtime. Teachers were supposed to be in the teachers' lounge, that hallowed ground forbidden to students. Every student was supposed to be in the large, echoing cafeteria, clattering trays of single servings of undefinable pressed meat and gluey mashed potatoes, limp green-gray beans, and a slurry of applesauce on the side. Those without trays would be elbow-deep into brown paper bags lovingly packed by stay-at-home moms— by fifth grade we were all far too cool to carry around metal lunchboxes. As each student completed the line, whether to get a full lunch or just the small carton of milk that we were repeatedly instructed was absolutely necessary to healthy bone growth, most would lift their heads, like deer scenting the wind. Avoid the wolves; find the herd. Off they'd go—in ones, twos, sometimes threes—to search out their own kind.

Except the wolves of course.

They also completed the lunch line, but when they exited, they knew exactly where they were going. Their eyes would scan the room, too, but for prey, on their way to specific varnished wooden benches secured to varnished wooden tables that they had decreed as theirs. Or, which was rather new, to pose or preen to the other wolves on their way.

Georgia Pillard was a wolf. She didn't always hunt for prey; she wasn't actually one of the mean, hungry ones. We'd been friends, sort of, early in elementary school. But now, on the brink of junior high, the stakes had risen. I wasn't sure how or when or why, but it was different. Maybe if I'd had an older sister or brother, or even cousins, they could have told me. But Georgia was one of the girls who knew exactly where she would eat lunch each day, and with whom. She frequently preened on her way to her selected spot that was always open when she got there. But she didn't seem ridiculous when she did it, the way so many of the other girls appeared to me.

I watched her, sometimes, out of the corner of my eye, from my own seat among the deer and other unaligned, lesser animals of prey. Georgia could walk and talk and preen all at the same time. Her chin and lashes would lower just a bit as her lips quirked upward, her head tilting slightly if she deigned to notice one of the posing boy wolves; she would toss her long, flowing, blond hair in dismissal if she chose to communicate that she didn't notice, not really. I'd practiced a few times at home in front of the long mirror in Mother and Papa's bedroom. I'd given it up as a lost cause pretty quickly. I'd never be a wolf. I wasn't a deer, but I refused to relegate myself to the status of unaligned prey.

I didn't know what I was.

Other than discovered, in that excruciating moment as my teacher and Georgia stood in the classroom doorway looking at me. "Margaux?" Mrs. Harrington repeated. Her eyes scanned the scene around me. I'd taken all twenty-six classroom copies of *The Last of the Mohicans* off the low bookcase shelf at the back of the classroom and stacked them around me in a circle, the twenty-sixth copy in my lap. I'd been leaning over it, chanting, whispering, imploring it to speak to me as it had every day that week as my classmates had read aloud—agonizingly slowly—the story of Magua, Cora, Alice, Hawkeye, and the others who were each so tangled with one another and America's unfolding history, and yet so alone.

"Margaux, what are you doing?" Mrs. Harrington's voice lost its incredulity and instead had the same tone it'd had when she'd called on me to read earlier that morning. I'd scrambled to find where to start, since I had been skimming ahead, bored with the tired, uninspired, droning voices of my classmates. The book had been talking to me, in multiple voices from multiple desks around the classroom—all at the same time—and I'd been trying to find among the pages who was saying what. If I could just read it all, I'd thought, as fast as I could—swallow it whole— the book might give me time to digest it, understand why it was barraging me from all sides. Which had led me to this strategy. With everyone at lunch—or so I'd thought—I could spend time with the books to inveigle them to tell me *why*? Why did they insist on all talking at once? And why talk to me at all when they apparently had absolutely no interest in having a conversation? Why talk *at* me instead of *with* me?

Why was this happening only to me?

I knew that was likely to be a version of my teacher's next question.

I shifted my eyes from hers, buying time. And noticed something interesting. Georgia Pillard glanced away when my eyes met hers. She shifted slightly, as though to be hidden behind our teacher.

She doesn't want to be here, I thought. And that couldn't possibly be because she doesn't want to embarrass me. It dawned on me. She doesn't want me to embarrass *her*.

I tilted my head, mimicking, a little bit, what I had practiced in front of Mother's mirror.

"Hello, Georgia," I said.

Mrs. Harrington glanced over her shoulder. Seemed to remember the girl she'd brought with her.

"Never mind," she said brusquely. "Margaux, put those books back on the shelf immediately."

I did as I was told.

But there were twenty-six of them. I knew; I'd counted. There's only so fast a person can carry and shelve twenty-six books.

I heard an impatient intake and exhalation of breath from Mrs. Harrington.

"Georgia, would you mind helping her? Just to quicken things a bit?"

I didn't look at Georgia when she knelt beside me. The books were blessedly silent. I could feel the pressure of her pent-up breath, caught the scent of an overly flowery perfume as we stacked the worn, hardback copies, the old cloth rasping against our young hands as we shelved them where they would wait for students to manhandle and dogear their pages and drone through their words.

"If you ever tell anyone that I was here for tutoring, I will make your life a living hell," Georgia whispered in a flat voice.

She could do it. She hadn't, yet. She wasn't that kind of wolf.
But she could be. I just nodded.

The books shelved, I left without looking at either of them.

I never told a soul that Georgia Pillard needed special tutoring with Mrs. Harrington.

But it became apparent that she thought I had.

Five

It was lunchtime again, a couple of weeks since the disaster with *The Last of the Mohicans*. The class had finally finished droning through it. We were now reading *Where the Red Fern Grows*. I'd never read it, which helped in the classroom, but I had a foreboding of sadness to come. I didn't have a friend at school to confide in about it.

Well, not one that would be eating lunch, anyway.

Instead, I snuck out of the cafeteria to the library. I'd been thwarted in the classroom, but this could be my opportunity to try out the library aspect of my plan. The new librarian, Miss Monroe, would likely be away having her own lunch in the teachers' lounge. I knew from long experience that the library doors were rarely locked. I snuck down the hall, knowing I was headed in the opposite direction of the girls' bathroom and so I'd have no good excuse for leaving the cafeteria. Reaching the library's double doors, I opened one with authority and stepped through, glad to be out of the exposure of the hallway, ready with a lie if Miss Monroe or someone else were there to challenge me.

The large room appeared empty of other people, light streaming in from long windows on one side to shine with benediction on more books than I'd be able to read before moving on to junior high. The bookshelves didn't go all the way up to the ceiling, the way the shelves in Papa's office did, but there were more of them, evenly spaced in rows that had often provided me sanctuary. If I tiptoed, I could reach books on the top shelf. There were small wooden stools scattered around for those who needed one, and the shelves in the fiction section were shorter. Miss Monroe called the rows and rows of bookshelves "the stacks," and I'd begun to do the same. So many stacks of books, far tidier than the piles in my room beside my bed and on my window seat. Our school library was carpeted—only the office and the teachers' lounge also had such a luxury. The carpet was worn and had more than a few suspect stains, but it contributed to the overall hush I associated with libraries. There were tables for reading, and a section set aside with big pillows on the floor. That section was new this year. A lot of the teachers didn't approve, but Miss Monroe had just graduated from college, hired when Mrs. Galloway had retired, and I'd heard when the teachers' lounge door was left open that Principal Blocke was giving her some leeway to try new things. I loved the smell of libraries, but I was most comfortable in them when I was alone, or nearly alone. The shelves were quieter then.

I nonchalantly checked the stacks, ducked my head into Miss Monroe's small office, chock full of books and folders. I felt a sudden urge to step inside, look at the titles. What did Miss Monroe like to read?

I glanced at the big moon-faced clock on the wall above the library doors. I only had twenty minutes before the bell would ring, signaling the end of lunch, and another five before I'd be expected back in Mrs. Harrington's classroom.

Twenty-three minutes with the library all to myself.

I pulled a number of my favorite books from the shelves, looked for a secluded stack where I didn't think anyone would happen to venture if they dropped by the library, not even Miss Monroe. The 800s seemed pretty safe. I sat on the floor and tucked the books close around me. Maybe having them actually *touch* me would make a difference.

I'd been holding *Half Magic* in my lap and talking to it in low tones, thinking at least one of the children in the book would identify with me trying to connect, when I heard giggles and shushes. I froze, keeping my eyes on the page in front of me. Martha had just made her wish and, not yet understanding how the magic worked, had only *half*-disappeared. She was dismayed. So was I. I heartily double-wished that I could be in the book with her. I knew I could help her out of her predicament. She clearly wasn't able to help me out of mine.

More giggles, more shushing.

I felt my cheeks redden, glad the fall of my hair hid them from whoever was watching me over the tops of the books one stack over. I snuck a sideways glance. I thought I recognized Georgia Pillard and the two or three girls who had lately hovered around her, enhancing her glow of popularity while at the same time trying to swallow it for their own in gaping, grasping gulps.

Georgia wasn't truly a wolf, I reminded myself. She liked to play a role. To preen.

I will make your life a living hell.

But I hadn't told anyone.

I hadn't.

There was no easy way out of this. I set *Half Magic* aside, stood up, and walked out of the library. I kept my face emotionless and my chin up. Didn't look at the girls who evidently had decided to follow me, spy on me, were now openly laughing at me, making fun of me and books. I ignored them. Told myself they didn't matter.

I kept my pace steady. Heard their mocking voices and laughter.

"She has an invisible friend!"

"Margaux, what's your invisible friend's name?"

"She has to have an invisible friend—otherwise she wouldn't have any friends at all!"

I pushed open both doors, one hand firmly on each—anger warring with embarrassment, anger winning by just a little bit—and walked through them down the middle. And then the doors swung shut behind me. I didn't hear anything. I stood alone in the hallway. I headed toward my classroom. I was grateful the girls had stayed in the library instead of following me to class with their taunts and laughter.

I shouldn't have been.

I'd left *Half Magic* behind.

That was a mistake.

I DIDN'T TYPICALLY like to stand up in front of a group of people and talk, but I was excited about this assignment. Everyone was to choose a poem—any poem—to recite in front of the class. Mrs. Harrington had spent a lot of time reciting examples, talking about cadence, how a poem could tell a story, evoke a mood, recall history. It interested me because I'd never spent a lot of time with poetry. It didn't talk to me, but maybe that was because I hadn't spent a lot of time with it. She'd read to us "The Spider and the Fly," and I'd been hooked. Though I was a bit wary of Mrs. Harrington after that. She'd read the spider part just a little too well.

I practiced in front of my mirror and, after I got the nerve, in front of Mother and Papa. After all, Papa had said, if you're going to recite in front of an audience, it can't hurt to practice first with a small audience who loves you. I'd chosen "A Bird Came Down the Walk" by Emily Dickinson because it reminded me of times spent with Mother in her garden.

The big day came, and I felt confident. Mrs. Harrington had posted a list of suggested poems, and so there were more than a few recitations of "Being Brave at Night" by the boys, because poetry was acceptable when it included the word "ain't," which Mrs. Harrington didn't usually allow in speech or papers. She cut off Gerald Smolinski before he got to the last line of his limerick, which Mrs. Harrington agreed was technically a poem but said was not appropriate for the classroom, even if it was written by his uncle. A number of the girls read "I'd Love to Be a Fairy's Child," which didn't surprise me. The intensity of Betsy Fruebecker reciting "Paul Revere's Ride"—the whole thing from memory!—made me think I'd like to get to know her better. Of course, after what happened when I recited my poem, she didn't want anything to do with me. Georgia recited "The Adventures of Isabel" and did it really well. She was like a miniature Mrs. Harrington, a born actress. Even the boys in our class seemed more in awe of her than usual as she calmly folded her paper and took her seat, tossing her blond hair over her shoulder and accepting the enthusiastic clapping as her due.

And then it was my turn.

I walked to the front of the class, my paper with the words of Emily Dickinson's poem in hand, though I didn't really need it. I'd practiced again in front of my mirror after making notes of Mother and Papa's suggestions on inflection, so the flutters in my stomach were more from nervous excitement than stage fright. I looked to Mrs. Harrington, who smiled and nodded. I began.

"A Bird, came down the Walk;
  He did not know I saw –
  He bit an Angle Worm in halves
  And ate the fellow, raw."

It was then I felt the first paper airplane hit my cheek. There was a muffled snort. I ignored both.

"And then, he drank a Dew
  From a convenient Grass –
  And then hopped sidewise to the Wall
  To let a Beetle—"

A paper airplane hit me in the mouth, cutting off my phrase, at the same time another hit my forehead and a third my throat. I glanced at Mrs. Harrington, ignoring the source of the assault.

She had her pen poised and was focused on her notes—about my performance, I hoped—and hadn't seen. I swallowed and picked up where I'd left off.

"To let a Beetle pass.

He glanced with rapid eyes

That hurried all abroad—

They looked like frightened Beads, I thought,

He stirred his Velvet Head

Like one in danger, Cautious"

I didn't get any further. The torrent came.

Paper airplanes soared from all over the classroom, all aimed at me. I felt like Gulliver facing the Lilliputians. I swatted at them, knocking them to the floor, feeling others hit me, not hurting, except for the sting of them being thrown at all. Mrs. Harrington finally noticed I'd stopped talking amid an undertone of muffled giggles and snorts.

"Enough!" I heard her commanding voice from the desk. Several final paper airplanes made their landing, one sliding in front of my feet. I looked down at it, rather than at anyone in the room.

And then I saw.

It was a page ripped out of *Half Magic*.

They'd torn apart the book.

They'd dismembered it.

They'd killed it.

Because I'd been reading it. And talking to it.

And then had left it behind.

I dropped to the floor, gathering up the pages, clutching them against my chest with one hand as I scraped the floor, pulling the rest toward me with my other hand. There were so many pages, scattered everywhere. I scrambled on my hands and knees, trying to collect them all. Some were neatly torn; others had ragged edges, sentences and paragraphs ripped with disregard from their binding. Jane, Mark, Katherine, and Martha pulled apart, a family, a story, eviscerated, separated, no way to put it back together.

I heard a whimpering, choking sound, and only when I felt a hand on my shoulder and heard a deep, growled denial did I realize the sounds were coming from me. Hands grasped my upper arms more firmly and I was lifted to my feet, pages cradled in my arms and in clenched hands pressed against my chest as others slipped from my grasp to join their still neatly folded companions on the linoleum floor. Mrs. Harrington led me from the room.

I STAYED HOME the next couple of days. I didn't want to go anywhere—certainly not back to school—and Mother didn't make me.

I didn't read or visit with any of my books. I think it was the longest period of time without a book in my hands since I'd been given one to hold before I could even read. I didn't feel I deserved them. I was tainted. I'd betrayed them. They would know. Somehow they would know.

And now they'd never talk to me.

And they didn't, those two days that I stayed mostly in my room, watching them on my shelves, stacked on my window seat, knowing they were watching me.

None of us talking.

Six

I have no idea if anyone in my class was ever reprimanded for what they did, but I sure dealt with repercussions. Someone at the school—probably Mrs. Harrington—got Mother worried enough that she decided I needed to see a psychologist.

Papa didn't agree. But he didn't veto Mother either, and so to the psychologist I went.

The psychologist was a woman. She was petite and had reading glasses that she wore on a chain of colored glass beads around her neck. She had a soft voice, kind eyes, and was very nice.

I lied to her, of course. The very fact that I was sitting in a psychologist's office—sent there by my mother on the recommendation of my teacher—confirmed that hearing books and wanting to have a conversation with them wasn't normal. It was weird and maybe even meant I was crazy.

Weird makes people uncomfortable.

Crazy makes them send you to a mental hospital.

Sitting that first time in the psychologist's waiting room with Mother, I remembered a sunny June day a couple of years before. I'd been helping Mother in her garden when she'd drifted off to a "Yoohoo!" from one of the neighbors. Papa called them "fence klatsches" and said they were like a telegraph from backyard to backyard and better than the local newspaper for learning what was going on around town. Maybe so, but Papa still read the paper every evening, even after hearing most of the news over dinner from fence klatsches Mother had had with the neighbors on either side and behind us. Mrs. Bradford tended to be loud, and among her repeated compliments of Mother's garden that day—I know she was hoping for some strawberries—I heard her say that maybe Aunt Trudy would still be alive if Uncle Owen had sent her to a mental hospital after news of the first son's death in the War had come.

I didn't mind so much being considered weird. It was what differentiated me from the deer and unaligned prey.

But I didn't want anyone thinking I was crazy.

Although that was why I was sitting in this waiting room, right?

So, for the psychologist, I made up a story about wanting to be an actress. An actress had to be able to take on many different roles, and since so many movies were drawn from books, I needed to *envelop* myself in art to truly access my acting talent. Okay, I admit, I was channeling Georgia more than a bit when I described this. If I could get this psychologist to think that I was just some overly dramatic fifth-grader, that would be far better than her thinking I needed to be sent away to a mental institution. I tossed my hair as I'd seen Georgia do and stressed that this was *acting*, not *pretending*, which was childish. I was very sincere about it all.

She took a lot of notes.

She asked a lot of questions.

I spent six sessions, one a week for six weeks, exploring with the psychologist my feelings about growing up, about our house, our family, my school. I think I was really good at guarding what had happened at school, although I have to say I liked that she smiled, her eyes on her notepad, when I, feeling more comfortable by our fourth visit or so, told her about the wolves and the deer and the unaligned prey.

She really latched on to the acting versus pretending thing. Which was fine. We even talked about my feelings about living in the bedroom whose last occupant had died before he'd grown up. (My bedroom had belonged to Howard, the boy who had been killed while riding his bicycle.) We spent two whole sessions on that topic. After the sixth visit, Mother took me to the paint store and I got to pick out colors. She painted my room for me; butter yellow for the walls, spring green for my bookshelves, and a fresh coat of white for the window frames and ceiling. It was lovely, and I didn't have to go back to the psychologist again.

After that, I did my best to tune out the books while I was at school and was mostly successful. I felt guilty about it. They'd obviously forgiven me. They were talking again, and here I was ignoring them. But I couldn't risk trying to find an opportune moment to explain it to them.

As always, none of the books in my bedroom talked to me when I was there by myself, which was most of the time.

I focused on trying to be normal, to fit in.

I didn't go to the school library unless someone made me. It was rare that someone made me.

I'm sure *that's* in my "permanent file" somewhere.

Thankfully, there were always kids in school who had either just recently moved to the village or who were not part of the "in" crowd either. I didn't have any close friends, but I could eat lunch without feeling like a pariah.

I never became a deer. I like to think I helped at least a couple of others avoid becoming unaligned prey.

I'd already been prey. Not unaligned. Very specific prey. And yet here I was: whole. Unconsumed. Wolves, deer, unaligned prey. I'd made up those categories; hadn't fit myself into any of them. There was more than just me in this non-category. So what should I call it?

I never decided.

Never gave it a name.

That made me smile, sometimes unexpectedly, sitting in the cafeteria with the brown paper bag lunch Mother had packed for me, as the school year went on.

I continued to read, often while sitting high in the huge beech tree at the far end of our backyard. It had large spreading branches, and I used an old rope and bucket I found in the garden shed and a brick I pried up from one edge of the walkway to the garage to make a pulley system so I could get my books up in the tree without having to hold them or tuck them into my shirt while climbing. There was one particular branch that was so wide it seemed slightly flat along the top, growing out perpendicular to the smooth trunk of the tree. Here I would settle myself, book retrieved from the bucket, hidden by the leaves. I mastered *The Swiss Family Robinson* and moved on to *Pride and Prejudice* and *Treasure Island*, which had come together in a package from Great Aunt Genevieve and seemed an odd combination. Both were tough reads.

I didn't remember my great aunt, although I was told she'd visited when I'd been three years old. Papa's mother had died when he'd been ten, and I knew Great Aunt Genevieve had moved in to help take care of Papa and his younger brother, Matthew.

It was almost a year after the sessions with the psychologist had ended that Papa told me Great Aunt Genevieve was coming for a month-long visit. People didn't travel distances so frequently and as easily as they do now, so when they did travel, they tended to stay long enough to make it worthwhile.

"You remind me so much of her," he said. "I don't suppose you remember the last time she came to visit us?"

I hated to disappoint him, but I shook my head no. It was a Sunday afternoon in late September and we were in Papa's study. Right after the War, he had gone to college to become a lawyer. After working for another firm for a number of years, he was now trying to start his own practice, something I could tell made Mother nervous. She'd expanded what had been Aunt Trudy's Victory Garden during the War, and we now had enough canned fruits and vegetables to see us through a lengthy siege.

Like most of the furniture in the house, the desk and chairs in the study had belonged to Great Uncle Owen. The desk was large and made of a heavy, dark wood. It had a lamp on it that seemed to have grown out of one corner. Neat stacks of files, books, and papers would be in different places nearly every time I was in this room, but that desk lamp never changed position. The chairs were also heavy wood, with seats and backs upholstered in dark green leather, although the one behind the desk had a much higher back and could rock and swivel. Heavy, floor-length curtains with dark green trim framed two long windows that faced the street. On three walls, interrupted only by doors to the hallway and the dining room, wooden built-in bookcases reached to crown molding that edged the high ceiling. Books lined just over a quarter of the shelves. The rest were bare or were decorated with a smattering of knick-knacks—several Hummel figurines that had been handed down to Mother, some framed photographs including one of me in a child-size rocker, a vase that had come from the hotel in Niagara Falls where my parents had honeymooned, a collection of pipes Papa had inherited from his father but never smoked. The overall feel of the room was like being in a comfortable burrow under the roots of a large tree. It was a burrow I entered only with Papa's permission and only when he was there.

I sat in one of the chairs by a window, he behind his desk. He rocked and swiveled the chair, something he did when he was relaxed and feeling conversational.

"Well, it *was* a while ago," he said. "I thought we'd visit her before now, but time just seems to slip away. I know you were young, but I thought maybe you'd remember because of her dog. For the first two days she was here, you followed that dog everywhere. After that, he followed you everywhere. We've got some pictures tucked away somewhere. He was a dachshund, but a standard, not a miniature like Mrs. Ponce's that had the run-in with the minister's cat."

I widened my eyes and nodded. The run-in had been epic and had ended with Mrs. Ponce verbally taking out of the minister's hide what his cat had taken out of her dog's. The minister's cat was a cranky cat. So was Mrs. Ponce, after the ambush.

Papa smiled and continued.

"Aunt Genevieve's dog was about thirty pounds, I'd guess. Short legs, of course, and long wiry hair that made him look like he had a mustache. Sweet as could be, though he had quite the bark if he thought someone was making you do something you didn't want to do. Bath time was a challenge. The two of you were quite the pair."

I shifted in my seat, trying without luck to conjure some memory of this dog. "What was his name?" I asked.

"Colonel Brandon," Papa said. He smiled. "The Colonel Brandon that will be coming with Aunt Genevieve on this visit is actually the third Colonel Brandon she's had."

I thought it was odd to give the same name to multiple dogs, but I didn't say anything. Papa seemed suddenly lost in thought, and the swiveling and rocking slowed.

"I remember when I was a boy and Aunt Genevieve first came to live with us to take care of my little brother and me. Your grandfather was a lawyer, like most of the men in our family, but he did much of his work in Washington and had to be away a lot. He needed somebody to keep us in line, and his little sister offered to help." Papa looked at me over steepled fingers and smiled. "You have her eyes," he said. "Light blue-gray with long, dark lashes—I remember telling her one day that she had a lash on her cheek. She ran to the hall mirror to see, put the lash on her fingertip, and then made me go outside with her into the yard. She held out the finger with the eyelash on it, told me to make a wish, and then blew the lash into the breeze."

I smiled. I had a hard time picturing my father as a boy, but I could imagine a young woman balancing an eyelash on her fingertip, blowing on it, and watching it catch the breeze.

"When she first came to live with us, Aunt Genevieve used to ask me about books," Papa said after a moment of reflection. "She'd ask me what they said to me." He cocked his head at me. "I told her that they didn't say anything. I wasn't a big reader," he added. "I have to admit, I thought her question was along the lines of what my teachers would ask: 'What does this story *tell* us?'" This last Papa said in a high nasal voice, and I laughed, wanting him to continue to tell stories of when he'd been a boy. "We actually had to read Seneca in seventh grade—mighty dry stuff for a thirteen-year-old, let me tell you.

"So all this leads to a question I have for you, Margaux," Papa said. "This isn't about pretending or acting. I'm going to ask you, in all seriousness, what Aunt Genevieve asked me. What do books say to you?"

I drew my knees up to my chin and wrapped my arms around them. This was a turn in conversation I hadn't expected, and it caught me off guard. I thought about the look on Mrs. Harrington's face when she and Georgia had caught me with twenty-five copies of *The Last of the Mohicans* tucked around me on the floor and another on my lap, the sideways looks I'd gotten sometimes from classmates afterward—even from un-aligned prey—and, feeling a twist in my gut, the guilt I'd felt when I'd realized *Half Magic* had been dismembered as a joke because the wolves had learned I loved it. I thought about what I'd heard the neighbor say to Mother about how Uncle Owen should have "erred on the side of caution" and checked Aunt Trudy into a mental hospital, how relieved Mother had seemed when we'd been at the paint store picking out colors, and how much work she'd put into painting my room, thinking she was solving the "problem" by covering up old, bad memories with a clean, fresh coat of color.

I took a breath, but not too deep, so that he wouldn't see.

"Books don't say anything, Papa," I said.

He stopped rocking, leaning forward instead to put his elbows on his desk and rest his chin in both hands. It was a casual, disarming gesture I'd never seen him do before, and I had a flash of what he must have been like as a boy. He gazed at me for a moment. "Don't they?" he finally asked softly.

I wrapped my arms a little tighter around my legs and tilted my head to press my mouth against my knees. We'd always been close, Papa and me. I'd never felt I had to be anyone but myself around him. But he hadn't overruled Mother when she'd decided I should see a psychologist. It had taken six weeks and a lot of careful planning to convince everyone that I wasn't crazy, that no one needed to "err on the side of caution" and send me to a mental hospital. And Papa was a lawyer. It was his job, he had once told me, to get to the truth.

I'd just never thought he'd be a lawyer with me.

"I like books," I said, lifting my chin just high enough from my knees so that I wouldn't sound muffled. "I like them a lot. But they're just ink on paper. They can't say anything." I swallowed and felt the weight of his second-hand law volumes on the shelves bearing down on me. The law books never spoke to me, but now they seemed to be present in silent judgment. "Can I go to my room now?"

Papa didn't answer for a moment. Then he sighed and leaned back in his chair. "Of course, sweetheart," he said, finally.

He seemed disappointed, and I felt a pang of remorse for lying to him. He continued to look at me, giving me time, and I wrestled with myself. But it was too big a risk. Mother would be sad and worried again and want to send me back to the psychologist—or worse. Papa hadn't overruled her last time; I had no confidence he would if it came up again. I walked over to hug him and kiss him on the cheek.

"Thank you for telling me about Great Aunt Genevieve, Papa," I said. "I liked the story about the eyelash."

"She'll be here in a couple of weeks," he said, returning my hug. "I think it will be good for the two of you to get to know one another."

I was almost to the door when his voice made me turn.

"By the way, do you know why Aunt Genevieve names all her dogs Colonel Brandon?"

I shook my head.

"Colonel Brandon is a character in a book called *Sense and Sensibility*. He was very honorable and kind. Aunt Genevieve would say that he knew how to keep a secret, ride a horse, and truly appreciate a woman with spirit. She used to carry that book with her everywhere and said that when she met a Colonel Brandon, she'd marry him. I used to wonder how having that book with her would let her know when she'd met one. Around the time Matty graduated from high school, she got a dog instead and named him Colonel Brandon. I asked her once if the dog could ride a horse, and she replied that no, he couldn't, but he could keep a secret, and that was more important."

I waited to see if there was more to the story, but Papa just smiled and started shifting the folders and papers on his desk.

"Did you ever ask her about the book?"

He looked up. "About the book?"

"You said you wondered how having the book with her would let her know. Did you ever ask her?"

"I did." He paused a moment, then put one elbow on his desk and his chin in his hand, a near mimic of his previous gesture, a slight smile on his face. "I don't remember exactly what she said, but I do remember that I didn't quite believe her."

I felt my heart thump.

"G'night, Papa."

"Good night, darlin'. I'm always here if you want to talk some more."

I climbed the stairs to my room, grabbed *Misty of Chincoteague* and a flashlight, and went out in the twilight to my beech tree.

Seven

reat Aunt Genevieve arrived with three suitcases and Colonel
Brandon. I came home from school to find Papa in his study,
catching up on work he'd put aside to drive to the train station
in Washington, DC, to pick her up. I set my schoolbooks on the
hall table and followed the sound of female voices to the kitchen.

Mother saw me as I shadowed the doorway, taking in the
woman who sat at the kitchen table as Mother cut up a chicken
on the counter. The woman was definitely older than my parents,
but she didn't look like my classmates' grandmothers and great
aunts, whom I saw from time to time. She was slim and wearing
pedal pushers and a fitted sweater, for one thing. Her hair was a
light blond that glinted silver in the sunlight streaming through
windows I'd helped wash with vinegar and water the weekend
before. It was pulled back from her face and pinned in a roll at
the back of her head in a style I had seen in magazines.

"Margaux, you're home!" Mother said. "Come and kiss your
Great Aunt Genevieve hello."

I did as I was told, catching myself when I almost slipped on
the newly waxed floor, aware of the dog watching me with alert
eyes from under my great aunt's chair. I knew he wasn't the same
dog, but he looked just like the one Papa had described from
my great aunt's previous visit, including the wiry mustache on
his snout. He didn't wag his tail.

My great aunt's arms came up and pulled me into a tight, brief
hug when I leaned over to kiss her upturned cheek. She had a

faint scent I couldn't name, but it reminded me of the perfume counter at the department store in the city, the time Mother and I had gone Christmas shopping there as a special treat.

"'Great Aunt Genevieve!'" she repeated. She pronounced "Genevieve" like it was a man's full name, "John V. Ev," running the words together. "That sounds rather formal, don't you think? Has the same ring as 'Oz the Great and Powerful,' and we all know what a charlatan he turned out to be." She held my hands in hers. They were warm but dry, the skin on the back of them thin and papery. She had lines around her eyes that made me think she smiled a lot. "You should call me Aunt Vieve," she said, pronouncing Vieve with two syllables, like the middle initial and last name of the imaginary man I'd conjured. "Don't you agree, Audrey?"

"It's fine with me, Genevieve," said Mother. Mother smiled but seemed a little tense, not as relaxed as the visitor in her kitchen. She was wearing the apron she saved for cooking holiday dinners.

"If your father insists on more formality, we'll switch it to 'Marvelous Aunt Vieve.' 'Marvelous' rolls off the tongue so much better than 'great'—don't you think?"

I nodded, and I felt my shoulders relax as her hands squeezed mine. The dog came out from under the chair and sniffed my feet and legs. I looked down at him, still holding Aunt Vieve's hands, and he wagged his tail.

I HAD TO go to school again the next day, and I didn't see Aunt Vieve before I left. I wondered what she thought of her bedroom. Mother had painted the back bedroom a robin's egg blue within days of learning the woman who had had such a role in raising Papa was coming for a visit. It was a corner bedroom, like mine, although hers overlooked the vegetable garden, largely spent now that it was October. Mother had collected a bouquet of asters and late-blooming yarrow from the cutting border and placed them in a milk-glass vase on the small table beside the bed. She had also aired one of her mother's hand-made quilts and covered the bed with it, in place of the everyday blanket that had been there since before Great Aunt Trudy's middle son had gone off to war. When I came through the front door that afternoon, Aunt Vieve was sitting in Papa's chair behind his desk. I'd never seen anyone sitting there other than my father, and the sight stopped me dead in my tracks as I walked past the open double doors. Colonel Brandon was lying in front of the desk, where he could keep an eye on comings and goings. He raised his head to look at me, and the metal tags on his collar jingled slightly. At the sound, Aunt Vieve raised her eyes from the book she was reading.

"Margaux! You're home. How lovely. Come sit down and tell me about your day."

I hesitated, then shook my head. "I'm not allowed in Papa's study when he's not here, and then only with his permission," I said. I felt my face flush, as though I were admitting some failure on my part, some lack of gumption or strength. I doubted Aunt Vieve had asked Papa's permission.

She leaned back in his chair and cocked her head in a way that was familiar, then rocked and swiveled slightly as she looked around the room. Colonel Brandon continued to watch me, but he didn't get up. After a moment she smiled. "So James finally got his tree fort," she said. "Right down to the 'no girls allowed.'"

I didn't say anything. I felt like I was holding my breath, even though I wasn't.

She continued to look around the room as though she hadn't really noticed it before. She got up and walked toward me, running her fingers along the shelf that held the pipes. She picked one up, smiled, and stuck it in her mouth. "I remember my father smoking this pipe," she said around the pipe stem, holding the bowl with one hand. A slight frown wrinkled her brow as she viewed all the empty shelves. "We need to do something about this." She was looking at the law books, not at me or Colonel Brandon, when she said it, and I didn't think she was talking about a collection of pipes that were never smoked anymore. I didn't hear the law books say anything in reply. They only felt present, as they always did.

She set the pipe back on the shelf, walked to where I stood in the doorway, and leaned down just far enough to whisper in my ear. "We won't tell your father I violated the sanctity of his tree fort," she said. "It'll be our secret." She beckoned to her dog. "Come, Colonel Brandon," she said. "Margaux is going to do us the honor of inviting us into her bedroom." She turned to me. "We are invited, yes? I clearly am the type to invade the sanctity of my nephew's tree fort, but I would never, ever, enter a woman's space without her express permission."

I thought of Aunt Vieve sitting in Mother's kitchen the day before and wished I had been there when she'd first arrived. It took me a moment to realize she was expectantly waiting for me to invite her and the dog. I cast about in my memory. I had, in fact, made my bed before leaving for school, and my floor was mostly picked up. It was only later, in my bed that night, that I pondered and savored Aunt Vieve referring to my bedroom as a 'woman's space.'

"Yes, please," I said, trying to adopt Aunt Vieve's tone. She had an ability to sound very formal and yet very intimate at the same time. I liked it.

We went up the stairs to my room in a sort of procession: I in the lead, Aunt Vieve just behind me, and Colonel Brandon bringing up the rear. I walked through the doorway and went to sit on my bed facing my visitors, feeling it mimicked my aunt sitting in Papa's office chair. Aunt Vieve took a few steps in and looked around. Her eyes lit up at the sight of my crowded bookshelves and the window seat overlooking the side yard with a short stack of volumes on the cushion. She looked over her shoulder and addressed the dog.

"Colonel Brandon, be a dear and watch the door for us," she said.

I noticed she stressed the word "watch." Colonel Brandon seemed to hear the same thing. The dog looked up at her, cast a glance at me, and, with a perfunctory wag, went out into the hallway and sat down, his back to us. Once he was settled, Aunt Vieve shut the bedroom door.

My books began to speak as soon as the door swung closed.

"You are the gull, Jo, strong and wild, fond of the storm and the wind, flying far out to sea, and happy all alone."
"Let us be elegant or die!"
"Why sometimes I've believed as many as six impossible things before breakfast."
"Her peculiarities must not be punished."
"Many strange things happen in this world."
"She made herself stronger by fighting the wind."

I swiveled my head, feeling reverberations from multiple books: *Little Women* and *Heidi* on my shelves. *Through the Looking Glass* on my bedside table. *The Secret Garden* in the stack on the window seat cushion. I'd never heard so many different titles speak at nearly the same time. They seemed to be conversing—not talking over one another but taking turns—except it wasn't really a conversation. I looked at my great aunt, and I saw that she was watching me intently. I felt a brief moment of panic—what would she say of my odd behavior, sitting on my bed, turning my head here and there as though I saw mice skittering in the corners?

She smiled.

It crept over her face, reached her eyes, and her chin dipped. The books didn't say anything more, but they seemed to thrum, a faint vibration I felt rather than heard. Aunt Vieve walked to my window seat and pulled out *The Secret Garden* from mid-stack. She held it a moment, as though weighing it, then opened it and turned through some of the pages. All the time the smile never left her face. I watched her. Many times in the months and years that followed, I thought about that smile, the look on her face as she seemingly ignored me and the only sound to be heard in my bedroom was the rub of paper against paper as she turned pages of the book like one would run fingers through someone's hair, sometimes feeling individual strands and sometimes thicker locks.

"I love this book," she said quietly, not lifting her gaze from the pages.

"I do, too," I said, after a moment.

"What's your favorite part?"

"When the robin shows Mary where the door to the secret garden is, and she uses the key she finds to get in."

"Know what mine is? When Mary decides she can trust Dickon and then Colin, and the garden is a secret the three of them share, and they spend all those lovely afternoons in it, tending it and watching it come alive."

OVER DINNER, AUNT VIEVE complimented Mother's garden, lamenting that she didn't have one of her own. Her flat was in the old section of Quebec City, she said, and so it had thick walls with wide windowsills where she was able to keep pots of herbs. She also had a narrow French balcony where she put potted tomatoes during the warm months, but "nothing like you have here, Audrey. It's positively a Garden of Eden!" Mother blushed and seemed pleased. I saw Papa look from one to the other, a smile playing around the corners of his mouth. He looked at me and winked.

In my bed that night I went over the afternoon and evening in my mind, beginning with seeing Aunt Vieve sitting behind Papa's desk. I thought again about the reaction to her presence I'd heard from my books, and the hour or so we'd spent in my room before dinner, talking about the stories we'd read. I recalled what my father had said about Aunt Vieve asking him when he'd been a boy what books said to him. As I fell asleep, it occurred to me that she hadn't asked me that question because she already knew the answer. My last thought was wondering what my books had said to her about me.

Eight

I came home from school one day after Aunt Vieve had been with us about a week to find her acting as sous chef: peeling, coring, and slicing the fruit that Mother was mixing with her special blend of sugar and spices to create the apple sauce that would fill one shelf of the butler's pantry. The two of them were laughing and talking, and it struck me how different the atmosphere was compared to the first afternoon I'd seen Aunt Vieve in this kitchen, with Mother wearing her holiday-best apron and cutting up a chicken to make a Sunday dinner on a Wednesday evening.

I think I watched Aunt Vieve more closely than I have any other person, before or since. She hadn't said anything more to me about books, but I remembered her expression when she had picked up *The Secret Garden* from my stack on the window seat, what she had described as her favorite part of the book, the glances she had cast at my shelves that first afternoon while we'd talked. I was sure she could hear books, and pretty sure she knew I could, too. But, so far, we were keeping our secret gardens separate.

I CAME OUT of the house after my chores on a Saturday morning to find Mark Robbins pumping up the tires of a bicycle in our driveway. Aunt Vieve was supervising; Colonel Brandon was sitting alert at her side, watching the boy closely. Mark lived three doors down and was two grades ahead of me. He had curly chestnut hair and deep brown eyes. He played sports and had a paper route. Suffice to say, we didn't move in the same social circles. The bicycle was one I vaguely remembered seeing hanging on two large wall hooks in the back of the garage. It was an adult bike, but it didn't have a cross bar. It must have belonged to Aunt Trudy. I'd always just thought of her as the woman who had gone to bed and never got up again after the last of her children had died. Seeing the bright blue paint, the white seat, and the gleaming handlebars of this freshly washed bicycle standing in our driveway made me realize that she had been a real person who had done more than grieve herself to death. There had been a before.

Mark finished pumping up the tires and Aunt Vieve thanked him and gave him some coins she took out of her pocket. He accepted them, said a few words I couldn't hear, and then, seeing me on the back steps, lifted his hand in what could have been a wave or just a swat at an errant fly before turning to jog back to his house.

"What a nice boy," Aunt Vieve said, seeing me. "He was walking by and I commandeered him. It really doesn't matter the age, boy or man, males like to be given something useful to do." She picked up a small stack of books I hadn't seen sitting on the driveway on the other side of Colonel Brandon. She tucked them into the white wicker basket attached to the front of the bike. "So what do you think? I saw this lovely bicycle hanging in the garage, and it looked like it hadn't been touched in ages, so I didn't imagine anyone would mind if I took temporary ownership."

"It's pretty," I said.

"Do you know Mark?"

"Not very well." I really didn't want to talk about my social standing—or lack of it—in the neighborhood and at school. "He's a couple grades ahead of me. He's in high school." In other words, there wasn't a need to forge a friendship—he had moved on to a different world.

"Keep half an ear tuned to that one," she said casually as she got on the bike and flipped up the kickstand with her heel. She was wearing pedal pushers again, wine-colored this time. "He doesn't know it yet, but he's got chivalry to his core. That's always a good trait." She pursed her lips and a slight frown creased her brow. "There's something else there, too, but I'm not sure exactly what. It's curious. Well, he's young. Hopefully the chivalry will win out." She turned her attention to Colonel Brandon. "Stay here and keep an eye on things, Colonel. I'll be back in a bit."

She rode down the driveway and turned right toward Main Street, three smallish, cloth-bound books in her basket. I followed Colonel Brandon to the steps of our front porch and sat down beside him. After a few minutes, he laid his head on my lap, although he continued to watch the street in the direction Aunt Vieve had taken.

I did, too.

LATER THAT AFTERNOON I looked down from my usual perch in the beech tree to see Aunt Vieve holding a book and examining my pulley—the bucket, rope, and brick that I used to get books up into my tree. Her eyes followed the rope from where it was tied around the brick lying in the grass up to where it looped over a branch not far from my seat and ended at the bucket that had brought up *A Tree Grows in Brooklyn*. I looked around for the ever-present dachshund and saw him nosing along the fence.

"What a marvelous contraption," I heard my aunt murmur.

I watched her and gave a small wave when our eyes met. I scrambled down the tree, leaving the book on the wide branch where I had been sitting. I felt a touch of pride; no one knew this tree as I did, and my descent was fluid and assured—a scene

right out of *The Swiss Family Robinson*. I jumped down the last
few feet and was rewarded by the admiration I saw on Aunt
Vieve's face. She didn't call me a monkey.

"You must climb this tree often," she said.

"It's my favorite place to read."

She touched the rope. "Ah, so this must be your book trans-
port." She looked at the tree, taking in its height and the thick,
widespread branches. Her eyes narrowed and she pursed her
lips. "May I?" she asked me.

At first I didn't know what she was asking, and then I realized
she considered the beech tree to be mine.

"Sure," I said, not sure at all. Grownups did not, in my experience, climb trees.

Aunt Vieve lifted the brick by the rope, allowing the bucket
to descend within arm's reach. She deposited her book in it,
then let the weight of the brick raise the bucket up to the branch.
She went to the trunk, shucked her shoes, wrapped her hands
around a low branch, and set one foot into the crotch of the
tree where the main trunk split into two. I had an urge to help
push from behind, but I didn't think she would appreciate it,
and, as it turned out, she didn't need the assistance. Colonel
Brandon let out a single, sharp bark and Aunt Vieve shushed
him. It took a little while, but she made her way, branch by
branch, up to a spot not far from where my book waited for me.
She settled herself on a nearby limb, one not as wide as my
usual seat, but strong and growing out nearly perpendicular
to one of the two trunks.

"Fetch my book, if you would, Margaux," Aunt Vieve said,
sounding satisfied but a little out of breath.

I realized I was biting my lip and hadn't moved so much as
a muscle since she'd started up the tree. Feeling somewhat cha-
grined, I climbed, going up my usual route, took her book from
the bucket, and gave it to her. Colonel Brandon had come to the

base of the tree and stood looking up at us. The foreshortened view of his mustached snout and stout legs made him seem to bristle with disapproval.

"*Fahrenheit 451*," Aunt Vieve said. "I typically prefer books that have been around for a while, but Mr. Bradbury is a very promising writer. This one is a bit of a horror novel," she added. "The critics call it a dystopia. But any story that has book burning at its core must be considered a tale of horror, in my estimation."

I settled back on my branch, my book in my lap, but I didn't open it. Aunt Vieve didn't open hers either, but she looked around, bits of color from the world beyond visible through the October-gold leaves and the taupe and gray branches of my haven.

"What a perfect place for a private conversation," she said. "I love your bedroom, and I'm quite envious of your window seat, but this is even better, albeit not as cushioned." She shifted a bit on her branch. "So, my dear Margaux, what did your books tell you about me?"

The question caught me off guard, even though I'd been thinking about Aunt Vieve and books a lot since that first afternoon. She waited for a moment; then, when I didn't respond, she continued.

"Why is it, do you think, that people accept that some things can be unseen or unheard by most, yet be valid and real, yet other things unseen or unheard are judged to be figments of imagination or signs of an unstable mind? It's well accepted, for instance, that dogs can hear sounds and smell scents that people cannot, and this is embraced as a valuable trait. Why, then, are most so suspect of similar traits in people?" She looked at me, and the indignation on her face faded away. "If you have the gift I believe you do, I want you to know that it is, indeed, a gift. It is not a curse, and you certainly are not mentally unstable."

I bit my lip. I felt a swelling in my chest, a tightness in my throat. The memory of the shame I'd felt after the time I'd been caught whispering to books in the school library crossed my mind, followed quickly by the effort I'd put into ignoring the murmuring of the books in my classroom. I thrust away the memory of the feel of paper airplanes pricking my face and throat, the sound of my classmates' jeers, the anguish I'd felt in seeing *Half Magic* dismembered. And then there was Mother's worried insistence that I see a psychologist, the change I'd felt in my relationship with Papa since our conversation in his study, the weight I'd carried since realizing I had to lie to all of them.

Aunt Vieve must have seen some of this on my face, because she leaned over as far as she safely could reach to touch the tips of her fingers against my leg.

"You and I, dear Margaux, can hear books speak—can we not?"

I took a deep breath. Within the shelter of my beech tree's leaves, cradled high above the ground, I decided to trust the woman who had once sent an eyelash on the breeze to carry a wish.

"Yes," I said.

And the world, in that moment, became a different place for me.

We talked for a long time in my beech tree that afternoon. Actually, Aunt Vieve did most of the talking. I listened, feeling her words soak into me and fill places I hadn't realized were empty.

No, empty probably isn't the right word, although there was an element of that. She filled the loneliness. Until that afternoon when Aunt Vieve talked about the gift we shared, I hadn't realized how lonely I had felt.

"It's my belief, based upon several cryptic remarks made by my uncle before he passed, that this is a family trait—an errant gene, if you will, that appears every generation or so," said Aunt Vieve. "Best used, it can help you recognize the good in people, as well as their motivations, strengths, and weaknesses. It can also help you discern deceit and warn you of those who are up to no good."

She said that she'd only ever heard fiction books speak and, even then, it was typically books that had been read by many over time that seemed to have the strongest voices. Books that were new or "churned out in haste to satisfy the masses" seemed to have little voice. "I will say I'm not sure why I've never heard a biography speak—perhaps it's because such books are about people who have actually lived and breathed and there is no bringing back the dead?"

Not that I needed the push, she said, but she encouraged me to read. There was simply nothing so frustrating as to hear a book speak and not be able to identify the volume so that you could get a better idea of what message it was trying to impart. Once you knew a book well, any copy of it would practically thrum, so that you could recognize it and find it even if you'd never been in that room before.

"But books can be cryptic," Aunt Vieve cautioned. "And books can also be fickle. They don't speak on cue nor respond to our desire to have them speak. And, frankly, sometimes they just won't shut up." In such instances, she advised, the best course of action was to remove yourself (or the book) to a safe distance. Proximity was required in order to hear a book speak.

"I have a lot of books in my bedroom. Why do they hardly ever talk to me?" I finally asked. The tightness in my throat was gone. Other than my single-word reply to her earlier question, it was the first time I'd acknowledged my ability out loud. It felt weirdly invigorating.

"Did they talk when I was in your bedroom with you?"

I nodded. "Four of them did," I said, and then I blushed, wondering if I could remember exactly which book had said what, if Aunt Vieve asked me.

"Books will not speak to you about you," she said. "'Know thyself' is attributed to Socrates, and apparently books rely on you to do just that. In fact, it's rare that they will speak to you about those closest to you, particularly blood relations. If they do talk about those close to you, pay attention. Something important is afoot. We're blood relations, of course, but you didn't really know me at all that first day I arrived." She smiled. "I suspect your books might not have much to say to you about me now. If you want to hear those particular books talk, take them with you places. See what they have to say then."

I smiled back. I liked the idea that books would judge Aunt Vieve and me to be close. She didn't ask me again what my books had said to me about her, and I didn't ask what she'd heard them say to her about me.

By now the shadows were getting long, and Aunt Vieve had made it a habit to help Mother with dinner. It was my job to set the table. Aunt Vieve handed *Fahrenheit 451* back to me and I put it in the bucket along with *A Tree Grows in Brooklyn*, realizing that I hadn't heard from either book during the time we'd been in the tree. I didn't think she had, either.

"I'm so glad we were able to have this talk, Margaux," she said. "I've been waiting for just the right time and place, and I think we were lucky enough to find both." She sighed contentedly and swung her legs, neatly crossed at the ankles. "Now be a dear and go fetch your father to bring me a ladder."

Nine

One day the following week, I woke to sunshine streaming in through my window. I stretched, my hands pushing against the headboard of my bed and my toes nearly reaching the end of the mattress. Then I sat up suddenly, a surge of panic running through my chest. Sunshine was streaming through my window? What time was it? I'd be late for school! Why hadn't Mother woken me? Had I slept through her call?

I got out of bed, tangling one foot in the covers in my haste and nearly falling headlong to the floor. I hurried down the hall to the bathroom to wash my face and brush my teeth. I glanced in the mirror and sighed. Growing my hair out hadn't helped—despite the added weight, it still refused to be tamed into flowing waves like Mother's, instead keeping the errant curls that tended toward frizz. I heard conversational voices wafting up from below. I considered this while scrubbing my teeth and then brushing my hair and tying it into a ponytail of submission. No one downstairs seemed concerned that I wasn't in school—why should I be?

I entered the kitchen, still in my nightgown, to see Mother and Aunt Vieve sitting at the kitchen table with cups of coffee. They both seemed relaxed, although Aunt Vieve was more dressed up than usual, wearing a camel-colored pencil skirt and white blouse rather than her usual pedal pushers.

"Ah, finally, Sleeping Beauty awakes," my mother said, smiling. "I was just about to come get you. Hurry up and get dressed.

Your father is going to want to leave soon. I'll have some breakfast waiting for you when you come back down, but you'll have to eat fast."

I stood there, looking from one to the other while racking my brain for the plans I'd obviously missed during last night's supper conversation.

"You get to play hooky today," Aunt Vieve said. "Your father has some meetings in Washington and you and I are hitching a ride with him. We're going to have lunch at the Carlton."

I must have looked comical, because Mother laughed. "Go on now and get dressed before I rethink this whole thing and send you to school with an excuse note for being late."

I ran.

I'D NEVER BEEN to the Carlton. It's changed hands and names in the decades since and, while it's still elegant, I don't think it has quite the panache it did then. But that morning when I was twelve years old and sitting in Papa's car wearing my Sunday best, it was one of the fanciest hotels in Washington, DC. During the drive there, Papa told me President Truman had often gone there to meet with official guests. He said the president more than once had entered and left the hotel through a side window to avoid the press. I pretended to be interested in this story, but what had really captured my imagination was Mother's whisper to me just before we'd left that I should keep my eyes peeled: Audrey Hepburn and Elizabeth Taylor often stayed at the Carlton, and who knew?—they might even be there now.

Aunt Vieve sat next to Papa during the two-hour drive. As we pulled up in front of the hotel, she smiled at me over her shoulder and told me to sit still until the car door was opened for me. A man in a long blue coat with lots of brass buttons opened the door for my aunt, and she leaned over to kiss Papa's cheek before swinging both legs out and accepting the man's gloved hand to stand up. She waited expectantly as he then opened the rear car door and offered me his hand. I imitated Aunt Vieve, holding my legs together to swing them out of the car and taking his hand. It all felt very elegant, and I was glad that Papa had washed the car.

The Carlton was the grandest building I'd ever seen up close, other than official places like the Lincoln Memorial on school trips, and it was a little intimidating. But Aunt Vieve held me by the hand, and I watched her nod and smile at the doorman when he tipped his hat as we walked through the doors of shiny brass and smudgeless glass and into the lobby. She gave my hand a quick squeeze and I knew that as long as I was with her, no one would think I was out of place.

I'd never seen anything so beautiful as the lobby of the Carlton. I've traveled quite a bit since then, but my memory of those first steps into that hotel is unequaled. There were people standing and chatting in small groups. Others sat, leaning forward or relaxing back on overstuffed, velvet-trimmed sofas and ornate chairs that looked like they might break if the occupant shifted unexpectedly. They were dressed like they were going someplace special—or had arrived someplace special—and that it mattered that they fit their surroundings and that those around them agreed they did. There was a huge, sparkling chandelier in the center of the lobby filling the space with its faceted light. Bright crystal sconces on the walls reflected back the light. Between the sconces were mirrors with small tables underneath that held cut-crystal vases of fresh flowers or sculptures and, on one, a telephone with gold trim and an ornate handle. Between the sconces and mirrors were paintings in ornate gilded frames that reminded me of pictures in my social studies book of collections in famous museums. But the Carlton wasn't hushed like a museum; it was alive. I heard voices, both lilting and deep, some with accents I'd never heard before, all accompanied by a background of elegant music that came from I didn't know where. The deep carpet we walked on mellowed the sound, didn't allow it to echo. Crossing the room with purpose or stationed behind the large registration desk were hotel staff, alike in their black and white clothes and deferent expressions, different in the way they wore them. It seemed like a movie set waiting for the actors and actresses to make their entrances.

I let myself be led as I tried to look at every face, searching for someone famous. My popularity would get a boost at school if I could reliably report having seen Audrey Hepburn or Elizabeth Taylor. I wondered if Gregory Peck ever came to the Carlton. *Roman Holiday* was Mother's favorite movie. For just a moment, I regretted not investing in one of the movie magazines so many of the girls at school pored over. I could be looking at a famous actress or actor and not even know it. The regret was just for a moment, though. I'd have to go into the store owned by Georgia Pillard's parents to buy one.

Aunt Vieve led me to the dining room and gave her name to the man who stood behind a narrow, high desk with a large book on it. He wore a formal suit and tie, smiled at my aunt, and gave me only a cursory glance. I flushed a little, thinking about the precious minutes I'd spent that morning trying to pick just the right dress to wear to someplace like the Carlton while still getting ready before my mother might decide that the whole hooky thing was a bad idea. The man ran his index finger down the page, then looked up at my aunt and asked her to please follow him. I trailed in their wake, weaving past tables draped with thick white cloths, noticing businessmen with expensive suits and gray in their hair, some of whom turned their heads to watch as Aunt Vieve went by. She walked with a sway in her hips that was accentuated by her pencil skirt, and her hair was woven into a complicated knot on the back of her head that left the nape of her neck exposed above the tailored collar of her blouse. She looked very different than she had sitting up in the beech tree or slicing apples in our kitchen—but just as much at ease.

Reaching a table by a window, the man pulled out a chair first for her, then for me. Aunt Vieve set her oversized leather handbag on the floor between us. Almost immediately another man, this one with black pants, a white shirt, and a white apron tied around his waist that nearly reached his ankles, appeared at the table with large, stiff menus. These he handed to Aunt Vieve and me before leaving with an assurance that he'd be back shortly. Another man, dressed in the same manner, came directly afterward to fill the water glasses, expertly pouring a sluice of ice and water from a silver pitcher beaded in moisture and swathed in a cloth napkin. The water and ice sloshed in the glasses without spilling over, and Aunt Vieve thanked him.

I watched her interaction with all these people and was struck by how she had an ability to be very formal and elegant without appearing haughty or cold. Yet I knew from watching her for weeks that this wasn't her typical demeanor; it was an attitude she'd selected for this afternoon, like a coat one would choose from a closetful depending upon the weather.

This was something I wanted to learn.

I looked at her and she smiled at me over her menu. There was a mischievous gleam in her eyes. She had the air of someone who wanted to tell a secret.

And then suddenly I felt like I was back in school again, hearing a book talk with lots of people around me.

"Under the guidance of our leader, Comrade Napoleon, I have laid five eggs in six days."

"Can you not understand that liberty is worth more than just ribbons?"

"They had come to a time when no one dared speak his mind, when fierce, growling dogs roamed everywhere, and when you had to watch your comrades torn to pieces after confessing to shocking crimes."

"Four legs good, two legs better!"

"Don't you just love George Orwell," Aunt Vieve said, her voice pitched to carry no farther than my side of the table. "I can always count on *Animal Farm* to talk in a crowd like this—politicians and businessmen, hangers-on and wannabes, all engaged in oh-so-important conversations." She reached into her handbag and pulled out a copy of *Animal Farm* that looked just like the one I had in my room. "I know I sent you a copy a while back, but I also brought mine from home. I thought it would give us something to talk about over lunch."

The waiter appeared at her elbow, and she slipped the book back into her bag. She ordered a Waldorf salad and a glass of sparkling water without even looking at the menu. I glanced down at my menu in a panic, feeling the waiter's eyes bore into the top of my head as he towered above me, pen poised above the small notepad he carried. The menu was filled top to bottom with elegant cursive lettering under bold headings that made me promise myself to take French when I got to high school.

"The same," I said, trying to look and sound self-assured while I wondered what was in a Waldorf salad and whether sparkling water tasted different from what the waiter had already poured.

He made a notation on his pad, inclined his head to Aunt Vieve, collected our menus, and left.

Aunt Vieve raised her water glass in a toast. "She made herself stronger by fighting the wind," she said ceremoniously.

I remembered hearing *The Secret Garden* say that very line the first afternoon Aunt Vieve had come to visit. I looked around the crowded dining room. "You have that book with you, too? Is there someone here who is like that?"

"No and yes. Pick up your glass, dear, my arm is getting tired."

I did as I was told and we clinked glasses. I started to put mine down, but at a quick shake of Aunt Vieve's head, I took a gulp first. The water was so cold I could feel it all the way down my throat and into my stomach.

"You must always take at least a sip after a toast. It brings on terrible bad luck otherwise. In some countries, it's also considered quite an insult to whoever was giving the toast."

I nodded, acknowledging the etiquette lesson. "No and yes?" I prompted.

"No, I don't have that book with me. And, yes, there is someone here who is like that. One for sure, and I like to think two."

The waiter arrived with a large chilled bottle and two wine glasses, each with a lime perched on the rim, and a covered basket of breads. Aunt Vieve waited while he poured, murmuring her thanks when he told her our salads would be out shortly. I waited, too.

"Why did you ask me in the beech tree what my books said about you when you already knew?" I asked as soon as the waiter left.

"*The Secret Garden* told you that about me?" Aunt Vieve looked delighted. "How marvelous. It's always been one of my favorite lines but, as I told you, you never hear books talk about you—just about other people. I'd always hoped *The Secret Garden* would feel a kinship with me—and that line, in particular—and now I know for sure. Thank you, Margaux." She took another sip from her glass, looking for all the world like someone who'd just received the perfect gift. "As for your question, we're both the daughters of lawyers. My father always said you should never ask a question to which you don't already know the answer. I'm sure you've heard the same from yours." She lifted the napkin of the breadbasket and selected a small roll encrusted with seeds.

"That's in court," I challenged. I felt a cold lump in my stomach, like the ice water had settled there and refused to be warmed.

Aunt Vieve paused, her long fingers and perfect nails stilled in the action of pulling the bread apart. She set the roll down on a small plate. "You're right, Margaux. And I never want you to think that what you and I discuss is a court. It certainly wasn't that afternoon in the tree. That was a sharing, and it was magical, and something I'd hoped for and sought out for a very, very long time."

I thought of Papa telling me about Aunt Vieve asking him when he'd been a boy what books said to him. I remembered how I'd felt that afternoon, knowing there was someone like me, that I wasn't crazy after all. I remembered not feeling as lonely as I had before. I looked at Aunt Vieve across the table, watching me, waiting, like this *was* a court, and I was both judge and jury. She was beautiful, but she was old. Not old in a used-up kind of way—the glances she continued to get from the men in the room were evidence of that—but she had been a kid, and then a teenager, and then a grown up. She was older than Papa. Had taken the place of his mother after she had died. And if I understood what she was telling me, all that time she had been on her own with this. That was a lot of one-sided conversations.

"Okay," I said, and I saw Aunt Vieve let out a breath I hadn't known she was holding.

She picked up her glass again, this time the wine glass. She squeezed the lime into the sparkling water and dropped it in, then held the glass up to me. "I was toasting you, Margaux. Let me be more plain this time. To Margaux, who has made herself stronger by fighting the wind."

I paused, suddenly shy. Aunt Vieve nodded to my glass, her eyes never leaving mine. I picked up my wine glass, holding one for the first time, and squeezed the lime as I'd watched her do, dropping it in and seeing small bubbles fizz up around it. I lifted my glass to meet hers, and I smiled at the sound of the clink, different from the one made by our water glasses just a few moments earlier. I drank. The taste was slightly bitter, but offset by the tang of the lime and the feel of the effervescence in my mouth. I set the glass down and smiled.

Aunt Vieve smiled back and leaned toward me across the table. "It was the first thing your books said to me about you, Margaux, and, oh, it lifted my heart to hear it. My favorite line from a book I've read and reread all my life, and the very first time I heard the book say it aloud, it was about you."

The waiter arrived with our salads.

"It was not for this that she and all the other animals had hoped and toiled," said *Animal Farm* suddenly.

I leaned back in my chair and dipped my chin to glance at Aunt Vieve's handbag under the table. The waiter saw me and leaned back, tilting his head to do the same. I saw Aunt Vieve demurely cross her ankles and smile up at the waiter with one raised brow. He flushed, finished serving our salads, and left.

I flushed, too.

"It takes practice," said Aunt Vieve, placing the starched linen napkin in her lap and picking up her fork. "That's one of the reasons I brought you here. You need to become accustomed to your gift, even in a crowd. At best, you can learn to use what you hear about people: their motivations, their intentions, something about their character."

"And at worst?"

"At worst." She seemed to consider this. "How not to be over-whelmed," she said, finally. "Having dozens of voices come at you from all sides at once can be disorienting, to say the least. That's why I only brought one book today. Someone in this crowd might have a novel or two with them, but it still was pretty safe. My advice is to avoid places where you have lots and lots of different types of people along with lots and lots of novels. I'd avoid the New York public library, for instance." She shuddered and closed her eyes briefly. "That's nothing less than a cauldron."

"I've felt that way in school sometimes."

"School is good practice."

The offhand way she said it made me think I had a long way to go before I could look and act as self-assured in any situation as Aunt Vieve apparently could.

Two men, led by the suited maître d', sat down at a table adjacent to ours. As soon as the maître d' left, one of them leaned forward, speaking to his companion in a low, urgent tone.

"The cat joined the Re-education Committee and was very active in it for some days. She was seen one day sitting on a roof and talking to some sparrows who were just out of her reach. She was telling them that all animals were now comrades and that any sparrow who chose could come and perch on her paw; but the sparrows kept their distance," said *Animal Farm* in a conversational tone.

Aunt Vieve didn't react at all but instead speared a slice of apple, lifted it to her mouth, and neatly cut it in half with her front teeth. She chewed, and she smiled at me.

I did the same.

Ten

Two days later, Papa drove Aunt Vieve and Colonel Brandon to the train station. Helping her to pack, I realized that one of the three suitcases she had brought with her had been devoted to books. It was one of the many things I learned from her. I never travel without books, although I always spread them out among my suitcases, insurance against one being delayed or lost in transit, leaving me bereft.

I didn't want Aunt Vieve to leave. Even at the time I realized my moping was likely hurting Mother's feelings, but I'd found a kindred spirit and a role model in my great aunt, and I simply couldn't hide my long face. As I sat on the steps of the front porch, Colonel Brandon took pity and came to sit by me and lay his head on my lap. The two of us watched Papa load the suitcases into the car. I heard the screen door shut, and then Mother came to sit beside me.

"It was a nice, long visit," she said, putting her arm around me.

"Uh-huh." Diction becomes more difficult when one's chin is wedged against the top of one's knees.

"We talked, your great aunt and father and I, after you went to bed last night."

I didn't respond. I wasn't worried. I knew Aunt Vieve wouldn't have told our secret. And I'd been learning from her. There would be no more trips to a psychologist.

"We decided that it might be nice for you to spend some time with her in Quebec City next summer."

Colonel Brandon gave out a startled yelp as I suddenly un-furled and leaned over to hug Mother tight around the neck. When I finally let go, Aunt Vieve was standing at the bottom of the porch steps.

"I take it you shared our news?" she asked Mother.

"We need to leave now if you're going to make the two-fifteen," Papa called from where he stood by the open door on the driver's side of the car. He tried very hard to sound impatient, but I could see he was happy at my reaction to the plans for next summer.

"Write to me," Aunt Vieve whispered as she hugged me fiercely and pressed her lips to my cheek. "Write to me and read, read, read."

SCHOOL BECAME A lot easier for me after Aunt Vieve's visit. It wasn't as though I skyrocketed in popularity or anything, but Mark Robbins said hi to me in the village a few times where others saw and heard, and Georgia Pillard sat next to me at lunch because she wanted to talk about my great aunt who had, apparently, spent some time one afternoon chatting with her mother and father at the sundry store they owned on Main Street. Was it true Aunt Vieve had been the nanny to a baron's children in Europe? Had I ever met the baron? Was there a baroness, or was he a widower? Her eyes gleamed at the thought of a love affair between European royalty and the elegant woman who had carried on a conversation in her parents' store. The fact that I hadn't any details at all for her (she knew a lot more than I did—Aunt Vieve a nanny?) didn't deter her. Between Mark's public acknowledgements and Georgia's acceptance of me, I moved out of the "weird" category—which was similar but slightly above what I'd designated in elementary school as unaligned prey—into the broad middle caste of our junior high's hierarchy. It also helped, I suppose, that I felt more comfortable in my own skin since Aunt Vieve's visit.

I wrote to her a lot, compiling a letter over a week or so like entries in a diary, then riding my bike to the post office to have the envelope weighed and stamped *Par Avion*.

Letters from Aunt Vieve were usually tucked into a book, and the collection in my room grew. Frequently these missives were short, signed with just her initial. *"When you read, Margaux, don't just read of heroes and happy times, although these are important,"* read one. *"Learn also of villains—especially those who may not appear to be villainous. It's important to recognize those, perhaps most of all."*

I drew Xs across the days of a calendar I received for Christmas—marking down the time to when school would let out and I would ride the train to Quebec City. My parents gave me a brand new suitcase for my birthday, a clear sign that Mother was fully supportive of my promised summer trip.

Eleven

I'd been indignant when told Papa would escort me all the way to Quebec City, not just to the train station in Washington, DC. Now thirteen, I felt I'd left childhood behind and was ready to step out on my own. I'd been thorough in my planning for my month-long trip. My suitcase had been packed for more than a week, and I had two carefully selected books in an embroidered satchel I'd found in our attic. Surely *Treasure Island* would warn me of anyone I should avoid.

Now, standing in the enormous Union Station, people swirling in and out of doors and arches and stairways with luggage and children and sometimes small animals in tow, confronted with a large board listing arrivals and departures that whirred and changed at a dizzying speed and with an array of train platforms that could lead you where you wanted to go or in an entirely wrong direction, and assaulted by smells of food and tobacco and sweat and a noise level that made me long for the muffling carpet of the Carlton, I was glad Papa was beside me. I felt a little like Alice, and I wished I'd brought *Through the Looking Glass* with me. We could have commiserated.

Instead, I didn't pull away when Papa took my hand, and out of the corner of my eye, I saw his mouth quirk at the corners.

"See the fourth one down on the left?" he said, pointing up at the large board with his free hand. "That's ours. There will be stops, but we won't have to change trains."

He tucked his small valise under one arm, picked up my larger suitcase, and led me confidently through what appeared to be all of humanity milling and churning.

Meanwhile, *Treasure Island* and *The Secret Garden* contributed a running commentary on those around us.

"Sir, with no intention to take offence, I deny your right to put words into my mouth."

"If you look the right way, you can see that the whole world is a garden."

"There's never a man looked me between the eyes and seen a good day a'terward."

"People never like me and I never like people."

"The workpeople, to be sure, were most annoyingly slow."

"Two things cannot be in one place."

"The man's tongue is fit to frighten the French."

This constant barrage from my books—I'd only brought two!—the smells, the sound, the sheer number of people—some talking, some calling out, others just standing around looking perplexed or bored or calculating—all while I tried to associate each observation from my books with someone close by, was making me a little dizzy. But I needed to be able to do this. I kept walking, glad of the feel of Papa's hand around mine. This was supposed to be easier by now. I remembered what Aunt Vieve had said about avoiding being around lots of books in places with lots of people and was glad Mother had insisted I bring only two books with me. Aunt Vieve had an entire library, she'd pointed out; there was no need to bring mine. I tried to focus, to practice what I'd been doing at school. Focus, and no one will notice you're different; no one will think you're weird or, worse, insane . . .

"Laugh, by thunder. Laugh!" *Treasure Island* roared in my head just as a group of older girls and boys went by, laughing and smiling, intent on each other and whatever adventure lay

ahead. One bumped against my shoulder, hard, and I lost my footing, pulled up by Papa's strong grip just before my knee hit the pocked marble floor.

"You okay?"

I nodded but didn't dare speak. I clenched my jaw, gritted my teeth together like a wall built without mortar. *Treasure Island* roared while *The Secret Garden* continued an unending stream of observations. I heard more voices than I'd ever heard before, all talking at once—Dickon and Colin and Mary and Ben and Mrs. Medlock and Jim Hawkins and Long John Silver and Israel Hands and Ben Gunn—how could there be so many different people in one place at once? I didn't have time or space to separate and connect to the people all the people so many people going in every direction around me. I stopped so I could get my bearings. Pulled my hand out of Papa's and brought up both of mine to cover my ears. Shut up, I thought, shut up shut up shut up just for a little while just until I can get on the train and sit down and close my eyes and focus like Aunt Vieve said. Just shut up shut up shut up until I can get some space and time to focus. Someone bumped my shoulder hard from behind, and I heard a man swear under his breath as I stumbled.

"They're letting it die!" wailed *The Secret Garden* suddenly in an apparent attempt to drown out *Treasure Island.*

"Th' world's coming to an end!" agreed another voice from *The Secret Garden.*

"We must go on, because we can't turn back," said *Treausre Island* in a quieter voice. *"I'm not sure whether he's sane,"* it added sagely in a different tone.

I heard new voices, voices outside my head, voices not from my books, concerned voices, but I couldn't make out what they were saying. The noise inside and outside my head was deafening. I clenched my eyes shut and tried desperately to focus. It didn't help. I felt someone take my arm. I slapped at it and dropped to my knees, the pain of hitting the marble floor a welcome, solid thing. I let the wall tumble down.

"Shut up shut up shut up!"

The words I screamed raked my throat raw even as I expelled them out of my mouth, aimed at the tall, stone ceiling of the train station, where they struck and ricocheted back at me.

I felt a hand along the side of my face. I heard a soothing voice and knew the hand was Papa's. It was wet in spots and lines. No, it wasn't his hand that was wet. I had tears on my face. Papa's hand was pressing my tears into my skin, making me absorb them again.

Like the words I shouldn't let anyone know I heard, I shouldn't be showing these tears. His hands moved to hold mine.

"Darlin', look up," I heard him say softly, his breath tickling my ear. "I want you to tilt your head all the way back and open your eyes. I won't let you fall."

His voice was soothing, as was the feel of his hand as it left my face to tuck an errant lock of hair behind my ear and then move to the small of my back as I knelt on the floor. His other hand still gripped mine. I felt his strength through his grip, his support through the hand that held me steady. He wouldn't let me fall. I tilted my head back and opened my eyes.

Sunlight streamed in through a series of elaborate arched windows, making the gold leaf of the vaulted ceiling's honeycomb pattern gleam. Solemn statues gazed at one another across the divide, ignoring the congestion and semi-organized chaos churning below them. I focused on them, one by one—their poise, their calm. Noise continued to rise and bounce and echo, but it didn't penetrate the serenity of that space any more than my scream had. Nothing marred the surface of lustrous white and gold; nothing happening below pocked the dignity of the statues. I felt myself center, felt the panic ease in my chest, felt my skin absorb tears shed. I heard continued muttering from

Treasure Island—it apparently felt a particular affinity with a number of people here—but it was muted now, not an insistent yammering in my head.

"Better?"

I brought my gaze down from the ceiling to look into Papa's eyes. I smiled. "Better," I said.

"Good."

He took my hands and helped me to stand.

"Is she okay? Does she need a doctor?" I realized that we—I—had attracted a small crowd. Faces circled us, some concerned, some judgmental, and others already turning away, deeming the show to be over.

"She's either sick or ill-mannered," I heard someone mutter.

"She's fine," Papa answered the woman who clutched a small handbag to her chest. "Thank you." He smiled at the crowd, nodding several times as they started to drift away.

"Sick or ill-mannered," someone repeated.

"Or both," someone replied.

"Thank you for your concern," Papa said again to no one in particular. He looked at me and tilted his head toward doorways through which I imagined I would see train tracks stretched to the horizon. He picked up our suitcases. "Shall we?"

AUNT VIEVE HAD an apartment in the old section of Quebec City. The taxi's tires made a rumbling noise over the cobblestone streets once we passed under an archway of the imposing walls that encircled the historic district. We stopped in front of a three-story building of flat-faced fieldstone with wrought-iron balconies that jutted out no more than a foot beyond French doors with mullions and trim painted a deep red. Many of these were open to the late June breeze, cooler than in Virginia. The balconies had potted plants of varying sizes and design and window boxes perched on the railings, these draped with geraniums, petunias, and other flowers I couldn't identify but knew Mother would have known on sight.

Papa paid the taxi driver while I took all this in, and then the first-floor door flew open and I was engulfed by Aunt Vieve, her scent at once department-store elegant and comfortingly familiar.

"You're here! You're finally here! How was the trip? Margaux, I'm convinced you grew three inches since I saw you last! James, stop dawdling and come in, come in! The skies are going to open up on us any minute!"

I glanced up, noting the leaden clouds and almost tasting the rain to come as the breeze became a gust. Papa kissed Aunt Vieve on her upturned cheek as he came through the doorway, then sighed and took a tighter grip on his valise and my suitcase as he followed us up flights of wide, worn marble steps to our destination on the top floor.

Aunt Vieve's apartment had a large front room with a high ceiling, two sets of balconied French doors that looked out onto the street, and tall wooden bookcases with painted trim on both adjacent walls that drew my eyes like magnets. As we came in, Colonel Brandon jumped down with a sharp bark from an overstuffed armchair.

"Colonel!" reprimanded Aunt Vieve. "Barking at invited guests is bad enough, but this is family!"

At the first sharp word, the dog's head had dropped. Now he came over, his tail slowly waving an apology. I dropped down to my knees to rub him behind the ears and get reacquainted, remembering how he'd laid his head in my lap the last time I'd seen him.

Aunt Vieve gave me a tour of the apartment, which didn't take long. From the back of the living room where we'd entered, a narrow hallway lined with photographs, etchings, and draw-ings ended at her large bedroom, with a smaller bedroom and bathroom to the left and a kitchen and pantry to the right. There weren't any closets, just tall, wooden wardrobes and built-in shelves. There was a claw-foot tub in the bathroom, but no shower. A small window in the kitchen looked out onto the slate tile roof of the building next door. Aunt Vieve's bedroom had a skylight and two windows through which I could see more buildings of brick and stone and a small patch of grass that seemed to be struggling to survive, hemmed in by a board fence that had seen better days. The second bedroom didn't have any windows, but someone had painted one on the far wall above the twin-size bed, so real it looked like you could reach out and feel the breeze. The painted window had actual wood trim, a windowsill, and a rod that held up ivory lace curtains.

"Trompe l'oeil," said Aunt Vieve. "This is where your father sleeps when he visits. You're welcome to this room once he leaves tomorrow, but I've prepared something else for you that I thought you might like. She crooked her finger and led me to the French doors in the front room, then turned me by the shoulders to look back the way we'd come. To the left of the hallway, a narrow corkscrew staircase of wrought iron led to a loft tucked into the eaves of the ceiling.

"I usually use that for storage," said Aunt Vieve, "but I decided it was time for some housecleaning anyway. It's a tight fit, but I think you'll be able to stand up straight without hitting your head. There's a bed up there now, and your suitcase should fit under it. And you can move whatever you like from the shelves to make it yours. What do you think?"

"It's perfect," I said.

I saw Papa look dubiously from my suitcase to the narrow spiral staircase and up to the loft, so when he took his valise to the back bedroom, I seized the opportunity to lug my suitcase myself. They both must have heard me as the hard case thunked against each step, reverberating the entire length of the iron structure as I lifted it to arrive ahead of me, but I eventually got to the top without anyone coming to tell me that maybe this wasn't such a good idea after all. I pushed the suitcase aside to make room for me and stepped onto the floorboards of the loft.

Even with the exposed beams, I was able to stand with a few inches to spare. Against the far wall, tucked beneath a triplet of square windows cranked wide open, was an iron bed stand. Its white paint was chipped in places, but the bed was made up with a patchwork quilt and pillowcases embroidered along the edge with what looked to be swallows. There was a small nightstand of some blond wood that had two shelves and a single drawer. On top of the nightstand was a gilded monkey gazing up at a lightbulb he held aloft in one hand. He didn't look too happy about his chore. An extension cord dribbled over the lip of the loft under the wrought iron railing and disappeared behind the staircase.

I slid my suitcase under the bed and peered more closely at the lamp. I loved my loft, could picture lying in bed and watching through the square windows as the stars came out, but the monkey would have to go. I'd seen enough episodes of *The Twilight Zone* to know that right away.

I came down the stairs and followed the aroma of something delicious to the kitchen. I found them there, Aunt Vieve setting the small table, Papa relaxing in a narrow chair with a tall glass of beer in front of him and Colonel Brandon stretched out at his feet.

"Aunt Vieve, I absolutely love the loft—thank you so much! But, um . . . " I held up the monkey I grasped firmly around the neck.

"Chester!" Papa's face broke out in a grin. He looked up at Aunt Vieve. "Still have your guardian, I see."

She rolled her eyes but smiled. "He's your daughter's guardian, now. See that you don't play any pranks on her. Age hasn't mellowed him a bit, you know."

My heart sank. The creepy monkey lamp was a family heirloom? Great. "Chester?"

Papa held out his hands and I gladly relinquished it.

"When your great aunt first came to live with us, me and my brother—your Uncle Matthew who lives out in California—were quite the terror of the neighborhood. The last straw came when Mrs. Pelton said she was going to call her lawyer on us because our shenanigans had caused her hens to stop laying. Which Matty and I thought was funny, of course, since our father was the Peltons' lawyer. We stopped laughing when Mrs. Pelton pointed out that we'd likely get what we had coming twice: once from our father Mr. Belcourt and a second time from Mr. Belcourt her lawyer." He grimaced. "She was right. I couldn't sit for a week, which was about the length of time it took me to write the apology letter to Mrs. Pelton that my father assigned and the five-hundred-word essay on good citizenship that Mrs. Pelton's lawyer assigned."

"Oh, you exaggerate," said Aunt Vieve, seeing my eyes widen. "Gerard was a gentle soul."

"Gerard knew how to swing a strap," said Papa ruefully. "Well, and we likely deserved it. And in a way it was good for him, too. He'd been walking around in a fog for months—ever since our mother died. I think a lot of what Matty and I did was just to try to get his attention. And probably to work off some of our own grief. But Mrs. Pelton showing up at our door wearing her Sunday hat and asking to speak with her lawyer woke him up." He set the lamp down on the table, patted the monkey's head, and took a long sip from his glass. "Wouldn't be surprised if that wasn't her plan all along. She actually was a really sweet lady. I want to go on record that it was Matty's idea to light the firecrackers under her chicken coop, by the way," he said, looking over his shoulder at Aunt Vieve. She rolled her eyes at him again.

"What does this have to do with a creepy monkey lamp?" I didn't know what disconcerted me more—the monkey, standing on its hind legs as though primed to leap, or the image of my grandfather whipping his sons with a belt, fog or no fog.

"Gerard sent me a letter, asking me to come live with him and the boys," said Aunt Vieve. "Just until everything got settled, he said. So I did. And, because I got a hint of what was going on by reading between the lines, I brought Chester with me. I found him buried in the back of an old jumble shop."

"Jumble shop?"

"Junk store," said Papa.

"Jumble shop," said Aunt Vieve firmly. "When I brought him out of my suitcase and placed him on my bedside table, of course Matty and James wanted to know why I had such an exotic thing."

"I don't think we used the word 'exotic.'"

"I'm sure that's what you meant. You just needed your vocabulary expanded a bit." She donned heavy mitts, opened the oven door, and brought out a steaming shepherd's pie. The ambient aroma in the room grew more intense, and my stomach growled.

Papa eyed our supper and made an appreciative noise. "Anyway," he said, getting up and fetching another bottle of beer from the refrigerator, "your great aunt introduced us to Chester and told us this amazing story about rescuing him in the nick of time from certain destruction—I think there was a large garbage compactor involved? Only to find, to her amazement, that the lamp could actually come alive."

"'I am Ch'es tk re, and I am in your debt,' he said," Aunt Vieve intoned, standing still and regal, waving one mitted hand in a sweeping gesture, her eyes moving between Papa's and mine. "'I once was truly alive, the trusted servant of a Mayan shaman. But he did battle with a rival shaman and was defeated. A stone curse was placed on me. For centuries I waited to be found. Eventually, I was. But it wasn't enough to break the curse. I have waited for someone to claim me and place me in a position of trust, which would break the spell. I have been wrapped in cloths, boxed, and stored as dross. Again and again, I have been found and unwrapped, only to be placed on a shelf to collect dust. I had hope when I was once again made useful, tasked with holding up the magic of illumination, just as I once held up the sacred saucers of flame for my master. But it was no use. I was not placed in a position of trust, but rather in a corner of an inconsequential room.

"'But now, now it is different. You, fair lady, have placed me beside your bed, set to watch over you as you slumber. This is a position of trust. After so many centuries, the spell on me has hardened and can no longer be completely broken, but it can bend. I will protect you, my lady. No one will disturb your slumber. No harm or mischief will come to you while I am on guard. My eyes may appear to be fixed, but they see all. The claws of my hands may appear to be docile, but they are not. I am on guard. And when darkness falls, woe betide any that mean you mischief or harm.'"

There was silence in the room as Aunt Vieve finished her story. I heard rain begin to strike against the window. She winked at me and brought the shepherd's pie to the table.

"Wow. I'm impressed. I think you recited that word for word," said Papa. He turned to me. "It scared the hell out of my brother and me. Suffice to say, with Chester next to Aunt Genevieve's bed, Matty and I found other outlets for our pranks." I noticed Papa had never changed to the "John V. Ev" French pronunciation of her name. ("I've known her a lot longer than Quebec has," he'd said.)

Aunt Vieve moved Chester to the kitchen counter, and I sat down. She ladled out shepherd's pie onto thick plates and Papa said grace. As I put my cloth napkin on my lap and picked up my fork, I looked over to where Chester sat. His vacant eyes stared at the light bulb he held aloft. I'd always thought of monkeys as being from Africa, not Central America. But Kipling's *The*

Jungle Book had been about India, I reminded myself, so why not monkeys in the land of the Maya, too? Savoring the taste of mashed potatoes, spiced ground beef, corn, and peas, I thought about Kipling's monkey temple and wondered if monkeys had taken over ruins in Central America, too. I looked over at Aunt Vieve, who was laughing at something Papa was telling her. I could picture Papa and his brother—the Uncle Matthew I could vaguely remember from a long-ago visit—as young boys listening, enthralled, as she wove her tale of magic, despair, and loyalty.

When dinner was done, I cleared the table and washed the dishes, including the one that Colonel Brandon had licked clean. I rubbed the dachshund's belly and behind his ears for a while, then kissed Papa and Aunt Vieve good night. I took Chester and, cradling him in the crook of one arm, carried him up the spiral staircase back to my loft. I set him on my bedside table and connected him to the extension cord. I pulled *Treasure Island* and *The Secret Garden* out of the embroidered bag, stroking their covers in forgiveness for nearly getting me committed in Union Station. I read for a while by the light of Chester's magical illumination, then clicked off the light and settled in to listen to the rain as I drifted off to sleep, confident that between Chester by my bedside and Papa in the bedroom downstairs, no harm would come to me.

Twelve

Papa took the early afternoon train back to Virginia. Aunt Vieve tried to get him to stay a few days, but he said he was due in court at the end of the week and still had some preparations to make. I kissed him good-bye, accepted some folded money he gave me, and then watched his taxi rumble away over the cobblestones, an odd feeling in the pit of my stomach. A month. I'd see him again in a month. He'd asked me to write to him and Mother.

Aunt Vieve put her arm around me.

"C'mon," she said. "Let's go up and fetch my market basket. We've got some shopping to do."

As always, Aunt Vieve wasn't going anywhere without books. I came down from the loft with *The Secret Garden*. I left *Treasure Island* behind. Aunt Vieve came out from her bedroom with a large wicker basket on one arm and went to her bookshelves.

"*Sense and Sensibility*, of course," she said. "At my age, it's become habit more than anything, but you never know. What else?" She tapped one long index finger against her pursed lips. "How about *The Great Gatsby*? Maybe we'll run into a Daisy Buchanan or, better yet, a Jordan Baker. Always good to identify those—particularly if the Daisy is about to get behind the wheel of a car." She put the book in her basket. "And Mark Twain is always good company." Two more volumes went into the basket. That was four, yet she continued to peruse the shelves.

I started to get nervous. Maybe I should leave *The Secret Garden* behind. I set it on one of the end tables. The movement caught Aunt Vieve's eye.

"Oh, sweetheart, we can certainly bring that one, as well."

"That's okay. We don't need so many."

She looked at me for a moment. "How thoughtless of me. Of course we don't." She took all the books out of her basket except for *Sense and Sensibility*. "I'm so accustomed to my little corner of the world, but it's all new for you. And you're still learning." She walked over to me, picked up *The Secret Garden*, and tucked it under the patterned tea cloth she had in the basket. She put her hand alongside my face. "James told me you got a little overwhelmed at the train station. Quite a crowd there, I understand."

I nodded.

"How many books did you have with you?"

"Two."

"Well, then. We'll take no more than two. And the crowds will be far thinner here. Come along, Colonel."

I followed the two of them down the marble steps. Once on the street, I glanced down at the dachshund that trotted purposefully at my great aunt's left. "He doesn't need a leash?"

"Colonel Brandon? Certainly not."

We walked half a block.

"Does Papa know?"

"I imagine he's noticed I never put one on him."

"No, about the books. You said he told you about the train station."

Aunt Vieve stopped in front of a sundry shop. "I need dish soap, but we can pick that up on the way back. No need to lug it all over town."

She continued on, this time at a stroll. There were other people on the sidewalks and in the shops, but we were able to walk side by side, the dog now trailing close behind.

"Your father has always been very observant, even as a boy. I picked up on that right away. It's one of the things that's made him a good lawyer. He'd collect bits and pieces of information from things he saw and heard and eventually put them together, like a puzzle. Matty—now Matty was the imaginative one. For a while I thought maybe he could hear books, but I came to realize our trait had skipped a generation. Matty was just a daydreamer. Still is. I can't believe he married a Daisy Buchanan. I told him before he proposed that he'd never be able to afford Liza's tastes, but he was smitten." She shook her head. "I suspect he's got a bit of Gatsby in him, although by the time that would have come through, books weren't talking to me about him anymore. That disappeared pretty quickly when I came to take care of the two of them." She smiled at the memory; shook her head again. "Gatsby, I suspect, but definitely without the money."

I was far less interested in Uncle Matthew and Aunt Liza than I was in finding out if Papa had figured out our secret. "Papa is good at chess, but Mother beats him sometimes." We had a fancy chess set that had been a high school graduation gift to one of the cousins before he'd gone off to war. It mostly got used in the winter, since during the other seasons, Mother was typically in the garden in the evenings.

"Does she?" Aunt Vieve laughed. "Well, your mother is a fine woman and definitely a match for James." She looked at me sideways. "That's a good thing. Does he ever play anyone other than Audrey?"

It felt a little weird to have a conversation about my parents using their first names, but I shrugged it off. Maybe this was Aunt Vieve's way of recognizing I was growing up. "Sometimes. He used to play with Mr. Stevens pretty often—he's the president of the local VFW chapter. They'd sit on the porch and Mr. Stevens would smoke a cigar because his wife won't let him smoke at their house, not even outside. But Mr. Stevens said last summer that he was tired of losing, so now he still comes over, but they don't play chess."

"Doesn't surprise me. James seems to lose a little of his analytical perspective when it comes to those closest to him. So he might lose to Audrey, but I'll bet he's a force to be reckoned with when anyone else is on the other side of the board." She nodded to her left and we turned to cross the street. "So, no, I don't think he knows about the books—at least not that I can tell. But I imagine he's been putting pieces together for a very long time. What makes you think he might know?"

I told her about the conversation we'd had in his study the previous year just before her visit.

"He came right out and asked, did he?" Aunt Vieve was thoughtful. "And you didn't tell him the truth?"

She was tall, but not that much taller than me, not anymore. I matched her look. "You never told him. I didn't want him to think I was crazy and send me off to some mental hospital. Mother had already made me see a psychologist. How was I supposed to know that I wasn't crazy? I thought I was the only one."

We came to a store of pink brick with green awnings and *Jean-Alfred Moisan – Épicerie* written in gilt script on the windows. Aunt Vieve grabbed the brass door handle.

"The only one," she repeated. "Yes, that can certainly motivate a lot of actions. Colonel, be so good as to wait here."

She stepped into the store without pausing to see the dog sit down on the sidewalk next to a water dish set out for canine passersby. I followed her through the door.

WE RETURNED TO the apartment about two hours later, me carrying a sizable loaf of bread and the plastic bottle of dish soap, neither of which fit in the full basket, and never having heard a peep out of *The Great Gatsby* or *The Secret Garden.*

"No, NOT THAT one." Aunt Vieve kept walking.

I cast a glance over my shoulder at the display in the store window. We were shopping again, this time to buy stationery so I could fulfill my promise to write home.

"Why not? It looks like they have a lot of different kinds."

"If you'd heard what *Les Misérables* had to say about the couple who owns that store, you wouldn't so much as darken their doorway, let alone actually buy anything there."

I shrugged. After only a handful of days in Quebec City, I was used to this. Aunt Vieve didn't have a car; we walked everywhere. There were shops she'd frequent and those she wouldn't. People with whom she'd stop to chat and those she assiduously avoided. She always dropped a coin or two into the music case of the accordion player who stood near the funicular that connected the upper town with the lower, but never the trio who played near the stairs, even though we passed that way more frequently and I thought they sounded better. We even took a carriage ride one afternoon because *The Little Prince* spoke up just as we were passing by a particular driver standing at the head of his horse, crooning to it in a low voice. I think what really touched Aunt Vieve was that we didn't have that book with us; it was sitting on the driver's seat of the carriage.

We took the stairs down to Lower Town, Aunt Vieve again ignoring the trio, and wound our way through narrow streets to an open square. On the far side was a bookstore with a café next to it and tables shaded by large umbrellas clustered in front of both. It was market day in the square, and Colonel Brandon and I followed Aunt Vieve as she made a beeline through the crowd. She selected a table and sat down.

I looked around. It was mid-morning and the bookstore had obviously just opened. A woman was pushing a rolling cart of books out of the shop, no doubt setting up the day's display. I could see the title on one oversized volume—a history of Russia with annotated maps. Non-fiction, then. I let out a breath, but I eyed the doorway as the woman went back in.

"Have a seat, Margaux. We'll have a cup of something and then go in. They have a marvelous selection of writing papers and cards."

"Is it a specialty bookstore?"

"Specialty?"

"Just history books and maps and that kind of thing."

"Oh, no. They've got everything. I actually purchase quite a few of my novels here. They have an extensive selection of second-hand books, mostly from estate sales, so the prices are quite good."

"So a lot of books." I looked around at the market of vegetables, fruits, meats, cheeses—and customers. "And a lot of people."

"Come sit down, Margaux. This will be good for you. I won't let anything happen to you. Besides, I've told you—you need proximity to hear books."

No sooner did I sit down than the woman came out of the shop again wheeling another cart. From where I sat, I could see *A Tale of Two Cities* in gilt lettering along one spine.

"And here comes the proximity," I said.

"We'll have a hot chocolate, a café crème, and three croissants, please," Aunt Vieve said to the waitress who appeared with a smile and two menus.

I looked up at her, trying to distract myself by noting how the sunlight made her hair seem an odd shade of orange, accentuated by a large gold-colored barrette that tethered her long bangs to one side.

"The crime of suicide lies rather in its disregard for the feelings of those whom we leave behind," I heard *Howards End* say

from its place on the cart. I looked quickly away and focused instead on two women standing in front of a cheese vendor. They looked like mother and daughter and they were in disagreement about something. The cheese vendor looked like he wanted to be someplace else.

"At times our need for a sympathetic gesture is so great that we care not what exactly it signifies or how much we may have to pay for it afterwards."

"Mr. Duffy lived a short distance from his body."

"No, he is not tactful, yet have you ever noticed that there are people who do things which are most indelicate, and yet, at the same time, beautiful?"

I became aware of other murmurs, other books trying to get my attention as people walked by. It was a steady, growing hum, and I had no idea just how loud it was going to get, how many different voices were going to try to force their way into my head, clamoring to be heard. I felt a small swelling of panic and shut my eyes. *Here we go again,* I thought. I tried to conjure from my memory the image of the serene statues aloft in Union Station, unperturbed by the continued turbulence below them.

"Margaux."

"You are inclined to get muddled, if I may judge from last night. Let yourself go. Pull out from the depths those thoughts that you do not understand, and spread them out in the sunlight and know the meaning of them."

It wasn't working. The insistent words were pushing in from all sides.

"Margaux."

I felt Aunt Vieve put her cool hand over my clenched ones.

"Margaux, open your eyes and look at me." Her voice was kind but firm.

I felt a sudden yearning for the creepy monkey lamp, but I did as I was told.

"*A Room with a View,*" I said, feeling a little desperate. "I think it's *A Room with a View.*"

"I think you're right."

"But there's something else there. I think it's about him, the cheese guy. What book has a Mr. Duffy? Why is he living apart from his body?"

"Margaux. Stop. Listen to me. Focus on me."

"*Better pass boldly into that other world, in the full glory of some passion, than fade and wither dismally with age.*"

"There it is again!" I stood up, my chair grating against the granite stones of the square. "Let me go look at the cart. I'm sure I can find the book if I go look at the cart."

"It's James Joyce, Margaux, it's *Dubliners.* You don't have to go look at the cart. Sit down, sweetheart, please."

I saw a nearby couple look up from their menus at me. I put my hand on the table to steady myself.

"You're sure?"

"I'm sure. Have you ever had someone go out of their way to annoy you?"

"What?" I sank back down into my chair, wishing the couple would stop looking at me and just go back to their menus and conversation. I felt the birth of tears sting my eyes. Did Aunt Vieve think I was doing this to annoy her?

"Perhaps in school? Somewhere you can't just get up and leave, and someone is there purposely trying to annoy you? To get under your skin?"

Hello, I had just survived junior high school. "Of course," I said.

"And what did you do?"

"No one will know the difference," I heard behind me from the mother at the cheese stand, her voice raised in exasperation.

"*Respect was invented to cover the empty place where love should be,*" I heard from *Anna Karenina.*

I opened my eyes and turned my head from the cart to the women arguing over cheese, feeling set upon from all sides. I felt a strong pinch on the back of my hand.

"Margaux," Aunt Vieve said sharply. "Don't pay attention to them. Pay attention to me. What did you do? When that person was annoying you and you couldn't just get up and leave. What did you do?"

"I ignored him."

"How did you do that?"

"I just—I just focused on something else. I just acted like he wasn't even there."

Laughter came from the table beside us.

"Laugh, by thunder. Laugh!"

Damn *Treasure Island*. I was beginning to harbor a distinct dislike for that book.

"Margaux. That's what you need to do now. Let it all become background noise. Don't focus on anyone but me. Don't try to connect what you hear from the books with any particular person. Just ignore it. Don't let it into your head. It's like shutting a door and the noise is on the other side. It can't get in if you keep the door shut. Let it become background noise on the other side of the door."

I tore my eyes away from the mother and daughter as they left the cheese stand, empty-handed. I let my gaze pass over the three laughing men at the table next to us and the couple who, thankfully, had stopped looking at me and now only had eyes for one another. I felt Colonel Brandon lean against my leg and focused on how his rough coat felt on my bare skin. I inhaled deeply, taking in the familiar scent of Aunt Vieve's perfume as she leaned in toward me. I made my hands unclench.

I shut the door.

The sound from the books became a murmur, barely heard over the clatter of the waitress setting plates and saucered cups on our table.

"Better?"

I nodded and picked up my cup, sipping the hot chocolate and letting it coat the inside of my mouth, savoring the creamy sweetness and warmth.

Aunt Vieve tore one of the croissants into pieces, set them on her saucer, and placed it on the ground beneath our table. I felt the dog leave his place by my leg.

"It took me a long time to figure out how to do that," she said, picking up her own cup. "It takes practice. And a conscious commitment not to let yourself get out of practice." She took a sip. "I've found that to be the most difficult thing," she added, almost under her breath.

I looked over to where the waitress was smiling and taking an order at another table. She laughed at something the man sitting there had said.

"I think she's unhappy," I said.

Aunt Vieve followed the direction of my gaze. "I think you're right. But I don't think there's much we can do about it. And them," she said, inclining her head to the table of three men next to us. "The laughter is all a show. There isn't anything genuine between any of them."

We sipped from our cups and ate our croissants in companionable silence. I focused on the taste of the buttery bread and the sound of the crunch when my teeth pierced the flaky crust; the richness of the hot chocolate, now cool.

"The woman at the large fruit stand at the front of the square is worried," said Aunt Vieve after a while. "Any time I hear Mrs. Dashwood speak up that loudly or that quickly, I know someone has some serious concerns top of mind—usually about taking care of family. We'll stop there on the way home and give her a bit of business. On a lighter note, there was a young man who passed us on the staircase who I suspect is going to pop the question sometime very soon."

"I didn't hear anything about those two."

Aunt Vieve shrugged. "It was *Sense and Sensibility* talking. We've spent so much time together by now that I hear from it more than any other book, a lot of times just quick little snippets, but it keeps me company." She leaned back to look under the table. "Done with your croissant, Colonel? Let's go buy some paper."

I noticed she left a much larger tip than usual for the orange-haired waitress.

Colonel Brandon parked himself against the brick wall of the building and watched Aunt Vieve disappear into the bookstore. I paused a moment, peering in. There was no more than a handful of people in the shop. I cleared my mind and stepped in. The beloved scent of paper, ink, and leather greeted me and I relaxed. This was no harder than the library at school, and I'd learned how to deal with that. I could do the same here.

Aunt Vieve beckoned to me from the recesses of the store, and I went to her.

WE TOOK OUR time walking home. In addition to some stationery, Aunt Vieve had insisted on buying me a copy of *Dubliners*. I flipped through the pages, reading passages at random out loud. It felt therapeutic—I'd had enough for one day of books reading themselves to me.

"One by one, they were all becoming shades. Better pass boldly into that other world, in the full glory of some passion, than fade and wither dismally with age," I read. "That's it, that's the passage I heard."

"Yes, I heard it, too."

"It's beautiful, isn't it?"

"It is."

"Do you have *A Room with a View* at home?"

"I'm sure I do."

"I know I was starting to freak out a little bit back there, but those lines are really beautiful."

"That's why we read, darling; that's why we read."

"HAVE YOU EVER met one?"

It was raining again. We were doing what we typically did when it rained, which seemed to be fairly frequently, judging by the last two weeks. We read.

Aunt Vieve didn't look up from her pages. "Met one what?"

"Met a Colonel Brandon. Papa said that when you were raising him and Uncle Matthew, you were waiting for a Colonel Brandon. And I don't think I've seen you ever leave the house without that book. So—have you ever met one?"

"Yes. Several, in fact. One fairly recently, come to mention it."

I'd been draped over the sides of the overstuffed chair I'd come to think of as mine. Now I swung my legs off and leaned forward. "And?"

"And it wasn't a fit."

I fell back against the chair, deflated. "But I thought . . . "

Aunt Vieve turned a page.

We'd left the French doors open for the breeze, but now the wind changed direction and a smattering of rain hit the hardwood floor. Aunt Vieve cut her eyes at me and raised her brow. I sighed and got up to shut the doors, turning the handle that adjusted the hinges the way she'd taught me so that the doors leaned open from the top, letting in air while keeping out the rain. I went back to my chair, picked up *Emma*, and then put it down again.

"Why wasn't it a fit?"

Aunt Vieve sighed and put *Mrs. Dalloway* on her lap. "Well, let's see." She counted on her fingers. "The first time, he was actually a she, and that simply doesn't work for me. The second time, he was already married, with three children." Aunt Vieve smiled. "A darling man, and a part of me is in love with him to this very day. But to be a Colonel Brandon is to have honor. If he broke his vows, he wouldn't be much of a Colonel Brandon, now, would he? So we parted as friends. I received an invitation to his daughter's wedding a few years ago. I sent a gift, but I wasn't really up for a trip to Europe." She looked over toward some framed photographs on one of the bookshelves and seemed lost in thought for a moment. "And the third time, I'm afraid," she said finally, "either I was born forty years too early or he was born forty years too late."

I waited for her to say more, but she didn't. It all seemed very sad, and I didn't want to read *Emma* anymore. I got up and put it back in its place on the shelf and went prowling for something else. Bradbury, maybe, or even Tolkien. I meandered to the framed photographs that had drawn my aunt's eye. An eight-by-ten black-and-white showed a formal family portrait. The man was tall with dark hair and wore a uniform with ribbons on it. He had one arm around the shoulders of a young boy, and the other rested on the back of a chair where a lady with her hair done up sat in a demure pose. She held a child on her lap. A third child, a girl, sat in a frilly dress on a small chair bracketed by her parents. There was another photo, smaller, that looked to be taken at the same time. In this one, the same children sat on a striped sofa surrounding a young woman. I look closer. The young woman was Aunt Vieve.

"It appears that the wind shift has carried away the rain. Let's go for a walk," I heard from behind me.

I felt I'd been caught spying and took a quick step back from the bookcase, almost tripping on Colonel Brandon. "What?" I hissed at him. He sidestepped but continued to look up at me. I grabbed a book from the shelf above the photos and joined Aunt Vieve at the door. She had her market basket. I knew what book lay in the bottom of it, below the patterned tea towel. She held the wicker basket out to me and I slipped my book into it, noting I'd grabbed F. Scott Fitzgerald's *The Beautiful and Damned*.

I'd started but had never been able to finish that book. Somehow it felt a very appropriate selection.

Thirteen

"I've invited Mr. Lederle to coffee this afternoon," said Aunt Vieve. "We'll need to go to the bakery just as soon as you've finished breakfast. I want to pick out a nice torte and some of those little petit fours they make. By noon, the selection will be down to nothing."

I dribbled a few more blueberries on my cereal and tried to remember what I had in my suitcase or draped over the end of the bed that was clean. I'd been meaning to do laundry, but Aunt Vieve wasn't a stickler about chores and I wasn't very good about imposing them on myself. "Why are we having Mr. Lederle over for coffee?"

Mr. Lederle was one of the many street artists who painted local scenes. Most of these he sold to tourists. Aunt Vieve had introduced me to him one afternoon when we'd cut through rue du Trésor, a narrow street where some enterprising art students had started displaying their work. He was tall and lanky with light brown shaggy hair that usually half-covered his intense blue eyes, which was probably just as well, since when he turned them on me full force, my knees became butter, even though he was probably close to thirty years old. He and Aunt Vieve typically spoke French with one another. It made me feel left out and contributed to my butter knees at the same time.

"Why not?"

"No reason. It's just that I've been here three weeks and you've never had anybody over."

"That's not true. Mr. Martel came by just last week."

"That was to drop off a package that didn't fit in your mailbox."

She shrugged. "Still, he could have left the slip in the mailbox downstairs letting me know to come to the post office to pick it up. Instead he came all the way up the stairs, knocked on the door, and I opened it. That constitutes a visit."

"I suppose it does."

"You can wipe that grin off your face, young lady."

I laughed, seeing the curl at the corner of her mouth. The package had come all the way from Belgium, Mr. Martel had said, and so he'd felt it might be important, and Madame should have it right away. It had been wrapped in thick brown paper and secured with twine. An array of colorful stamps had covered the upper right corner. She had taken it from his weatherworn hands and given him her sincere thanks, which had made him blush. I couldn't remember ever seeing a man blush, much less one who was at least as old as my great aunt. She'd invited him in and he'd looked torn for a moment, but he'd demurred and then left with a jerky bow that had seemed both rehearsed and an afterthought. She'd closed the door and held the package for a moment. She'd looked up to see me perched backward on my usual chair, avidly watching with just my nose and eyes visible over the cushioned back, then had spun on her heels to take it to her room and shut the door, ignoring my call of "Who's it from?"

"Are you done with your cereal?"

I abandoned my spoon and lifted the bowl to my mouth to drain it. "Done," I said.

AUNT VIEVE SET the coffee table with the delicate china set I'd never seen outside of its glass display case, the good silver I'd polished for her that morning, and patterned napkins so gossamer I could see through them when unfolded and held up to the sunlight. When she went to the kitchen, I ran my fingers along the scalloped edge of a plate. It was trimmed in gold with painted ribbon swirls of royal blue and gold and raised embellishments of white. I picked it up carefully and turned it over. *Tirschenreuth 1838 Baronesse* was stamped on the bottom. It was beautiful, and I suddenly wished Mother were here to see it—that she were coming to coffee and not Mr. Lederle. I set it down gently when I heard Aunt Vieve's heels on the hardwood floor mark her approach, and I took a step back to watch her carefully set in the middle of the table the matching china platter bedecked with the torte, now sliced, and petit fours we'd selected at the bakery.

The French doors were open to the breeze, and I caught the scent of the herbs and cherry tomatoes on the shallow balcony heated by the sunlight that striped the hardwood floor and worn Oriental rug. I looked around, taking in the tall bookcases with all those volumes and cherished relics of family history and travels abroad, the swirl of iron staircase that led to my loft, the overstuffed chairs facing the high-backed sofa across the expanse of the now-laden coffee table, the plump cushion on the floor where Colonel Brandon had left a permanent indentation, and decided that this definitely edged out my beech tree as my favorite place in all the world.

MR. LEDERLE ARRIVED promptly at three, which surprised me a little. I didn't think of artists as the type who paid all that much attention to punctuality. He crossed the threshold at Aunt Vieve's invitation. Not tentatively and with a blush, as Mr. Martel had done, but with one single, confident step. She lifted her face to him, and they kissed one another—a brush of first one cheek and then the other. It was called a *faire la bise*—I'd looked it up after seeing it done so often here in Quebec City. I stood to the side, a hand on the railing of my staircase. Half of my mind was rethinking what I had chosen to wear—jeans and a peasant-style blouse that I'd bought with the money Papa had given me because it echoed ones I'd seen worn by girls much older than me holding the attention of boys that looked like younger versions of Mr. Lederle. The other half of my mind catalogued the ease with which Aunt Vieve interacted with him.

"*Je suis ravi que vous soyez ici, Monsieur Lederle. Vous vous souvenez de ma nièce Margaux?*" Aunt Vieve said as she turned his attention to me.

I smiled and nodded, understanding the gist of the exchange, trying to appear at ease and natural. This was home while I was in Quebec City, after all. In this apartment, *he* was the visitor, I told myself as he turned to me. The muscles of my face suddenly locked up. I hoped I didn't look insipid.

"*Mais bien sûr. Comment pourrais-je ne pas?*" he said. He walked over and greeted me as he had my great aunt. "Mademoiselle, how nice to see you again," he said, switching to English.

His breath brushing my left cheek then my right removed any hope I'd had of mimicking Aunt Vieve's casual yet welcoming air. I could feel heat rise in my face, instantly incinerating any words that might have been ready to exit my mouth.

Thankfully, he turned again to Aunt Vieve. "I can't tell you how delighted I was to be invited into your home, Madame. It's an honor. I know you've always insisted on formality, but surely this allows us a bit more familiarity. You must call me Thierry."

Aunt Vieve smiled. She loved charming men; she'd told me that more than once. She especially loved the ones who could, as she said, "dance the fine line between rogue and all-too-perfect gentleman." Don't you mean walk the fine line? I'd asked, remembering a phrase Papa used on occasion to describe working with his law clients. Why walk when one can dance? she'd replied over her shoulder, and then pirouetted on the spot, swinging her market basket wide, there on the parapet where Upper Town overlooked the river. When we got back to the apartment, I'd practiced pirouettes in the privacy of my small loft until one spin had nearly sent me over the rail.

"Thierry, then," she said. "And you must call me Genevieve."

Her name rolled off her tongue in soft consonants and breath in a way that made me think she knew a bit about that dance, herself. I'd never get my name to sound like that. I had an expensive name, a teacher had once told me—pay for seven letters but only actually hear five.

I looked at the bookshelves. Nothing to say? I thought at them. Of course they didn't answer me.

Mr. Lederle—being only thirteen, I didn't think the first-name invitation included me—sat down in one of the chairs. When Aunt Vieve gracefully sank to sit in the hostess position in the middle of the couch opposite him, I took my usual spot, mimicking her by perching on the edge of the cushion and crossing my legs at the ankles.

"So, Thierry, what news from rue du Trésor?"

She poured a stream of steaming coffee into his cup. His hand as he picked it up looked exactly as I thought an artist's hands should look: one soft palm cradled the bottom of the fragile thing while two long fingers of the other, a trace of blue paint that matched his eyes visible along the cuticle curve of one nail, looped through the cup's handle. It was graceful and masculine all at the same time, and I felt a flutter in my stomach.

"It's going well. The word is getting out, so we're all having to consolidate our space a bit to let more artists in—which has gone more or less smoothly, as you can imagine. But I agree with Pierre and Harry—it benefits all of us if more artists and more people come to think of rue du Trésor as a place to see the true art of Quebec. Not just art for tourists, but for lovers of art and lovers of Quebec City."

"What vision those two had," said Aunt Vieve. "I do love seeing artists at work around the city, but rue du Trésor—a treasure, indeed." She poured only half a cup of coffee for me, knowing I'd fill the other half with the steamed milk and a sizable helping of sugar. "And are you getting many art lovers?"

He shrugged. "Mostly tourists. Enough to pay the rent and buy more paint and canvases." He accepted a plate from Aunt Vieve. "But it's my hope that will change. Bringing in additional quality artists will help, I think. I've discussed this with Pierre and Harry—we have to uphold the quality. It can't just be about who knows whom. I know they founded rue du Trésor—had the vision, as you say, made it happen—but there is so much more that it could be. Not just streetscapes and landscapes—how many versions of Château Frontenac does the world need? It could be a true inspiration for artists and lovers of art alike. 'It is through art and art only that we can shield ourselves from the sordid perils of actual existence.' Oscar Wilde."

"I don't want realism. I want magic! Yes, yes, magic! I try to give that to people. I misrepresent things to them. I don't tell the truth, I tell what ought to be the truth. And if that's sinful, then let me be damned for it!" a high, female voice interjected from the shelves.

It took me a moment, and then I realized it was *A Streetcar Named Desire*, which was unexpected. And the voice had been Blanche DuBois's, which was even more unexpected.

"Sordid, indeed," said Aunt Vieve. "'It is through art and through art only that we can realize our perfection.'"

Mr. Lederle set down his cup and leaned forward, his elbows on his knees. He seemed contemplative. Aunt Vieve sipped from her cup. I heard a car honk in the street, a yelled retort, another honk in response. The sounds seemed to melt once they reached our room, the books absorbing the short, bright cacophony. All here remained serene. Colonel Brandon didn't even look up from where he lay on his cushion.

"I've no aspirations to be rich and famous, Genevieve," Mr. Lederle finally said. "I know a lot of my compatriots—and I count

Pierre and Harry among them—want the gallery openings, the write-ups in the newspaper, the invitation to exhibit in Montreal. This may sound a bit pretentious, but money and fame really don't mean all that much to me. Of course I want to have a roof over my head, clothes on my back, and meals on the table, but beyond that—give me paint, give me canvas." He shrugged.

I buried my face in my cup. This was confusing. I couldn't tell if Aunt Vieve had also heard Tennessee Williams's *A Streetcar Named Desire.* I'd read it one rainy afternoon just last week. I had felt the heat rise in my cheeks and low in my belly as I'd finished it by the light of my guardian monkey lamp, knowing Mother wouldn't have thought this an appropriate selection from the many, many books Aunt Vieve had on her shelves. It had taken me a long time to fall asleep after I'd finished the last page. I hadn't liked the play; didn't like how Stanley got away with what he did to Blanche; how her sister Stella hadn't believed her. In the last scene, Blanche was taken away to a mental in-stitution—her tale of rape the last bit of proof needed to show she was crazy, I guess. I had lain in bed, looking out my trio of square windows for stars that the city lights made invisible.

But the voice I'd heard from the shelf was not Stanley's—and I just wasn't sure how to connect the very self-assured and mas-culine artist sitting to my left now exchanging news about mutual acquaintances and goings-on in the neighborhood with what *Streetcar* was telling me through the voice of the fragile Blanche.

"He should have known better," said Aunt Vieve with a dis-missive wave of her hand in response to the latest bit of gossip disguised as news.

I didn't know what they were talking about—I'd missed it during my ruminations and scanning of shelves, willing some-body to say something more. I felt like I was back in school again.

"We both quoted dear Mr. Wilde earlier," she continued. "But in my experience, art alone is *not* enough—and perhaps in yours as well, although I'm willing to keep that tidbit just between us." She tilted her head, a coquettish smile on her lips. "'Give me books, French wine, fruit, fine weather, and a little music played out of doors by somebody I do not know.' Keats. I can make do without the fine weather, as we all mostly have this last month or so, but books and wine—surely you don't include those as part of the 'sordid peril'? May I offer you more coffee, or perhaps something that comes in a stemmed glass?"

He smiled. "Genevieve, nothing that comes from your hand could ever be sordid."

I took this as my cue and got up to fetch the bottle of white wine from the fridge and decanter of tawny port from the counter, as well as the tray of glasses prepared in advance. I focused on carrying these to the coffee table without letting them rattle. I noticed Mr. Lederle and Aunt Vieve had hardly touched their plates, so between trips I surreptitiously took mine with its scattering of crumbs back to the kitchen.

Not that either of them noticed me at all.

"Keats. I've not read him for a while. Been too engrossed in my painting to take time for poetry—but I see now that this is a failing I need to correct."

"I have always depended on the kindness of strangers."

"I agree one shouldn't be overly engrossed in the pursuit of riches, Thierry, but you do appear to have a certain—revulsion—about the topic."

"I've seen how the pursuit of money can corrupt art, Genevieve."

"Run for your life from any man who tells you that money is evil. That sentence is the leper's bell of an approaching looter."

I had no idea what book this was. The voice was coming from behind me. I turned my head, oh so nonchalantly, and looked to those shelves. My eyes scanned lots and lots of spines of cloth and leather. About a third of the way up in the bookcase to the left, I thought, but beyond that I hadn't a clue which book had spoken. I turned back around and caught a wink from Aunt Vieve.

Mr. Lederle saw the wink and looked at me, as though remembering I was there at all. He raised his glass of wine.

"To the beauty and charm of my hostesses; you are the inspiration for art."

I felt my cheeks grow red, but I reached over and picked up the glass of wine Aunt Vieve had poured for me. It was less than a third full, but I felt like Eve as I lifted it to my lips.

"So what are you working on now?" asked Aunt Vieve. "I've not seen you at your easel around the city lately."

"I'm working on some new pieces. Something a little different. Portraits, of a sort. Portraits of the city, you might say. A friend has a loft down in the lower town—lots of windows, the most amazing light. I've been staying there."

"It sounds marvelous—both the work and the space. Will you exhibit in rue du Trésor?"

"Possibly. I haven't decided yet. Although I know I owe Pierre and Harry a great deal."

"There are no white lies, there is only the blackest of destruction, and a white lie is the blackest of all."

"I don't believe in 'guilt.' I don't believe in villains or heroes—only right or wrong ways that individuals have taken, not by choice but by necessity or by certain still-uncomprehended influences in themselves, their circumstances, and their antecedents," replied *A Streetcar Named Desire* to the book on the shelf behind me.

"Well, you must let me know when and where I can see this new work of yours when it's ready. Now that you know my address, there's no excuse for not keeping me apprised." She said this with an arched brow and a glance over the glass raised to her lips.

I squashed my immediate impulse to practice raising only one eyebrow. I had never been able to do it before; I doubted seeing her do it yet again with such ease and effect would convince my facial muscles to mimic hers.

"Of course. And, in the meantime, if there's something particular you'd like to add to your own collection, I do, of course, take commissions." He took a sip from his glass and cast his eyes around the room. It seemed to me he took it all in, and I wondered what stood out, what faded to background. "I'd like nothing better than to create a piece for you that would enhance this room."

The air felt thick to me all of a sudden, and Colonel Brandon raised his head, his mustache appearing to me particularly bristly. Enhance this room? This room was perfect.

"I've actually been considering a piece for another room," said Aunt Vieve smoothly. She looked down at Colonel Brandon. He pointedly ignored her and continued to stare at our visitor. I inwardly applauded him.

Mr. Lederle didn't notice the dog or me. He set down his glass.

"What did you have in mind? I'd be happy to give you several sketches. We could work from there."

"I'm not quite sure yet precisely what I want," said Aunt Vieve with a wave of one hand. "I'll have to think on it a bit more." She took another sip then set down her own glass. She smiled at Mr. Lederle.

He took the hint.

"Well, you know where to find me. Thank you so much for your hospitality, Genevieve," he said, standing up. "I can't remember when I've enjoyed an afternoon more."

"It was our pleasure, Thierry," said Aunt Vieve.

At the inclusion, I set down my own glass and trailed after them to the door. They exchanged another *faire la bise*. I felt the heat rise in my cheeks again in anticipation, but Mr. Lederle simply gave me a small wave and Aunt Vieve a long look before leaving. I heard the smooth shuffle of his shoes against the worn marble steps before Aunt Vieve shut the door.

She sighed. "Well, that was a bit of a disappointment. I'd *so* hoped for *Fahrenheit 451*. I really want a *Fahrenheit 451* artist for this piece. 'Stuff your eyes with wonder, he said, live as if you'd drop dead in ten seconds. See the world. It's more fantastic than any dream made or paid for in factories.'" She sighed again and strolled over to the stack that held the book I hadn't been able to identify. "I took it with me to rue du Trésor several times, but thought maybe the book just clammed up with so many people milling around. Wishful thinking."

"What piece?"

"A painting I want done," she said. "Something I've had in mind for a few months now, but I have to find just the right person to create it for me. When I want to really understand the motivations and inner workings of someone, I invite them over for coffee and let the books speak as they will. I can't possibly tote around every option, after all. What they say is just a guideline, of course, but it definitely helps cut through appearances. Now which of you was it?" This last was addressed to the spines on the third shelf from the top.

"I heard *A Streetcar Named Desire*, but that was from the other side of the room," I said. "I didn't know who it was over here. You don't either?" I'd never known Aunt Vieve not to be able to identify a book right away.

She turned to look at me, the brow again arched. "You read *Streetcar*?"

I nodded. A little embarrassed, I wandered over to scratch Colonel Brandon behind his ears. He rolled over to give me access to his pink tummy.

"So what did you think of it?"

"I didn't like it."

"Hmm. It's an excellent play, actually—I'd love to see a live performance one day. But I can see where you might find it a bit disturbing." She turned back to the shelf. "All artists—good ones, at any rate—have a bit of the fanciful about them, but I have to admit I wouldn't have pegged Thierry Lederle as a Blanche DuBois. Ah, there you are." She pulled a thick volume off the shelf and smoothed her hand over the cloth cover.

I craned my neck from where I sat, trying to see the title.

"*Atlas Shrugged*," she said, holding it up for me to see. "I got it with a box of books I bought at an auction. Hadn't gotten around to reading it yet."

"How do you know that's the one if you haven't read it?"

"Sometimes you can tell which book speaks, even if you aren't personally acquainted with it. You know that sort of hum, that vibration, you feel that lets you know where the book is that spoke? The way you knew exactly on which shelf *Streetcar* was?" She waited for my nod. "A lot of times that vibration lingers for a while, sort of like a church bell that's been rung. If you don't wait too long, you can hone into the specific book by following that vibration." She opened the cover and flipped through some of the pages. "Plus, I've read all the other books on this shelf, and it wasn't one of them.

"Yes, a live performance of *Streetcar* would be just the thing," she continued, turning back to the title page of *Atlas Shrugged* and running her long fingers along the ink as though introducing herself. "This whole afternoon felt a bit theatrical, don't you think? Maybe Thierry was meant for the stage."

Her voice trailed off and I knew I was losing her. I smiled and gave the dog's tummy one last rub. Aunt Vieve wandered to the coffee table, absently drained off her glass, and then picked up the wine bottle with the same hand and strolled down the hall to her bedroom, glass and bottle in one hand and already engrossed in the book she cradled with the other. I watched her bedroom door close, then went to the coffee table and drank the rest of the wine in my glass before going up the staircase to my loft to find my own book.

Fourteen

"Why won't they talk to us?"

I kept my tone conversational, but, hearing my voice as I said it, I sounded like Mother when she tried to make caramel on a humid or wet day. It just never worked out and her frustration always came through.

It was certainly wet in Quebec City that June and July. Everything felt damp.

Everything *smelled* damp, an earthy fragrance from the pots and window boxes of flowers and herbs on the French balcony overlaid with a faint mustiness from the carpets and drapes.

"Who, darling?"

We were all tucked into our usual spots in the front room—Aunt Vieve, Colonel Brandon, and me. The red-mullioned French doors were wide open, letting in the damp summer breeze. Aunt Vieve had called today's weather "merely a mizzle"—a cross between a mist and a drizzle—and hadn't even bothered with an umbrella when we'd taken Colonel Brandon out for his morning constitutional.

I hadn't seen the sun in days. No one came to visit. The street cafés were empty. Tourists didn't meander as they typically did, providing entertaining people-watching opportunities. The street musicians and *plein air* artists were absent, waiting for the skies to clear. Few voices or laughs came drifting up from the street. The most frequent sounds were tires shushing over wet cobblestones, Colonel Brandon's gentle snores, and the rasp of paper against paper as Aunt Vieve turned the pages of *Atlas Shrugged*.

Which wasn't saying anything out loud.

None of the books were.

"The books," I said. It came out with more exasperation than I'd intended.

"Why would you expect them to?" Aunt Vieve didn't look up from the page.

I considered that.

At length.

Thought about how to say it. It had been bothering me for a while.

"Well, they've spoken up plenty of times—sometimes all at once—when it would have been better that they didn't." I avoided looking at the books or Aunt Vieve when I said this, instead focusing my gaze on Colonel Brandon. The dog snored on.

"Better?"

I felt a wave of indignation. It was a question? She knew what had happened at school. I was sure Papa had told her. And she knew about the train station. She had been there that first time at the outdoor café here in Quebec City. Didn't she remember? Didn't she understand?

I heard another page turn.

I tamped down my indignation. Wouldn't let it coalesce into anger. Forced it to sluice away. This was a conversation. Not an argument. And I could never be angry with Aunt Vieve anyway.

Ever.

"It's just, at a time like this, when it's so quiet, just a lot of rain—well I know it's only mizzle today, but there's been a lot of rain—and so now it's just us, and there's not a lot going on, it just seems like it would be nice to, well, hear them. There are so many times they talk—why not now? To maybe have, I don't know, maybe a conversation. Or they could have a conversation, and we could listen. Sort of like listening to the radio." I knew I was rambling. I finally managed to stop.

Aunt Vieve still didn't say anything. She didn't have a radio. Or a television. Or even a phone, for that matter. Papa and Mother had Mr. Keinwitz's number, who lived below Aunt Vieve on the second floor.

The silence stretched.

I decided to bring up something else I'd been thinking about.

"Do you think they talk to each other? And we just can't hear them?"

"Interesting notion," said Aunt Vieve. She didn't look up from her book.

I waited, but she didn't say anything more.

I set my book aside. Cast my gaze across the bookshelves and all the volumes in the room.

"Why won't they talk to us?" I repeated.

After a moment, Aunt Vieve closed her book on her lap. She kept one finger in it to mark her place.

"You said they won't talk to us about family, most of the time," I went on, encouraged. "And that they won't talk to us about ourselves ever. But why? It would be so nice, especially on a day like this . . ." My voice trailed away as she tilted her head and raised one brow.

"On a day like this," repeated Aunt Vieve.

She took her finger out of the book and folded her hands on top of it. She turned her head to look around the whole of the room, slowly, seeming to take it in as though seeing it for the first time. I watched her. I knew from memory what she was seeing, feeling a seed of chagrin and disappointment in myself plant in my chest. This was my favorite room in the world, I reminded myself. From the chair I sat in now, from my loft, from the kitchen, from the doorway as we entered coming back from errands or walking Colonel Brandon, turning from a shelf after selecting a book—from all those viewpoints and more I'd viewed this room and taken it in, grateful beyond measure that it existed and that I had a place in it, belonged in it, was claimed by it.

I huffed the seed out of my chest. I *did* love this room. Anything to the contrary wasn't what I had said, implied. It was just the endless rain, or mizzle, or whatever it was—the ever-present damp, I guess—was getting to me. It wasn't about the room. But Aunt Vieve seemed to take it that way.

Her gaze ended on Colonel Brandon, curled up with his tail nearly tucked under his snout. Her expression softened, but there was something else there I couldn't name, especially only seeing her face in profile.

"Be careful, Margaux. Be very careful what you wish for." Aunt Vieve looked at me. "And be especially careful of what, in your wishing, you unknowingly wish away."

I still can't name what caused it, but I felt an involuntary shiver ripple over me, even as a warm, damp, summer breeze came through the French doors and riffled my hair.

WISE WORDS. I'D remember them, later.

Fifteen

Papa arrived several days later to escort me home.

I couldn't decide how to feel. I was truly happy to see him, hugged him tight as soon as he'd set his suitcase on the floor, burying my face in his shirt, imagining I could smell the scents of home in the creases of the cotton instead of just the sweat of so many hours spent on the train. But as I peered over his shoulder to see Aunt Vieve waiting her turn, my throat tightened. How could I leave? This place was home, too. Aunt Vieve, Colonel Brandon, this room, my loft, the accordion player by the funicular that Aunt Vieve always tipped, the trio who were better musicians that she never did, the artists in rue du Trésor, the woman who always set up her easel in the same place on the parapet overlooking Lower Town and the river but whose paintings were never repetitive, the lady behind the cheese counter at *Jean-Alfred Moisan* who had something "special" for us every time we came, the sad waitress with the orange hair and lilting laugh at the café in the square, Mr. Martel who had climbed our stairs again just yesterday, gray-bearded Mr. Keinwitz on the second floor who liked to speak to Colonel Brandon in Latin—how could I leave them all behind, not knowing when or if I'd ever see them again? And the books! There were so, so many I hadn't read yet. I thought about my fledgling library in my bedroom in Virginia and felt like someone going from a banquet to rations of bread and water.

Papa hugged me tight in return, and I felt him press his lips against the top of my head. He stepped back and held me

at arm's length, his eyes roving my face, my body. He smiled,
then kissed me warmly on the cheek.

"That's from your mother," he said. "I promised."

I'd been missed.

He turned to Aunt Vieve. I couldn't make out the murmur
between the two of them as they embraced, but Aunt Vieve's eyes
were shut tight and her fingertips whitened where they clutched
Papa's shoulders. I looked down to see Colonel Brandon watching
the two of them. He noticed me and wagged his tail, but slowly.
He knew what a suitcase meant.

THIS TIME PAPA had arranged to stay a few days. We made the
most of them. We went several times to the café in the square,
always sitting at one of the tables in front of the bookstore. It
had become a part of our routine, a chance for me to practice
being around a lot of different kinds of people along with lots
of books. We rented bicycles and rode to Montmorency Falls,
where we had a picnic. We visited rue du Trésor. Papa was
going to buy a streetscape watercolor from one of the artists—
not Mr. Lederle, whom we hadn't seen since his afternoon
visit—but Aunt Vieve led him instead to the woman on the
parapet. While she spoke with her, market basket, as ever, on
her arm, I helped Papa select a painting for Mother. I favored
a scene that showed the city in the rain—a familiar sight in
the month I'd been here, although everyone said it was somewhat unusual for this time of year—but Papa chose one that
showed a narrow cobblestone street with stucco-and-timber
buildings that seemed to lean forward so that you could imagine the flowers in the window boxes might reach across to
entwine with one another.

On our last evening in Quebec City, we took a carriage ride
with the man who had had *The Little Prince* on the driver's seat.

It wasn't there anymore, but it still seemed the perfect ending to my stay. The driver let me feed a carrot to the horse and told me its name was Fox.

THE NEXT MORNING, I put everything in order in my loft. I even kissed my creepy guardian monkey lamp good-bye. You just never know. I thought about asking Aunt Vieve if I could pack him in a box and bring him to Virginia with me, but I decided against it. I liked the idea that he would guard my loft until I could come back next summer.

And I would come back next summer. Over dinner Papa had given Aunt Vieve and me his solemn word that I would be allowed to return as soon as school let out. Aunt Vieve had winked at me, and I'd noticed her eyes were bright with unshed tears.

I would be missed.

Mine didn't stay unshed. They dripped. It wasn't long before my nose joined in. The taxi driver didn't say anything, and Papa just hugged me around the shoulder and gave me a clean handkerchief, but I'm sure I was a blotchy mess by the time we boarded the train. I watched the city disappear behind us as the rhythm of the rails became a staccato. It was a soothing sound and, after a while, I slept. When I awoke, we'd left Canada behind.

Sixteen

I didn't get to visit Aunt Vieve the next summer. Nor the one after that.

"It is kind of exciting when you think about it," said Georgia one spring afternoon our high school sophomore year.

I lifted my head from the floorboards of my bedroom where I'd been lying, indulging my exasperation, Aunt Vieve's latest letter in my hand. "Exciting how? She's still in California taking care of my cousins because my talentless Aunt Liza left my clueless Uncle Matthew to become a movie star. Which apparently means living with some producer. Or director. Or something." I wasn't entirely clear on this last part but had heard enough of conversations between Mother and Papa to draw my own conclusions. "Bottom line, I don't get to go to Quebec City this summer. Again. How is this exciting?"

As unthinkable as it had been before Aunt Vieve had come into my life, Georgia Pillard and I had become friends. School scars being as enduring as they are, I hesitated to call her my best friend, since I wasn't sure the feeling was reciprocated. Georgia had a lot of friends. I'd only caught her attention via the mystique Aunt Vieve had cast that afternoon she'd spent in the Pillards' sundry shop talking about her time as nanny to a baron's children in Europe. I hadn't had a clue what Georgia was talking about when she'd first brought it up, but then I remembered Mr. Martel climbing the worn marble flights of stairs to Aunt Vieve's apartment on the third floor to deliver a package from Brussels and the framed photographs on the bookshelves. Georgia had started talking to me when she'd found out through the grapevine that I'd spent a good part of the summer in Quebec City with Aunt Vieve. One day the fall after my trip to Quebec City, out of the blue, Georgia had turned around in her seat in history class and asked me about an assignment. About a week later, she'd invited me to sit with her and some of the other girls at lunch.

I'd been guarded at first, wary of a trick. It had all fallen into a kind of routine and others had accepted me because Georgia had, I'd started to relax. It was nice to have people who included you in conversations, who laughed with you instead of at you, who shared M&Ms passed surreptitiously around the classroom when the teacher turned her back to write on the blackboard, who saved a space for you on the bleachers in the school gym to watch a basketball game.

I realized that I'd changed, too. Part of it was the influence and tutelage of Aunt Vieve, who continued to write regularly. I had some new clothes, which helped how people saw me, I guess. More important, though, I just felt more confident, since the month spent in Quebec City. Maybe that changed how people saw me, too.

Another part of it was, well, I was growing up. I'd gotten used to the at-first uncomfortable feel of a bra strapped around my chest. The first week, I'd felt like my undershirt had ridden up. And then had come blood. And cramps. I'd read Genesis in my Children's Bible back in elementary school. More than one month, I'd lain in bed with a hot water bottle pressed against my belly, planning what I'd say to Eve about the ramifications of her life choices if I ever got the chance.

I'd solidified our friendship when I'd saved Georgia from a disastrous relationship our freshman year. Keeping an arsenal of novels in my locker had its advantages. Georgia's locker was just a few to the left from mine, and boys would come by to talk sometimes. Mostly they talked to Georgia, but a lot of times it was to both of us. Sometimes it was just to me.

It was nice having a girlfriend, I'd decided then.

"You're so self-centered, Margaux," sighed Georgia now. She was sprawled on my bed perusing the latest issue of *16 Magazine* she'd "borrowed" from her parents' store. Her hair cascaded like a smooth blond waterfall over the edge of my bed. "How do you know your aunt doesn't have talent? And just because she's living with someone doesn't mean she's sleeping with him. It could be like a commune—they have those in California, you know. Emily's sister joined one last year after graduation. Oh, and I meant to ask before: is her name really Liza, or did she just make that her name, like Marilyn Monroe was really Norma Jean Mortenson? I can't believe she killed herself. Marilyn, I mean."

I had diligently tried to get my hair to mimic Georgia's, but to no avail. Mine stayed thick, wavy, and very brown, although Mother insisted it was "warm chestnut" and that all it needed was one hundred strokes every night with the boar-hair-bristle brush she'd bought me. That routine had lasted all of a week before I'd abandoned the effort as futile.

"I think her name is really Elizabeth, but I've always heard her called Liza, so I don't know." I let my head thunk back against the floorboards and stared up at the ceiling. It was very white, very bland. Like a blank piece of paper waiting for words. "Why am I self-centered?"

"Liza Belcourt. It *sounds* like a movie star name. Why shouldn't she want to give it a shot? I wonder what her maiden name was? I could never marry a guy with a gross last name. Cheri Butz has got to be just dying to get married. Anything would be better than Butz. I don't care how often she says it's pronounced 'boots.' I'm surprised anybody even dates her brother, although he *is* cute.

But still. I can't believe my parents named me after a state. Like I don't know it's where they honeymooned. Daddy calls Mama his 'peach' all the time. It's gross." I heard her flip through a few more pages of the magazine.

"She had soon begun tormenting him with her rather touchy vanity. One day, for instance, alluding to her four thorns, she remarked to the little prince, "I'm ready for tigers, with all their claws!"'

I smiled, knowing exactly where on my shelves this voice was coming from and feeling my annoyance at being called self-centered fade away. I'd heard this book—and only this book—speak of Georgia so many times. So I didn't think of her as a state and didn't associate her with a peach. I thought of her as a flower. She was Rose.

For the longest time, not a single one of my books had connected with her. Well, maybe one or two had when lots of books had talked at the same time in the library or classroom and Georgia had been there, but I hadn't been good yet at connecting specific books with specific people and had spent most of my effort at school trying to tune them out. I'd been so expectant the first time she'd come here to my bedroom after school to study for an English test. But nothing. After a while, it had put me on edge, like Georgia and my books had been in cahoots to keep a secret from me. They were *my* books—whose side were they on?

And then a package had arrived from California, my name and address written in the strong, elegant hand I had recognized immediately. And inside had been the book *The Little Prince* and a framed copy of the photo Aunt Vieve had asked the carriage driver to take of her, Papa, and me standing by the horse named Fox that last evening before Papa and I had left Quebec City. The very next time Georgia had been at our house I'd heard *The Little Prince* speak. It piped up every time Georgia and I escaped to my bedroom, always lines about the little prince and his vain but somehow endearing rose.

"Oh my God. I am *so* cutting out this picture of Ricky Nelson," said Georgia. "Don't you think that new guy in our science class kind of looks like him?" I heard the bedsprings bounce as she flipped onto her belly and her face appeared over the edge of the mattress. She held up the open magazine and waited for my opinion.

"Just like him," I said. "So why am I self-centered?" I repeated.

Georgia tossed the magazine aside, propped her head on her hands, and gave me her full attention. Her eyes were a startling blue and fringed with thick lashes she coated in mascara because she said they were too light. Until recently, she'd always worn makeup in an attempt to cover up the sprinkling of freckles that ran over the bridge of her nose. That had stopped when somebody had told her that she'd heard from somebody else that another somebody had said he thought her freckles were cute. Georgia knew all the somebody names, their hierarchy and trustworthiness. I just couldn't keep track.

I knew the look I was getting from Georgia now. It was the same look she gave me when instructing on what I needed to do with my hair or how I should wear green eyeshadow to accentuate my eyes or why my wardrobe needed a new certain something and tips for haranguing my parents for shopping money.

"I know it's horrible that she left your uncle and all, but this isn't just about you. So what if you can't spend the summer with your Aunt Vieve? She's taking care of those twin boys and you know that she is *amazing*. If she was trusted with a baron's children, I'm sure she can handle your cousins. They *need* her. Your uncle can't be expected to take care of kids. And just think: your Aunt Liza could become famous." Her eyes widened. "Oh my God! Margaux, you have *got* to promise me here and now that if she does you'll take me with you to California."

"She left her family, Georgia. What makes you think that if she becomes famous she'll come back to them?"

"Because it's drama! Of course she'd come back to them! She didn't leave because she doesn't love them—she left to pursue her career! Her passion! You can't just ignore that if it's burning inside you. Besides, your uncle is kind of cute. Your dad showed me a picture, remember? He's kind of got a Paul Newman look—I mean, he's old but still, you know . . . "

"If she comes back—and Uncle Matthew takes her back . . ." I paused, remembered overhearing my parents talking about this very subject. Mother thought Uncle Matthew should have already sued for divorce, citing child abandonment. Papa was more conciliatory.

"She'll be famous. Of course he'll take her back."

"If," I said firmly. "If on both counts. And if it happens, I'm not going to California. If Aunt Liza comes home, and if Uncle Matthew lets her, that means Aunt Vieve can go back to Quebec City, and that's where I'll go, too."

Georgia rolled her eyes. "I don't understand you. How could you not want to go to California? What's so great about Quebec City?"

What was so great about Quebec City?

The first thing that came to mind was the front room of Aunt Vieve's apartment. The tall bookcases, filled top to bottom with enough novels to outlast months and months of rainy afternoons. The French doors with red-painted mullions that opened onto the two narrow wrought iron balconies, overflowing with pots of fragrant herbs and rail boxes of trailing geraniums, the rumble of tires over cobblestone streets, and the call of voices drifting up and over the railings to be absorbed by the thick Oriental rugs and overstuffed furniture. I thought of my loft. The three perfectly square windows that looked out onto rooftops and a sky that never got quite black enough to show the stars that I could see in Virginia, but that I loved all the same. Colonel Brandon was undoubtedly in California at the moment, but my guardian monkey lamp holding up its magical illumination was in Quebec City. As was the parapet overlooking Lower Town where I liked to stand to feel the wind against my face and watch the rain clouds sweep in over the river. There were people who knew me there. Not just Aunt Vieve. Other people who smiled when they saw me and said hello, who remembered the last time we'd spoken because they'd always pick up the conversation where we'd left off. "And have you had a letter from your mother?" they'd ask. "Did her strawberries bear as she'd expected?"

"It's home," I said to Georgia. "This is home, but Quebec City is home, too. I wouldn't mind visiting California one of these days, but I miss being with Aunt Vieve in Quebec City."

"They don't make movies in Quebec City."

"No, they don't."

"You can't get discovered in Quebec City."

I turned my gaze from the wordless ceiling to look at her. "And you think I would in California?" I said, knowing she hadn't really been talking about me.

She paused, then reached for the discarded magazine. "I still think your Aunt Liza will come back. She's pursuing her dreams, but I can't imagine her leaving her children forever. That's just bad karma."

I looked back at the ceiling. "You have no idea how much I hope you're right."

Seventeen

Dear Aunt Vieve,

Thanks for the copy of The Hobbit. *It's amazing how J. R. R. Tolkien can build a whole, complex, nuanced world like that in a book—not just a little part of one world, which it seems most books have. I'll put it in my locker at school; I wouldn't be surprised if Thorin speaks up if my gym teacher ever walks by. If I find a Gandalf, I'll want him or her for a study partner.*

We read Lord of the Flies *last year, and I guess Freshman English must be reading it now, because there are copies of it all over the place. I didn't like the book. Have you read it? I was at the varsity basketball game last week and somebody must have had it with them because I kept hearing Jack and even sometimes Roger—but I couldn't tell who the book was talking about because there were so many people in the bleachers. (We were playing against the team that beat us in regionals last year.) Anyway, it was spooky to think there could be some normal-looking, sick, sadistic bastard sitting close by, maybe right behind me, while everybody is screaming and shouting. And what if I suddenly heard Simon? Or Piggy? What would I do? How could I protect them from Jack and Roger—if I could even figure out in that crowd who was who? I got kind of freaked out and left and then walked home . . .*

My dearest Margaux,

Had I known of your recent brush with Lord of the Flies— *no pun intended—I never would have sent you* The Hobbit. *While I stand by my original advice that it's important to read of villains so that you can identify and avoid—or perhaps thwart—them, there is such a thing as overload. I insist you reread* The Secret Garden *immediately. Consider it a prescription for good health. It's your touchstone book, dearest, just as mine is* Sense and Sensibility *(as I'm sure you've noticed), and you should go back to it whenever you need to re-center yourself. Just in case your copy is getting hard to read, I've enclosed two more for you. Keep one at home and one in your school locker.*

I put the letter down. Hard to read? Why would it be hard to read? I set aside the two copies she'd sent and fetched mine from the stack on the window seat. I settled myself on the bed to obey doctor's orders, turning the pristine pages that didn't have so much as a dog-ear.

Eighteen

Another summer went by with no trip to Quebec City. I found myself wishing Aunt Liza would get discovered, get some big role in a movie, and play out the fairy tale Georgia had spun months earlier. I didn't want Aunt Liza to be rewarded for abandoning Uncle Matthew and my cousins—let alone taking Aunt Vieve from me—but at least it would end the exile. The twins were seven years younger than I was, which meant they were only nine now. Aunt Vieve had stayed with Papa and Uncle Matthew until both had graduated high school and gone off to college.

It was a depressing thought.

I ALMOST MISSED it the next time I got a book-sized package wrapped in thick, brown paper and addressed in Aunt Vieve's elegant script. But when the dark chocolate bar from *Jean-Alfred Moisan* slipped out of the package, I snatched up the brown wrapper from where I'd discarded it next to me on the bed.

Queen Elizabeth II serenely looked out into the middle distance, the blue tattoo of a cancellation stamp marring her otherwise pristine complexion.

The stamps were Canadian.

Aunt Vieve was back in Quebec City.

"Well, if I were Matty, I wouldn't get too comfortable. She could pull the rug out from under him again any time." Mother handed Papa his plate with two pork chops and a generous scoop of mashed potatoes on it. "And who knows what she may have brought home with her. You know how those Hollywood people are." She glanced at me and then pursed her lips.

I put some green beans on my plate and passed the bowl. Papa hadn't been home more than fifteen minutes, but dinner was on the table and Mother was picking up the conversation right where she'd left it the evening before, as though it had been sitting there waiting for her next to the salt and pepper shakers.

Aunt Liza's return to Uncle Matthew and the boys had occupied two dinner conversations. Then Mother had moved on to her views on the reconciliation and its likelihood to endure. That had taken just one dinner. Now, apparently, we were reviewing it all again. It reminded me of being at Georgia's house when her older brother Brad raked the leaves while listening to a football game blasting on his transistor radio. Papa was required to give the play-by-play—he was the one who'd spent a small fortune in long-distance phone charges talking first to Uncle Matthew and then to Aunt Vieve—while Mother provided the color commentary.

"And those poor boys," said Mother, smoothing her dress to sit down. "What must they be thinking about all of this?"

"They're thinking they're glad their mother is home," said Papa firmly.

"Gone almost three years . . . "

"Not quite two and a half."

"Oh, of course. Not quite two and a half. That does make all the difference."

For a few moments the only sound was the scraping of cutlery on plates. Nobody made pork chops as good as Mother's. A crusty sear on the outside, but always moist and perfect on the inside.

I'd tried a couple of times, but I didn't seem to have inherited her knack for cooking.

"I'm sure there's plenty of talk in the neighborhood . . . " she continued.

"Theirs or ours?"

I glanced at Papa. He seemed tense, and I wondered if something had gone wrong at court that afternoon. His client, Mr. Garrigan, had come to meet with Papa late last week here at the house. Papa had shut his office doors for privacy, but I'd been on the front porch doing homework when he'd walked Mr. Garrigan out nearly an hour later. After the man had driven away, I'd told Papa I thought he was guilty. Of course I didn't tell him why I thought so. That was between *The Scarlet Letter* and me. Papa had given me a long, considering look and then told me that every man was entitled to a defense and if I knew something that he should know before standing in front of a judge representing Mr. Garrigan, he was all ears. Truth be told, I didn't even know why Mr. Garrigan needed my father to represent him; what it was that he was accused of doing or not doing. I just had known that he was guilty of doing or not doing it. Papa ran his practice out of his office here at the house, but he was very particular about privacy and confidentiality. I had felt my cheeks go red as he'd stood there, an open and patient look on his face. "No sir," I'd said, and, after another moment, Papa had gone back into the house. I'd wondered then if the sudden knot in my stomach matched the one that surely must be in Mr. Garrigan's.

"You can't just pick up where you left off, you know," Mother was saying. "When you leave your husband and children to go gallivanting around movie sets, you don't just get to come home and start attending PTA meetings like nothing ever happened. Although it *is* California. From what I read . . . " She glanced at me and didn't finish her thought.

"I doubt that the *National Enquirer* is a reliable source to judge the entire state of California."

Mother put down her knife and fork. "You know I don't read that trash."

"Sorry."

"I'm not talking about the entire state of California. I'm talking about a prevalent subculture there that values fame above marriage and family."

"A lot of people value things they shouldn't above marriage and family. It's not a California thing, it's a people thing."

Mother didn't pick up her knife and fork but continued to look at Papa. He didn't return the look, but rather scooped mashed potatoes into his mouth. Check and check, I thought. He was buying time. It was impolite to speak with your mouth full, after all.

I occupied myself with my green beans and didn't look up. I'd hoped to veer the conversation to going to Quebec sooner than the summer—maybe over the Christmas break—but now clearly wasn't a good time. I'd heard Mother talking with Mrs. Olssen over the backyard fence, a bowl of the last of the beets from the garden balanced between them. You'd think California and its contaminated culture was the next town over and threatening to invade. Mrs. Olssen had been positively indignant.

"And I don't want you going to see that movie, young lady."

I looked up at Mother, suddenly feeling I was on the chessboard.

"What movie?"

She pursed her lips again.

I looked at Papa. "What movie?" Criminy, had Georgia's prediction come true?

"Technically, there isn't a movie. I don't think it has a final title, let alone a release date," said Papa.

"Aunt Liza is in a movie?"

"So she says," said Mother. She picked up her fork again but just picked at her food. Georgia said that was why she stayed so slim. Watching Mother move her fork around her plate reminded me of watching her in the garden with her hoe.

I felt a flutter of butterflies in my stomach.

"Is it a big part?" I asked.

"I have no idea. I wouldn't give Liza the time of day to discuss it if she were sitting here in this very kitchen, let alone spending good money on a long-distance call."

I looked at Papa. He was the best source of information, since he was the one who'd accepted the reversed charges from California when Uncle Matthew had called. I was glad he'd been the one who'd picked up the phone when it had rung.

He shrugged.

I sighed. Personally, I didn't really care about Aunt Liza and her Hollywood career. But I could already hear the exasperation in Georgia's voice if I didn't have any details to offer.

"Do you think it will make her famous?" I asked.

"Enough about Liza," said Mother. "I don't want any more conversation at the dinner table about her."

"Okay," I said, pushing my food around with my fork. I knew better than to say that she was the one who'd brought it up—four evenings in a row.

"It's your Aunt Genevieve who's the saint in all of this. Dropping everything to travel across an entire continent to take care of those two children. And not just for the month or so Matty said it would take. Nearly three years!" Mother shook her head. "Genevieve is due some time with family that doesn't include babysitting and housekeeping." Mother picked up her glass of water and took a sip. "Which is why I called her yesterday and asked her to spend the Christmas holidays with us."

Even after all these years, I still wince to think of it, but I do believe I actually squealed—one of those high-pitched squeals that only dogs should be able to hear—as I dashed around the table to hug Mother tight around the neck.

Nineteen

2019

I set aside my writing and go to the kitchen. I stir the Brunswick stew again and cut a thick slice of bread to take with me back into the library. I have a microwave oven, but Adele insists food tastes better heated slowly on the stove—and stirring often so the bottom doesn't scorch—and I'm set enough in my ways to agree. We use the microwave to reheat coffee.

I turn on the outside lights and peer through the window of the kitchen door. Thick flakes are falling, just as they have been since before it got dark. Only the top step of the three leading up to the small, covered porch is visible, though like the porch, it's blanketed in white. There is little wind, just the ceaseless drop of slivered artistry that silently demands full attention by obliterating from sight everything else. I turn off the light, extinguishing my view of the performance. I take my tray and go back to the library.

Snow—lots of it—but so far, no ice.

Three kinds of weather always make me think of Aunt Vieve: rainy summer afternoons, ice storms, and snow in April.

Twenty

1965

There were pockets of ice storms up and down the eastern seaboard that December Aunt Vieve was supposed to visit. Her train was cancelled, and the one after that and the one after that. Papa said it was just as well, since he wasn't sure he'd be able to safely get to the train station to pick her up anyway. I did get to speak to her on the phone for a few precious minutes, and we made a pact that I'd take the train up to Quebec City the day after school let out for the summer.

That night I woke to the sound of loud cracks and pops. I turned on my bedside lamp, but the room stayed dark. I got out of bed to go to the window. The floor was cold against my bare feet. I pulled a blanket over my shoulders and settled myself on my window seat, nightgown drawn over my knees and feet tucked under me. By the faint moonlight, I saw tree branches and the large, bare forsythia bush near the neighbor's yard crystallized and unnaturally bowed, as though they were being sucked to the ground by some increased pull of gravity. A clump of small birch trees Papa had planted several years ago looked like a grouping of large croquette wickets. The ground glistened, but not with snow. The world had lost its color and was a palette of blacks and grays and whites. I heard another loud crack. The trees, their branches coated in heavy ice, were breaking. I opened my window a few inches and ran a finger along the outside painted sill. It was slick with ice. I felt and smelled the cold, wet air swirl in. I pulled the blanket closer around me. The world was ice. I watched and listened, weirdly fascinated.

I woke with my head on top of a pile of my books and a crick in my neck. The room was bracingly cold, even when I shut the window. The small wind-up alarm clock by my bed said seven o'clock, but the room was dim. I got up and flipped the overhead light switch. Nothing. Pulling on a pair of jeans, I looked out my window. The trees and forsythia bush were still bowed. Then I saw the top third of an elm across the street had broken and now hung at a contorted angle. It looked shocking, evidence of violence that had been witnessed by no one as I'd slept with my head resting on my books. I thought of my beech and rushed downstairs, my heart in my throat as I pulled a sweater over my head. My hands were shaking as I pulled on boots. I didn't bother trying to zip my coat.

An ice storm encapsulates both the breathtaking beauty and pragmatic destruction of nature. There is nothing so beautiful and yet so heartbreaking as a mature tree after an ice storm. Each branch, each individual leaf-bare twig, is coated as though by an artist's brush with painstaking attention. The ice captures the weak rays of winter sun and magnifies them, making each strand of the tree glisten.

Ah, but the weight.

I knew my tree like I knew my books. And my tree was struggling to hold up the exquisite burden that had fallen from the sky. Branches were bowed that should be reaching for the solstice heavens. I startled at a loud crack followed by a scraping crunch of wood, like a thunderclap that alerts you the lightning strike was nearby, maybe to the roof of your house. The sound reverberated.

In the night, the scene and sound of bent trees and breaking branches had seemed removed, my window a protective barrier, even when I'd opened it and let the elements in to where I'd sat. I had felt no fear, no alarm. I had been a spectator. Had fallen asleep while the trees had fought to survive their weighty aggressor.

Now I stood among them, beneath their branches, felt the damp cold bite my face and hands. The wind blew raw, sharp pins that pricked through the loose weave of my sweater to my skin where I hadn't zipped my jacket. I didn't feel serene.

I saw that one of the maple trees next door had split where the trunk branched into two about fifteen feet from the ground. One half had fallen onto the Olssens' garage, leaving its twin to stand alone and exposed, witness to the violence of torn shingles and crushed boards.

I went to my beech tree.

It still stood, but on the ground were scatterings of twigs and leaves that had stubbornly clung despite November gales. An aggressive gust hit my face and made me squint my eyes. I heard a sound like muffled wind chimes, accompanied by several pops farther afield. More twigs fell to the ground near my feet. I looked up into the branches. A part of my brain told me I really should move out from under them. I shushed it and stepped closer to the trunk. This was my tree. It would never hurt me.

I saw the branch where Aunt Vieve had sat swinging her legs, waiting for Papa to arrive with the ladder while Colonel Brandon had paced anxiously below. It was still attached to the tree, but hanging at an awkward angle, pale shards of the thick inner wood thrusting into the cold air like a fractured bone. I felt tears on my cheeks. They were warm against my skin. They didn't freeze.

I didn't try to climb the tree to where that appendage hung. The branches were far too slick and the last thing my tree needed was additional weight. But I did wrap my arms around the trunk. I pressed myself full against it, my cheek against its bark, my eyes shut, willing my strength into it. Letting the heat from my body melt the ice that clung in rivulets along its length. Speaking to it in low, comforting tones. I stayed that way a long time, my eyes closed, hearing irregular pops and cracks close by and farther afield.

MOTHER COULDN'T UNDERSTAND why I was so upset about that branch. The tree had survived, after all, unlike so many around our neighborhood. I couldn't adequately explain it, myself. I guess my heart knew more than my mind did.

My mind would learn, soon enough.

Twenty-One

I read like a fiend and got quite good at sorting out people.

I knew Mrs. Talbot, who taught algebra and trig, was pregnant long before she wrote $1 + 1 = 3$ across the top of the blackboard.

I knew when Gracie Henderson was pregnant—and then when she suddenly wasn't anymore.

I knew Mr. Grenville, our affable and even-tempered assistant principal, was not so even-tempered at home, and I wasn't surprised when he no longer wore a wedding ring.

When things were going her way, Georgia bragged that I had a sixth sense about people, and she seemed to take personal credit for my rise in popularity. In private or when I told her something she didn't want to hear—or worse, didn't tell her anything at all when she thought I should—she called me spooky and gave me sideways looks. I tried to avoid that by sneaking books I trusted out of classrooms, the library, and even our house and stashing them wherever I could. They routinely disappeared, leaving me grasping for answers at inopportune times.

"Remember back in elementary school when you used to whisper to books when you thought no one was looking? You were _so_ weird! It's hard to believe we even became friends!"

I met Georgia's look. "Yeah, hard," I said.

PAPA FINALLY LEASED a small law office downtown. He still kept his home office, but now his clients came to the second floor of an old brick building a couple of blocks from the county courthouse. The floors creaked and there were a few water stains on the high plaster ceiling, but the rugs were thick and the furniture heavy and substantial—all bought from the prior tenant, who had moved his practice to Richmond.

Mrs. Thomas, a substantial woman herself, had been Papa's secretary since he'd started his practice, coming regularly to our house or meeting him at the courthouse to pick up his hand-written papers and then delivering them in neatly typed stacks. Now she had a desk in the small reception area, and she took her new duties seriously. She was friendly to the postman and court courier, professional with Papa's clients, stern with the salesmen who periodically dropped by, and warm to Mother and me. Mother she didn't see often, but I now had an after-school job as Papa's file clerk and research assistant. I got paid every other Friday, and I squirreled away what I didn't spend on books I found at yard sales and thrift stores.

The new set of law books didn't speak to me any more than the ones at home did, but, like those, I often felt they were on the brink of it. A lot of the court cases in them were interpretations of the law. Scouring volumes for precedents, reading accounts from plaintiffs and defendants—each telling a story they hoped would sway the judge and jury—I frequently felt the element of fabrication. Which is, of course, fiction. Someone hadn't been telling the truth, the whole truth, and nothing but the truth. The law books knew it, and they seemed to want to join their fiction brethren in speaking to me. But the law is the law, so they didn't. But I could still sense them. They quivered on the brink of telling what they knew about the people who came into Papa's office. I hoped that whatever bound them would never break, because I suspected that the

onslaught—should they ever be free of their constriction—
would have me running for the door.

I hid novels behind the law volumes, tucked them in file
drawers or on the windowsills behind the heavy drapes. Mrs.
Thomas didn't care for blinds and Papa didn't care one way or
the other, so the previous tenant's blinds had been pitched along
with the framed print of the Battle of Chancellorsville.

"Stonewall Jackson was mortally wounded by his own men in
that battle," Mrs. Thomas had said solemnly, holding up the print,
which had easily been three feet across. "I had a great-great
uncle who fought at Chancellorsville. Thank goodness he wasn't
near the front lines. I don't know if he could have lived with
himself if he thought he'd had a part in that horrible mistake."
Looking around for Papa and seeing he wasn't there, she'd put
the squat heel of her sensible shoe through the print, cracking
the frame in the process. "Oops," she'd said. She'd looked at
me calmly. "Things do break during a move. I'll just take this
out back to the dumpster to get it out of the way. Your father will
never miss it."

Papa would often go into the office on Saturdays to get caught
up on paperwork, and I'd join him to get in a few more paid
hours. We'd usually have lunch together from brown bags Mother
packed for us, papers and portfolios placed out of harm's way.
I'd have a Coke and Papa an orange Nehi. Aunt Vieve had never
let him have orange Nehi when he'd been growing up, he'd told
me more than once. He always seemed to take such satisfaction
out of that first swig.

Over lunch, I'd try to drop a few hints to Papa about his clients, courtesy of what I'd heard from my books that week. I had
to be careful, though, not to repeat the mistake I'd made telling
him about Mr. Garrigan.

Papa would ask me questions, probing me about what I
said—was it opinion or based on fact? Could I back it up? He

conceded that intuition had its place, that juries could be swayed by something other than the facts. But a lawyer shouldn't be so swayed, he said. Intuition could be a start, but it was only a start. I learned to be observant of details that could support what I knew from my books and, wherever possible, to remember facts and precedents that put me on firmer footing.

Those Saturday conversations were like a whetstone for my mind.

Looking back, I like to think that Papa treasured them as much as I did.

Twenty-Two

I had almost half the days of April marked off on the calendar that hung on my closet door when I came home to find Mother sitting at the kitchen table with a cup of tea instead of out in the garden, where she'd been most afternoons lately, turning the soil and planting the seeds that could withstand a frost—lettuce, peas, and collards. She pressed her lips together when she saw me and beckoned me toward her.

The telephone call had come shortly after I'd left for school, and Papa had taken a mid-morning flight to Canada. Aunt Vieve had contracted polio.

We rarely think about polio anymore, but when I was a child, it was a disease that crippled children and haunted parents. After Jonas Salk discovered a vaccine, the country breathed a guarded, collective sigh of relief. I'd been vaccinated at school, along with all my classmates. I hadn't thought much about polio. Until then, no one I personally knew had ever contracted it. I'd seen March of Dimes posters, though, in our school and in the drugstore in town. The posters showed children wearing leg braces and clutching crutches. The words encouraged parents to get children vaccinated. There weren't any pictures of adults in braces on those posters. It hadn't occurred to me that adults could get polio.

"Papa took a plane? Not the train?"

Papa never flew. Train travel was already a luxury—a distinct step above taking the bus—but air travel . . . Air travel was reserved for people who had money to spare . . .

Mother didn't answer. She reached to place her hand over mine where I'd steadied myself against the kitchen table.

"Why didn't he wait for me? Why didn't you come get me from school?"

"Margaux . . . "

"How long before she's better? Did Papa go to bring her here? So we can take care of her?"

I had a sudden image of Aunt Vieve climbing my beech tree, of her bicycling down our driveway and making the right turn toward town, of her walking assuredly through the dining room of the Carlton Hotel as men turned their heads to watch her go by, of the day she'd pirouetted on the parapet where Upper Town overlooked the river, her market basket swinging wide. *Why walk when one can dance?* she'd said. Of the posters of children in metal braces holding themselves up with wooden sticks tucked into their armpits. I pulled my hand out from under Mother's and touched the spot on my left arm where I'd received the vaccination shot. I tried to remember if polio was contagious. Had Mother and Papa been vaccinated?

We would need more books. If Aunt Vieve could no longer walk, pedal, and dance her way through the world, I'd bring the world to her. She could live here. Papa could bring along some of her favorite novels, and I'd scour the thrift stores and yard sales to find more. There would be flowers from the garden and breezes through the windows of the corner room where she had stayed last time she'd been here and which we'd make hers. After I graduated high school next year, we'd move back to the apartment in Quebec City. Or maybe we'd need to find another apartment—one in a building with an elevator. It would be hard to leave the third-floor haven with its bookshelves and French doors and loft, but we could find someplace just as wonderful. Or even if it didn't start out wonderful, I'd make it wonderful. For us. It would have her books, her art, Colonel Brandon, and me.

I brought myself out of my planning haze when I realized Mother hadn't answered me.

"She's in the hospital?"

Mother nodded.

"How long before she's released? If it's going to be more than a day or so, I should go there. I can take care of Colonel Brandon and pack Aunt Vieve's things. I know which books she'll want to have with her—and other things." My voice trailed off. At the look on Mother's face, I realized I shouldn't put such an emphasis on books. To anyone other than Aunt Vieve and me, there would be items far more important to bring to Virginia.

"Margaux." Mother stopped and cleared her throat.

Mine constricted.

"Genevieve has a rare form of polio. It affects the spinal cord and brain, and that affects—other parts of the body." She reached for my hand where it hung limply at my side. "That's why your father took a plane. To try to get there in time."

Planes were for people who had money to spare, which we didn't. Or when, apparently, there was no time to spare . . .

I didn't return her squeeze.

"I have to go, too," I said, my throat tight, my voice barely more than a whisper.

Mother shook her head. "There's no point, Margaux. It'll be too late."

I snatched my hand out of hers. "I can't believe you didn't come get me from school. That he didn't take me with him."

She didn't reach for my hand again. "Sit down, Margaux." Her voice was firm.

I didn't sit. I looked at her with new eyes. Recognized what my twelve-year-old self hadn't. Aunt Vieve had been competition. Was still competition. That was why I wasn't in Quebec City right now. Why we all weren't in Quebec City right now.

"You told him not to bring me."

She paused. "I did."

I'd read in books of people being so angry they saw red. For the first time, I could truly understand that. A number of retorts rose in my throat, names I'd heard hissed between even white teeth and over pink-glossed lips in school hallways and the cafeteria and in the locker room getting ready for gym class. But my upbringing prevailed, and I choked on the epithets before I could hurl them at my mother.

"You were always jealous of her," I finally spit out, swallowing the jagged, more hurtful, hateful words I had almost said. I kept my voice low and even. I didn't shout. My eyes dared her to contradict me.

I felt the sharp sting on my cheek before my mind registered her hand moving through the air.

"Young lady, you have a lot to learn about life before you make those kinds of judgments about anyone. And even more to learn before you make them about me or your father." Mother stood and set her cup and saucer carefully in the sink. "You can apologize when you're ready."

I clenched my lips tight and went upstairs to my room. I still felt the sting of her slap but didn't look in a mirror. The slap had surprised me. The most violent thing I'd ever seen Mother do was squish the slugs she found on her cucumber plants. She'd never even spanked me.

And Papa. Despite Mother's urging, how could he have agreed to leave me behind? He *knew* what Aunt Vieve meant to me. He'd *encouraged* it. It felt like a betrayal.

I considered throwing myself on the bed and having a good, long cry, but that felt like capitulation. I looked around my bedroom for something else to throw, instead. My eyes lighted on *The Secret Garden* on my window seat.

It was silent, as always when I was alone.

I realized what I needed in that moment—in the face of Mother's violence and Papa's betrayal and possibly losing Aunt Vieve—was to hear the words. The words Aunt Vieve had said *The Secret Garden*—the book she said was my touchstone—had spoken to her about me. The words it had said to me about her, that afternoon when the sun had been shining and I had been on the brink of discovering that I wasn't the only one, that hearing books talk was special, not crazy. I needed to hear those words out loud and no one was here to say them to me, to give me the reassurance I needed at that moment. I walked over to the book, stood over it, my hands clenched into fists by my side.

The book lay there, quiet, looking for all the world like it was no more than ink on paper.

"Don't act like you can't talk. I know you can. I've *heard* you, remember?"

The book remained silent.

Frustration welled up in me. I struck at it, knocked it off the top of the stack. The book took a few others with it. *Stuart Little* faced me now, the cover showing the valiant mouse setting off for adventure in his birch bark canoe. I looked at it. It was silent, too.

After a moment, I picked up *The Secret Garden* from the floor.

There *was* someone here to say the words.

"She made herself stronger by fighting the wind," I said out loud in a clear voice. I held the book unopened in front of me in my upturned hands, like a talisman. I closed my eyes and repeated the words twice more. Then, with a pat on its cover for apology, I set *The Secret Garden* on top of *Stuart Little* and, after peeking out my door to make sure Mother hadn't come upstairs, went down the hall to my parents' bedroom.

We had three telephones in our house, the most of anyone on our street. The one in Papa's study had its own line. The telephone in the kitchen was used most often. And there was a telephone on Papa's nightstand.

I dialed Georgia's number. Her mother picked up. I glanced at my parents' bedroom door and hoped Georgia would get to the phone before Mother decided our conversation wasn't done and came upstairs.

"Hello?"

"Georgia, it's me. Is Brad working today?"

"Yeah, till six. Why?"

"I need a ride to Union Station in DC."

Twenty-Three

I left Mother a note taped to the bannister that I was very upset about Aunt Vieve, needed company, and so was spending the night at Georgia's house. I wrote that I was sorry about what I'd said. It was a lie, but then so was the part about spending the night at Georgia's house. By the time Mother figured out I wasn't there, hopefully I'd be halfway to Canada. Once in Quebec City, I'd take a taxi to Aunt Vieve's apartment building. One of the neighbors would know which hospital she'd been taken to.

But first I had to get to Union Station.

It had been raining most of the day and still was as I waited impatiently in the shadows of our front porch. I tried to imagine this was like the rains in Quebec City the summer I'd been there, that this weather was the city beckoning me to come, but the drops were heavy and cold and I couldn't quite get the imagery to work. Even the forsythia looked miserable, and in the fading light, I could see the cups of Mother's daffodils drooping on their thick stems.

I checked to make sure the satchel on my shoulder was closed tight. In it, I'd packed *A Streetcar Named Desire*, *Fahrenheit 451*, and *The Secret Garden*. At the last minute I'd added *To Kill a Mockingbird*. The first two books were to give me a heads up on people to avoid. I brought *The Secret Garden* because I wanted Aunt Vieve to see I was keeping my touchstone near me, the way she did *Sense and Sensibility*. I included *To Kill a Mockingbird* because I was feeling a little guilty about Brad driving more than four hours round-trip on a rainy night and hoped to hear the book confirm he was okay with it.

My mind warred between emotion and logic. Worry for Aunt Vieve and trying to recall everything I'd ever heard about polio. Anger at Mother for telling Papa he should go without me and determining the logistics of getting to Quebec City without running out of money or into trouble. Hurt at Papa's betrayal and planning what I'd say to him when I arrived, unexpected and without permission. And, of most immediate importance, maintaining a calm, albeit concerned, façade for Brad while reinforcing with Georgia my dire straits to ensure she remained my fervent but discreet ally.

I was starting to debate whether I should sneak back into the house to get a heavier jacket when I heard the familiar ping of Brad's Ford Galaxy, something it did whenever it drove below thirty-five miles an hour. Georgia had always said that was why he'd gotten so many speeding tickets in high school—he didn't want to hear that noise and it was too expensive to fix. When Papa had heard that, he'd said Brad likely could have paid to have the engine repaired for what he'd spent on fines and court fees. Of course, that was before Brad had gotten so serious about the family business. Now he was working at the store six days a week and taking night classes at the community college. Everyone heard the Galaxy ping a lot more now than they ever had when he was in high school.

I ran down the driveway and was waiting at the curb as the Galaxy pulled up. Mother was far less likely to notice a car stopping in the street than the gleam of headlights swinging into our driveway. I jumped into the back seat, pushing aside a small pile of business books and pulling my suitcase in behind me.

"Hi! Thanks! Let's go!" I said brightly.

Brad looked at me over his shoulder, then at Georgia next to him on the front seat. She was turned around, facing me, and biting her lower lip.

"Sure," he said. He pinged away from the curb.

I would have bet money that Georgia would absolutely love the drama of my sneaking out of the house to get to Aunt Vieve's bedside. That her mind would be awhirl spinning the story she'd tell in school the next day. But she just looked worried. Well, so was I—I was trying to push out of my mind what Mother had said about Papa taking a plane to try to get there in time—but I couldn't afford to show too much. Brad was the chivalrous sort. If he thought I was close to falling apart, he wouldn't let me out of his sight until he was sure I was in my father's.

"So you're meeting your dad at Union Station?" Brad said.

"Yes, he had appointments in DC today. Then Mother got the call about Aunt Vieve being so sick. She called Mrs. Thomas and got my dad's schedule. You wouldn't believe how many secretaries she had to talk to before she finally got hold of him. So he decided to just take the train from there rather than come all the way home and then drive up to the city again. He keeps some clothes and stuff at Aunt Vieve's apartment, so it's not a big deal. He'll probably have to buy a razor or something, but that's about it. And he wanted to have plenty of time to get the tickets. You know, in case there was a line. I mean, he probably could have asked one of the guys in the meeting to send their secretary or something, but he really hates imposing on people." I realized I was rambling. I wished Georgia would say something, help with the conversation. She'd turned back around, and all I could see of her was her perfect blond hair. I had an urge to yank it.

"Well, he wouldn't have been coming back home just for clothes, right?" I saw Brad look at me in the rearview mirror.

"He had to finish his meetings. That's why we're taking such a late train." I craned my neck to see the instrument panel. A little less than half a tank. He'd probably have to stop for gas on the way back. I looked down at the satchel beside me. Not a word. I remembered Aunt Vieve's caution to me: *And books can also be fickle. They don't speak on cue nor respond to our desire to have them speak.* I looked again at the back of Georgia's head. Fine. I'd do this by myself. "I know this is kind of imposing on you, Brad, but my dad thought you'd be okay with it. Not that you're okay with people imposing on you, but that, you know, we know each other pretty well—not like the secretaries. He doesn't know them. I mean, he might know their names or something, but he doesn't *know* know them. And Mrs. Thomas hates to drive at night. She's talked a few times about how bad her night vision is, so he didn't want to ask her . . . " I bit my lip to make myself stop talking and looked out the window. We were past the town outskirts now, nearing the highway. I breathed a little easier. "I really appreciate you driving me, Brad. I'll pay you for gas money as soon as I get back." I was nearly positive I had enough for the train ticket, but I'd also need cab fare in Quebec City. I would have to be careful. I thought of the two Almond Joys and the cellophane wrapper of Lorna Doones in my satchel. It was all the food I'd had in my room, and I hadn't wanted to chance a trip to the kitchen.

"I can get it from your dad."

"Actually I thought you could just drop me off in front of the train station. So you don't have to worry about finding parking."

Again I saw Brad's blue eyes in the rearview mirror. Georgia had twisted around again in her seat to look at me, but she hadn't yet said a word beyond a quiet greeting when I'd first gotten in the car.

"I meant when y'all get back into town. Your dad comes into the shop for his newspaper most mornings."

Brad was expected to take over the family sundry shop—it had been started by his grandfather as a general store just before World War I. He didn't seem to mind that everyone had considered this career path a foregone conclusion pretty much since he'd been born. I glanced at the business books on the seat beside me.

"Oh, right. Sure."

The silence stretched.

I rummaged around in my satchel and pulled out the old train schedule I'd saved from my trip to Quebec City four years before. Back then there had been a train at ten twenty that had had a lot of stops but had gone straight through to Quebec City and beyond. I knew schedules changed, but I was counting on it being similar.

The streetlights thinned as we left town behind us. The two-lane road stretched ahead, the Ford's headlights making it shine in the rain. It was only a few miles to the junction with the main highway that would take us north to Washington, DC. It wasn't long before I saw the sign indicating the turn coming up.

"Let's make a stop," said Brad, breaking the silence in the car. He turned into a parking lot, pulled the car between two others, and turned off the engine. Through the windshield I could see a giant clock, symbol of the diner. It was already after seven. The highway was tantalizingly close, the entrance ramp just on the other side of the Sinclair gas station.

"I'm really not hungry. I'll eat at the station. With my dad."

Brad looked at Georgia, then at me. "Let's get some coffee. My treat. We can have pie. Even when you're not hungry, you can always eat pie. Georgia loves their peach pie." He grinned at her but didn't get the usual reaction. I got out of the car. I saw him put the keys in his jacket pocket.

"Very funny," Georgia finally said. She got out of the car and walked toward the restaurant without looking at me.

I LOOKED AROUND as we entered the building. We weren't far outside of town, but I didn't see anybody I knew. Then again, even if I did, this wouldn't be a bad thing for someone to report back to Mother. I had said I was going to Georgia's house. I was here with Georgia and her brother. Her kind, generous, older brother who had offered to take us out for coffee and pie.

For what I hoped would be very quick coffee and pie.

Georgia scooted in along the red leatherette bench on one side of the table and immediately began flipping through the offerings on the tabletop jukebox. I sat down beside her, my satchel between us. Brad sat down across from us.

I returned his steady gaze while Georgia tucked two quarters into the tabletop jukebox and punched in the letters and numbers of her selections.

And I knew.

Brad wasn't going to drive me to Union Station.

I thought about the keys in his jacket pocket. I did have my driver's license, after all. If Papa hadn't taken our car to the airport, all of this would have been so much simpler.

Brad smiled at our waitress, an older lady who looked like her feet hurt, and ordered three coffees and asked what kind of pie was good that evening. Georgia smiled too, first past me at the waitress, then at me. She seemed nervous. A few of the names I'd been ready to hurl at my mother swirled around in my mouth, but I swallowed them. The problem was that, while Georgia was definitely *The Little Prince*'s rose, I knew from homework sessions in the Pillards' living room that Brad was *To Kill a Mockingbird*'s Atticus Finch.

Honorable, ethical, empathetic Atticus Finch.

To Kill a Mockingbird might be mute for the moment, but it was definitely Atticus Finch now looking at me across the worn, yellow Formica tabletop.

"I'm so, so sorry about your aunt, Margaux," Brad said. "I met her, did you know? She came into our shop once a few years ago—I guess she was in town for a visit—and I was restocking shelves. She changed the whole atmosphere of the place, just by walking in. I'd never seen someone who was so classy without being stuck up. And her laugh! She got talking to Mom and all Mom's stress just seemed to melt away."

The waitress came with three thick mugs of steaming coffee. My mind started to go down cobblestone streets to revisit scenes of Aunt Vieve chatting with shopkeepers, her ever-present basket in the crook of one arm, Colonel Brandon keeping watch at her feet, but I pulled it back. I wanted to hear about Brad's memory. Maybe it could help me convince him to take me to the train station. This had to have been the day Aunt Vieve had discovered Aunt Trudy's bicycle hanging in the garage and commandeered Mark Robbins to bring it down and pump up the tires for her. I remembered watching her put a small stack of books in the basket and pedal away toward town. I never did find out which novels she'd brought with her, what they'd told her that had led her to the Pillard Sundry Shop, but the time she'd spent there had helped ease my path in school society. In a way it had led me here, sitting in a diner with Georgia and Brad Pillard. The bike was back on the garage wall—had been since Aunt Vieve's visit. I said a silent, brief prayer for Mark Robbins, who, I'd heard, had received his draft notice just over a month earlier and would be headed to Vietnam. I turned my attention back to Brad. If we kept the conversation on Aunt Vieve, surely he'd see how important it was for me to get to her. We had time for coffee and pie, I decided, because she wasn't going to die. That had to be Mother being dramatic. Nobody actually *died* from polio, right?

"I remember that, too," said Georgia. "She talked about raising that baron's children in Europe."

"She talked about raising a lot of children, starting with your dad and uncle, Margaux," Brad said. He shook his head. "I had no idea your dad had been such a hell-raiser. All mostly harmless stuff, but still." He sipped his coffee. "Of course, most of that was before Miss Genevieve showed up."

"She came to help take care your dad and uncle when they were kids," Georgia said importantly.

"His mother had died the year before," I said. I remembered Papa telling me the story of Aunt Vieve arriving to help her older brother when it had become clear raising two boys on his own had been beyond him. I wondered if she had told Brad and Georgia the story of the eyelash, or if that story was more Papa's memory than hers.

Brad nodded, breaking the crust of the pie the waitress had brought with a fork that had a bent tine.

"Your dad was eleven, I think she said. And that made your uncle, what, eight or so?"

I nodded.

"Mom and Miss Genevieve must have spent ten minutes just talking about what it took to get a house back in order when it's been a while since a woman has been in charge. Remember that *Mary Poppins* movie that came out a couple years ago? Mark was babysitting his little sister and talked me into going with them to see it."

"You went to see *Mary Poppins*? With Mark?" Georgia laughed. "I wished I'd been there to see that! Why didn't he take Stacey?"

"They hadn't started dating yet. And it wasn't a bad movie, actually," Brad said. He looked at me. "Partway through I realized I was thinking about your aunt. From overhearing her talk to Mom that day in the store, it was like she was Mary Poppins—but without the magic, of course."

I sipped my coffee. Of course.

"And the other difference is that Miss Genevieve was an aunt—a close blood relative—not a hired nanny. I imagine she became like a mother to your dad and uncle. They were pretty young when their mom died. So it's not like it was just a job she left once they didn't need her anymore."

"She left the baron's children when they didn't need her anymore," said Georgia.

"That was a job."

"But she still kept in touch. It couldn't have been just a job." Georgia turned to me. "Right? She kept in touch."

I thought about the packages arriving from Belgium. "She did," I said. "She does," I amended.

"And who knows? Maybe she'll be invited to visit. I wonder if the Baron lives in a castle or just one of those big mansions."

"But back to your dad and uncle," said Brad. He set his fork down, reached across the table, and took my hand.

His touch was unexpected and I nearly jerked away, but he held on, his grip warm and firm. I met his gaze, and the feelings of the old, unrequited crush I'd had on him rose in me again.

"Margaux, I can't drive you to Union Station."

A different kind of crush, as I felt my plans crumble beneath the weight of reality. I had known this was coming since Brad had put the car in park outside the diner, but I still felt the tears spring to my eyes. I put my free hand on my satchel, ran my finger along what I knew was the spine of *The Secret Garden*. Fight the wind, I thought to myself.

"I have to be there," I said in not much more than a whisper.

"No, you don't. I know you *want* to be there, but the person who *has* to be there already is. And the last thing he needs is to be worried about his teenage daughter traveling alone eight hundred miles on an overnight train."

I kept my eyes on Brad. She'd told. The bitch had told him everything. I'd revealed to Georgia as much as I had because I'd thought it had been necessary to get her to talk Brad into this last-minute drive. I'd been so sure she'd see it as a dramatic story and want to play a part. I'd half-expected her to ask to come with me.

"Then you take me," I said to Brad. "If you take me, I won't be traveling alone." I had no idea how I'd pay for two tickets, but maybe Brad had some money.

He raised his brow, genuinely startled, and pulled back his hand. "Me? You're underage, Margaux. Your dad's a lawyer. Of course, my mom would kill me before he could have me arrested, but either way, the outcome isn't good."

I felt Georgia place her hand over mine. It was warm, as Brad's had been.

"Margaux," she said gently. "Quebec City isn't even in the United States. It's in a different *country*."

It was such a Georgia thing to say, but I felt like slapping her. I fought back tears of frustration and betrayal.

"It's in Canada," she continued. She looked around, then leaned in and lowered her voice. "Where Mark went."

"Mark went to Canada?"

"The draft," Brad said. He picked up his fork again. He clearly didn't want to talk about it. Georgia, on the other hand, seemed relieved at the change in subject.

"When?" I asked.

"About a month ago."

"What about Stacey?"

"She stayed here."

"I shouldn't have gone out so far, fish. Neither for you nor for me. I'm sorry, fish."

I went still. That wasn't *To Kill a Mockingbird*. Nor was it any of the other books I had with me. I withdrew my hand from Georgia's and looked around the diner. There was only a scattering of customers with the one foot-sore waitress making trips between tables and behind the long counter to bring order slips to the short-order cook and fetch pots of coffee from the warming burners. On one of the counter barstools, a skinny man in a worn leather jacket sat hunched over a plate of eggs and corned beef hash. He had a worn paperback copy of Ernest Hemingway's *The Old Man and the Sea* propped open in one hand.

I looked again at Brad.

"'I am sorry that I went out so far. I ruined us both,'" said *The Old Man and the Sea.*

The book's voice carried regret and remorse. When I focused on Brad, it had a slight resonance I'd come to recognize. *The Old Man and the Sea* identified strongly with Brad. But that didn't make any sense. Although maybe he was now regretting not taking me to Union Station so I could be with Aunt Vieve? Was that the regret? I looked at him again, searching for some wavering in his resolve.

There wasn't any.

I felt defeat creep over me. Mark Robbins could get to Canada, but I couldn't get any farther than The Clock Diner. I might have made myself stronger by fighting the wind, but that didn't mean the wind wasn't often still stronger than me. I lifted my cup to my lips, but the coffee had grown cold, and I put it back down.

Brad signaled for the check. "C'mon, I'll take you home."

"CAN WE MAKE one stop on the way?" I asked as we got into the car.

Brad looked at me via the rearview mirror. "So long as that one stop isn't Union Station."

I smiled. "No, but I'm hoping you can time it to miss a few red lights. I think they close at eight."

AS WE PULLED into the library parking lot, Georgia turned to look at me.

"The library?" She shook her head, but she was smiling, as though this was now familiar territory and we could pretend her betrayal had never happened. "Margaux, you are so weird about books."

Brad parked the car and got out with us, saying he wanted to look in the business section and also flip through the latest issue of *Fortune.*

"We have that at the store," said Georgia.

"Those are supposed to be for paying customers," said Brad. "People who buy magazines want pristine copies, not smudged and bent pages—or ones with photos cut out of them."

Georgia rolled her eyes.

Brad held the door open for us. Just as we crossed the threshold, she grabbed my arm so hard I almost yelped, years of library etiquette kicking in just in time.

"Oh my gosh, I just remembered," she said. "We're having a test on the first two chapters of *The House of Seven Gables* tomorrow, and I haven't read it yet. And I forgot the book in my locker." She looked at me, eyes wide. "How did you know I'd need to have it tonight? You aren't just weird, you are *spooky*." She cast her eyes around the library. "It'll be under 'H', right?"

"For Hawthorne, yes," I said. "Nathaniel Hawthorne. This way. I need an H, too."

WE'D ARRIVED A mere ten minutes before closing, and I heard the solid click of the door lock behind us as we left the building.

The cold raindrops had turned into fat snowflakes that swirled in the yellow light spilling from the library windows and the tall lamp poles that lit the way around the building to the parking lot. There was the barest coating of white on the sidewalk and grass.

"It's April! Enough with the snow already!" yelled Georgia to the sky.

"It won't last," said Brad. "But I heard they're really getting hammered up north." He looked at me, and I expected him to say something about this being yet another reason for me not to travel tonight. But he didn't say anything more. Neither did *The Old Man and the Sea*, which I'd borrowed from the library.

Georgia leaned in as Brad walked a few steps ahead of us to the car.

"Do you really think your Aunt Genevieve is going to die?"

"My mother does."

It was one more thing I couldn't forgive her for.

Twenty-Four

The Old Man and the Sea was a short read.

Brad had dropped me off at the curb and I had slipped through the front door of our house before the ping of his engine had turned the corner at the far end of our street. The porch light had been on as well as the usual squat electric candle on the small table near one of the front windows. But the house had been quiet, even though it hadn't been quite eight-thirty. The note I'd left for Mother had still been taped to the top of the bannister. There had been a slit of light showing at the bottom of her closed bedroom door. I'd taken the note with me into my bedroom, crumpled it into a ball, and thrown it into the far corner. It had bounced off the wall and rolled under my dresser to sulk.

That had been hours ago.

I closed the book and slid down against the pillows on my bed. My mind was in a boat on a darkened sea with an eighteen-foot marlin tied to the side and sharks coming at the both of us.

After no luck on the water for too long, Hemingway's old Cuban fisherman had finally hooked a fish that would ensure his fortune. But the fish had been as strong as it was beautiful, and it had pulled the old man's boat for most of a day and a full night and another day and another night and then again most of another day before losing the fight. The old man won. Too large a prize to fit in the boat, he had tied it to the side of his skiff and set his single sail for home.

But then the sharks had come.

I shouldn't have gone out so far, fish. Neither for you nor for me. I'm sorry, fish, the book had told me in the diner. It was quiet in my hands now, but I could still hear the words in my head, remember the warmth of Brad's hand covering mine as it spoke and the rock-steady trustworthiness of his gaze.

The book had been talking about him, I knew with certainty. But Brad was Atticus. *To Kill a Mockingbird* had told me so, more than once. The words from *The Old Man and the Sea* were about regret and remorse. The old fisherman talking more to himself than to the fish who couldn't hear him anyway. His realization that his actions, though seemingly so right at the time, had turned out to be so tragically wrong.

What could Brad have possibly done?

Twenty-Five

I woke to light streaming through the windows and books strewn around me like a litter of puppies. I lay there for a moment, knowing something was horribly wrong, waiting for my consciousness to wake up enough to remind me what it was.

My eyes lighted on *Sense and Sensibility*, and I remembered.

I also remembered it was Thursday. I glanced at the clock. School had started forty minutes ago. True, I usually got myself up for school—but still . . .

I heard the two house phones ring in tandem.

I leapt out of bed and ran down the hall to my parents' bedroom.

I could see Mother's profile as she sat on Papa's side of the bed. She listened and spoke quietly into the receiver she held with both hands, cradling it as though it were something precious and fragile. Her thick chestnut hair spilled around her shoulders, and I saw her suddenly curl her bare toes that peeked out from beneath the hem of her cotton nightgown. She turned to look at me, and I saw grief in her eyes and glints of silver in her hair. When had her hair started to gray? My hand tightened on the doorknob, ensuring I would neither run away nor stride across the room to snatch the phone out of her hands. She spoke a moment longer, and then there was a long pause. I waited for her to offer the receiver to me, but instead she placed it back in its cradle on Papa's nightstand.

"What's happened?" I asked, my voice coming out as a croak.

"She's gone."

"That was Papa?"

"Yes."

"Why didn't you let me talk to him? Didn't he want to talk to me?"

"Margaux . . . " Mother stood up. She started to cry. She held out her arms.

I wanted to rush into them. To feel them envelop me.

For the two of us to share this grief.

At the news of Aunt Vieve's death, I thought I'd think only of her, but seeing my mother standing there with tears running down her face and her arms open to me, what my mind's eye showed me instead was Mother. Mother waxing the kitchen floor until I could nearly skate on it, making a Sunday chicken dinner on a Wednesday night, painting the corner bedroom robin's egg blue and making sure there was always a fresh flower bouquet on the nightstand, arranging for me to skip school to enjoy a Carlton Hotel lunch with Aunt Vieve, buying me a suitcase and cheerfully waving as I set off for Quebec City, ladling out mashed potatoes as she told me she'd invited Aunt Vieve to spend Christmas with us.

This unimaginable grief.

Why didn't I step into her open arms? Fifty and more years later, it still haunts me. Instead I stood there, rooted, my hand clutching a green crystal doorknob as though it were the fulcrum of the world.

I WENT TO my window seat and tucked myself in among the book stacks. I put my hand against a windowpane. It was chill, but not cold. Brad had been right—last night's snow wouldn't last. I saw a robin hopping around the grass, avoiding rims and ridges of white where the sun hadn't yet touched, but it would be all gone by noon. Farther north it would linger, I knew.

I had forgotten to set my clock, but I knew Mother hadn't forgotten to come wake me. She had anticipated this morning's call. I reached for anger, resentment, injustice—but it wasn't there. Instead I had a tight, hairy knot of sorrow lodged at the base of my throat, making me rasp when I breathed, its loose fibrous tendrils dangling down into my chest, making it hurt.

With a last glance at the disappearing snow, I got up and put back all the books strewn on my quilt, made the bed, and got dressed. I peeked out my bedroom door to make sure Mother wasn't in the hallway and snuck downstairs. There was the smell of fresh-brewed coffee in the kitchen and the back door was open. I poured myself some coffee from the percolator pot, added milk and sugar, and then, imagining I could hear Mother's soft tread and the turn of the aluminum storm door handle, scurried back to my haven without the bread that hadn't yet popped up in the toaster.

Today would be about Aunt Vieve.

I wanted to be in Quebec City, to have been with her, there at the end. To have told her how much I love her and how much it meant to me that she had taken me under her wing and made me understand that I wasn't a freak or insane, had shown me who I could be. That I was a different person—a more confident, whole person, a person with friends, even popular friends!—because of her. I wanted to be there now, to hug and be hugged, to give comfort and be comforted. I would have taken Papa by the hand and we would have walked all over the city, stopping and speaking to the people who had known Aunt Vieve, either by name or by sight— the shopkeepers, the artists in rue du Trésor, the street musicians, the waitress with the orange hair at the café, Mr. Martell, the carriage driver with his horse named Fox. They would look down and see Colonel Brandon, and they would ask why Aunt Vieve wasn't with us and we would tell them, and their eyes would become sad and they would tell us how sorry they were, how beautiful she'd been—so full of life! they'd say—and then they'd offer a hug or maybe just place a hand on my arm. They would ask Papa if there was anything they could do, and Papa would say no, but thank you. And by the time we'd returned to the apartment building, word would have spread, and there would be bouquets of flowers by the entrance with small notes of condolence, because there wasn't a person who had ever met or seen Aunt Vieve who hadn't realized that the world was a better place with her in it.

I set down my coffee cup and went around my bedroom, taking books from the shelves, from the window-seat stacks, from the satchel I'd packed last night. I paused as I pulled out *Dubliners*, remembering the conversation with Aunt Vieve after my near-meltdown at the café in the square.

> *"'One by one, they were all becoming shades. Better pass boldly into that other world, in the full glory of some passion, than fade and wither dismally with age.' That's it, that's the passage I heard."*
> *"Yes, I heard it, too."*
> *"It's beautiful, isn't it?"*
> *"It is."*
> *"I know I was starting to freak out a little bit back there, but those lines are really beautiful."*
> *"That's why we read, darling; that's why we read."*

"That's why we read," I said aloud now, looking at the book in my hand.

I thought about taking the books out to my tree, but the leaves were still mostly buds, and I knew I'd feel exposed. Instead, I climbed onto the bed with my treasures.

I opened *Sense and Sensibility* first. It seemed as connected to Aunt Vieve as—well, as Colonel Brandon, whining at the base of my beech tree or trotting at her heels over the cobblestone streets of Quebec City. I flipped through the pages to the part where Colonel Brandon leaves his assembled guests for an emergency trip he won't explain, insistent that no time can be lost, the hell with the planned picnic.

"Yeah, and where the hell were you this time?" I hissed at Jane Austen's Colonel Brandon, who was leaving his guests in a cloud of dust as he wasted no time in getting to the bedside of a loved one.

Colonel Brandon, of course, did not reply.

I didn't throw the book across the room but instead slammed the flat of my hand against the page. "Where?" I demanded.

My hand stung. I glared at the words. Colonel Brandon continued his exit, hooves kicking up dust, ignoring me.

I stalked to my dresser, grabbed a pen from the dross in my top drawer, and went back to the bed. I wanted an answer, damn it.

I paused, though, as I felt the tip of the ballpoint press into the paper. Deface a book? Sacrilege, said a voice in my head.

Communication, I answered. Ink translated to spoken word. Spoken word translated to ink.

Where the hell were you? I wrote across the cloud of dust, chasing Colonel Brandon in his desperate race against time. *She waited for you! Years! Damn you!*

I lifted the pen. My blue ink looked like crude graffiti on the thick, cream-colored paper. I slammed the book shut to hide my sin and threw it across the room. It hit the closet door and slid down, stunned, pages fluttering to stillness like a nineteenth-century heroine in a swoon.

I threw the pen after it, then wrapped my arms around my knees, closed my eyes, and waited for my breathing to slow.

Had I really just scribbled all over a page of one of my books?

I picked up *Fahrenheit 451*. I'd first heard of it when Aunt Vieve had brought it with her the day she'd climbed my tree, declaring Ray Bradbury's latest book a horror novel. I didn't like horror stories, but *Fahrenheit 451* had become one of my favorite books. I'd read it at least a dozen times. I held it close, seeking absolution for the sin I'd just committed. It didn't say anything, of course—neither damning nor comforting. Books never spoke to you when you were alone, Aunt Vieve had instructed me. But they *were* here with me. Physically, at least. And perhaps more, just out of my range of hearing.

I flipped through the pages, found the section I wanted.

"'Everyone must leave something behind when he dies, my grandfather said,'" I read aloud. "'A child or a book or a painting or a house or a wall built or a pair of shoes made. Or a garden planted. Something your hand touched some way so your soul has somewhere to go when you die, and when people look at that tree or that flower you planted, you're there. It doesn't matter what you do, he said, so long as you change something from the way it was before you touched it into something that's like you after you take your hands away.'"

I thought of the photos on Aunt Vieve's bookshelves. Who would tell the Baron and his family? I pictured the post office in Quebec City, some disinterested hand reaching for a rubber stamp and affixing a "return to sender—recipient deceased" smear of ink on the box before tossing it into a bin to be sent back across the ocean.

No. That would be awful.

I played out a different scenario in my mind. Mr. Martel would see the box. With a gentle hand, he would write a note, telling those in Belgium—among them, I suspected, one of the three Colonel Brandons Aunt Vieve had said she had encountered during her life—that the beautiful Genevieve was gone. Mr. Martel would place the handwritten note in an envelope, affix the correct postage, and then tape the envelope to the box before sending it on its way back to Belgium with its tragic news.

I rubbed my eyes against my sleeve and flipped more pages. I read aloud from *Fahrenheit 451* again.

"'And there, at the bottom of the hayloft stair waiting for him would be the incredible thing. He would step carefully down, in the pink light of early morning, so fully aware of the world that he would be afraid, and stand over the small miracle and at last bend to touch it. A cool glass of fresh milk, and a few apples and pears laid at the foot of the steps. This was all he wanted now. Some sign that the immense world would accept him and give him the long time he needed to think all the things that must be thought. A glass of milk, an apple, and a pear.'"

I knew it was impossible, but I felt as though the book had warmed in my hands. That my reading aloud—something I never did except when called on in class—was causing the book to try to bridge the gap, to speak to me as it normally didn't, or couldn't.

A glass of milk. An apple. A pear.

I looked at my cup of coffee and didn't want it any more. And not just because it was cold.

I closed the book and held it against my chest. "You're only warm because my hands have been holding you," I said.

I was *not* crazy.

I looked around my room and spied the framed photo of Papa, Aunt Vieve, and me with the carriage horse its driver had named Fox. I picked up *The Little Prince* and flipped through the pages.

"'"Good-bye,' said the fox,'" I read aloud. "'Here is my secret. It's quite simple: One sees clearly only with the heart. Anything essential is invisible to the eyes.'"

I thought of the day Aunt Vieve had first talked to me about hearing books. The way she had explained that just because not everyone could hear or see something, that didn't mean it wasn't there—like dogs hearing high-pitched sounds or bees seeing colors that people can't. Invisible. I thought I was the only one,

I'd told Aunt Vieve in Quebec City. Well, now I was again. Or I might as well be.

I picked up *The Secret Garden*, the book Aunt Vieve had said was my touchstone, like *Sense and Sensibility* was for her.

"'She made herself strong by fighting the wind,'" I read aloud. I looked out the window. The branches were not moving. "That doesn't mean the wind's not coming again," I told the book. I flipped a few more pages. I came to Colin's speech in the garden.

"'It's something. It can't be nothing!'" I read to all my books, glancing up from the page to include them as though reading a storybook to children. "'I don't know its name, so I call it Magic. I have never seen the sun rise, but Mary and Dickon have, and from what they tell me I am sure that is Magic, too.'" I paused. "'Magic is always pushing and drawing and making things out of nothing . . . So it must be all around us.'"

I didn't like to think of hearing books talk as magic. It was just something I could do, the way dogs could hear sounds that people couldn't, or the way Mary Beth Henderson at school had been able to turn a cartwheel on the balance beam without falling off on her very first try, or the way Mr. Sprichwort seemed to pick up languages as easily as some people caught colds. He'd told our French class that when he traveled, words and phrases just hung there in the air and he simply gobbled them up as he walked.

I set aside *The Secret Garden* and looked again at *Fahrenheit 451*. I turned the pages until I found what I wanted. "'The magic is only in what books say, how they stitched the patches of the universe together into one garment for us.'" I loved *The Secret Garden*, but I felt more of an affinity with *Fahrenheit 451*. "What books say," I repeated.

I turned more pages and stopped at the passage I remembered Aunt Vieve quoting. "'Stuff your eyes with wonder, he said, live as if you'd drop dead in ten seconds. See the world. It's more fantastic than any dream made or paid for in factories.'" That was Aunt Vieve. I thought about the milk, the apple, and the pear sitting at the bottom of a hayloft staircase.

"Everyone must leave something behind when he dies," I recited again, this time from memory. "Something your hand touched some way so your soul has somewhere to go when you die, and when people look at that tree or that flower you planted, you're there."

I thought about Mother's garden, the open back door. She'd be there this morning, checking on the peas and collards and lettuce she'd planted in March, readying the soil for the more tender vegetables she'd plant in the weeks ahead. My eyes went to a green cloth spine on the shelf, an antique book I hadn't touched in a very long time. "'When you are Real you don't mind being hurt,'" I murmured. I wasn't quite sure it was true, the wisdom of the Skin Horse notwithstanding.

I went down to the kitchen, threw out the cold toast still in the toaster, and poured a glass of milk. Sipping on it, I found a pear in the fruit bowl on the kitchen table, but no apple. There was one, albeit a bit wrinkly, in the bottom of the refrigerator's fruit and vegetable bin. I ate and drank and wandered from room to room, seeing evidence of decades lived in this house—my father's fledgling law practice that had kept the roof over our heads, my mother's touch everywhere that made it a home, the ghostly underlay of an aunt, an uncle, and three vibrant cousins I'd never known but who had lived here, too.

I put the empty glass in the sink and threw away the fruit cores.

I found Mother in the garden, as I'd expected I would. I stood just outside the latched gate and waited for her to notice me. To invite me into her woman's space.

Twenty-Six

P apa came home about a week later, bringing Colonel Brandon
with him.

I was a couple blocks away, walking home from school, when
I saw our car pull into the driveway. I ran.

He turned from speaking to Mother and she let go of his hands
as I came through the door. He hugged me, a tight embrace, and I
felt his chin rest for a moment on the top of my head. Then he held
me at arm's length and looked at me solemnly without speaking.

"Thank you," he finally said. "For staying here so your mother
wouldn't be alone. And for understanding where I needed to be."

These were not the words I'd expected. They gave me a lot
more credit than I was due. I looked at Mother, but her expression
gave no clue. Had she not told him about my outburst when they'd
spoken on the phone? Or had Papa simply presumed I'd acted in
the manner he'd wanted? My rehearsed speech died in my throat.

"We'll talk more later," he said, when the silence stretched.
He pressed a kiss against my forehead and let go.

He went through the double doors into his study, Colonel
Brandon trailing slowly after him. Papa set his briefcase on his
desk, opened it, and pulled out a green and blue Fair Isle sweater
that I remembered from Aunt Vieve's tall cupboard, although it
had never been cold enough when I'd been with her for her to
wear it. Papa spread the sweater on a cushion I'd seen Mother
bring down from the attic several days ago and hang on the
clothesline to air, the wooden clips spread wide but clinging with

tenacity. Mother had set the aired cushion in a corner of Papa's office where she'd said the dog would be able see all comings and goings but still feel a bit secluded. As Papa swung the doors shut, I saw Colonel Brandon sniff the sweater. I didn't see either of them for the next two days.

THE BOXES FROM Quebec City finally arrived. I came home from school to find a half dozen of them stacked in the hallway and a few more in Papa's study.

I knew from dinner-table conversations that most of Aunt Vieve's belongings had been donated or sold. I tried not to think about the apartment being dismantled. Much as I'd wanted to be there, I was glad I had missed that part. Uncle Matthew had been there to help. He'd arrived too late to see Aunt Vieve before she'd died—there'd been some complications other than just the polio, details I didn't want to know—but he'd stayed to help with the aftermath.

They had scattered her ashes around Quebec City.

"That can't have been legal," Mother said.

"I didn't ask," Papa said, loading up a fork with tuna noodle casserole. He loved tuna noodle casserole.

I pushed mine around the plate.

"But . . . " Mother looked distressed. "Aren't there laws about that sort of thing? You can't just scatter ashes wherever, can you? Walk around town with an urn where people are stepping, and . . . " She shook her head. "It just doesn't seem fitting."

"It was Matty's idea, and I thought it was a good one. And we didn't walk around town with an urn. We got some small paper bags and we cut off one bottom corner when we got to where we wanted to be. Then we just . . . walked. Matty, me, and Colonel Brandon. We visited all the places she loved." He looked at me.

I nodded. It was perfect, and my opinion of Uncle Matthew went up a notch.

GOING THROUGH THE boxes in the hallway, I was looking for two specific things.

I didn't find either of them.

I peered through the doorway into Papa's office. There were three travel-worn cardboard packing boxes on his desk. Old habits die hard, and I hesitated. But I was his research assistant now, a member of his legal team, in a sense. I strode into his study and rifled through the open cartons. One was nearly empty, and the others had variations of what the hallway boxes contained: books, a few small pieces of artwork, knickknacks.

Mother came by the doorway and saw me.

"Could you please shelve the books? Your father said they should go over on the far wall." She pointed out one of the bookcases that had been cleared, the contents moved to shelves closer to Papa's desk. "He said if there were any books you wanted for your room, go ahead and take them."

The whole room looked better once I was finished. I remembered the day I'd come home from school to find Aunt Vieve in Papa's chair behind his desk. She'd looked at all the empty shelves and told the law volumes, "We need to do something about this." I doubt this was what she'd had in mind at the time, but the shelves now looked comfortably full. I got a damp dust rag and cleaned everything, even my grandfather's pipes. I took particular care with the one I remembered Aunt Vieve holding. I clenched the stem between my teeth as she had done and kept it there as, under the watchful gaze of Colonel Brandon from his sweater-bedecked cushion, I finished my work. I heard a chuckle from the doorway.

"Not sure that's a habit your mother would condone," said Papa.

I smiled at him and carefully set the pipe back, making sure he could see the dust rag in my hand.

"Thanks for shelving the books for me. Did you find any you want for your room?"

"Some, yes. Thanks." I hesitated and watched him walk over to his desk to set down his briefcase. "There was one particular book I was looking for, but I didn't find it."

"Oh? Which one?"

"*Sense and Sensibility.*"

"That's got to be here. I remember packing it. In fact, I remember packing two or three. She had multiple copies of a handful of titles, but she had probably a half dozen of that one." He looked affectionately at Colonel Brandon, whose nose—the hair noticeably grayer than it had been when I'd lived with him in Quebec City—was once again set firmly between his paws.

"I found those copies, but there was one that she always carried around in her basket that summer I was there. It was a hardback—green cloth."

"Green cloth. Well, I know Matty took some books, too. I can ask him about it when I talk to him next." He snapped open the briefcase and took out some manila file folders. He'd been working late to catch up. After the first two nights, Mother had asked him if he could please come home for dinner and then work here, rather than staying at his office in town "until the wee hours." She had a hard time falling asleep until he came home, and the electric candle lamp by the window was never turned off until the three of us were home safe and sound. It was the job of the last person in the door to turn it off. If Papa was away or I spent the night at a friend's house, it stayed on all night. "What was the other thing?" Papa asked.

I felt my face redden. "Remember the monkey lamp that Aunt Vieve put in my loft?"

"Chester?" Papa grinned, and a quizzical frown creased his brow. "I didn't think you liked that lamp."

"Well, it kind of grew on me. I mean, you know, the story you and Aunt Vieve told about her bringing it with her when she came to stay with you. That makes it sort of a family heirloom, right?" I would have preferred just to find my creepy monkey lamp and take it up to my room, no one the wiser. A cold thought hit me. "That's not one of the things you and Uncle Matthew gave away, is it?" I knew it definitely wouldn't have been on the "sell" list.

"Give away Chester? Perish the thought! He's family. No, Matty took it back with him to California."

California?

"I'm sorry, sweetie, I didn't know you wanted it. You didn't seem that thrilled to find it in the loft that first day in Quebec, and when Matty asked . . . "

"No, no, it's fine. I just wanted to make sure it didn't get tossed or broken or something," I lied.

"It just seemed sort of poetic. Full circle. She brought it with her when she came to take care of Matty and me, and then she took it with her when she went to California to look after Matty's two boys. I guess they'll fight over who gets it one of these days."

I nodded. An image came to my mind of two scowling boys facing off, fists raised, the lamp safely set to one side as I watched, hidden among the trees. They tussled, intent on one another, and I swooped in, grabbed my creepy monkey lamp, and disappeared into the trees. Moments later, two disheveled boys stood, mouths agape, aghast and convinced that their altercation had caused Chester to once again come to life, this time to desert them.

"I'll keep an eye out for a green cloth copy of *Sense and Sensibility*, and I'll ask Matty about it next time I write to him. If he has it, I'm sure he'd be willing to send it to you."

"Thanks, Papa."

I picked up the stack of books I'd set aside for my room as I heard the phone ring. Mother answered it and then called out from the kitchen that it was for me.

It was Georgia.

"Margaux! What are you doing right this very minute?"

I rolled my eyes, hearing the dramatic note in her voice. "I'm standing in the kitchen, holding a stack of books, and talking to you." As soon as the words were out of my mouth, I wanted to edit them, leaving out the part about holding a stack of books.

"I need your spookiness. Put down the books for once and meet me at Grady's. But don't go inside. I'll meet you out front."

"Now?"

"Yes, now." Her voice got low. "Remember who dropped everything for you when you called?"

Yes, and betrayed my confidence by telling your brother what I was planning to do, I thought, but I swallowed the words.

"I remember. I'll see you in fifteen minutes."

"Wait! On second thought, bring some books."

I heard the rattle as she clumsily hung up the phone and the line went dead. I stood very still with the receiver still pressed against my ear.

She couldn't possibly have figured it out, I told myself.

Twenty-Seven

G rady's had been a hardware store until the Great Depression. When Mr. Nathan Grady had lost nearly everything and the bank had been about to foreclose, he'd locked the doors, pulled down the window shades, and refused to come out or let anyone come in for nearly a week. Our neighbor, Mrs. Randolph, had been just a girl then, but she said she remembered all the kids loitering around, waiting to hear the gunshot, while Mrs. Grady came periodically to stand outside the store and yell loud enough for the whole street to hear that she couldn't believe Mr. Grady would shame the family name and how this was no way for a civilized and respectable man to act.

"She'd stand there on the sidewalk in front of the hardware store, in the same flowered dress she wore to church every Sunday, bellowing for Mr. Grady to act like a man and come out of that store," Mrs. Randolph had related to me more than twice. "Mrs. Blenkin would come out of the post office, careful to post the 'closed' sign in the window, and try to get Mrs. Grady to come with her out of the street, but Mrs. Grady wouldn't have it. She stood there, every day, yelling at the windows with their lowered shades until she was good and ready to stop. The sheriff came out once in his patrol car, but he said that Mr. Grady wasn't breaking any laws, and until he did, there wasn't any reason to break down the door. He did tell Mrs. Grady that she was disturbing the peace with all her yelling and he might have to give her a ticket if she kept it up. Mrs. Grady told the sheriff that just because she hadn't gone to prom with him when he asked was no reason to get on his high horse now. 'Dodged that bullet,' the sheriff said," and Mrs. Randolph would laugh.

It was an early Saturday morning when everyone had seen the window shades were up and the door propped open at Grady's Hardware. A neat, hand-lettered sandwich board on the sidewalk had read "Grady's Soup & Coffee" in big letters and, underneath in smaller letters, "First Cup of Each is Free."

Mr. Grady had taken apart all the shelves in his hardware store and made tables and counters out of them, using sawhorses, paint cans screwed together, oil drums, and whatever else he could find in the store to make the trestles. Crates and wooden boxes served as seats or people just stood. He'd spoken to the pastors at both of the churches in town—Baptist and Methodist—and even the nuns at the small Catholic school the next town over. They had all pitched in. Anything that couldn't be used for the Soup & Coffee had been stacked in the back room and creditors had been invited to take what they wanted to settle debts. A little notice had said that whatever wasn't gone in a month would be free to whoever wanted it.

There were some who had complained that Grady's Soup & Coffee had brought the wrong element downtown, but as the Depression had worsened, it had become a lifeline for a lot of people. The first cup of each was always free, up to three times a day, but it had become a tradition for those who could afford it to stay for a second or third cup—or pretend that they did—and leave a little money behind to help keep the place running.

Then the letter had come. It had been on White House stationery, addressed to Mr. and Mrs. Nathan Grady and signed by the First Lady, Mrs. Eleanor Roosevelt. Mrs. Roosevelt had praised the tenacity, idealism, and charity of Mr. and Mrs. Grady, holding up Grady's Soup & Coffee as an example of what is best about America and her people. Mrs. Grady had never yelled at her husband again and had been seen most mornings chopping vegetables for the day's soup, typically standing so that anyone looking at her would also see the framed letter hanging prominently on the wall above her. The bank, recognizing it could either alienate most of the town (and potentially the First Lady) or take part of the credit, had decided not to foreclose and instead had forgiven Mr. Grady's loan.

THE FIRST CUP was still free. The tables of planks, sawhorses, and paint cans had been replaced with more modern booths, tables, and chairs, and I followed Georgia to a booth at the back of the diner.

"No, sit next to me where you can see," she said as I started to sit across from her.

I thought we looked a little funny sitting next to one another, but maybe people would think we were waiting for someone. Which, apparently, we were, except that Georgia didn't seem to want to be seen. She was hunched behind a menu in the far corner of the booth. I tossed my satchel onto the seat across from us. It landed with a noticeable thunk. I saw Georgia look at the satchel as it hit the bench, then at me, and nod.

"See what? Or who?" I wasn't sure how to act. Georgia was the closest thing I had to a best friend, but she was also *The Little Prince*'s prickly rose. And she'd specifically asked me to bring books. That was new. It had me on edge.

The waitress came over and we ordered our usual. Soup-of-the-day, Coke, and a sandwich to split between the two of us. Grady's didn't make a lot of money on high schoolers.

"I'm supposed to meet Stacey here," Georgia said, still peering over the menu she hadn't surrendered to the waitress.

"Why?"

Stacey was rarified air, the golden prom queen who had graduated the year prior with Brad and Mark. Brad and Mark were best friends, and Mark and Stacey had been glued at the hip since their junior year in high school, but that didn't translate to a friendship between Stacey and Brad's little sister.

"I don't know why. She called me and asked me to meet her here. That's why I need you. You have to tell me what's going on before I sit down with her."

I felt a flutter in my stomach. "Georgia . . . "

She thrust her chin at my books. "Do whatever it is you do."

"I don't know what you mean."

"Of course you do." Georgia looked tense. "I'm not kidding, Margaux, and don't make fun of me. If those books are your version of a black cat, so be it. If all those times I saw you whispering at books you were practicing spells, fine."

"You think I'm a witch?"

"You know things. Things you shouldn't know."

"I'm just observant. There are no such things as witches."

Georgia snorted. "Fine. Have it your way. If it were me, I'd rather have people think I'm a witch than just plain weird." She turned to the doorway and lowered herself in her seat a bit more. "Turn your observation skills to what just walked in the door."

Stacey Mulholland seemed a bit tentative as she looked around the restaurant. She didn't notice Georgia hidden in the corner and certainly didn't register my presence. She sat down at a table for four where she could see the door. A young waitress, obviously someone who knew Stacey from school, was by her side instantly to take her order.

I felt Georgia kick me under the table. I sighed and reached for my satchel and held it on my lap, feeling the familiar spines of a half dozen books. At the same time our soup, soda, and sandwich arrived, Stacey had soup and a cup of tea placed in front of her. I saw her lift a spoonful of the soup to her lips, then hurriedly set the spoon down again. I tried a sip of my own. Split pea and ham. It was good, with just a little kick to it.

"Well?" Georgia hissed.

My books were silent. It was the lull between breakfast and lunch, so the diner wasn't crowded. I held the satchel and focused on Stacey, willing them to say something, anything. In the back of my mind I was weighing what Georgia had said. Weirdo or witch? Did it have to be one or the other? Was there another option? How long can secrets be kept?

Stacey sipped her tea, the cup of soup pushed to the far side of the table. She had her strawberry blond hair pulled back in a ponytail, and she looked pale. I saw her suddenly straighten and turn her head. From my angle I could see the small, uncertain smile and the way she put one hand on her belly.

"I shouldn't have gone out so far, fish. Neither for you nor for me. I'm sorry, fish."

It was Hemingway's *The Old Man and the Sea* again. I'd brought it along with *Dubliners*, *Sense and Sensibility*, and *Fahrenheit 451*. I followed Stacey's gaze and saw Brad standing in the doorway, looking at her.

"I am sorry that I went out so far. I ruined us both."

Brad walked to Stacey's table and sat in one of the chairs. She said something to him, dipping her head. He hesitated. Then he put his hand over the one she had resting on the table.

"I ruined us both," I heard again.

"Oh, God," I said.

Atticus, I thought. The man who always did the right thing, no matter the cost.

I turned to Georgia. How long can secrets be kept? "He has to marry her, Georgia. Brad got Stacey pregnant."

Twenty-Eight

It was a small, June wedding, held at the Methodist church with a reception in the Pillards' backyard. I thought both bride and groom looked a little shell-shocked. Georgia was maid of honor.

Stacey and Brad were a beautiful couple. Brad wore a dark suit with a crisp white shirt and a white flower in the lapel. With his hair slicked back instead of hanging to his eyebrows, he looked like a somewhat nervous, blue-eyed, blond otter. Stacey wore a simple, white, empire-waist gown and a garland of flowers twined through hair that flowed in strawberry blond waves down her back. The gown had come from Stacey's grandmother; the flowers from my mother's garden. Mrs. Pillard had spent a lot of time in Mother's kitchen the weeks leading up to the wedding, the two of them talking in low voices over coffee, Mother's hand frequently patting Mrs. Pillard's.

I'D SLIPPED OUT of Grady's shortly after Georgia had taken a deep breath and joined her brother and Stacey at their table to hear the news and help plan how best to break it to the rest of the family. Georgia had never shared with me the details of that conversation, but she sought me out more frequently at school that fall semester, and I'd catch her looking at me expectantly. I think she considered me her personal early warning system—ready, willing, and able to alert her of any ambushes that might be coming her way. I knew what it was like to need a friend, and so I helped as much as I could. There were a few snide remarks and whispered conclaves that ceased when Georgia and I would arrive, but I was able to help her shut down some of them. There's nothing so tantalizing to high school girls as scandal. And the love triangle of Mark, Stacey, and Brad was just too much to resist. Those who live in glass houses shouldn't throw stones, though. *Sense and Sensibility* proved useful. I learned quickly that anyone who got Lucy Steele chattering away was someone who would smile and defend Georgia and her family to her face while stabbing her in the back without thinking twice. Armed with this knowledge, Georgia held her own.

I was glad to be her champion, her private oracle, and our friendship strengthened. In some ways, I was happier than I had been since my summer in Quebec City.

After the wedding, Stacey and Brad moved into the Pillards' attic. The only bathroom was on the second floor, but the attic had a full staircase leading up to it, not just a pull-down, and dormer windows that faced the backyard to let in lots of air and light. Stacey scoured the thrift stores for a window fan, colorful rugs, and an old record player. She painted the slanted walls, sewed curtains and a slipcover for the old couch that had been in the attic for decades, and created a small nursery in the corner. Brad took on more hours at the store and supplemented that income by making deliveries for the local florist. The ping of the Ford Galaxy was heard more frequently than ever.

Things had settled into a routine and the gossip had pretty much spent itself by Thanksgiving.

And then the baby came more than a month earlier than expected, just before Christmas. A healthy, six-pound, nine-ounce baby girl with brown curls, big brown eyes, and dimples.

The spitting image of Mark Robbins.

My breath was making puffs of smoke in the cold morning air when I felt someone grab my arm hard and spin me around. I almost lost my footing, but I caught myself to face Georgia, her face blotchy and her Cupid's bow mouth curled up in a sneer.

"Stacey I may or may not have believed, but you I trusted. And you said it was Brad's baby." Her hands were in fists clenched at her side. She looked like she was working hard to keep them there.

I'd been expecting this. Been bracing for it. I'd talked to my books about it. Multiple times. They hadn't offered any advice. Of course they hadn't. That wasn't what they did, right? Even though they'd gotten me into this mess.

I was on my own.

As usual.

"No, I said Stacey was pregnant." I kept my voice calm.

Georgia leaned forward. She glared. "No, Margaux. Believe me, it's seared in my brain. You said, 'He has to marry her. Brad got Stacey pregnant.' Just like that. Just those words. Oh, yeah— you said 'Oh, God' first. You invoked God in this, Margaux. You know that means you're going to Hell, right?"

My heart fluttered. She was right. Those had been my words. But that didn't mean I was going to hell, did it? I was pretty sure it didn't. "Well, did he say any different? It's not like I was there when she got pregnant, for crying out loud. What did Brad say?"

Georgia took a deep breath. She looked around, but we were alone, standing on the sidewalk a couple of blocks from school. "He didn't tell me then, but I got it out of him after the baby was born. They had sex. Once. Two weeks after Mark left for Canada. Stacey called him, all upset, he said. He meant to just be there for her, a shoulder, he said. Try to convince her that the whole Vietnam thing would blow over soon, that Mark would come home, or that once he got settled with a job and a place to live, he'd contact her and she could meet him in Canada. But Stacey just kept crying, he said, and one thing led to another. He was trying to *comfort* her, he said." Georgia snorted. "Of course we all know now that she was already pregnant. She *used* Brad. Then she made him believe it was his baby. And what is so infuriating about it all is that I *helped* her to do it."

Spittle flew from Georgia's mouth as she leaned in toward me to hiss these last words. She either didn't notice or didn't care. I didn't wipe away the droplets that hit my chin, my neck. I deserved this.

"I helped her, Margaux," Georgia continued, after taking a breath to compose herself. "I helped her because I trusted you. That day at Grady's, I told Brad I'd help him explain to Mom and Dad. I never even questioned Stacey's story. I didn't question that Brad had to marry her. *I* didn't question any of it and so he didn't feel *he* could question it. He said once he saw how I accepted it, he knew it was the right thing to marry her. And all the while that bitch sat there knowing she was lying and not caring whose life she ruined in the process. She'd arranged for both of us to meet her there. She thought she was ambushing me just like she ambushed him. But I could have questioned it. I should have questioned it. I *would* have questioned it. But I didn't. And you know why? Because I trusted you."

She stepped back, her arms loose at her sides, her anger for the moment spent. In place of the anger I saw hurt and guilt. There was bitterness, too. It was there in her eyes. Georgia had always been an open book. The hurt and guilt was that of a little sister, a daughter. The bitterness was toward me.

And justifiably so.

I felt bile rise in my throat and I swallowed it back, the taste stinging and bitter.

I'd been sure. Why had I been so sure?

It had been because of the diner, what I'd heard in The Clock Diner from *The Old Man and the Sea* held in the hand of a skinny guy in a worn leather jacket perched on a stool at the counter eating greasy eggs and corned beef hash. I'd gotten cocky by then. I'd been right—or not proven wrong—so many times.

That was the bottom line. I'd gotten cocky.

Brad was a standup guy. He was an Atticus. An Atticus who'd made a mistake. What I'd heard in the diner—I now knew—was guilt about having sex with his best friend's girlfriend. But I'd made a different leap that day at Grady's. A leap that had him responsible for a child that, as it turned out, wasn't his. A leap that had had a town gossiping about a shotgun wedding to cover the birth of an illegitimate child fathered by the son of one of the leading families in town. I remembered Mrs. Pillard crying in our kitchen, Mother comforting her.

"Georgia, I'm so sorry. I never meant . . . I shouldn't have said anything. I just knew she was pregnant and that Brad was feeling guilty when he walked in, and the way he looked at her . . . " I swallowed again.

"How did you get it so wrong? This one time when it was so important? Do you have any idea what this is doing to my mom? To our family? I've been your friend. I was your friend when no one would have anything to do with you." Georgia took a deep breath. "Did you do it on purpose? Was this supposed to be some sort of life lesson for me?"

"On purpose? No! Of course not!" I realized we were going down a dangerous path here.

"Then what happened? How do you know stuff like this any-way? You always nail it. What people are really thinking. When they're being honest and when they're blowing smoke. How do you know what you know?" She gestured with her chin at the satchel by my feet. "Let me guess. The books tell you? Someone swears on a Bible or something and forever afterward any book can tell you if they're lying? Or are you into the occult? That's what my mom thinks. That your family used to be into some sort of occult thing. That maybe it runs in the family. She said she remembers your mom's Aunt Trudy started acting weird after her son got hit by a car riding his bike and died. And then the two other sons died. And then she died and not long after that her husband died. Watch what you're mixed up in, Margaux. My mom thinks your whole house may be hexed. Just be glad I haven't told her your part in getting Brad to marry Stacey when you knew it wasn't his baby."

"Georgia! I didn't know that! I never meant for any of this to happen!" This was getting out of hand. Georgia wasn't being logical.

"Well you sure had me fooled." Georgia was calm now, back in control. "But never again. Stay away from me and stay away from my family." She stalked a few steps, then looked back at me over her shoulder. "Feel free to continue your friendship with Stacey."

"I never had a friendship with Stacey," I said.

But Georgia was already out of earshot.

I turned around, went home, and climbed into bed, not even bothering to take off my shoes. I pulled the covers over my head so that I couldn't see any of my books.

I doubted they noticed or cared.

Twenty-Nine

Things got uncomfortable for the Pillards after that. Which meant they also got uncomfortable for me. It became obvious very quickly that Georgia was having nothing to do with me and, faster than weeds in my mother's garden, rumors grew around the cause.

I don't know if Georgia followed through on her threat about telling her mom my role in the whole mess, but Mrs. Pillard no longer came to have coffee in our kitchen. The entire Pillard family seemed to draw into itself, as much as was possible for business owners who relied on the good will of the community.

By spring, Brad found a job in Richmond and moved his small family to an apartment there. Georgia started working more at the store, and it wasn't long before there was an additional line of nail polish available and customers didn't have to flip through magazines before purchasing to make sure they were intact.

IT WAS SENIOR prom night when Papa came tapping on my bedroom door. Not surprisingly, no one had asked me to be their date, although prior to Christmas, Georgia and I had already been planning what we'd wear, how we'd style our hair, and discussing the list of boys who might get up the nerve to ask us and what our response would be to each.

He entered with two heavily laden ice cream bowls balanced on a cardboard box.

"I thought it might be a good evening for ice cream. And not just any ice cream. I splurged and got the good stuff—raspberry chocolate chip. And I have something else for you."

I scooted over on the bed to make room, sliding college pamphlets and forms to one side and a ball of tissues under the pillow in the process.

"I was just going over paperwork, making sure I've sent in everything I need to send in," I said.

"Studious work for a Saturday night."

I shrugged.

He set the box on the floor, handed me a bowl, and sat down on the bed with the other. "You know, final decisions aren't due until next week. You could still pick a Virginia school."

I shrugged again. I'd applied to several Virginia colleges to make Mother happy, but I knew there was no way I would stay so close to home. I needed some fresh air. "I think it would be good for me to live outside Virginia, at least for a while. I used to think about going to college in Quebec City and living with Aunt Vieve. I'd get really good at French and then talk you and Mother into letting me have a semester or two in Paris." I smiled and looked up at him sideways. Enough time had passed that I could talk about Aunt Vieve without feeling sad. And it was because of her that there was the money for me to go to pretty much whatever college accepted me. "I don't want Quebec City anymore, but Charleston seems like it will be a good fit for me."

Papa patted my leg. "I'm sure Charleston will be an excellent fit. And, if it's not, you can transfer back." He winked. "That's what I told your mother, anyway. 'She can always transfer back if she gets homesick.'"

"Living in a dorm will be a little weird. I'm trying to narrow down which books to take and which to leave here, but I'm not making a lot of progress." I motioned with my spoon at the shelves and stacks of books that made my bedroom look like a small, cluttered library.

Papa sighed. "I can see renting out your room while you're gone won't be an option. I'm surprised you can find your bed at night." He nodded at the pen on my nightstand. "Have you taken up writing, too? I've heard it's a good idea to keep a pen and notebook next to the bed. So that when you wake up with just the right words in your head, you can jot them down before you fall back asleep and forget them."

I looked at the pen and away again, my eyes avoiding the small stack of books near the nightstand. The first time I'd ever defaced a book had been the morning after my botched attempt to get to Quebec City and Aunt Vieve's bedside. *Where the hell were you? She waited for you! Years! Damn you!* I'd written in my copy of *Sense and Sensibility*, pressing down hard enough with the ballpoint pen to score the words into the paper. These past few months, I'd found myself picking up my pen again, usually right after I got home from school or in sleepless pre-dawn hours, venting my hurt and frustration on *The Old Man and the Sea* or confiding in *Fahrenheit 451,* among others. I had three copies of *Fahrenheit 451.* One sat under the ballpoint pen. Another, margins chock-full of ink, was mid-stack by the nightstand. It seemed a better alternative to screaming, and the one night I'd tried to shut everything out by sneaking a bottle of wine and drinking the whole thing had resulted in a horrible headache and feeling awful the next day.

I'd learned—as Aunt Vieve had—that books wouldn't talk to me when I needed them most. Which was when I was solitary—left to be solitary, chose to be solitary. When I scoured my books, seeking connection, trying to find my way.

When I so needed a confidant.

By now I was sure that books—or at least certain books—listened to those around them. The books that listened, that spoke, were those that, like the Skin Horse in *The Velveteen Rabbit* , had become real. There was a reason, a poetry, that this had been the first book I had heard speak to me, all those years ago when the wind had made my dresses dance as headless marionettes and the storm had billowed like rising bread dough and mother had left an afternoon's work to fend for itself and instead had scooped me up to cradle me and read the words of wisdom of a toy horse abandoned and left to memory.

How many books were left to memory? Rarely chosen? Rarely read?

Couldn't those loved and read and reread and reread and reread again become Real, as had the Skin Horse and the Velveteen Rabbit?

They *chose* when to speak and with whom. They chose when to speak to me. And it wasn't when I needed them. No, that couldn't be it. Aunt Vieve had been the one to tell me that books didn't speak about the ones who heard them, and what was there to talk about otherwise? Which brought me to the essence of my aloneness: Aunt Vieve was gone, her ashes scattered around the places she'd loved best by two men who had loved her for who she'd been. There was no one left for me to talk to. So I talked to my books through writing directly in them. I'd decided it was like a blood transfusion, in reverse, but lifegiving nonetheless. Or if not lifegiving—I didn't have much of a life these days, especially compared to my exuberant classmates celebrating the last months of our senior year in high school—at least it kept me sane.

Or so I told myself.

"Just some notes to myself," I said. I hoped he didn't notice there wasn't a notebook on my nightstand. Just the pen and *Fahrenheit 451*. I finished my ice cream and saw he was looking at me intently, his spoon left dormant in a half-full bowl.

"You seem to be a little tense these last few months. You doing okay?"

"Sure. Of course. Finals and all, you know, but I'm fine."

"I haven't seen Georgia around lately."

I set my bowl aside. "We had a falling out. No big deal."

"It's been a rough year for the Pillards. Anything the two of you can fix before graduation? People tend to drift apart after that. You might come to realize that whatever it was could have been fixed, but the more time that passes, the harder it can be."

I pressed my lips together and shook my head. I didn't want to talk about Georgia. I nodded toward the cardboard box on the floor. "What did you bring me?"

"Ice cream—the good stuff, mind you—isn't enough?" He smiled and lifted the box onto my bed. "Something from Aunt Genevieve."

The box looked the right size to hold the creepy monkey lamp that Uncle Matthew had spirited away to California for his boys, but when Papa lifted the cardboard flaps, I saw it was full of books. A familiar green cloth volume was on top.

"You found it? You found Aunt Vieve's copy of *Sense and Sensibility*?" I lifted out the book and held it on my lap. "I know she had other copies, but this is the one she carried with her everywhere we went that summer I visited her."

"You're right, she had a lot of copies." Papa continued to empty the box, and, when he was done, there were seventeen other volumes of *Sense and Sensibility* on the bed around us, all different printings with different covers. He set the box aside and nodded toward the book on my lap. "Open it," he said.

Words, scribbles, drawings. On page after page, in different colors of ink, Aunt Vieve had held a one-sided conversation with this book. Some pages had letters written to various characters. Some had messages obviously written in anger, sometimes one or two words scrawled across an entire page. There were smears and fingerprints of a brownish-red color. Old, dried blood, I realized, matching my own fingertip to one of the marks. I felt Papa watching me. I dipped my head, allowing my hair to become a curtain between my face and his. Turning pages, the sound of paper against paper the only sound in the room, I noticed the fingerprints had something in common. Every one of them had been carefully placed over a character's name. A spell? A talisman? A wish? This was no longer a novel. It was a diary. Aunt Vieve's diary. I felt like an intruder.

I shut the book.

Anyone who didn't know Aunt Vieve and had come upon this book would have thought it was the work of an unhinged mind. Which was why, I knew, Papa had hidden it, hidden all of them. Until now.

"They're all like this?" I didn't touch the other books on the bed.

He nodded.

"Do you think she was mentally unstable?" I wouldn't say crazy. I wouldn't say insane. I would approach this as an adult. An adult who was not going to let herself be locked up somewhere.

"I think she felt very alone with a secret too big to keep completely inside herself. It had to have an outlet somewhere. This was hers."

"What secret?" He and I had been dancing around this since the day in his office when I had been eleven years old and he'd told me the story of the eyelash. A wish sent out on a breeze.

"The same one that you have."

There. It was out. Sort of.

I waited.

He got up and walked to the window. He put his hands in his pants pockets and looked out. I looked past him to see what he was seeing, but it was dark outside and all I could see was the reflection of my room the light of the bedside lamp cast on the windowpane.

"Remember that day I had to bring the ladder out to get her out of the beech tree in the backyard?" Papa said after a moment.

"That's how I like to remember her. Stuck out on that branch, daylight fading, but still laughing and having the time of her life. She'd got up there just fine on her own, knew someone—you— was up there with her to keep it fun and interesting, and knew that someone—me—would come to get her back down when she was good and ready. She wouldn't be stranded out there alone with night coming on." He turned to look at me, a wistful smile on his face. "I wish she'd trusted me to bring a ladder at other times, too. Times when she felt alone with night coming on. I'd have done it for her. I'd have done just about anything for her. She and I talked about it—that last time we talked."

He walked back to sit on the bed beside me, eighteen copies of the same book—and yet no longer the same book—scattered around me. He took my hand.

And that's when I knew he wasn't bluffing. She'd told him our secret.

I'd always thought I'd be angry if I learned she'd told.

I wasn't angry.

"The only one," she'd said once, *"Yes, that can certainly motivate a lot of actions."*

Alone with night coming on.

I made a decision.

"I can hear books," I said, looking Papa in the eye. "They talk to me, read themselves to me. Sometimes. Not always." Somehow it suddenly seemed important that I be the one to tell him, not the other way around.

He nodded and reached over to kiss me on the forehead. "There's something else in the box I think you should have," he said. "It originally went with Matty to California—he thought Liza would like it—but he just recently realized it was meant for you."

He reached into the side of the box and withdrew a small, rectangular package wrapped in brown paper and tied with string. He handed it to me.

I pulled the string and the paper fell away.

It was a painting. Right away I knew it was the parapet in Quebec City overlooking the Lower Town. It was different, though, from the many paintings I'd seen in rue du Trésor. This one would likely not appeal to the tourists. The day depicted was blustery, the paint strokes and colors evoking wind and rain. The unframed canvas was small—no more than ten inches long by four inches high. I saw that the scene was populated, despite the inclement weather. To the far left, a painter worked at a canvas as though it were the brightest, clearest day of the year. To the far right, a figure with outstretched arms seemed to ignore everything and everyone. Her arms were outstretched and one leg was raised. She could be mid-pirouette.

"What made Uncle Matthew decide it was for me?"

"He looked at the back. I don't know how we both missed it before."

I turned the piece over. I recognized Aunt Vieve's elegant script on the inside of one of the wood stretcher bars that held the canvas.

She made herself stronger by fighting the wind.

I felt my throat tighten. "And this is how he knew it was for me?"

"She said it to me—about you—that—" he paused. "That last time we talked," he finished. "Matty wasn't there, but I told him about it. Not everything she said," he added, seeing the look on my face. "Just that part. She said you'd need to be reminded now and again."

I nodded. The painting didn't have a signature in the lower left corner, but I knew Mr. Lederle had not painted this. Aunt Vieve had gone elsewhere for this commission. I touched the figure of the painter and remembered the woman who set up her easel in the same spot every time, but whose paintings were always different. Maybe it was signed, after all.

"He's right," I said, finally. "She meant this painting for me. To remind me."

Part II

Thirty

1973

It would be good to get out of DC for the weekend, to spend some time with Mother and Papa, enjoy the fall colors. I hadn't seen my beech tree bedecked in its glorious gold for a couple of years.

On Saturday morning I could go into town and visit some old haunts—Grady's, the library, the bakeshop that made petit fours that reminded me of Quebec City. Maybe even Pillard's Sundry Shop. Maybe enough time had passed. It had been more than seven years, after all. No doubt Aunt Trudy's bicycle was still hanging in the garage. I could take it down, pump up the tires, put some books in the basket, and ride it into town. That way I could make a quick getaway if Georgia or Mrs. Pillard starting throwing things at me—bottles of nail polish remover or dagger looks. Georgia, I recalled, had terrific aim.

On second thought, maybe I'd skip a visit to Pillard's. Maybe I'd skip a visit to town altogether. A nice, quiet weekend with Mother and Papa. That was all I needed. I could help Mother in her garden, play a game of chess with Papa on the porch. The weather was supposed to be nice.

But first I had to get through this evening. I glanced at my watch, then at the speedometer as my car crawled south through I-95 rush hour traffic. I had planned to be a little late—avoid the pre-dinner chitchat—but now I was going to be *really* late. Mother wouldn't be pleased.

THERE WAS A Porsche in the driveway and two other expensive cars parked on the street in front of my parents' house. If the Porsche had moved up, at least one of the other cars would have fit, but I wasn't surprised to see it positioned for maximum admiration. I tucked my VW Rabbit in behind the Porsche, not caring that I blocked the sidewalk, and thought about tapping the bumper just to see what would happen. Maybe it would set off an alarm. I glanced at the house windows and then looked over my shoulder at the books in my back seat.

"Waddaya think? Just a little tap could prove entertaining."

They didn't answer.

I shrugged and pulled up carefully.

Getting out of the car, I examined my handiwork. Close enough for a copy of *Anna Karenina* between the bumpers, but *War and Peace* wouldn't have fit. Perfect. Let the owner wonder. I grabbed my overnight bag and leather satchel from the back seat and did my best to slide through the front door unnoticed. The electric candle by the window was turned off. A reminder that this wasn't home anymore—not really.

I was halfway up the staircase when I heard Mother in the foyer.

"Margaux, you're late."

I stopped and turned. She was as trim as ever, wearing a modest but brightly colored sheath dress, her hair pulled back with a matching band to let thick waves of silver and chestnut frame her face. I had the sudden thought that if I looked up "perfect wife of successful lawyer" in the encyclopedia, her image would be right next to the definition.

"I know. I'm sorry, Mother. There was a lot going on at the office. And traffic was a bear."

"Come down and join us. Dinner is over but everyone is still here. Margaux, please don't give me that look. You know there's someone your father wants you to meet." She glanced at the doorway through which drifted the murmur of conversation. A laugh that sounded like Papa's. "Save me the stress of another client dinner party by meeting him at this one?"

I replaced whatever "look" I apparently had on my face with a smile. "Will do. Give me five minutes and I'll be down."

"And you have to stay at least twenty minutes. And for goodness sake, brush your hair!" I heard Mother call up in a stage whisper as I turned down the upstairs hall toward my childhood bedroom.

I tossed my overnight bag and satchel on the bed and went into the bathroom. I grabbed a hairbrush, wincing as I worked out the tangles incurred from leaving the car windows open. Setting the brush aside, I looked at my reflection. I widened my eyes and bared my teeth in a dazzlingly fake smile—the kind the receptionist at our office reserved for certain visitors—then stuck my tongue out at my reflection. I pointed an index finger at the mirror. "Behave yourself," I said with raised brows and mock severity. "I know you can be charming when you're willing to put in the effort. It's important to your father." I switched off the light to leave, then switched it back on. I looked at my reflection for a moment. I picked up a tube of lipstick from a ceramic tray on the bathroom counter, twisted its base, and considered the color. With a shrug, I swiped it across my mouth several times. I pinched my cheeks until they bloomed a bit. Then I switched the light off.

Going back into the bedroom, I went to my shelves. Most of my books were in my small studio apartment just across the river from Washington, DC, but I kept a shelf or two here, along with my childhood books. It wasn't just that they wouldn't fit in my apartment; having them at my parents' proved useful on evenings like these—this wasn't the first time Papa had had someone he wanted me to meet.

Charleston had been a good choice. And if Papa was disappointed that I hadn't pursued a law degree, he never let me see it. I didn't want to have people's lives and happiness resting on decisions I made and the advice they'd look to me to provide. I'd learned my lesson.

Instead, I'd earned a bachelor's degree in architecture, then a master's in architectural preservation. There was something about rescuing and preserving the beauty of the past that appealed to me, like finding a gem of a book on a back-corner shelf of a used bookstore. The outer layers might be peeling, worn, and in disrepair, but the bones of older buildings had a strength and grace I just never sensed in newer architecture, particularly the buildings that had been seemingly thrown together in the flurry of growth following the end of World War II. It was a puzzle of sorts, too, to properly restore a historic property, to find the pieces that fit and made it whole.

I had spent an entire summer internship amid dust, dirt, rust, and cobwebs, scouring old warehouses in three states looking for crystal doorknobs, bathroom fixtures, gas lamps, fireplaces and irons, and other items for a boutique hotel restoration. I'd always brought a few books with me on those forays, tucked in the leather satchel that doubled as my purse. *Catch-22* had proven helpful in identifying several conniving Milo Minderbinders among the warehouse owners and managers. *To Kill a Mockingbird* had been my barometer of trustworthiness for years. Of course I always had a copy of *Fahrenheit 451* with me. Depending on my mood, I sometimes brought *Sense and Sensibility*, but I had yet to come across a Colonel Brandon. Or someone who was looking for the peace and space of a glass of milk, an apple, and a pear.

My efforts that summer had paid off. The following spring I'd been invited to the gala celebrating the grand reopening of the 1890s-era Hotel St. Christopher and had seen firsthand what dedication to detail—and a lot of money—could accomplish. Over champagne cocktails, the owners had personally thanked me for my efforts. During dinner, I'd chatted with the chair of the local board of tourism and learned of another property owner who would be interested in hearing about renovation possibilities. Sipping an after-dinner glass of port, I had passed this information on to the CEO of the company that had given me the summer internship. Before I'd left that night, the CEO had made me a job offer.

I ran my index finger along the book spines, considering. I took one off the shelf and two out of my satchel and went downstairs to meet my parents' guests.

Per the instructions in Aunt Vieve's will, my father had sold her Quebec City apartment and most of its contents. A few family pieces and many of her books had been carefully crated and shipped to our house, including the cardboard box of eighteen identical titles that I had repacked, thoroughly resealed, and tucked away in the back of my closet. The proceeds of the sale had been divided between Papa and Uncle Matthew, with trusts set aside for my college education and that of my twin cousins. Papa had invested most of his inheritance in his law practice, which had grown in size and success, much to the relief of Mother, who, over time, had felt secure enough to convert about half of the vegetable garden to rose bushes, perennials, and other flowers. She chaired a garden committee that brought fresh arrangements to area nursing homes. Old habits die hard, however; every year, she still canned tomato sauce, bread-and-butter pickles, and fruit preserves from the largesse of our backyard.

I came down the stairs quietly and slipped into Papa's study through the hallway doors. For a number of years now, I had ignored the rules of sanctity around what Aunt Vieve had called my father's "tree fort"—although it still seemed more of a burrow to me. He didn't seem to mind. Through adjacent doors to the living room, I could hear bits of conversation and the clink of glasses. I set the books I'd brought on one of the shelves near the doorway to the living room. Proximity was important. Aunt

Vieve's novels filled much of what had been empty space on the shelves, but I still liked to bring a few of my own to these gatherings. Papa may have accepted that I'd never be a lawyer, but, at age twenty-five, he clearly felt I should be dating. I think he wanted to know that I'd have someone ready, willing, and able to fetch a ladder to get me out of whatever tree I climbed, should there come a time that he couldn't. I knew he meant well, but these dinner parties were one of the reasons I didn't make the trek home very often.

One of the reasons.

It was bittersweet, coming here. While I had been away at college, every time I had come home, the electric candle in the window near the front door had been turned on. It wouldn't be turned off for the night until everyone was home—the tradition I'd known for as long as I could remember. All those weeks—a couple of months, sometimes—between trips home from college, it would be left on. I'd thought about that sometimes, when I'd been getting settled in Charleston, when I'd felt homesick or that I didn't quite belong. I'd made some friends, but no one really close. I'd dated a few times, but nothing that had stuck. I'd gotten good at creating a façade, a cover for everyone to see. I'd let one or two people read the Margaux book jacket. But I kept my pages shut. I let people judge me by my cover. I guess I was keeping people at arms' length, waiting for my wounds to heal after the debacle with Georgia. Some healing takes a while.

But, as I'd written on page ninety-two of my current diary, I had had a place that had claimed me. That had known me. A place where a light had been left on to guide me home. I had dogeared that page so I could easily find again those words I'd written over the words already printed. For the times I'd need to remind myself.

The first time I'd come home after graduating and moving to DC, I had been up the walk, across the porch, through the front door, and halfway up the stairs before the niggling in the back of my mind had coalesced enough to grab my attention. I had turned around on the staircase and looked at the window next to the front door.

The electric candle hadn't been on.

Which had meant everyone had been home. Even before I'd gotten there.

It had been my decision, of course, to move to the city rather than settle back in our little town. But it was in that moment I had realized this was now my *childhood* home. Past tense. My parents had accepted my decision to make a life, my home, elsewhere.

More than a year later, though, I was still working out where home was.

Walking to the sideboard near Papa's desk, I selected a lead-crystal decanter and poured a glass of tawny port.

The lilt and buzz of conversation drifted over me as I took a sip and strolled across the study to the doorway. I saw Mother notice me, look me up and down. I hadn't changed clothes, but apparently the blue wrap dress I'd worn to work passed muster. Or maybe she just was confirming I'd brushed my hair—not always a sure thing. I smiled at her, knowing the stress she felt at these dinner parties, particularly when Papa had decided there was someone I needed to meet. She murmured something to the woman at her side and made her way to where I stood.

"Finally. That was more than five minutes. Now please come and meet your father's guests." She gave me a meaningful look. "And behave yourself. I know you can be charming when you're willing to put in the effort. It's important to your father."

Mother could be so lovingly predictable. "I'll be charming. I promise."

She paused. "Well, not *too* charming," she amended.

I leaned over to kiss her powdered cheek, taking in her scent—grass, fresh air, and just a hint of Chanel No 5—thinking of the

Sense and Sensibility volume I'd left on the bookshelf. "Yes, Mrs. Dashwood," I said. Used to my literary references, Mother just gave a small harrumph. I strolled to Papa's side. The men were discussing the latest legislation that had passed in Richmond.

"Darlin'! You're here. I'm so glad." Papa put his arm around me. "Margaux, I'd like you to meet some clients I'm rapidly coming to think of as friends." He gestured with the hand that held his usual glass of bourbon. "This is Mr. Dempsey, his son Colin, Trey Janus, and August Locke. Gentlemen, my daughter, Margaux."

I knew from a phone conversation with Papa and a follow-up prep chat with Mother that Trident Investment Group was the latest client of my father's law firm and already the third largest. I nodded to each man in turn, accepting Papa's introductions with the grace and poise I'd learned from Aunt Vieve. There was Cole Dempsey, the aging yet elegant founding partner. His tailored suit exposed a monogrammed French shirt cuff as he shook my hand in the slight, little-lady-I-don't-want-to-hurt-you manner that always aggravated me to no end. His son and heir apparent, Colin Dempsey, looked to be in his thirties and was a more attractive, slightly shorter version of his father, with a genuine smile that exposed dimples as he nodded when we were introduced. Trey Janus looked a lot like Steve McQueen in *The Thomas Crown Affair*, except that he wore his blond hair slicked back a bit. I suspected the Porsche in the driveway belonged to him. At our introduction, he nodded to me, as well. A half-smile played on his lips and he had a look in his eyes that made me decide the Porsche was definitely his. It was distracting, and I almost missed the last introduction. I caught the name of August Locke as his hand took mine in a warm, firm handshake. I looked up, a little embarrassed, to see light green eyes looking at me intently. August smiled.

"Pleased to meet you, Margaux," he said.

During the years since Aunt Vieve and I had spent an afternoon in the beech tree, I'd added to the list of book proclivities.
Focus on one person in hopes of gleaning some truth, I'd learned,
and books would often pretend to be merely ink on paper. They
could not be inveigled to speak. But when a number of people
were present, books seemed to almost compete with one another
to be heard, each wanting to outdo the other in identifying a
kindred spirit. The trick was to then untangle what I heard and
attach the right book voice to the right person and figure out
what it all meant.

And to do it without getting it wrong. Without hurting anyone.

I'd brought three books to Papa's study—*The Swiss Family
Robinson* because I admired those who could turn adversity to
advantage, plus the father was a bit of a know-it-all and it never
hurt to pinpoint those; *To Kill a Mockingbird* to identify weakness,
strength, morality, and villains; and *Ulysses* because James Joyce's
depiction of a single day in Dublin exposed the inner thoughts
and motivations of more people than most novels I'd read. I kept a
copy of *Fahrenheit 451* and of *Sense and Sensibility* permanently
and strategically shelved in Papa's study. I had started to toy with
the idea of getting a dog and naming him Colonel Brandon. I made
a mental note to cut some late-blooming flowers from Mother's
garden and a sprig of golden beech tree leaves tomorrow and
place them on the small mound near the back fence.

" . . . completed her master's in architectural restoration a
little more than a year ago," Papa was saying. "She's working
now at the firm where she had her internship. They knew not to
let a good thing go, didn't they?" His arm around me squeezed
my shoulder.

"I think it's more that they had a big project underway and
needed a lot of worker bees," I said.

*"The troublesome ones in a family are usually either the wits
or the idiots."*

I lifted my chin at the sudden, loud voice from *Middlemarch* and cast a glare at the doorway to the study. George Eliot may have been a woman, taking on a man's name for a penname to suit the times, but I'm not sure we would have been friends. Someone here thought my being late meant I was troublesome? And possibly an idiot? Really? And, which, pray tell, of my father's guests thought that, would you mind telling me? George and her book, of course, declined to elaborate.

"Is everything okay?"

It was Colin, his head bent solicitously toward mine. His auburn hair curled around the backs of his ears, and I caught a whiff of sandalwood cologne. Out of the corner of my eye I saw Mr. Dempsey glance at us and smile.

"Yes, thank you." I gave him my attention. I really shouldn't write him off just because my father—and apparently his— thought we were a good match. Colin had Irish good looks, could hold an intelligent conversation, and apparently didn't care if a woman was late. All admirable qualities. I took another sip of port. Mr. Dempsey and my father moved away, deep in discussion, apparently content the proper introductions had been made.

"And when all was said and done the lies a fellow told about himself couldn't probably hold a proverbial candle to the wholesale whoppers other fellows coined about him."

This came from *Ulysses*. But I was looking Colin in the eye when I heard it and it just didn't seem to connect, fellow Irishman or not. I took a sip from my glass and nonchalantly cast my gaze around the room, trying to determine the connection. I disliked hearing this line—had heard it a few times since first reading the novel—but it was better to know than not. As a result, Joyce's book was one of my mainstays, particularly at business and matchmaking gatherings.

"So I understand you worked on the restoration of the St. Christopher Hotel," Colin said, drawing my attention back to him. "I was there last month for a seminar. It's stunning."

"It is stunning, isn't it? But I didn't really 'work' on it. I was an intern and did some search and rescue to find bits and pieces that were used in the restoration."

"Search and rescue?"

"The green crystal doorknobs? One of my finds."

"The place just wouldn't be the same without the green crystal doorknobs," Colin said gravely.

"Yes, everyone agreed with you. I think that's why they offered me a job." I lifted my glass to my lips. He really was very handsome. The evening had become promising.

"May I fill your glass?"

I felt a hand come up under my elbow, and I started at the unexpected touch. It was Trey, and he smiled as he poured more port into my half-full glass. I recognized the cut-crystal decanter as the one in the study from which I'd poured. He noticed my reaction and withdrew his hand, sliding his fingertips along my bare skin. His touch was warm and I felt a curl in my belly.

"Pardon me," he said. "I didn't mean to startle you."

He looked at me. A smile tugged at the corner of his sensuous mouth. I recognized that look; had seen it before. It said I was a book he already knew, even though he'd never read me. That I was like so many other books he'd read over the years.

There is a fine line between confidence and arrogance. I decided he'd crossed it.

I ignored the flutter in my belly and forced a slow breath. I resisted the urge to rub the underside of my arm to smudge away the shiver I'd felt at his touch. I glanced at the decanter, then gave him the look I'd perfected during my internship; what I called my there's-no-way-in-hell-this-is-authentic stare.

"Actually, I was drinking Madeira," I lied.

He looked at my glass, then up at me. His eyes held mine. They were a piercing blue, set above high cheekbones and a strong jawline.

"You will always be fond of me. I represent to you all the sins you never had the courage to commit."

My eyes widened. This wasn't from one of the books I'd left on the shelf. Who was speaking? I caught myself as Trey's smile deepened. I could sense Colin's annoyance at the interruption, but he merely pressed his lips together and didn't say anything.

Trey held up both hands in mock surrender, one still holding the decanter. "Sorry. Let me get you a new glass." He took the glass from my hand, his fingers brushing mine ever so slightly, and placed it on a nearby tray. His touch sent tingles through my hand and up my arm and I wondered just what sins he might represent. "August, you've steered me wrong once again," he said loudly over his shoulder, his eyes not leaving mine. "The lady says she is not drinking port; she says she's drinking Madeira." He shook his head in mock regret. "We've been friends since elementary school; you'd think I'd learn by now not to trust him when there's beauty involved."

Dorian Gray, I thought, reaching for stability, something familiar. It's *The Picture of Dorian Gray*. I sensed the volume and remembered precisely where on Papa's shelves Aunt Vieve's book lived. It was a fair distance from that side of the study to where we now stood. The novel had clearly felt a strong kinship.

August stepped through the doorway of the study into the room, two fresh glasses in one hand and an open decanter in the other. "Wouldn't be the first time you've been wrong," he said amiably. His green eyes met mine, and I knew he knew I had lied—and he didn't mind a bit that I had. I remembered what *Ulysses* had said just a few moments ago and reminded myself that books would never talk to me about me. Aunt Vieve had said so. So I couldn't be the liar the book was identifying, right? Who was? Colin still said nothing, seemed suddenly subdued. I wondered why the son of a founding partner—the heir apparent—was deferring to the older men, allowing the conversation to be redirected. My eyes skimmed the three of them, then glanced at Mr. and Mrs. Dempsey talking with my parents on the far end of the room. I was certain it was Colin Papa had wanted me to meet.

August arrived at my side. His hair was the chestnut color of mine, but gray at the temples. His face had a weathered look; he clearly didn't spend all his time in the offices of Trident Investment Group. He was at least ten years older than Colin, with lines at the corners of his eyes and mouth that deepened as he smiled at me.

"... *till the expression of his eyes, which are uncommonly good, and the general sweetness of his countenance, is perceived.*"

"May I offer you a glass of Madeira?"

"Please."

He poured, gave me the glass. Unlike Trey, his fingers didn't presume to touch mine. He lifted the decanter in offer toward Colin, who shook his head slightly, raising a glass of bourbon in explanation. He then poured some for himself in the second glass he held and set down the decanter. He lifted his drink slightly in a silent toast to me before raising it to his lips.

I sipped, tasting Madeira for the first time, the balance of wine and spirits that was similar but different than port, and tipped my head toward August. "Perfect," I said. "Thank you."

"My pleasure."

"*Every romantic woman dreams of Willoughby. However, every wise woman's heart knows Colonel Brandon would take care of her when she was sick, love her when she was well, and know her worth every day that she breathes.*"

I saw Trey watching us, relaxed, confident. Biding his time? His hands were in his pockets. August hadn't offered him a drink. I thought about the curl I'd felt in my belly when Trey had brushed the soft skin on the underside of my arm, the tingle when his fingers had touched mine. What sins? I wanted to ask him. I took a swallow of Madeira to drown the question welling up in my throat. I thought of Aunt Vieve and her lifelong, elusive search for a Colonel Brandon, and I instead kept my focus on August.

"So tell me about yourself," I said to him.

Thirty-One

"Have you told him yet?"

The sun was coming through the pristine plate glass window of the small brasserie in Richmond where Papa and I met for lunch on days when he was in court and I could make an excuse for a search and rescue trip. It was bright and made the sizable diamond on my left hand sparkle. I picked up my water glass to buy a few seconds of time to frame my reply and surreptitiously watch the play of light on the ring.

I saw Papa look from my face to my hand and back again. He'd always been an observant man.

"I haven't found the right time yet. But I will."

He picked up his own water glass.

"It won't matter to him, Papa. It won't change anything. I know him."

"Do you? Six months doesn't seem very long to get to know someone."

I gave him a level look. "I've had help."

I'd had a lot of help, actually. I hadn't had so many books talk to me about a single person since Aunt Vieve had walked into my bedroom and shut the door all those years ago. There were some contradictions. *Sense and Sensibility* had connected August with Colonel Brandon, both on that first evening and a few times afterward. But that didn't quite mesh with *The Most Dangerous Game* reminding me twice that perfection was a bore and repeated curious mutterings about death and what people thought of you after it from *Captains Courageous*. I liked to focus on what *Far from the Madding Crowd* had said—it had been the most romantic. *"I shall do one thing in this life—one certain thing—that is, love you, and long for you, and keep wanting you till I die."* Who could say no to a marriage proposal after hearing that? I remained convinced I'd found my Colonel Brandon. And who wanted to be married to a one-book man anyway? Complexity was good.

"When was the last time a book spoke to you about him?"

I hesitated. "Two weeks ago."

"That's a little odd, isn't it? So much from so many and then— what, nothing? Like maybe they decided you weren't going to listen anyway so what was the point?"

I rolled my eyes at him. "Papa, you're giving the books too much credit. That's not how it works."

Though he could be right, I thought. I'd made up my own mind over the months I'd gotten to know August. And why shouldn't I? If some of my books didn't agree with my decision—well, I didn't need their approval. I would've liked to have Papa's, though. Wasn't it odd that tradition was a father gave his daughter away? Like a thing? Like a book?

"Are you sure?"

"Yes, I'm sure I want to marry August," I said, purposely misunderstanding his question. I looked around the restaurant. "Do you see our waiter?"

It *had* been odd. August and I had met for drinks in Alexandria, across the river from DC. We'd picked the café because it had already had its outside tables set up. The air had carried the chill of early spring and tall heater lamps had been placed between planters of daffodils. With a mild breeze riffling his hair, August had taken my hands and looked into my eyes in a way that had made me certain *Far from the Madding Crowd* would speak up again from inside my leather satchel to cement this as the most romantic moment ever.

And then *Sense and Sensibility* had spoken.

"It is not time or opportunity that is to determine intimacy;—it is disposition alone. Seven years would be insufficient to make some people acquainted with each other, and seven days are more than enough for others."

I had been a little confused. This wasn't a passage about Colonel Brandon. It was Marianne defending emotion-based decisions about Willoughby to her sister, Elinor, who was far more circumspect. But all that had become unimportant when, at that moment, August had done it. He'd asked me to marry him.

I'd reminded myself that it was Marianne who had been the object of Colonel Brandon's love. Decided on the spot that the book was connecting with August having a ready reply if I said we hadn't known each other long enough.

I hadn't said that.

I'd given him a heartfelt yes. And he'd slipped the ring on my finger.

"I thought you said once you were close with someone, books didn't speak to you about them anymore," Papa said conversationally, signaling to our waiter.

"That was what Aunt Vieve said. I hardly think there are hard and fast rules about this. There's no manual. And maybe that's why I haven't heard from a book about him recently. We're engaged now." I ignored the bit of contradiction in saying I knew how this worked and that there were no real rules around it.

Papa ignored it too. I was relieved. The waiter arrived and I asked for a glass of sauvignon blanc.

My relief was short-lived.

"It took a ring to make you feel close to August?"

"No, that's not what I'm saying. I'm saying . . . " I paused. What was I saying? I took a breath. Reminded myself this wasn't a courtroom. I didn't have to answer every question put to me. I took a different tack. "Believe me, Papa, books don't care how I feel. They talk when and if they like." I sipped my water. Papa watched me from across the table.

The waiter arrived with our food and my glass of wine. I was grateful for the interruption.

After Papa said grace, I picked up my fork and pierced the quiche. Perfection. I decided to break the silence with a question of my own—one that I hoped would maybe make Papa feel more at ease with my decision. I did love him. Both of them.

"How long did you know Mother before you got engaged?" I asked.

"That's different. It was right after World War II." He picked up his fork. "A lot of things were different because of the war."

I thought briefly of the current war that seemed to be coming to a close. A lot of things were different because of Vietnam, too. I thought about Mark Robbins every now and again. I wondered if he'd ever been in touch with Stacey. And what she'd told him if he had.

"What was different was that time seemed more precious," I conjectured. "Time is precious for August and me, too. We're not kids. We don't need to date for two or three years to know this is what we want."

"Well, one of you certainly hasn't been a kid for a long time."

I knew it bothered him that August was closer to his age than to mine.

"Can we talk about something else?"

He chewed, looking at me across the table, then swallowed and nodded. "Sure."

I opened my mouth to talk about the latest renovation project I'd been assigned, working with a local artist to replicate a specific wallpaper pattern from the 1920s.

Papa raised his fork, forestalling me. "But tell him, Margaux. Before you marry this man, you need to tell him."

"I will," I said.

He looked at me. The lawyer look. I knew it well.

"I will," I said again.

Thirty-Two

It had taken me a solid year and a spring break trip back to Quebec City to regain my equilibrium and some modicum of confidence after the debacle with Georgia and Brad. Logically, I knew it hadn't been my fault. Sure, I had blurted out the wrong thing, had been dead wrong interpreting what *The Old Man and the Sea* had told me. But that hadn't been the only action that had led to Brad marrying the mother of his best friend's child and living in Norfolk instead of running the family business, as had been his parents' plan since his birth and Brad's own chosen path—until an afternoon when Georgia had called me and asked me to meet her at Grady's. In my experience, however, when logic and emotion get in a wrestling match, emotion often wins.

Logic and emotion were at it again since my talk with Papa.

I took the diamond ring off my finger and laid it between August and me on the peeling green paint of the park bench, careful to avoid the openings between the slats.

"There's something I need to tell you. And I don't think I can wear this ring, or any other ring you give me, until I do."

I'd picked our meeting place carefully. We were in a small park across the street from a bookstore. I suspected the street between it and me created too great a distance to hear anybody, but it gave me a level of comfort just knowing it was there. My personal "olly olly oxen free" to rush to, if needed. I'd also arrived early, tucking under the bench my usual leather satchel plus a stout Macy's shopping bag. In these, I had every book I'd ever heard speak about August and a few more besides. It had been a long, heavy walk from the Metro.

August had greeted me with a warm smile and a kiss. I had savored that kiss, returned it ardently. It was possible it would be our last.

With the ring he'd placed on my finger now on the bench between us, his brow furrowed. I had expected him to look wary, guarded. I hadn't anticipated the way his eyes seemed to shutter, hiding behind them all emotion, once I told him I had something to say. He seemed to be leaving, the emotional distance between us already greater than the physical measurement of space from my body to his, the ring on the bench midway.

I took a deep breath. It was always best just to get done what had to be done. Rip off the bandage. Shove your foot through the framed print. Dawdling wasn't going to make this any easier. I'd be calm, logical, and look him in the eye. If he thought I should be locked up in an attic while he found another love, better to know it now.

"When I was a girl, I realized that I could hear books talk. They read themselves to me. Only I can hear them. Well, one other person—that I know of—could, but she's dead now. I'm not delusional and I'm not making this up. It's just something I can do."

I waited, the ring on the bench between us. I heard a bus stop on the street beside us, pause, then move on. I smelled the plume of its exhaust. Knew my path to the bookshop was now clear. Imagined myself standing up and pulling my books out from under the bench, leaving August and his ring and all it signified behind, walking across the street, pushing open the door. A bell would announce my arrival. Olly olly oxen free.

I imagined it, but I still waited.

August seemed to relax. He let out a breath and smiled. "Well, I'm sure that made story time easy when you were growing up.

Your mom could just get you settled with a book, get on with her day, and come switch it out for another after a while."

I blinked. This was *not* the reaction I expected. I resisted an urge to punch his chest. Not hard, of course. But it had taken every ounce of courage I had . . .

"Don't make fun. I'm serious. It's not like I hear the whole book, just bits and pieces. And I don't get to pick which bits and pieces. It depends on who is in the room with me and which book identifies with that person at the time."

Now he looked wary.

I took a deep breath. This had been a whole lot easier when I had finally told Papa. I placed my hand over August's, his arm slung over the back of the park bench. His remained inert. "Just let me finish." I told him about the first time I'd heard a book speak to me, the day of the storm when I'd thought a bed-sheet on our clothesline was trying to suffocate Mother and she'd taken me up to my room and read from *The Velveteen Rabbit*. About my whispers to books in school. About being discovered. About paper airplanes thrown at me, crafted from torn pages of the book I'd abandoned in the library. About the psychologist. About Aunt Vieve and the conversation we'd had in my beech tree. About admiring how she'd lived and moved in the world. About becoming a part of it in Quebec City.

"I wish I'd known her," August said, when I paused to catch my breath. His eyes had unshuttered. He was listening.

I felt my shoulders relax a bit. "Me, too," I said.

I didn't tell him about the sealed cardboard box in the back of my closet, eighteen copies of *Sense and Sensibility* with Aunt Vieve's thoughts and yearnings and rants scrawled over their pages. I didn't tell him she was still my north star.

We were silent for a space, as I gave August time to let what I'd said sink in. He dropped his chin to his chest so I couldn't see his face. I watched him closely. I waited. I half-expected him to pick the ring up from the bench. To get up and walk away with it. Hidden in my satchel and the Macy's shopping bag beneath the bench, my books were silent. *Tell me*, I pleaded silently with them. *Warn me.*

I realized August's shoulders were shaking. My angst was replaced with a rising anger as I realized he was trying very hard not to laugh. And failing. I felt the urge again to punch him in the chest. Maybe a little bit hard.

"What is so funny?"

He picked up the ring, looked at it, and closed his hand around it. My anger drained away and my heart sank.

"This is what you needed to tell me?"

"Well, yes. The gist of it."

He tilted his head back, closed his eyes, and laughed out loud. "God, I love you, Margaux. Although you may have taken a few years off my life just now. Do you have any idea what was running through my head when you took off this ring?" He reached for my hand, slid the diamond back on my finger, and kissed me. "Beauty, brains, and a sense of humor. I can see you're going to keep me on my toes."

I pulled back my hand, though not sorry the ring was again on it. "Wait. You think I'm joking? You think I'm making this up?" I had been prepared to have to convince him that I wasn't crazy, but not prepared for him to think this was an elaborate hoax.

He raised his brows, a smile playing around the corners of his mouth.

"This is real, August." I realized I was indignant. "I hear books talk. Frequently."

"Okay. So what are they saying right now?" He leaned forward and tilted his head, directing his glance at the bags beneath the bench.

So much for tucking them out of sight.

"Well, nothing right now. I can't make them talk. They do it when they want to."

"Sounds like some clients I have."

I looked away. This was better than him walking away, convinced I was a loon, but it annoyed me.

"Have they ever talked to you about me?"

I felt my cheeks redden.

"What did they say about me?" He ran his fingers along my chin, up under my hair, and rubbed my neck. "Something good I hope?"

His touch was warm. Okay, so he kind of sort of believed me. Maybe. But I'd fulfilled my end of the bargain with Papa. I'd told him. It was out in the open.

"The first time was the evening I met you at my parents' house," I said, relenting. "*Sense and Sensibility* identified you with Colonel Brandon. *Middlemarch* identified first with Colin, but then it got a little muddled." I thought about the line I'd heard with Colin, Trey, and August grouped around me and Mr. Dempsey a few steps away talking with Papa. "*And when all was said and done the lies a fellow told about himself couldn't probably hold a proverbial candle to the wholesale whoppers other fellows coined about him.*" I still wasn't sure who had prompted *Ulysses* to speak that line—maybe more than one person? I decided not to mention what *The Picture of Dorian Gray* had had to say—and about whom.

"And is identification with Colonel Brandon good?"

"You know, you really should pick up something other than *The Wall Street Journal* once in a while. Yes, it's very good."

"Any peep from your books about Dempsey or Trey?"

I hesitated.

"Let me guess. James Bond."

"Now you're making fun of me again."

"Not at all. The women just seem to flock to Trey. Maybe it's his car."

I thought about the brush of his hand along the underside of my arm, the steel-blue eyes and strong jawline. *What sins?* I had wondered. Sometimes, lying in my bed at night, with no one around to see or judge, I still wondered. If it hadn't been for *Sense and Sensibility*, I might have been intrigued enough to find out.

"Jealous?" I asked.

"I think he just might be."

Thirty-Three

We married in June, a garden wedding at Lockeswood, August's family estate. It was two hours west of my parents' home, a stone's throw from the quaint but isolated village of Drakes Forge, nestled in the undulating Virginia Piedmont that leads up to the Blue Ridge Mountains.

I'd heard people say that you don't remember a lot about your own wedding—that it all goes by in a blur and, when it's over, you realize you've forgotten to eat. I didn't understand this until my own wedding. A lot of it, honestly, *is* a blur in my memory. But there are moments of that day that have stayed with me—for better or for worse, as the saying goes.

It was a small gathering—maybe forty people or so. I got ready in one of the bedrooms in the big manor house that had been built in the 1870s on the fieldstone foundation of the old manor house that had burned to the ground during the War Between the States. Or, as Mrs. Thomas, Papa's longtime secretary, called it, "the War of Northern Aggression." From what I'd been able to piece together, the burning of Lockeswood Manor hadn't had anything to do with that war, but rather someone careless in the kitchen. But it sounded more dramatic—more historic—to say the house had been "rebuilt following its destruction during the War Between the States," and so that was what it said on the bronze plaque the county's historical society had presented and ceremoniously mounted near the front door in the 1920s. Of course the plaque was still there. It was kept polished and legible.

Mother helped me get ready. I'd chosen an ivory satin dress I'd found on one of my search-and-rescue missions. It wasn't terribly old—barely qualified as vintage, in my estimation—and had yellowed a bit, but the triad of Mother, baking soda, and persistence had restored the masked beauty that had initially caught my eye. It did have an ungodly number of buttons up the back, and, as I felt Mother work her way from my hips to my neckline, I blushed at the thought of other, masculine fingers working in the reverse order. With as much patience, I hoped— for the sake of the dress.

It was just the two of us, and we spoke, Mother and I, as she helped me dress and put on makeup in that beautiful room filled with furniture older than the years of both of us put together and the grace of a bygone era. I won't write here—despite all the years that have passed—what we talked about. I still think of those hours with Mother as very private, even for these pages I suspect no one will ever read. But I will say that I hoped, as I put on my grandmother's pearl earrings lent to me by Mother, that perhaps some of the grace and elegance of that room would rub off on me. That I could carry it with me, like collected pollen, if just for this one afternoon, down the broad staircase and out the French doors at the back of the house and across the bluestone terrace to where Papa waited. Waited to walk with me past flower- ing borders, over a lush lawn set with chairs where well-dressed people—and one particular man—also waited. And then to give me, his only daughter—his only child—into the care of that man.

Those hours with Mother have stayed with me.

The moment Papa turned to me when we reached the end of our walk has also stayed with me. He looked at me, eyes searching. He leaned in close to kiss my cheek.

"Tell me you're sure," he said on an exhaled breath. No one else would notice, I knew, that he had said anything at all. Had done anything but lean in to kiss my cheek. I need only say two words and he would turn and, without further comment, escort me past the minister and the man who waited, past the guests in their chairs, past the elegant house, and away.

Away to where?

"He's my Colonel Brandon, Papa," I responded in a low tone I knew he, and no one else, would hear.

I'd expected that would set his heart at ease, but I was a lawyer's daughter, and I saw a shadow of uncertainty in his eyes as he lifted his head, as though my answer wasn't quite enough to convince him.

But he smiled anyway. And it was genuine, which made me doubt what I thought I'd seen. Then he turned and placed my hand in August's. After a quick squeeze, he let go and stepped back to stand beside Mother.

Watching him—watching them—my breath caught, and I felt a moment of misgiving. Then I felt August place his other hand atop mine. I looked at our joined hands. The minister started speaking. His words seemed a droning in the background. I honestly don't remember what he said. August's two hands engulfed my one almost completely. I looked down, expecting to feel too enveloped, suddenly encased. Trapped. I couldn't even see my hand. It seemed my arm ended at my wrist, the rest of it devoured by the weathered, lined, strong hands of the man standing next to me. Who was this person, that I'd allow him to do such a thing? My other arm with its own hand hung at my side. It could come to the aid of the trapped hand. Or the trapped hand could rebel, pull away.

Trapped? What kind of word was that at a wedding?

My eyes followed the topmost hand up its accompanying arm. Up the long expanse of sleeve to a wide shoulder. Laterally across a collarbone held in place by a charcoal gray formal jacket to a throat threatened with asphyxiation by a wing-tipped shirt collar and a tie seemingly knotted with the express purpose of choking its occupant. North over a strong chin and lips that were almost too sensuous to belong to a man, past a nose with a slight bump at its bridge, to the eyes.

August's eyes. Green eyes. Green like the forest looks when the leaves turn underside up, anticipating life-giving rain. Green like my books say the sea sometimes looks, though I'd never been and could only imagine. But I *could* imagine. I looked into August's green eyes. Which were looking at me.

Waiting for me.

Looking into his eyes, my hand no longer felt trapped, but treasured.

Looking into August's eyes as he watched me, I saw he was waiting.

The minister hadn't waited. Tradition had been observed. The bride had been delivered; Papa had given me to the groom, had stepped aside. August and I were there before him. No one objected when given the opportunity. The minister continued with the words of a ceremony he'd likely performed countless times. For the guests behind us, it was probably also routine. One of many weddings they'd attended.

It wasn't routine for August and me.

He wasn't listening to the minister, either, I realized. He was still waiting.

I'd told him yes. And then told him yes again on a park bench with a diamond ring set between us and beneath us a Macy's bag stuffed with books I'd lugged from the Metro.

Three times. It wasn't just fairy tales, although I'd cut my teeth on those. Three was a magical number.

August was waiting. I saw in his eyes the waiting. The waiting to find Home.

I could give him that.

And find it for myself, I realized.

There was a ripple of laughter from the seated guests. I'd missed a cue.

I squeezed the hands that enveloped mine. I was used to catching up quickly after I'd let my mind wander. "I, Margaux Brigitte Belcourt," I began . . .

THE REST OF the day was mostly a blur. Hugs and kisses from well-wishers. An afternoon banquet under benevolent skies. A lot of toasts. More than a little drinking.

All a blur.

Except for one more figure who stands out in my memory. Who will always stand out in my memory.

There was another Mrs. Locke at the gathering when the minister presented August and me as man and wife and we were greeted with cheers and clapping and laughter. And while I completely understood why my new mother-in-law, her cane by her side, didn't rise from her chair to join in the applause, I did suddenly wish Lockeswood's library were closer. Or that I'd figured out a way to include stacks of books in the outdoor wedding décor.

I dearly wanted to know what book might speak to me about the cold look I saw in my mother-in-law's eyes.

Thirty-Four

Lockeswood was a big fieldstone house with two main floors, a main staircase, and another near the kitchen. There was a full attic with small windows in the eaves, accessible by a narrow staircase behind a door at one end of the second floor. I wasn't a guest. This was where I lived. I hoped—needed—to make it feel like home. Right now, home was August.

But August wasn't here. He was in New York City for several days of meetings.

And I was in search of one particular room.

I could have asked, of course. But ever since August had casually mentioned a library, I'd decided I wanted to find it myself. To be alone when I first introduced myself. If this was going to be home, I wanted to make sure I got off on the right foot with the books.

I went down a long hall that branched off from the two-story foyer by the front door. I passed by a room and paused. It was an office, with a large desk and built-in shelves. It was dim at the moment, interior shutters closed and heavy curtains pulled nearly shut. I could discern neat stacks of folders on the desk, shapes on the shelves. I took a step inside, my hand feeling for the light switch on the wall, but then stopped and stepped out again. Yes, I was interested in learning what my husband's office could tell me about him, much the way Aunt Vieve had investigated Papa's all those years ago, but I was on a particular mission at the moment.

I heard the low tones, just above a whisper, before I found the library. I walked quietly, not wanting to disturb whoever was in quiet conversation in the room ahead on my left, sunlight spilling through the double doorway into the dim hall. I couldn't imagine who could be there. I didn't think anyone else was in the house at the moment.

I stepped into the spill of sunlight. The voices stopped. I let my eyes travel around the room before I entered it. I'd found the library.

The left side of the room was styled like a public or school library, with shelves along the wall and three perpendicular book-cases jutting out, creating four alcoves. These alcoves weren't as deep as the ones in the public library called "the stacks" but they were tall and most were filled with volumes, some spines gleaming, others faded, most books upright but others lying flat.

At the back of the library was a series of tall, narrow windows, hinges on the side, each with a dozen individual panes of wavy glass, here and there a pane of stained glass. There were no curtains, allowing the sunlight to pour in. Several of these windows were open, and I heard birdsong and the sound of some sort of machinery—a farm tractor, maybe. There was a faint scent of new-mown hay. I could see the rolling landscape, several outbuildings, and the Blue Ridge rising in the distance.

On the right side of the room was a large fieldstone fireplace with a strong, thick mantel of what looked to be oak. Above it hung an oil painting of a detailed fox hunt scene, including elaborately costumed men on horseback and brown-and-white dogs milling about and bounding into the nearby forest. I peered at the painting from the doorway and could just barely make out the fox standing on a log, one elegant paw raised, looking back at its hunters in the distance. There was no fire set in the hearth at this time of year, but instead some ivory-colored candles of varying sizes. In the middle of the library was a large round table, oversized books upon it, several cushionless wooden chairs drawn up to it. More comfortable seating, two deep leather chairs with small side tables close to hand, were set in a vignette near the fireplace. The one in my line of sight was empty. I stepped into the room, ready to introduce myself to whomever was in the chair with its back to me.

The chair was empty.

I walked around the room, peering into the alcoves created by the bookcases.

No one was here but me.

I stood in the middle of the room and turned completely around. True, there could be some sort of hidden door in the wood paneling on either side of the fireplace—wouldn't that be very Sherlock Holmes?—but the double doors through which I'd entered seemed to be only ones in the room. The windows seemed a bit narrow for anyone to climb out of, and what would have been the point of that? And I'd have seen them, in any case.

I cast my eyes over the books. Hundreds, likely thousands of them. How long had they been here, together? Rarely leaving their shelves?

I was wrong. There were a lot of somebodies here besides me. I just had never heard books talking unless I was in the room. I flushed, thinking how vain it was to think books would only speak when I was there to hear them. Why shouldn't they talk with one another to pass the time? I had *not* imagined the low voices I'd heard coming down the hall.

"Hello," I said to the shelves in a voice I hoped sounded strong and confident. "I'm Margaux Bel—" I caught myself. "I'm Margaux Locke. August Locke and I married here last week. Outside, in the garden." I pointed at the windows. Noticed again the view. "You can't see it from here. I guess it's on the other side of the house. Anyway, I've come to live here."

The books remained silent.

I decided not to take any of them from the shelves, bring them back to my room, as I'd initially planned. I looked around at the chairs again. A cozy spot to read, but not right now. I didn't want to come across as presumptuous or ill-mannered. This was different from Aunt Vieve's private library. She'd brought me there. Had so clearly welcomed me. At Lockeswood, I'd just walked into the room. I could be anyone off the street. No one was here to vouch for me being who I said I was.

If I wanted this room to become a particular place of home—and I realized I desperately did—I would need to do it slowly, let the books become accustomed to me. To decide I was who I said I was. A part of the Lockeswood family.

"I'll be going now," I said. "I'll be back again soon. I'd really like us to get to know one another."

I waited, hoping, but the silence continued.

I left, doing something I'd never, ever done in my life. I left a roomful of books without so much as touching one.

I stopped a few steps down the hallway and listened. After a moment, the low voices, barely above a whisper, began again.

Thirty-Five

Walking down the center aisle of the stable, I was once again grateful that I wasn't allergic to dust or hay. Still, the air had a thick, musty smell, and I was careful not to scuff my boots along the floor and churn up any more detritus.

"I have to ask, why on earth did you let the place fall apart like this?" I said as I looked around. Any attempts I'd made to talk about the stable prior to today had been deflected. The main doors had always been securely locked, the side stall doors to the paddock locked from the inside. I'd tried picking the lock a couple of times, urged on by memories of the Nancy Drew books I'd inhaled as a child, but my skills had fallen far short of hers. So I'd never been inside this stable.

I was now.

Something had changed.

"Me? I was away for almost fifteen years," said August. "You think this all happened in the five years since I've been back?"

I looked around the stable with a professional eye. "Point taken. But still. Everything else at Lockeswood is maintained and gorgeous. Why not the stable? And why let it continue to deteriorate once you moved back?"

"I did it for you."

I looked sidelong at my husband. "You did it for me," I repeated.

He nodded, walking ahead of me and ducking slightly to avoid a large spider web that would have made Charlotte proud

as we moved farther down the row of stalls. He was wearing
khakis and a white linen shirt, the sleeves rolled up to just
below his elbows. The light was muted and dappled with dust
motes. It streamed in through the outside stall doors August
had thrown open and the spaces in the roof where clay tiles
had dislodged over time. Looking at him, I could picture the
scene in sepia tone, like an engraving in a book protected by
a page of tissue paper, and I stopped to fix it in my mind. Tall,
handsome, accomplished, and mine, I thought. God, I loved
this man.

"I knew that one day I would fall in love with a woman whose
heart I would win by promising her an 1890s fixer-upper stable to
renovate." He looked back over his shoulder at me and grinned.

"The hell you did. And this isn't a renovation; it's a complete
restoration. It's amazing the place hasn't fallen down before now."
I walked past him into one of the twelve stalls. My comment was
hyperbole. The stable was definitely in extreme disrepair and
would need a lot of work, but it had been solidly built. It's the
bones of a building that count. I noted dovetail joints, heavy
rusted hardware that could be revived, wide weathered floor
planks that looked to be oak or maybe chestnut, and an oversized dented water bucket in one corner with the verdigris of
aged copper. From Papa's research, I knew that in the twenties,
Lockeswood had had a reputation for steeplechase champions,
elegant yet hardy horses that could compete on rolling terrain
through water and over fences. The Great Depression had taken
its toll on the estate. By the fifties, a good chunk of the acreage
had been sold, the stable reduced to a handful of horses.

"And you love it." August came up behind me and slid his
arms around my waist.

"And I love it." I leaned back against him. The top of my
head fit snugly under his chin, and I crossed my arms over
his, relishing the feel of the coarse hair and muscle of his

forearms. "But really, why is the stable like this? Every other building is pristine—even the old chicken coop."

"It's a garden shed."

"But it started out as a chicken coop. Grant told me. And when your parents got married and your mother said she didn't want anything to do with chickens, your father had it converted into a garden shed. Except she hasn't used the shed in more than a decade, but it still gets a scrape and a new coat of paint every four years."

"Grant apparently is very informative. I had no idea the man was so talkative."

"Well, informative on some things, though I'd hardly call him talkative. I thanked him for spending so much time teaching me to ride and about horses when Lockeswood doesn't even have horses. He said Lockeswood did, indeed, have horses, but was down to three, and so that's why they're boarded at his place. Then he changed the subject."

"Well, Lockeswood does have just three horses."

"But if you don't keep horses at Lockeswood, why is Grant called the Lockeswood Stable Master?" Who had stable masters anymore, anyway, I wanted to ask, but I didn't.

"Because that's what he was called when we kept the horses here."

"And why don't you keep the horses here anymore?"

"The accommodations aren't exactly up to par." August pushed aside my long hair to nuzzle my neck. "Care for a roll in the hay?"

I tilted my head to give him better access. "You're as bad as Grant."

I felt August pause in his ministrations. "Grant asked you for a roll in the hay?"

I laughed, keeping it low in my chest, a vibration I knew he would feel more than hear. "Don't be silly." He didn't relax, which rather surprised me. I filed it away as something new

I'd learned about my husband. "I just mean he's as elusive in his answers as you are." I rubbed my hands again along his forearms.

August turned me around. I looked up at him and let him study my face. A barn swallow darted in through an opening in the roof, banked, and landed in an upper corner of the stall. I saw it had a mud dauber nest built into the eaves. I wondered if there were eggs in the nest, ready to hatch. I turned my eyes back to my husband. He was smiling, watching me watch the swallow.

"Fair enough," he said. "Here's the deep, dark family secret. At least one of them. You know my father died twelve years ago in a riding accident."

I nodded. I'd heard this several times at our wedding from various guests as they'd given me their family connection bona fides, as though I were keeping score on who should or should not be in attendance. Maybe they'd thought I was very particular, since my side of the aisle had been outnumbered by August's.

August walked to the Dutch door that led from the stall to the overgrown paddock. He unlatched the rusted catch and pushed on the top half of the door, pushing harder when the swollen wood resisted. It finally relented and swung open to slap hard against the outside wall. He leaned on the ledge of the door's bottom half.

I watched him and shared his view of a pastoral, early spring vista of greening copses and pastures, a meandering of sycamores that marked the flow of the creek, and the awakening Blue Ridge rising to the west. The swallow darted out over his shoulder, trilling its distinctive chirrup. The fragrance of new growth in damp earth greeted us and then mingled with the scent behind us of decade-old straw and rodent droppings. Lockeswood was more rural than where I'd grown up, with miles of dry-stack stone walls and blackboard fence delineating acres that sometimes were sold but often passed down from generation to generation. It was a region of both "gentleman" farmers and the farmers who typically only bothered to get all the dirt out from under their fingernails to go to church or for a holiday dinner. Neither looked down on the other—for the most part. I'd found that surprising, at first. Comforting, after.

"Lockeswood has been around a long time," August said. "It was originally a grant from the British Crown and extended all the way from where we stand now to that line of trees at the base of the Ridge—hundreds of acres. My however-many-times grandfather took a chance and sided with the rebels in the Revolutionary War. I don't know if he was an idealist or a gambler, but he picked the right side. After the war, he was able to keep his land when a number of Loyalists around him lost theirs. Unfortunately, the generations of Lockes after him haven't always been as astute. Lockeswood is down to fifty acres."

Only fifty? I almost said, but I caught myself. I wanted to hear this story.

"I didn't know it at the time, but without the life insurance money from my father—he'd always kept a sizeable policy—we'd barely have the ground the house stands on." August turned to me with a wry smile. "Maintaining first-class chicken coops isn't cheap, you know."

I watched him look out again at the vista. I remembered gossip I'd heard in Drakes Forge when I'd first arrived.

"You don't think it was an accident."

He didn't immediately answer.

I waited.

We'd learned that about one another. To be comfortable with a space of silence, even after a direct question. Or, in this case, a direct statement. It was a demonstration of trust, I'd decided. Of love. Love is patient, I'd been taught as a child.

"I still haven't quite decided," August finally said. "What I know is that my mother doesn't think so. She's never said it publicly, of course, but she thinks my father arranged that fall."

"If it was suicide, the insurance company wouldn't have paid on the policy."

"That's why I'm the only person she's ever told. Well, me and one other. And only the one time, the day it happened. Asa Locke was a very proud man. She said he did it to avoid the humiliation he'd have felt at losing the last of the land and Lockeswood becoming just a house. No matter what it did to her—to the rest of us. The coroner ruled it accidental death—there were plenty of people who saw him fall. So she let everyone believe it was an accident. The insurance company paid, and Lockeswood remains intact. The last fifty acres, at least."

He said it so matter-of-fact. But there had to be pain there. And a weight.

No matter what it did to her—to the rest of us.

I walked to August and put my arms around his waist and my cheek against his chest. I thought of my parents' home, the backyard with my mother's large vegetable garden and flower borders and my beech tree with its spreading branches. The whole thing encompassed about half an acre. Yet it had been a whole world for me growing up. "And what do you believe?" I asked.

"I don't know. I like to think it was an accident. But my father always had a need to be in control—to act rather than feel acted upon. There's a part of me that can believe he would rather play his last card and exit the game on his own terms than have the game play out with him the loser. There's a part of me that can even understand it."

I tried to look at him, not liking at all that last comment, but he tightened his hold around my waist, pressed his chin against the top of my head, and kept talking.

"Anyway, after Father died, Mother didn't want anything to do with horses. We only had three by that point—horses are bloody expensive to keep, especially the steeplechasers we had—but she wanted them gone. She had, however, always respected Grant's father, who had been Lockeswood's Stable Master before Grant, back when she came here as a bride, and he was the one who convinced her to board the horses at his place instead of getting rid of them entirely. He was sure that once enough time had passed, she'd want to ride again. And Brodigan is just up the road five miles or so. So the horses went to Brodigan and Mother put that huge padlock on the doors and forbade anyone to even step into the stable. That was just over eleven years ago."

"So why are we stepping into it now?"

I felt August take a deep breath. He kissed the top of my head.

"Because Lockeswood is mine now. And I fell in love with a woman whose heart I won by promising her an 1890s fixer-upper stable to renovate."

I made a face even though I knew he couldn't see it. "That isn't true. We've been married almost a year. Are you implying you didn't have my heart before this morning?"

He laughed. "I didn't think that through, did I? I should have waited a couple of months and made it an anniversary present. Damn, now I'm going to have to come up with something else for June."

I playfully slapped at his arm.

He leaned in and his breath tickled my ear.

"Okay, maybe I won your heart with my charm, but I intrigued you with the stable. Admit it, you've been itching to get your hands on this project since that first night I told you about it."

So tell me about yourself, I'd said when we'd met at my parents' home, after I'd heard *Sense and Sensibility* speak to me of Colonel Brandon. August had obliged with a brief self-sketch, then turned the conversation to my work in historic preservation and restoration, and then to the 1890s stable on the Lockeswood property that had "fallen into disrepair."

"Itching might be a strong word," I said.

"Itching is exactly the right word. It was all part of my plan to woo you and win you."

"You came up with that plan pretty quickly. We'd just met."

"The truth is," he said as he bent his head again to nuzzle my neck, "*I* was intrigued when you so thoroughly put Trey in his place while at the same time keeping Dempsey's puppy at bay. Discovering that the gorgeous woman who entered the room—albeit late—was also intelligent and talented just sealed the deal."

I closed my eyes and leaned into him. "I was late, wasn't I?" His hands moved from my waist, one higher and one lower.

"Very. Your mother had set a place for you at the dinner table. But you were definitely worth the wait. So how about that roll in the hay? We could christen the stable."

"What hay?"

"Use your imagination."

"I am. I'm imagining what this place will look like when I'm done with it. And there definitely will be hay." I moved my hips against him.

"Excellent. Lots of hay. For the more immediate need, there's a blanket in the tack room."

"I don't even want to think about what kind of residual blanket might be in that tack room. And the hay will be mostly for the horses."

"Of course. For the horses. Mostly."

"We could have horses here, August. Like there used to be."

"Fine. We can move the horses back from Brodigan. And it's a new blanket. I brought it out earlier this morning."

"Always planning. There are twelve stalls here."

"This one is fine, I don't have to get the blanket."

"We most certainly will need the blanket. I have some money to do this, you know. I still have some from what my great aunt left me."

"You don't need to use your money. I told you. This is my gift to you. I've got it budgeted. It was part of the plan."

His hand was inside my blouse. I heard a button hit the wood planks. I had wanted to talk to him about this dream of mine for a while, broach again the subject of the lock on the stable doors. But the lock had unexpectedly opened and my heart was pounding.

"You didn't need a plan."

"I always have a plan."

"Just promise me we'll talk about the horses later."

"I promise. And to think that twelve months ago you'd never even been on a horse."

"That's not true."

"Carnival pony rides don't count."

"Of course they do. Besides, I'm a quick study. Even Grant says so. And you know how stingy he is with praise."

"Enough about Grant."

I pulled his head down to mine. "Enough about Grant," I agreed.

"Can you tell me something?" I asked later as we walked back to the house.

He nodded. He tended to be quiet after we made love.

"You said you could give me the stable because now Lockeswood is yours. It wasn't yours before?"

August didn't answer for a few moments.

Love is patient.

"I was never in any hurry to get married. I came close a couple of times. But then I'd see a friend or someone I knew in business dealing with a divorce—often with kids involved." He shook his head. "I didn't want to get married just because someone decided it was time that I was married.

"Over a glass of bourbon on my thirty-fifth birthday, my father told me that he'd changed his will. It was time for me to settle down. He thought I needed an incentive. So, he said, in the event of his death, if I weren't already married, my mother would control Lockeswood until such time that I did marry. At that point, Lockeswood would become mine. I would, of course, be required to 'maintain' her at Lockeswood." August shook his head as he made the air quotes, looking at the house rather than at me. "That was all in the will. Like I'd ship her off somewhere. Or sell it out from under her. My father could be such an ass," he said.

"And if you never married?"

"Lockeswood would remain under my mother's control and what happened to it would be determined by whatever she put in her own will."

"Your mother hates me. I guess now I know why."

"My mother doesn't hate you."

I didn't reply.

August stopped. We were nearly to the bluestone terrace and the multiple sets of French doors, all open to allow the spring breezes—and sometimes the occasional errant frog—into the house. I saw multicolored pansies had been planted in the borders around the terrace that afternoon. I felt August's hand along my cheek, and I let him turn my face toward him.

"My mother doesn't hate you," he repeated. "Her moods have always been volatile from time to time over the years. Maybe—no, definitely—more often since Father died. That's another family secret for you, although it's really not so secret. Just ask around the village. It has nothing to do with you, Margaux." August pulled me close. "And when we give her a grandchild, everything is going to change. She is going to absolutely love you."

Thirty-Six

The stable restoration went fairly smoothly, although there were a few setbacks. Termites had taken a toll on the southeast corner of the building, and water damage due to missing roof tiles was more extensive than we'd first estimated. The wrought iron hardware of the stable doors was decorative as well as functional, and removing all of it without further damaging the graceful whorls was time consuming. I had boxed up and driven all the hardware to a small shop in southwest Virginia that a farrier in Drakes Forge had recommended to me, and it was well worth the hours in the car. Three of the 1920s-era light fixtures weren't salvageable, but I'd been developing the network I'd started during my St. Christopher Hotel internship project, and I found identical replacements.

The real find was on a shelf in the tack room, where I discovered a heavy metal box. Inside were old black-and-white photographs, newspaper clippings, and a number of ribbons—memorabilia from Lockeswood's heyday. I framed these and hung them on the walls of the stable. One showed August's father on horseback. The horse was white with gray-black flecking, the muscles of its extended neck taut and long as it carried him over a fence. Asa Locke was in the formal wear of a Hunt, and he had a cigar clenched in his teeth to one side of his mouth. I couldn't tell if it was lit. There was something I just loved about that photograph. The vigor of it. Looking at it, I could sense the grace and energy of the horse as it cleared the hurdle, the verve and vitality of the man on its back. I doubted my mother-in-law would appreciate my interior decorating, but I didn't expect she would ever enter the stable, so I wasn't worried about stirring that pot.

The most unexpected repair had been to the weathervane. Made of copper, showing marvelous verdigris, on it was a rider bent low over the neck of a horse clearing a gate in a fluid jump. The profile was a lot like the photo of Asa, minus the cigar. The vane had two bullet holes through it. I had them filled and the weathervane replaced on top of the restored cupola.

There was a waist-high maple desk in one corner of the tack room, meant for use while standing, with a separate, matching organizer of cubbyholes affixed to the wall behind it. There were enough mouse nests in its various recesses to make it look an apartment building for Cinderella's furry helpers. But they weren't here to clean. I unscrewed it from the wall and spent one long afternoon sitting on the wide planks of the swept floor of the tack room, removing years of grime and neglect. It took a lot of Q-tips and patience to get into all the recesses. As I rubbed in beeswax polish with a soft cloth, watching the gleam of maple grain emerge, I realized I was humming.

I smiled. I was happy.

Happy felt good.

I started to sing a Mary Hopkin song—an artist hardly anyone seemed to know, but Mother had had her album and had liked to play it with the window open so she could hear it while she gardened. A lilting melody about finding a pebble and happiness running in a circular motion. I didn't sing loud, and I knew I wasn't a soprano songbird like Mary Hopkin, but apparently it was still too much for my resident barn swallows. I hadn't gotten to the second verse before they glided from their mud dauber nests, past me, and out one of the open doors. I watched them, admiring their grace, until I couldn't see them anymore. I stopped singing and went back to humming.

I kept smiling, though.

The organizer cleaned and waxed, gorgeous again, I re-attached it to the wall. I tucked a hoof pick back into the cubby where I'd found it. Using the top of the organizer as a shelf, I arranged a volume of hand-written breeding records I'd found with the old photographs, several decades-old point-to-point race programs the mice had spared, and a few novels that I hoped wouldn't look out of place and would alert me if someone entered the stable who shouldn't be there. I trusted Grant's judgment in hiring the stable hand or two we would need once the horses arrived, but I trusted my books more. I'd come to know Grant fairly well, but it bothered me a bit that I still hadn't heard a book speak to me about him—it would be a couple of years before I'd hear *The Sun Also Rises* identify him with Hemingway's Jake Barnes. It uncomfortably reminded me how much I'd come to depend on books to know how to act with and around people other than August and my parents. I was more at ease sitting by myself on the floor of a half-restored building, singing off-key, reclaiming beauty from neglect and abandonment.

In all, it took nearly eighteen months before the Lockeswood stable was ready for its equine residents. I'd never spent so many frustrating, sweaty, dusty hours on something in my entire life.

It was wonderful.

Thirty-Seven

I had a bottle of Veuve Clicquot chilling in the tack room on the crisp afternoon that Grant was scheduled to bring home the three Lockeswood horses. I heard a low diesel rumble coming up the long driveway from the road and knew it wasn't August's car. I glanced at the angle of the sun and the lengthened shadows, then at my watch. August had been traveling a fair amount the last few weeks—Trident Investment Group had acquired a small firm near New Orleans, and he and Trey were leading the team that was integrating the two companies. His flight back should have landed at Dulles more than three hours ago.

Grant's late-model pickup truck with a long, white horse trailer came into view, following the gravel driveway as it curved around a stand of mature magnolias. Grant turned the pickup to position the trailer and cut the motor. He stepped down from the truck. "Where's August?" he asked.

I shrugged. "Not sure. On his way, I hope. He's been in New Orleans most of the week but was supposed to be on a flight home this morning. I went to the house to check for messages a few times, but so far, no word. There's nothing on the tack board and Leah went home about a half hour ago."

The thick cork "tack board" was the main method of communication at Lockeswood. Framed in oak and hung on the outside wall of the house's covered side porch, from March until Thanksgiving, it was where delivery invoices, instructions for the landscaping crew, and phone messages were hung. If

August had called and talked to Leah—the woman from the village who came three times a week to clean, cook, and run errands for my mother-in-law—she would have left a note on the tack board.

"Did you ask Gloria?"

Grant always called August's mother by her first name, with no title. He was in the minority. I always addressed her in southern fashion as "Miss Gloria." She'd never invited me to do otherwise.

"No," I said. "I went upstairs to ask her, but when I knocked, Vivaldi just got louder. I wasn't going to give her the satisfaction of standing there banging on the door while she pretends she can't hear me."

Grant grinned. "Gloria does love her Vivaldi. It's when she starts in with the Wagner that you have to watch out."

I made a face. While we had had our Wagner moments, my mother-in-law and I had reached a sort of détente. When August was home, we were cordial, sometimes even friendly. If August wasn't traveling, a few times a week—the evenings that Leah cooked—the three of us would have dinner together in the large, formal dining room. It was when August was away on business that Gloria seemed to recall that she was now "the dowager," as she put it, and no longer the lady of the manor. She would retreat to her suite of rooms on the second floor, have her meals brought up if Leah was there, have them delivered from the village if she wasn't, and pretend I didn't exist.

This reaction to my presence in August's life didn't surprise me anymore. I'd heard from Steinbeck's *The Grapes of Wrath* a few weeks after the wedding. "*She seemed to know, to accept, to welcome her position, the citadel of the family, the strong place that could not be taken . . . She seemed to know that if she swayed the family shook, and if she ever really deeply wavered or despaired the family would fall, the family will to function would be gone,*" the book had intoned one afternoon when I'd purposefully sat down in the same room with her, bringing what I'd considered a likely stack of novels. I'd set these on the floor next to my chair. She had looked at me, then pointedly down at the collection of books near my feet, and then had continued to flip through the latest issue of *The New Yorker*.

Even Mother had been unable to bridge the divide. Lockeswood didn't have a garden, per se, but it did have extensive borders and beds around the house filled with perennials, annuals, and flowering shrubs. I never touched them—these fell under the Dowager's purview. Mother had seen this interest in gardening as common ground. When she and Papa had come over for dinner one evening the summer before, Mother had complimented Gloria and tried to draw her into conversation. Gloria had been polite, but Mother had done most of the talking. The next day, Mother had gotten a call from the landscaping company. The man on the other end of the line had seemed a little nervous, but he had said that Miss Gloria had insisted he call, and was it true that she would like a job with his landscaping crew?

"You really like her," I said to Grant.

Grant shrugged. "Back in the day, Gloria Locke was one hell of a rider and absolutely fearless on horseback. And she didn't put up with anything. When I was a teenager, I once saw her go toe-to-toe with a contractor she was sure had shorted her on materials. By the time she was done, he'd all but shriveled up and blown away."

"I can picture it," I said drily.

Grant tilted his head. "I suspect you and Gloria are more alike than you are different. Now, if the two of you ever go at it, I'd pay for a ticket to watch. Not that I'm encouraging anything, of course."

We were interrupted by the sound of three loud bangs against metal. Grant turned to the trailer.

"Somebody wants out," he said.

"Somebody" was a spirited six-year-old named Rockefeller that August had had his eye on for a while. He was a beautiful bay, seventeen hands, who clearly did not appreciate being left confined in a tin can while pleasantries were exchanged in the open air. At Grant's direction, I willingly stepped back and limited my participation to admiration as the Lockeswood stable received its first resident in more than a decade.

Equine resident, I amended to myself, seeing several swallows dart through the eaves. I'd caused quite a bit of grumbling and consternation among the construction workers by insisting on it, but only two of the mud dauber nests tucked throughout the stable had been destroyed during the restoration. The swallows had scattered initially, but I was seeing them more frequently now that the racket had ceased.

Once I was sure Rockefeller was in his stall at the far end, I led Isolde down the ramp and into her new home. She was seventeen and the youngest of the three horses returning to Lockeswood. It was on her that I had learned to ride. I wondered if she recognized the place.

When the horses were settled and August still hadn't arrived, I suggested we open the champagne anyway, but Grant politely demurred. Watching his taillights disappear down the driveway, I resisted the urge to pop it open and drink it by myself.

I left the Veuve Clicquot to soak in the melting ice of the dented copper bucket I'd noticed that first afternoon August had led me into the stable and we'd made love in one of the stalls. I walked to the house to check the tack board again. There was a note in Gloria's looping, elegant hand asking the landscaping crew to trim back the boxwoods and forsythia. There were no notes about phones calls received. I went up to the second floor and paused before her door. Vivaldi was going strong and I'd have to pound to be heard. That was by design, I was sure. August had been delayed before. If he wasn't home by noon the next day, I'd revisit my options.

I went back downstairs to the kitchen. I opened a bottle of pinot noir and took a chunk of cheese from the fridge. I sniffed it. Maybe Manchego. I nibbled an edge. Not Manchego, but good. I poked around the counter and found a white paper bag. Its end was curled tight along two-thirds its length, the logo of the Drakes Forge Bakery discernable only because I knew it so well. I unraveled the end, opened the paper bag to stick my nose in, and inhaled. Lovely. Was there anything better than the scent of bread? With a free pinky finger, I hooked a wine glass as I exited the kitchen.

I climbed the stairs and made my way past the strains of Vivaldi slipping out from under Gloria's door to the bedroom I shared with August. The evening had grown chilly, but I left the windows open more than a bit to hear the song of insects and frogs calling to one another. I changed into cozy pajamas that were in no way seductive and settled under the bedcovers, the wine, bread, and cheese within easy reach. I looked over the stack of books by my bed and, after running my finger along the spines as I sipped from my glass, settled in to spend my evening with Elizabeth Bennet and her sisters.

It had been a good day.

There were horses again at Lockeswood.

And I was confident August would be home tomorrow.

Thirty-Eight

Two stable hands arrived early the next morning: young men in scuffed work boots, jeans that looked like they hadn't seen the inside of a laundry room in months, and flannel shirts with rolled-up sleeves worn over faded t-shirts. They were polite and introduced themselves as Joe and Joe.

"It is good people who make good places," I heard from *Black Beauty* on the shelf in the tack room, and I shook their hands and welcomed them.

Joe and Joe made short work of mucking the stalls and feeding the horses before leaving to continue their day at Brodigan. I busied myself puttering around the tack room, talking to the horses, opening the doors that led from stalls to the paddock, and watching them get acquainted with their new surroundings. During all the months of renovation, I had imagined what this would be like, and now it was here. After more than a decade of absence, horses were back in a place that had been built for them, and I reveled in the sight, sound, and smell of this nearly century-old building, brought back to vibrant life—by me.

A few hours later, August's car came up the driveway. I learned he had, indeed, called to let me know he wouldn't be home as planned. He had spoken to Leah—had I not gotten the message? I waved it off, changed the subject. He let me.

I did ask Leah about it later. She looked puzzled; said she'd left the message on the tack board. I checked again. All the pins were either green, white, or red—the colors of the Welsh flag and a nod to Leah's heritage. Leah liked using the green ones. Gloria tended to choose the red. I wondered if she knew the red of the Welsh flag represented a dragon—I was sure Leah did. Looking at the board now, I saw five green pins embedded in the cork in a neat row near the top right corner, reserved by everyone—even Gloria—for Leah. A sixth green pin had strayed to a random position in the lower third of the board. I suspected where the note had gone, but I didn't pursue it. Choose your battles, I'd learned from Papa. This one wasn't worth choosing.

Thirty-Nine

The horses settled in, and the scent of paint and new-cut wood was slowly replaced with the redolent smells of animals, straw, and leather. In the spring, I could hear chirping coming from the barn swallow nests in the eaves.

The first time I heard this evidence of new life, I was leading Isolde to her stall, back from a ride to a sycamore tree I'd found that had low, spreading branches. The branches weren't as wide as those of my beech tree, and I was no longer the gangly girl I'd been, but I managed. I took care not to climb so high that I'd need someone to fetch a ladder to get me down. It felt good to sit in a tree and read, Isolde cropping grass below.

I liked to think the books enjoyed these outings, too. I selected a different one from the library for each ride, replacing it on its shelf afterward so it could share its experience with the other books during the long, perhaps monotonous, hours when no one was there. I'd taken my time with the library. Long winter evenings with me quietly curled up in one of the leather chairs in front of the fire had sealed our relationship, I liked to think. The books had accepted me. Sometimes I now heard the whispering while I was in the library, not just in the hallway, and that made me smile. I couldn't make out any of the words—they weren't talking to me—but, who knew? Maybe one day they'd include me.

My favorite evenings were when August was there with me, he in his leather chair and I in mine. I didn't tell him about my campaign to win over the books or the whispering I heard from the shelves. There was a niggling in the back of my mind that said maybe this wasn't normal. Maybe it wasn't like dogs hearing sounds others couldn't, or bees seeing colors invisible to others, or Mary Beth Henderson being able to do a cartwheel on the balance beam on her very first try. I'd told August I could hear books, that they sometimes read themselves to me. I'd fulfilled my promise to Papa. My secret was out in the open between us. But we never talked about it. It was never part of our conversations. And so, there was that niggling. I ignored it—mostly successfully.

I hoped it didn't hurt their feelings, but I avoided books that centered on young mothers. August and I were coming up on our third wedding anniversary. It wasn't for lack of trying, but the room that had been his nursery remained empty.

Mother told me not to worry, that these things sometimes just take time.

Forty

A half dozen years—nearly storybook-perfect—went by. To limit my commutes to DC, I transitioned from full-time employee to contractor, which also gave me a lot more flexibility to pick and choose projects. I found I enjoyed the detailed "search-and-rescue" aspects of finding just the right piece for just the right place. Also working with the craftspeople who could bring back to life a relic that others might be inclined to toss onto the scrap heap. My network of novel-endorsed resources grew, and I stayed busy.

We bought four more horses, and I learned about steeplechasing, though I was always just a spectator. My riding skills didn't include jumps, except once, when Isolde and I got caught out in a rainstorm and an unexpected lightning strike to a nearby tree sent her off on a streak for the stable. I ended up simply hanging on for dear life. We cleared a fence before I realized it was in front of us. Grant gave both of us a tongue-lashing when we got back to find him pacing. At first I was contrite, but then I stalked out and got thoroughly drenched before reaching the house after he started in on me about Isolde's age. I pretended it was because he had insulted both of us and I was angry, but really I was shaken and close to tears. I don't think I fooled him. He was right—in human years, Isolde was close to sixty and certainly shouldn't be jumping fences. I should have stayed in control.

There were mishaps and misfortunes here and there. We had a couple of close calls with Gloria's health, and we lost a horse to a bad leg break. There were a few tense months when Papa's firm was defending Trident against a high-publicity fraud lawsuit that would have been devastating for both his firm and the investment company had it been lost, especially since we had sunk a sizeable chunk of money into Trident when August had become an equity partner. But Papa prevailed, although Mother later told me she was convinced it took five years off his life.

I didn't get pregnant.

Gloria added Verdi to her playlist.

These were bumps in an otherwise smooth road.

Maybe I became complacent.

Forty-One

1983

"Madeira? We have a nice one Grant brought back for us from his scouting trip. He reminded me it was Thomas Jefferson's libation of choice. I guess he got it near Monticello. Or would you prefer bourbon?" I had been listening for August's car and, as the hour had grown late, had known he would come directly to the library. He looked tired as he came through the doorway, tie loosened but still around his neck. I stood by the sideboard near the windows holding up both decanters. I waited for him to reply something witty about the Madeira, given its role during our first meeting. Something along the line of "Yours too, as I recall."

"Definitely the bourbon," he said instead, making his way to his accustomed chair and sinking into the leather upholstery. "How did his trip go? I haven't had a chance to talk with him yet."

"*. . . You should have seen how wisely I proceeded—with what caution—with what foresight—with what dissimulation I went to work!*"

I sucked in a deliberate breath as I turned and set the decanters down. It had been years since books had talked to me about August—and this was an entirely new voice. And it hadn't been said in a whisper. I forced my own voice to sound casual as I selected two glasses. "Pretty well. He said there's a mare we should strongly consider. Neat or on the rocks?"

"Neat, please." He looked at the fire I had lit in the large fieldstone hearth. November had come in wet and chilly.

". . . as the beating of a drum stimulates the soldier into courage . . ."

I carried a glass to August. His fingers caressed mine absently as he took it from me, and I leaned over for a kiss. He seemed distracted, the kiss perfunctory. I settled into the opposite chair with my own glass. I was fairly certain I knew from which shelf the voice was coming, but I couldn't identify the novel. It rattled me that a book was speaking about August.

He took a sip, nodding approval. Took a deeper one. "Is the mare in foal?"

"No, but she dropped one late last year that appears promising, Grant says. She's at that farm near Lexington he told us about. I saw photographs. She's beautiful. Wonderful lines, deep brown color . . . "

"Blakeford?"

I shrugged, sipped my Madeira, focusing on the sweetness of the wine and the warmth of the spirit that slid down my throat rather than the voice from the shelf that I wished would shut up. "I don't remember the name of the farm. But it's the one Grant said has had a string of bad luck the last three years running. That's why they're willing to sell the mare at all. Grant knows the trainer there . . . "

"Grant knows the trainers everywhere."

" . . . and the trainer would like to see the mare go to someone he trusts."

August leaned his head against the high leather back of his chair, looked again into the flames. "Think we'd be buying bad luck?"

. . . the mournful influence of unperceived shadow that caused him to feel . . .

"I think people who rely on luck don't know a damn thing about horses."

It was Poe, I realized. "The Tell-Tale Heart" had been a reading assignment in high school. I hadn't particularly liked Poe. No wonder it had taken me so long to recognize it.

August's green eyes always smiled more than his mouth. "You've already told him to buy the mare."

"She arrives next Thursday," I admitted. "Grant hasn't steered us wrong yet, right?" My heart was pounding and I drank again—this time not a sip—wanting to feel a stronger burn down my throat.

I'd learned over the years how to divide my attention between listening to a book and interacting with the people in front of me, but I hadn't had to do it with August since before the day I'd set my engagement ring on the peeling green park bench between us and fulfilled my promise to Papa. August and I hadn't really talked much since then about what I'd told him. I knew he wasn't sure if I'd been joking, looking for a way out of the relationship, or serious. I'd been content to leave it that way.

A little mystery was good for a marriage, right?

I tilted my head and looked at him from under half-lowered lids. "Consider it your birthday present to me," I said. I drank again and stood up to refill my glass. I'd been stingy on my first pour.

August chuckled and seemed to relax, which was good. The voice retreated to a mutter, which was better. "Grant Brodigan is a damn good trainer, but he's not infallible." August paused, looked into the flames again. "No one is infallible." A log shifted, sending up a dash of bright embers. It broke his reverie and he lifted his glass to his lips and looked at me. "And besides, you said to consider the last horse we bought your birthday present."

I wished he didn't look so tired, so worn.

I filled my glass, took another drink, and then held his gaze as I crossed the distance to him. I held out my hand. He took his time, his eyes never leaving mine, as he raised his glass to his mouth and emptied it, then handed it to me. I set both on the small table next to his chair and stood over him for a moment. He looked up at me. Beneath the tired, the worn, there was still strength. I could see it. I could help him rally that strength. I wanted to touch my finger into the small, vulnerable indent of his throat just above the loosened tie. Instead, I ran one hand through his hair, gray at the temples, graying throughout, but still thick and sleek as an otter's pelt.

A May-November romance, some had said. Surely more June-September, my husband had replied when he'd heard.

As I leaned down to undo his belt buckle and lower the zipper of his pants, he put his hands on my hips, slid them down until his fingertips reached the hem of my skirt. I closed my eyes, feeling a familiar, welcome rush that started in the pit of my stomach. "Good point," I whispered as I leaned in. "Consider it just a gift, then."

"Consider it done."

"The Tell-Tale Heart" went silent on the shelf.

Forty-Two

The mutterings from the third shelf of the far-left bookcase continued sporadically for weeks. It was nerve-wracking. Just as I would decide that whatever had caused the book to speak had resolved itself, the voice would start up again. I found myself watching August closely as we sat with our usual evening glass, searching for something suspicious—furtive glances, a disinclination to look me in the eye, aloofness. I dissected each of our conversations the following day in my head, looking for the thing that would tell me what was going on, what was hidden under the floorboards. But nothing August said or did shed any light on why "The Tell-Tale Heart" suddenly identified with my husband. Identified often and with vigor.

I analyzed what was different, compared it to what was the same. August spent more time at the office and on business trips, mostly to New Orleans. Challenges with the company they had acquired there, he said. Trey became a fixture in our home, coming and going at all hours. Gloria loved it. She smiled and patted Trey on the arm and said it reminded her of when August and he had been boys.

Forty-Three

I wandered into the kitchen, wearing just my chenille robe casually belted, to get a cup of coffee to take back to my bedroom. August had left very early to catch a flight. We'd been up late the night before as I'd made sure he knew just how much I would miss him. Maybe this time . . . My mind briefly touched the still-empty nursery on the second floor.

Trey was standing in the kitchen with a newspaper in one hand and a cup of coffee in the other.

I nearly turned on my heel when I saw him, but it was too late. He looked like he was ready for a photo shoot for a Bond Street tailor. He raised his head and then his eyebrows.

"Good morning, sunshine," he said.

"Good morning." I tugged the belt around my robe tighter, tucked what I knew must look like strands from a rat's nest behind my ear, and took a cup from the cupboard. When I turned, Trey had replaced the newspaper in his hand with the coffee pot. I held out my cup and kept my eyes on it as he poured.

"I have to say, there is something about seeing a woman first thing in the morning who has so clearly had a very invigorating and satisfying night," he said. "It's a wonder August made his flight."

I nodded my thanks for the pour and turned on my heel as he reached for the cream. I'd drink it black today, I decided.

Forty-Four

I finally locked the Poe book in a large, iron-banded trunk in the attic.

I realized, even at the time, that this was avoiding the real issue. Aunt Vieve's warning about books rang in my head: *"If they do talk about those close to you, pay attention. Something important is afoot."* But Aunt Vieve wasn't here and Gloria was. I couldn't afford to be on edge. The holidays meant a lot of visitors and entertaining. That was stress enough, even with Leah's help. And I knew firsthand that Gloria could scent weakness on a three-day-old breeze.

The trunk's lid was heavy and would keep out the mice in the attic that I imagined must be watching me from dark corners and the folds of shrouded furniture. After that, I didn't hear any voices from the library shelves when August was there.

I wished I could have felt relieved.

The whispers from the shelves when I was alone in the library stopped, too. I felt like I had in the days following the debacle with Georgia, when it had seemed our whole high school had known I'd done something terribly, horribly wrong—even if they hadn't known exactly what it was. I felt watched. Judged. I'd locked away one of their own, and the books seemed to know. Locked it away because it had spoken to me. The thing I had wanted. That I'd told them I'd welcome.

But the books couldn't know about the trunk in the attic, I told myself. About Poe locked away. I was imagining the stares, the heavy weight of judgment from the shelves.

It had to be just my imagination.

Forty-Five

"To recognizing the true treasures in life," said August, a glass of champagne in his raised hand and his free arm around me. "And may they increase in the coming year," Trey added as a dozen crystal flutes clinked against one another. On the television in the background, a crowd of strangers in New York's Times Square reveled shoulder-to-shoulder as they awaited the arrival of 1984. In tribute, I'd brought George Orwell's book of the same name with me to the Janus New Year's Eve party, stowing it in a purse that looked only a little out of place. The book wouldn't fit into an evening clutch. Outside the window, the Virginia countryside was blanketed in white, with only a sliver of moon in the sky.

The party was a small one by Janus standards, made up mostly of men from Trident and their wives. The women chatted about children, their book clubs, and Shirley MacLaine's performance in *Terms of Endearment*. The men gathered in small groups and talked about sports and politics. The senior Mr. Dempsey and his wife weren't there, but Colin was, representing the family. He looked at me across the room, and his glance cast me back to the first time we'd met, our banter about the green glass doorknobs at the St. Christopher Hotel while standing in my parents' living room. This time he had an attractive woman with him. He leaned over to murmur in her ear and then brought her over to meet our hostess and me.

"Hi, I'm Caroline," Colin's companion said, shaking my hand in the broken-wrist, delicate way women often did. Her voice was low, as was the cut of her sapphire blue dress.

"Caroline is our new executive secretary," Colin added, and I saw a flash of annoyance cross her features.

"It's such a pleasure to have you join us," said Jacqui. Jacqui was Trey's wife, an old-family southern belle whose debutante ball had been more than twenty-five years ago, but who still had a figure that could halt conversation—I'd witnessed it firsthand—and a standing weekly appointment at the salon that ensured her blond hair remained perfectly highlighted and styled. I'd been sure I'd hear from *Gone with the Wind* when I'd first met her. But it had been Virginia Woolf's *To the Lighthouse* that had identified with Jacqui Janus.

"*. . . for it was not knowledge but unity that she desired, not inscriptions on tablets, nothing that could be written in any language known to men, but intimacy itself, which is knowledge . . .*"

I saw Trey glance over from where he stood near a table brought in for the night to serve as a well-stocked bar. He dipped his head and said something that made the three men with him smile and look at us. He crossed the room, running his hand once lightly along the underside of his wife's arm in a gesture I remembered, but his focus was on the woman standing next to Colin.

"Caroline, what a welcome surprise," he said. He motioned to one of the jacketed waiters, and a tray of fresh champagne glasses was quickly brought to our group. Trey handed one to Caroline. "Welcome to my home," he said, offering a toast.

Jacqui swapped out her glass for a new one from the tray. She lifted her free hand to the diamond pendant around her neck and began to slide it back and forth along its gold chain. Her smile remained bright.

Colin asked the waiter to bring him a scotch, neat.

I shook my head at the proffer of another glass, excused myself under the pretense of freshening up, and went to move my purse from the foyer where I'd left it to a more central location. The book seemed to thrum, but that wasn't unusual in such a large group. I had only one book with me, but one was better than none.

From the television, Dick Clark announced that the Times Square Ball was about to drop, and I saw August look around the room for me, a full glass of champagne in each hand. I smiled and joined him, turning my face up for a last lingering 1983 kiss. We counted down with the others, and we welcomed in 1984 with a toast to the room and another kiss. This one tasted of champagne and the effervescence of new beginnings.

"Happy New Year, Love," said August. He kissed me again, and I leaned into him, a promise of how we'd ring in the New Year later.

I felt a touch on my shoulder and turned around. Colin held up his glass of champagne for a toast. We clinked and then he kissed me on the lips, a chaste brush. He winked over my shoulder at August. "It's New Year's," he said. "Tradition, you know."

"I'm glad it only comes once a year, then," August said.

Over Colin's shoulder, I saw Trey kiss Caroline. It was quick, but it wasn't exactly what I would call chaste. His hand skimmed down her back and rested for a brief moment along the rounded curve that filled out her dress. She looked up into his eyes as he did it.

I looked at Jacqui, who was a few yards away and laughing, her cheek held up to another guest.

One of the wives must have been watching me. She leaned over. "I hope Jacqui really enjoys that diamond necklace," she said under her breath. "I wonder what Trey got Caroline for Christmas?"

I saw Jacqui look around, no doubt seeking Trey's whereabouts. Her eyes found him.

"If you loved someone, you loved him, and when you had nothing else to give, you still gave him love," I suddenly heard from Orwell's *1984.*

I drained my glass. I was ready to go home.

JACQUI WOULDN'T HEAR of it. "But I have the most marvelous midnight buffet!" she said. "You and August can't leave yet." She took my elbow and I felt her squeeze. "Please don't leave yet," she implored softly.

I looked around, saw the wives in their clusters, one of them cutting eyes to where we stood. Leaning in to whisper to one another. The one receiving the whisper half-turned to look but reversed direction when she touched my steady gaze. Neither of them was the one who had spoken to me earlier.

I had an image of the school cafeteria back in fifth grade. The wolves. The deer. The unaligned prey.

Why did women do this to one another?

The men were in their own groups, laughing a bit too loudly, fueled by the abundant alcohol and the promise of a lucrative new year. I saw Trey walk with August down the hall toward the study. In the foyer, Colin was helping Caroline into her coat.

"Just a little while longer," Jacqui said. Her grip on my elbow was tight, as though she were mooring herself.

I nodded and moved with her toward the dining room, where I would admire the buffet. I wouldn't leave her alone with the wolves.

"If you want to keep a secret, you must also hide it from yourself," whispered *1984* to me as I passed by the sofa where I'd left my purse. I suspected Jacqui kept secrets well.

IT WAS MORE than an hour later. I was wearing my coat, had retrieved my purse and *1984*, and had said my goodbyes—twice—when I went looking for August. The low-voiced conversation between August and Trey cut off as I stopped in the doorway of Trey's mahogany-paneled study.

"There you are," I said, pasting a smile on my face. "Darling, it's nearly two o'clock. Everyone else has left. We need to let

Trey and Jacqui get to bed." I held up the car keys. "I'll drive," I said pointedly.

August gave me look that was a cross between sheepish and harassed. "Is it that late? Lost track, I guess. Trey and I were just discussing a little business."

"You're always discussing a little business," I said airily, coming into the room and taking my husband by the arm. "The business will still be there once we've all had some sleep."

"Truer words were never spoken," said Trey, following us out of the room and into the foyer. "I'll call you around noon, August. We can continue this discussion then."

"Power is in tearing human minds to pieces and putting them together again in new shapes of your own choosing," said *1984.*

"It's a holiday, Trey, *and* the weekend," I said. "Surely it can wait. Jacqui, tell your husband you have plans for him and all business will just have to be put on hold until Monday."

Jacqui smiled and gave me a "boys will be boys" shrug, which didn't really surprise me. Had the woman no backbone at all?

"I'll stop by around noon," Trey said as August and I stepped from the overwarm house into the cold night of a new year.

"I'll be there," said August over his shoulder. As we walked down the salt-strewn steps toward our car, he took my hand. His touch was cold.

Forty-Six

The monotony of winter set in. August was away for a few days, and I decided I needed a respite from Gloria and Trey.

Grady's looked much the same, but the menu had expanded. The first cup of soup was still free, but you pretty much had to know to ask for it: this tradition had moved from front-of-the-menu billing to a small notation at the bottom on the back side. Today's soup was cream of leek with bits of smoked ham. It was delicious, and I blew on another spoonful to cool it.

"Hey, Spooky," I heard someone say softly behind me.

I looked up from my soup and my book. Her hair was the same long blond waterfall, her eyes just as blue. I felt a wave of anxiety wash over me. This had been my friend, my closest friend, in high school. My closest friend ever, aside from August. And here I sat, feeling like a trapped animal, making sure it didn't show on my face.

"Do you have any idea," Georgia said conversationally, "how many times I've walked into this place imagining I'd see you here with your nose in a book? How many times I've played out in my head what I'd say to you?"

I set aside *Far from the Madding Crowd* and met her straightforward gaze with one of my own. "And what did you say, when you played it out in your head?" My voice, I was glad to note, matched hers. I didn't sound nervous. Or guilty.

"Oh, it's changed over time. You made yourself scarce for quite a while, so I've had plenty of opportunity to think it through. May I?" She indicated the chair across from me.

"Of course."

She slid into the seat, picked up the menu, and flipped it over. She wrinkled her nose. "Cream of leek with *ham*," she said. "I swear Ginny does it just to annoy me. She didn't even have cream of leek soup in the rotation until I gave her the absolute best recipe for a vegetarian version. So what does she do? She adds *ham*."

"Ginny? Ginny Lothrop?"

"Ginny Kosmatka, now. They bought Grady's last year. At least they had the good sense to keep the name. Somehow 'Kosmatka's' doesn't have the same ring."

A waitress, who looked like a slightly older image of the one I'd always had in my head of Pippi Longstocking, came to take Georgia's order.

"I'll have a grilled cheese on rye," Georgia said. "And a pot of green tea. Don't bring me those nasty tea bags Ginny has back there. I want real tea leaves. Tell the kitchen to use boiling hot water—boiling, write it down—and let it steep for seven minutes. I brought over a half dozen tea infusers from the shop a couple of weeks ago, so the kitchen should be accustomed to using them by now. Tell them to wait until the tea leaves are steeping to make the sandwich. And make sure they use the green tea; I brought Ginny a large tin of both the green and oolong blends, but I don't want the oolong today."

I noticed Pippi was looking down at her pad but her pen hadn't moved since Georgia had said "pot of green tea."

"If there isn't any green tea left back there—and I wouldn't be surprised, I told Ginny it would sell like crazy—just let me know and I'll run down and bring her some more from the shop. She can settle up with me later." Georgia raised

her brow. "We're good, right? Thank you so much. Oh, wait."
She turned to me. "Do you want some tea? It's *so* good when
it's allowed to properly steep." She didn't wait for an answer,
but turned back to Pippi. "Bring two cups with the pot of
tea, please."

Realizing she'd been dismissed, Pippi went directly to the
kitchen, ignoring an urgent signal from another table.

I waited. In the time she'd taken to give her lengthy instructions to Pippi, I'd erased my anxiety. I'd known we'd meet again.
Would need to come to terms—or not—with what had happened
so long ago. If I had wanted to avoid it for yet a few more years,
I wouldn't have come to Grady's, right? The situation with
August—the words of "The Tell-Tale Heart"—had me rattled
enough. I was ready to put this part of the past to rest. Georgia
had just caught me by surprise, that was all.

She looked around the restaurant, registering who was there,
nodding and smiling at a couple of tables. I kept my gaze on
her. "Spooky," she'd called me. But she'd made it sound like a
pet name, a nickname.

Still.

Georgia either would or wouldn't forgive me.

I'd forgiven myself.

She turned her attention back to me, and I knew she'd been
buying time. *Far from the Madding Crowd* was silent. I didn't
have any other books with me. I was on my own.

"So lay it on me," I said.

"What?"

"What you imagined you'd say to me."

She'd learned to be inscrutable. The silence stretched.

I let it.

A hand slapped the table between us.

"Georgia Peche, I've got more to do in this kitchen than coddle
your tea leaves."

The woman with her very broad hand on our table had a hairnet covering wiry curls of an odd red-purple color, plump earlobes, and an annoyed expression.

"Ginny, you don't coddle tea, you coddle eggs," said Georgia. "Which would be a great addition to your menu, by the way, but likely lost on this crowd. And brewing a good pot of tea from actual tea leaves is really very basic. I don't know why we're even having this discussion again. It's not that hard." She tilted her head. "Do you want me to come back and do another demonstration for your kitchen?" She lowered her voice. "Are you having trouble keeping staff again? Is that the issue? The new people don't know how?"

Ginny's mouth was a tight line. She turned on her heel and went back to the kitchen. "You can use a tea bag just like the rest of us regular people," she called over her shoulder.

"Peche?" I said, as soon as Ginny was out of earshot. "You married a guy named Peche?"

Georgia rolled her eyes. "I know, I know. He's French-Canadian. From Montreal. We met when he was here on an educational exchange. What can I say? He talked, I melted. It doesn't hurt that he's gorgeous, rides a motorcycle, and knows his way around the kitchen. There is no joke you can make that I haven't already heard at least five times from Brad." She leaned in. "Guess where we honeymooned."

I smiled and shrugged, still on my guard but drawn in nevertheless by the atmosphere she created. It was like we were high schoolers again, before the disaster. "Where?"

"Guess."

"Montreal."

"No. He's from there. That wouldn't be a honeymoon."

"Paris."

"Not on his teacher's salary. C'mon, you can guess." There was something in her look.

I paused.

"Quebec City?" I ventured.

"He told me it would be just like going to Europe, but without the jet lag."

I sat back in my chair. "You realize, of course, that Quebec City is in a whole different country."

"Well, sort of. We drove, and they didn't even ask me for my passport at the border, and I got one just for the trip. And it was a really good photo, too!" She leaned back and sighed. "What a beautiful city. We had a picnic on the wall overlooking the river. Remember when we tried to get Brad to drive you to the DC train station so you could go up there without anyone knowing?"

We. What an interesting pronoun to use. I was framing my reply when Pippi arrived with Georgia's grilled cheese, a thick ceramic mug of water, and a saucer with a selection of tea bags.

Pippi seemed nervous. "I made sure the water was really, really hot," she said.

"Thank you so much," said Georgia. "You know, I've just decided I'd like a cup of the soup after all. And a glass of water. With a lemon slice. There are actual lemons in the kitchen, I hope?"

We watched Pippi go quickly back to the kitchen, ignoring the same gesticulating table.

Enough dawdling.

"So how is Brad?" I asked.

Georgia took a bite of her sandwich. It was a delicate, thoughtful tear of one corner made by even, white teeth. She took her time. She chewed. Then swallowed. It was the prerogative of a wolf. I sipped on my soup, the kind with ham that Georgia had ordered but I knew she wouldn't eat. It was very good, actually. I didn't give Georgia the satisfaction of a fidget.

"He's in Norfolk now," she said, after half her sandwich was gone. "Working for a company that builds ships for the Navy.

I think he's okay with it. He didn't say much when Mom and Dad gave the store to me." She picked up the other half of her sandwich and, elbow on the table, bit off one corner. Her blue eyes watched me over her bite. There was a slight smear of her red lipstick on the bread.

I waited. I wouldn't ask. She'd either tell me or she wouldn't.

"Mark came back from Canada," she finally said.

I put my hand on *Far from the Madding Crowd*, feeling exposed despite my earlier bravado. I wished I'd brought other books. I'd fix that, I promised myself. I'd been frequenting Grady's since I'd been a kid. There were plenty of places to stash books where no one would notice them or, if they did, think they were out of place.

"Of course, he's *Uncle* Mark, now," said Georgia.

Pippi arrived with Georgia's soup.

"It has ham," I reminded her, after the waitress left to attend the ignored table. "Is that a problem?"

"Not for our cat. Our cat loves ham."

"You and—" I realized I didn't know her husband's first name, and I didn't want to call him Peche. "—your husband have a cat?"

"And three kids. Who really want a dog. But I just don't think we've got the room for that unless I can figure out how to convert the rest of the storage into living space and still have someplace to store stock." She stirred the soup, a moue of distaste on her face. "We live in the apartment above the store. Remember my parents used to rent it out? It started as just being convenient— and cheap—but it's turned into home. I've got flowerpots on the back fire escape. Corey down at the fire station kept telling me it's illegal and I had to get rid of them." Georgia rolled her eyes. "At the last Fourth of July in the park, I dared him to come up and get them. Okay, so maybe Stuart helped by looming—he's six foot three—and muttering in French. But Corey hasn't bugged me about it since. We knocked out a couple of walls to expand.

A one-bedroom just didn't work once we had kids. It makes it tight for storing stock for the shop—and for us, frankly, since Maurice was born—but, well, you know . . . " She smiled and set down her spoon.

Children? No, I didn't know, I wanted to answer. It might come out bitter, though, and she could be waiting for that, so I just smiled. I remembered that apartment. I'd helped Georgia and her mom clean it between tenants. Even with a knocked-out wall or two, it wasn't where I would have expected Georgia to set up house. She'd always had such grand expectations of life.

And yet.

And yet . . .

"Knowing you, Georgia," I said with heartfelt sincerity, "that apartment is heaven for your kids and fodder for a feature spread in *Better Homes and Gardens*."

She shrugged but was clearly pleased. She had always rewarded friends who pleased her, and this, somehow comfortingly, hadn't changed. My reward was information.

"I really thought Brad and Stacey would divorce once Mark came back," she said. "I even think Stacey asked for one. I don't know why Brad refused to give it to her. He was obviously just a fill-in. Cute baby, but clearly not his. And Mark snuck back from Canada when the baby wasn't even two yet. She'd never even have remembered Brad. He could have been free and clear and come back to take the store. Him inheriting had always been the plan. Lord knows I'd never intended to stay." Pippi had brought the water, complete with a slice of lemon, and Georgia swigged it like it was a much-needed shot of bourbon, ignoring the tea bags on the table.

It hurt my heart, but I knew exactly why Brad would hold faith with the marriage vows he'd made, regardless of the circumstances or fallout. Atticus Finch didn't shy away from what was hard, regardless of personal cost, and neither would Brad. Unlike Atticus, though, he hadn't had a Boo Radley to step in and avert disaster.

Mark should never have abandoned Stacey. But we'd all seen the images on television—I couldn't blame him for not wanting to go to Vietnam. Stacey shouldn't have made Brad believe he was the father when she'd found out Mark had gotten her pregnant. But she'd been young and scared. Brad shouldn't have let himself get lured into a one-night stand with Stacey. But he'd done the right thing when she'd told him the baby was his. Even though it was a lie, he hadn't known that. He'd acted on the information he'd had. Acted in line with his character.

And I should have just kept my mouth shut that day here in Grady's when my comment had made Georgia an ally and helped Stacey perpetuate her lie all the way to a wedding. But I'd become so cocky, thinking I knew exactly what books were telling me when they talked, and it had felt so good to be part of Georgia's "in" crowd. I supposed I should have been Brad's Boo Radley. Should that have been my role? *Would* that have been my role if I'd understood better why I was hearing what I was hearing—instead of arriving at a snap judgment? Would it have made any difference to Brad if he had known the truth? Stacey still would have been young, scared, and pregnant. Looking to him for help.

I'd never know.

The fact was that I had, at best, altered the course of two families' histories and lineage. At worst, I'd ruined three lives. Four if I counted Georgia, who had never wanted the life of a small-town shopkeeper. Five if I counted the child who might never know the truth about her parentage. Six and seven if I counted Georgia and Brad's parents and the anguish and embarrassment they had gone through. Eight and nine if I counted Mark's parents, who would never know their granddaughter.

I decided to stop counting.

I reminded myself that I'd forgiven myself.

I saw that Georgia was watching me closely. I raised my chin. It felt like school all over again. Wolves and deer and unaligned prey.

Except now I was stronger. I refused to be put into one of those three categories. I met her eye.

"I'll bet Brad is a great father," I said.

Georgia took another bite of her sandwich. "He is," she said, after making me wait again. "And the baby isn't a baby anymore, of course. She'll graduate high school next year. It's funny, she's about the same age we were when the whole mess started."

"Does she know?"

Georgia shook her head. "I think Brad and Mark came to an understanding about that when Mark first came back. Brad wouldn't go into details with me, just told my parents and me that he was Lucy's dad and that was that. I think she deserves to know the truth once she's eighteen, but it's not my call. Sometimes I wonder if she suspects, though. Mark is around a lot, from what I understand. And the resemblance is still there. Somebody is bound to have said something along the way." She looked down at her watch. "I've got to run. The kids will be home from school soon." She covered the ceramic cup of soup with a paper napkin and picked it up to take it with her. "Give my best to your parents. And your husband. What's his name again?"

"August," I said. We hadn't talked about me at all. Not surprising, really.

"Give my best to August. And come by the shop if you want to get some decent tea," she added, looking over my shoulder at the archway to the kitchen. Just before reaching the door to the street, she turned.

"Welcome home," she said, as though I were just now returning after being away all these years.

Forty-Seven

I set the phone receiver back on its cradle.

From down the hall, I heard Gloria giving instructions to Leah about how the table should be set. Trey and Jacqui were coming for dinner. My mother-in-law had invited them, and I anticipated an evening of trips down memory lane led by Trey, while Jacqui, as ever, performed her role of rapt and attentive audience. Gloria's pale, powdered cheeks always got a rosy glow when Trey regaled us with stories of when he and August had been growing up, pulling pranks and displaying the spirit and vivacity of young colts. I'd heard every story at least four times.

Given the news I'd just received, I wasn't in the mood.

The front door opened and August walked in.

"I know," he said. "I'm late. Trey and I got stuck on a call with the New Orleans office. He left a few minutes before me, but he needed to pick up Jacqui."

"We have to talk," I said. "Preferably in private."

"Unless it's a quick conversation, it'll have to wait until later. They're not more than five minutes behind me."

"I'm not sure how quick it will be, but I do know it can't wait. That ungrateful, backstabbing jackass Dempsey fired my father." In my head I could still hear Mother's voice on the phone, her shock, her concern.

August paused, then continued to take off his heavy coat and hang it up in the hall closet.

I waited.

"We'll have to talk about this later," he said. He looked tired but his jaw was set, like a soldier who knows there is at least one more wall to scale, one more hill to take, before any rest will be allowed.

"You have to do something about this, August," I said. "You need to get on the phone with Dempsey and fix this. Somebody needs to let him know that this is not how you treat a firm that's had his back for more than a decade."

August reached out to pull me into his arms, but I stepped back.

"I'm serious. You need to get on the phone and fix this. You're a partner. He'll listen to you."

August let his arms drop to his sides. "Trey and Jacqui are right behind me," he said. He walked past me, then turned. "And just so you know—so you're not surprised if you decide you can't wait until later and happen to bring up the topic over dinner—Cole Dempsey didn't fire your father's law firm. I did. And Cole didn't overrule me because you're right—he does listen to me."

I felt the breath leave my body, and then I saw Gloria standing at the end of the hall, dressed formally for dinner, her white hair coifed in a cloud on her head, her usual elegant cane in hand.

"Everything all right in paradise?" she asked.

August looked at me, then turned and went to his mother. He kissed the cheek she offered him. "Dinner smells wonderful," he said.

"That's the French onion soup. Nothing like soup for a first course on a brisk evening. And I had Leah make an herb-crusted pork roast. You need something that will stick to your bones when winter's about gone but spring's not yet come."

"Beware the ides of March," I quoted, and I walked past the two of them to the dining room. Behind me, the doorbell rang. I heard August and Gloria greet our guests.

Dinner was already a half hour late, so Leah wasted no time in having everyone seated at the table. August said grace. I put my hand over my wine glass when he offered to pour. I saw Gloria fix me with a steely blue gaze, and her chin rose. I'd seen men drop their eyes to the ground at that look, but I met it and didn't flinch. Unseen beneath the table, I placed one hand over my belly, my fingers splayed. I wanted to be sure before I said anything to August. Besides, I had too much shock and anger swirling around in me at the moment to have room for sharing happy tidings.

"So, Trey, I understand Trident will be in need of new legal counsel. Shall I fetch a Yellow Pages?" I said as we sipped our soup.

August shot me a look but didn't say anything. Jacqui asked Gloria to pass her the sherry.

"Not unless you have one for East Baton Rouge Parish," Trey said. He looked at August. "News travels fast."

"This news met me at the door."

"I'll bet it did." Trey cut a look at me, the slightest of smiles playing around his lips. "Don't take it so hard, Margaux," he said. "We need a firm that knows Louisiana law. And your dad is getting up there. Think of the positive side. You know he would never retire and leave the Trident account in the hands of some junior staffer. What would his daughter say? This gives him the opportunity to cut back on his hours, relax. Maybe he and your mom could travel."

How could I ever have felt drawn to this man? This arrogant, womanizing, selfish . . .

"You are an ass," I said.

Sound at the table stopped. Jacqui set down her spoon, lifted her napkin, and dabbed at the corners of her mouth.

Trey shrugged. "I've been called worse."

"Believe me, I'm thinking worse."

"Margaux." August's voice was flat.

"Maybe we should go," said Jacqui, setting down her napkin and pushing back her chair.

"Nonsense," said Gloria. "This is my dinner party and I won't hear of it." Her gaze at Jacqui was deceivingly benign.

Jacqui wasn't deceived. She lowered her eyes, scooted her chair back under the table, and put her napkin on her lap.

"Leah, bring out the main course, please," Gloria called. "August, please pour more wine. But not for Margaux, she's not drinking tonight."

I glanced at my husband, but August simply picked up the decanter, his lips a hard line. Trey looked amused. Jacqui's eyes didn't leave the napkin on her lap. I looked at Gloria, who was watching me as her son moved around the table, topping off four glasses.

Leah entered the dining room, accompanied by two girls from the village hired to assist for the evening. They cleared away the soup plates and brought out the pork roast and enough side dishes to feed a group twice our size.

"The wind was positively howling around the house this afternoon," said Gloria as forks and knives scraped against one another and the heirloom china plates. "It reminded me of that time you boys decided to make sails for your bicycles out of my best guestroom sheets. Do you remember that, Trey?"

Trey laughed. "I missed baseball season because of that broken arm!"

Across the table from me, Jacqui's shoulders visibly relaxed, and she smiled at her husband.

"Excuse me," I said, and I got up from the table.

"Where are you going?" asked August. "You've hardly touched your dinner."

"I'll be right back." I didn't look at him.

Jacqui glanced at me and then back down at her plate, her mouth a tight line but her brow, as always, unwrinkled.

Once out of sight of the dining room, I quickened my pace to the library. I needed an ally. Or at least the possibility of an ally.

I stood in front of the shelves.

"I need your help," I said to the books. If August had followed me, he'd think I was talking to him. But I didn't think he'd left the dining room. I found myself contending with a lot of doubt regarding my husband at the moment. What the hell was going on?

The books would either forgive me or they wouldn't. Either help me or remain silent. Nothing I said was going to make a difference with them. They lived by their own rules.

And I was done apologizing for every action I took, everything I said.

I paced along the shelves, grabbing books, my fingers finding volumes from memory. *The Picture of Dorian Gray*, *To Kill a Mockingbird*, and *The Hound of the Baskervilles*. I started back to the dining room, then turned. Went to the shelves again for Bradbury's *Something Wicked This Way Comes* and Milton's *Paradise Lost*. I also grabbed *Sense and Sensibility*, hoping to hear something that would let me know my Colonel Brandon hadn't been subsumed. I held the books to my chest as I went back to the dining room. Walking down the hall, I felt myself calm at the weight of them, comfort seeping from them into me where the bare skin of my arms touched cloth and leather. My breath was even and natural by the time I re-entered the dining room.

Trey was recalling taking tennis lessons while wearing a cast on one arm when I walked in, went to the sideboard, and set my stack of books on one corner. They sounded a thump as they hit the wood. Conversation stopped again. I took my seat, placed my napkin on my lap, and picked up my knife and fork.

"Some light reading to go with dinner?" asked August.

"Something like that," I said, taking a bite of pork roast.

"Wow," said Trey. "This is quite the judgment on my scintillating dinner conversation."

"Not at all," I said. "I've read all those books more than once—some even three or four times—and I still find them entertaining. It's no different from your stories, really. So please, Trey, continue."

Jacqui set down her fork but didn't get up from her chair.

I didn't look at August. I knew I was being rude—very rude—but I really didn't care. I heard a dry chuckle from Gloria.

"Trey, I realize it's a bit late in the game, but learning to deal with a woman of spirit would do you good," she said. She held Trey's eyes for a moment, glanced at Jacqui, and then seemed to dismiss both in favor of the plate in front of her.

"Oh, what strange wonderful clocks women are. They nest in Time. They make the flesh that holds fast and binds eternity," said Bradbury's *Something Wicked This Way Comes.*

It wasn't what I expected to hear from that book—or from Gloria. I looked at my mother-in-law. Was she actually defending me?

"And here I thought I'd learned that lesson from all the hours I spent in this house," said Trey. He didn't look at Jacqui—or at me.

"Did you now?" said Gloria.

I lost the next exchange of conversation as a volley of voices talking over one another came from the sideboard, as though Bradbury's book had broken the veil. I tried to listen to each one, to associate each spoken line with someone at the table—more importantly, each with the right person at the table.

"I don't want to be at the mercy of my emotions. I want to use them, to enjoy them, and to dominate them."

"When one is in love, one always begins by deceiving one's self, and one always ends by deceiving others. That is what the world calls a romance."

"Whenever a man does a thoroughly stupid thing, it is always from the noblest motives."

"I have grown to love secrecy. It seems to be the one thing that can make modern life mysterious or marvelous to us. The commonest thing is delightful if only one hides it."

Slow down! I thought. I can't tell what you're telling me! I can't tell who is who!

I felt August's hand on mine and turned to see concern on his face.

"Are you okay?" he asked.

I realized the table had gone quiet again. All eyes were on me. There was a splash of gravy on the jacquard tablecloth next to my fork. Had I said something out loud? Under the table, I put my hand on my belly again.

I felt suddenly drained, as though August's touch, the first of the evening, had penetrated a weak spot in the fortress I'd thrown up when he'd told me he was responsible for firing Papa. I decided I was done sparring for the evening. It wouldn't accomplish anything.

"I'm fine," I said. I picked up my fork and poked at the now-cold roast.

I wanted to leave the room, but getting up and walking out without my books felt like abandonment. I wouldn't do that. Never again. Fetching them and walking out would look petulant. So I sat there—resolved not to fidget like a nine-year-old—through reminiscences and postulations and a bit of village gossip, through the clearing of the main course and the greeting of Leah's walnut pie, through coffee and digestifs, and through Jacqui's measured looks at me across the table that let me know I shouldn't expect a guest invitation to the next Daughters of the American Revolution luncheon. I actually was a little sorry about that last—those women had marvelous connections when it came to architectural salvage and restoration resources—but I admit I felt some bit of satisfaction in remaining aloof, no matter that I likely resembled nothing so much as a proud but molting sparrow hawk.

Gloria retired to her suite of rooms right after dinner, as she always did. August walked Trey and Jacqui to the front door. Jacqui avoided looking at me as she left the room, trailing our husbands as they talked about the next day's plans.

Once they'd left, I picked up the stack of books from the sideboard and took them back to the library. I'd heard enough from *The Picture of Dorian Gray* over dinner to last me quite a while, but I put it back on the shelf with care and respect. I resolved to retrieve the Poe book from the trunk in the attic in the morning.

I needed all the help I could get.

"Thank you," I said to the books.

Forty-Eight

I felt the mattress shift under me as August got into bed. After a long moment, I stopped feigning sleep. He was looking at me, a question in his eyes. I met his gaze and then put my hand against the familiar mat of hair on his bare chest.

"Explain to me why," I said.

He put his hand over mine, enfolding it. "I need you to trust me."

"I do trust you."

"Good." He leaned in and kissed me.

I responded to the kiss, but held back, not willing to let go of the conversation yet. "But I need to know what's going on."

He lifted my hand from where it rested against his chest and kissed my palm, his eyes on mine. His lips were warm, but I didn't feel the stir in my core that I usually did.

"That's not trust, Margaux. Needing to know isn't trust. You must trust me without knowing. Trust that I'm doing what's best for you. For us."

I looked at him. I saw my Colonel Brandon. What had the book told me the evening I'd met August? " . . . *every wise woman's heart knows Colonel Brandon would take care of her when she was sick, love her when she was well, and know her worth every day that she breathes.*"

It had meant so much to me to hear those words. To discover that this man was, indeed, what the book had told me he was. But I wasn't a nineteenth-century damsel. And maybe, just maybe, Aunt Vieve hadn't had it entirely right to have spent her whole life searching for a man who would treat her like one. It felt a betrayal the moment the thought crossed my mind, but I pushed that aside to think about later.

"For better or for worse," I said. "We both promised. And that means we share with each other what's going on in our lives— good and bad. And something is going on at Trident beyond the usual office politics. I get that I don't know banking and investments and mergers and acquisitions the way you do. Frankly I don't want to. I'm not asking for all the intricate details. But help me to understand what's going on that's affecting our lives—yours and mine—the way it is." I squeezed the hand that held mine. "I'm not a child. I'm not the sharks parading as good ol' boys at the office, and I'm not the hired help. I'm your wife. I love you, August. You can trust me."

August put his hands around my face. "I trust you," he said. "I'm sure there are things about you that I still don't know. And there's plenty I don't understand. Like why you're constantly hauling books around. Why you left the table tonight to bring a stack of them into the dining room. But that's okay. Because I trust you."

Outside, I heard it start to rain, March gusts throwing the drops hard against the windows. I heard a growl of thunder. We hadn't talked about my books since that day on the park bench years earlier. It was as though he thought that conversation had just been some flight of fancy from a nervous virgin and, promise to Papa fulfilled, I had let him think so.

If he wasn't going to believe me, it was better than him thinking I was mentally unbalanced.

"Ask me anything you want—about books, about anything." I held up a finger as he opened his mouth to reply. "But I asked first, and I deserve an answer. What's going on in New Orleans?"

There was a long pause, and then he pulled his hand away and ran it through his hair.

"I trust you, Margaux. I can't believe you would think I don't."

"Well, then?"

"I'm sure you'll consider it an old-fashioned notion, but it's my job to take care of you, to protect you." He got up from the bed and checked the windows. The rain was beating against them hard.

I watched him move from window to window, reassuring himself that the latch on each was secure. The single lamp in our room threw his shadow, long and tall, against the gray-and-blue-patterned wallpaper I'd never liked.

"If there's something related to the New Orleans business that could hurt me, hurt us, I'd rather know than not know." I said quietly.

He turned to look at me. Something in my face made him come back to the bed. He pulled me close to him and I let him. He felt tense, and I nestled my face against his chest. After a few moments, I felt it rise and lower in a deep sigh.

"Nothing is going to hurt you. I'm not exactly sure what's going on in New Orleans," August said finally, his voice quiet but even. "It should have been a very cut-and-dry acquisition. Trident does them all the time. But there are just some things that aren't adding up, that don't make sense. So Trey and I have been tasked with making sense of it all."

"You and Trey?"

There was a long pause.

"Trey may be—in a bit of a bind. He led the acquisition team. Had actually been the lead on the due diligence prior to the buy and in making the recommendation that we move forward. So now, with all these—irregularities—and questions raised, he's in a bit of hot water. The Board wants to know why he would have recommended the buy in the first place, why a lot of this stuff didn't come to light until now."

"And you're helping him figure it out?"

August ran his fingers up and down along my back.

"Trying to," he said.

"And you fired Papa why?"

August's fingers stilled.

"You're going to have to trust me on that one, Margaux. Your father is good, one of the best. But it's like Trey said at dinner. We need a firm that knows Louisiana law inside and out."

I absorbed all this, listening as the rain seemed to beat a little less hard against the windowpanes.

"Okay," I said.

"Okay?"

"Well, I mean, we could go over your files in depth tomorrow, if you want. I don't know if you remember, but I was a pretty good research assistant for Papa when I was in high school. Then again, I don't want to put any of your people at Trident out of a job." I lifted my head and kissed him, then looked him in the eyes. The green eyes that had captured my heart the evening I'd met him in my parents' home. "See? Was that so hard?"

August let out a breath and a bit of a laugh. "Hell, yes, it was. I'm not used to explaining myself."

"And now I have something to share with you," I said playfully. "But it has to be a secret for just the two of us for a while."

"I like our secrets," said August, leaning in to nuzzle my neck as his hands started to roam.

"I think I might be pregnant," I said. And waited.

For a moment, he didn't react. Then his face lit up in a smile that started at his eyes, and the thought struck me that I hoped our child's eyes would be green like his.

"Darling, that's wonderful news." He kissed me, deeply. "And it explains a lot."

I ignored the last remark. "I don't know for sure. But I'm three weeks late." I felt a thrill of hope surge through me just talking out loud about the possibility.

"Did you make an appointment with the doctor?"

"Not yet, but I will."

August leaned over and kissed my still-flat belly. "Hello, little one," he said softly.

THERE IS A level of trust implicit in sleeping next to someone. In sleep, one is completely vulnerable. To sleep in the presence of another person is, at its best, to trust that other person completely. The middle ground is that you trust that the person adheres to a code of morality that keeps you safe. At a minimum, you trust that the person has a sufficient fear of repercussions, should they do you harm during your most vulnerable state, and so will refrain from inflicting any harm.

That night I made a conscious decision, again, to trust my husband completely.

I slept well and deeply, not waking until I felt the insistent tickling of sunlight through early spring tree branches that waved in the breeze.

Forty-Nine

A couple of days later, three envelopes of a thick, creamy stock arrived in the mail, each addressed in the same elegant handwriting and with the same return address.

As a girl, Jacqui had attended cotillion, learning the social graces and manners her mother felt imperative for a southern lady of good family. Among these was the requirement to send a handwritten note in response to nearly every occasion. The bakery in the village even had one of Jacqui's notes taped to its window, eloquent praise for the cake baked in honor of her mother's seventieth birthday.

I really wasn't surprised, then, to see three separate envelopes. I opened the one with my name on it. In it was a thick sheet of stationery and a smaller envelope. *Dear Margaux*, read the main sheet. *Thank you for opening your home to Trey and me the other night. It is always a pleasure to spend time with friends. Best regards, Jacqui.* I raised my brows as I read and couldn't help smiling. When August and I had first been married, Jacqui had decided to take me under her wing. It hadn't lasted long, but she had explained to me the art of writing a thank-you note. I saw at least one of her nuances here. Short and sweet, the note fulfilled Jacqui's perceived obligation. And she hadn't lied. It *was* a pleasure to spend time with friends—but her note didn't actually say that she had felt any pleasure on that particular night she and Trey had come for dinner.

I glanced at the other two envelopes. The letter in Gloria's name was undoubtedly more effusive. And Jacqui had known

Leah long enough to consider her more than just "the help," so I wasn't surprised that she had received her own thank-you note.

I picked up the smaller envelope that had been included with my thank-you, recognizing Jacqui's personal stationery. The envelope did not have my name written on it and it wasn't sealed. I slipped out the card that had *Jacqueline Evelyn Halloway Janus* engraved on the front in royal blue ink and opened it. The distinctive handwriting was, as ever, perfect.

It pains me to write this, but I am unwilling to remain silent any longer. I don't know all the details behind your actions, but I find them deplorable. You must be made to realize there are repercussions. Sometimes they can be a while in coming, but they do come. I take no satisfaction in being the agent of this, but feel it is necessary. Perhaps one day you'll agree I took the right steps.

She had signed it simply with her first initial.

Well, that's that, I thought, tucking the card back into its envelope and tossing it along with the thank-you letter back onto the hall table. Jacqui definitely had the influence to blackball me with every woman involved in everything from Daughters of the American Revolution to the Junior League to the hunt and country clubs in three counties. I didn't care about luncheons with petit fours and cucumber sandwiches, I didn't play golf, and I had no enmity toward foxes nor desire to chase them around on horseback, but those social organizations had been my go-to for valuable business leads. I actually was in need of another restoration project to keep my employment contract in force, so the timing of Jacqui's displeasure was a problem. I'd have to think about maybe actually apologizing.

I snorted. I'd think about that later. Maybe.

Fifty

Trident Investment Group hired a new law firm, one based in Louisiana. Mother enticed Papa to take her to Italy. She'd always wanted to visit Florence, she said. She planned to bring back olive oil and wine. I decided to wait until they came back to make the happy announcement that I wouldn't be drinking wine for a while.

Trey came by often, and I'd hear scraps of heated discussion escape August's study like bits of charred newspaper kindling swirling up the air column of a bonfire.

"What the hell good is it to have a Louisiana law firm if there's a federal investigation?" I heard my husband shout one Sunday afternoon.

"There won't be a federal investigation," I heard Trey retort. "That's why we hired the goddamn Louisiana law firm instead of keeping the goddamn Boy Scouts."

I had resolved to trust my husband. So I swallowed the questions I had, feeling them lodge in my belly like a weight. At least once each morning I threw up everything—breakfast and questions—flushed the commode, and watched it all swirl away.

My books had taught me not to trust Trey Janus. He was handsome, charming, and charismatic. I'd seen how easily he could draw in women. I blushed when I thought how I'd nearly been one of them. But of late his easy, jocular manner had been replaced by a watchful, coiled demeanor. I didn't take any satisfaction in this.

Boyhood pranks had evolved into adult business relationships. And he and August were tied together by knots I couldn't unravel.

I took to visiting yard sales and flea markets, looking for cast-off copies of novels that already lined our library shelves, were stacked by my bedside: the books I knew very well. I needed multiple copies and it was the least expensive way to get them. I tucked novels throughout the house wherever I could hide them. Fitzgerald, Steinbeck, and Wilde under various sofas. Bradbury, Woolf, and Hemingway among the serving dishes in the dining room sideboard. Joyce, Austen, and Lee tucked among the cookbooks in the kitchen. Faulkner, Hawthorne, and Poe behind the heavy drapes. Shakespeare anywhere I could find an unobserved niche.

I wasn't really worried until the day even-tempered Grant Brodigan stormed out of the house. August followed him out of the study a few minutes later, but Grant was already in his white pickup truck, gravel spitting, when August went out onto the front porch. I watched through the window as August stood there, tall and at ease, his head cocked slightly, watching his employee—who was so much more than just an employee—drive away. I clutched the windowsill, desperately wanting Grant to look in the rearview mirror, to notice August there on the porch and, seeing that, to turn around, come back, and talk out whatever it was that had caused him to storm out in the first place.

Maybe Grant did look in his rearview mirror.

Maybe he saw August standing there.

But Grant didn't turn around. At the end of the driveway, the red light of the pickup's right turn signal blinked a few times. The road was clear. The pickup turned and, in mere seconds, was lost to view.

August put his hands in his pockets and came back inside the house to pack. He was catching an afternoon flight to New Orleans. He'd be back in a few days, he assured me, definitely in time for the season's first point-to-point that weekend. He was registered to ride Rockefeller in the Owners Race. *Wouldn't it be great to have another win like the one last year?* he'd asked rhetorically. Yet another addition to the "pots and pans" of trophies that decorated the shelves of his study, I thought.

I had other goals on my mind.

"I have to admit, I've been reminiscing about the days before you were a partner, before Trident bought that New Orleans company," I said, sitting on the bed, watching him pack. "I thought you acquired them, not the other way around. Why don't they come up here, instead of you always going down there?"

"It does seem a bit upside-down, doesn't it," August said. "Well, sometimes the grownups have to go to the kids to get things straightened out, rather than sit around and hope the kids come to their senses. Think of it as practicing my parental muscle." He made a show of flexing his biceps as he closed the suitcase, then leaned over and kissed me thoroughly. "I'm doing this for us," he said. "Take care of yourself and our baby. I'll see you on Friday, at the latest."

Fifty-One

The pains woke me up the next night, a deep menstrual ache. I lay still in our bed and prayed. When I felt the first wetness, I got up and went into the bathroom. I didn't use the commode but sat down on a thick bath towel on the tile floor next to the claw-foot tub. I felt a flush of liquid leave my body between my legs. It wasn't like the relaxation of muscle when I peed. I couldn't control it. There was no tourniquet that could be applied to stop it. I sat there watching the blood change the marine blue towel to purple, seep over the white hexagon ceramic tiles into the grout between them, creep up to touch my nightgown, where it was absorbed into the yellow cotton fabric. I put my left hand over my belly, looked at my wedding ring, and let the tears come.

I didn't call out for anyone. I didn't make a sound. I was as quiet as the books in the house around me. All the books shelved and stacked and hidden. Not one of them could help me in this.

August was away. But even if he'd been here, he couldn't have helped either.

I looked at the blood. There seemed to be a lot of it. I felt lightheaded and empty. I took my hand away from my belly. There was nothing left to protect there.

I felt very alone.

Fifty-Two

August called Friday afternoon. Bad weather had caused his flight to be cancelled. He'd be on the first flight in the morning. I should go out to the point-to-point grounds with Grant; he'd drive straight from the airport and meet us there. I kept my voice light, commiserated about the weather, but didn't say anything about losing the baby. I didn't want to tell him over the phone. I'd wait until after the race, after we'd left the hubbub of the point-to-point behind and were back home. I wanted to lay my head against his chest and tell him, to feel him stroke my hair, to hear the rumble of his deep voice in his chest as he would reassure me that my womb was not an inhospitable place, that he loved me, and that, as the doctor had told me, sometimes these things just happen.

Fifty-Three

August arrived at the point-to-point grounds just forty-five minutes before the Owners Race. As he strode up to Grant and me, I noticed he looked harried and tired and was still wearing his business clothes, though without the tie.

"Parking was a bear," he said, kissing me. "I think the car is in the next zip code. How are we doing?"

We'd brought three horses from Lockeswood, and Grant had brought two from Brodigan.

"Not as well as I'd like," said Grant. "No wins. But Brandy looked good on the timber course. And it's only the first point-to-point of the season."

"No wins. Well, I'll just have to fix that, won't I?" August grinned and some of the fatigue seemed to drop off him. "How's Rockefeller?"

"Cranky. You sure you're up for this? You haven't been on him in weeks. No one has. And you know that tends to be a problem."

"Don't start that again. You sound like an old woman. Rockefeller and I have an understanding."

Grant put up both hands in surrender, but his mouth was set in a tight line.

I looked between the two men.

"What's going on with Rockefeller? Other than him being a demon horse, I mean." The horse was big, seventeen hands, and what my husband called "spirited." I remembered all too well the sound of his teeth snapping together mere inches from my shoulder a couple of years before when I'd gotten too close to his stall door. But I had to admit the bay thoroughbred was fast, and he negotiated jumps and water obstacles with a powerful grace that was breathtaking to watch. A number of our "pots and pans" trophies had been won by Rockefeller.

"Nothing's going on with Rockefeller that a firm hand and a good race won't fix," said August. He kissed my forehead, then put his hand on my belly and winked at me. "I need to go change. Send one of the guys to find a good spot at the rails for you to watch me win this race."

I waited until August got back from the clubhouse and walked with him to where we had the horses. I noticed him flexing his left fist a couple of times.

"I don't think a left hook is going to help," I said.

I stayed back as he greeted Rockefeller, patting his neck and talking to him. The horse tossed his head and stomped a few times but then whickered and seemed more at ease. One of the Joes saddled the horse while August checked the bridle, speaking in low tones to the horse. It was time. He walked over to me. He held my face between his hands and kissed me. It was a gentle, tender kiss. I leaned into him and we took our time. Then he looked into my eyes, kissed the tips of his fingers, and pressed them against my belly. I bit my lower lip and wished we were home, not here among hundreds of people. He was about to race; this was not the time.

"Good luck," I said.

"I never depend on luck." August mounted Rockefeller. He looked down at me as the horse danced a few steps to one side, then the other. He smiled, emanating confidence. "See you at the finish line."

AUGUST NEVER MADE it to the finish line.

Fifty-Four

Mama and Papa had cut their Italy trip short when they had gotten the news of August's death, and I was grateful. I don't think I could have handled making all the arrangements and dealing with Gloria by myself.

Grant had been the one to tell her about August. When I'd asked him about it later, he'd just shaken his head, and I hadn't pressed for details. The record player had been silent for days.

Gloria and I had sat together in the church, and then again at the graveside. It had been a very formal service; no one other than the minister had spoken. Gloria had worn an elegant black hat with a wide brim and a patterned veil that had completely shrouded her face. She had never lifted the veil. Not once. She had looked distant and imperious. We hadn't touched as we'd sat side by side, hadn't spoken at all, but she had taken my father's offered arm and allowed him to escort her to and from the gravesite. He and Mother had taken her up to her rooms as soon as we'd gotten back to Lockeswood. They had been up there a long time.

I'd stayed with my guests as long as I could stand it. Then I'd gone to my bedroom for the gun in August's nightstand, walked out to the stable, and done what I had done.

By the end of the following week the condolence letters and calls had petered out, and the world around me had gone back to its normal rhythm. It seemed to expect me to do the same.

I wasn't sure how to do that, or if I even wanted to.

I didn't go out to the stable, having no desire to spend time with horses, not even Isolde. I don't know what happened to Rockefeller's carcass. I was content to let it rot in the stall, but I hadn't ordered Grant to leave it there and, even if I had, he would have ignored me.

I decided I heartily disliked April, the month that had presided over the deaths of both Aunt Vieve and August. I ripped the month out of every calendar in the house—the big one hanging on a hook in the pantry where Leah kept track of who was coming to dinner when and the various delivery days, the smaller one on my writing desk in my bedroom, the day planner August had kept in his study. I didn't go into Gloria's rooms, of course. It's possible April lingered there. If it did, that was her business.

Looking back on it now, I know it was a bit ridiculous, but I remember that it gave me a modicum of satisfaction at the time, especially since I ripped each sheet into flushable pieces and sent them down the commode to the septic field under the side yard. It's been more than thirty years, but to this day I rip the month of April out of every calendar I own. It's become something of a ceremony for me.

Fifty-Five

M y husband had been a thief, I decided, to take a part of my soul away with him without asking me. That hadn't been in the marriage vows. Words mattered to me—immensely; I would have remembered. I might have given it to him, as I had my heart, but he hadn't asked. He'd just taken it and then gone away.

I had a chronic ache in my sternum, the bone that supposedly protects the heart from grievous injury. It was in my head, the doctor all but outright said. I could see it in the way he avoided my eyes as he poked and prodded and had me breathe in and out. But the hell with what he thought with his fancy M.D. Standing at the rail, watching August's body disappear from the back of the demon horse, I had felt the excruciating pain of an impossible weight press on my chest, flattening the thin flesh between my breasts to reach the bone beneath. In the moment before the concentrated weight had crushed my bones and sent shards into the vulnerable, vital organ that was pounding an alarm in my ears—it had lifted. And was gone.

And so was August.

As for that piece of my soul—the piece I'd felt leave with him . . . Where is the soul tethered in the body, anyway? And how? Does it have bone to protect it, the way the heart does? The eyes are the window to the soul, I'd heard so often. It sounded poetic, romantic.

Well, windows break. Fairly easily, actually.

I was off-balance. Dizzy a bit at times, or disoriented—more than once going down a hallway only to realize that I was looking for a room that existed in one of the buildings I'd helped renovate, not the one I was in—but I didn't tell the doctor that. After his last visit to the house, he'd left me a bottle of pills to help me sleep and another to help with anxiety. I hadn't taken any of either. I guess I was saving them.

For what, I wasn't ready to articulate, even to myself.

What I felt wasn't a hole, exactly; that would be too elegant, too much the picture of the mourning southern widow. Which I was, of course, but there was something else. Something in me was shredded—was that the right word? Maybe torn? No, that sounded like a pop song. But something was definitely askew within me since I'd looked at a house full of funeral guests, gone upstairs to August's nightstand, and then decided to take the gun out to the stable instead of using it right there.

I wouldn't have shot them. Of course I wouldn't have. They weren't guilty. But they'd just looked so damn complacent. Sorrowful, but complacent. And I did have a reputation to maintain for being just a tad "off," after all. Well, maybe I'd have shot Trey, but I hadn't had a clear line on my way to the stable, and then afterward I'd left the gun in the petty cash box in the tack room.

Good thing, I thought, remembering the storm swelling in my aching chest when Trey had raised his glass to toast me from across the room.

The thought had crossed my mind when coming down the stairs from the bedroom to make a dramatic yet silent entrance and hold the gun up to my own head. Wait to see who noticed, if anyone. They were here for August, after all. Remind myself, perhaps repeatedly, while waiting, not to pull the trigger. What gossip fodder would that have provided to the Junior League and the hunt club and the country club and the Drakes Forge Diner crowd and, and, and . . . ?

More importantly, which books would have offered new commentary on my guests? And what kind? Would someone have tipped his or her hand in that moment of violent threat, the books then revealing to me an answer to the question I had about August's death?

Would they have finally, in that last moment, spoken to me about me?

Or would they have held their collective breath, a titillating excitement rippling among the volumes I had long since scattered around the room, wondering what would happen next in a plot not yet fully written?

And if I had pulled the trigger, would some part of me have heard them, maybe the parts of my soul August hadn't taken with him exiting this life? Where do you go when you die if your soul is no longer whole? Maybe you just stick around? Communing with the books? I liked Lockeswood's library. So long as I could avoid *Treasure Island*. I'd had enough of "Laugh, by thunder. Laugh!" to last me a lifetime—and an afterlifetime.

But I did want to see Aunt Vieve again. I'd been taught since childhood that I would, in the afterlife. Of course, that had been before August had taken part of my soul. I was no longer whole. How do you fix that? When I'd asked the doctor, he'd given me the pills to help me sleep. And the ones for anxiety.

Which I was now saving.

The doctor—I couldn't recall his name—didn't know anything about Aunt Vieve. Or, it seemed, the afterlife.

When it came down to it, I couldn't have done it to Leah. Gloria would have left it to her, of course, to get the mess of my brains off the rug. It had been a long, arduous campaign to win Leah over. If I did join the library, I didn't want to take the chance that she would sense I was there and hold a grudge. The books wouldn't thank me for that. Leah was the one who kept the library pristine, who opened the windows to let in the breeze and the birdsong and the scent of new-mown hay.

Not that I'd had this cogent conversation in my head as I had descended the staircase, careful not to trip on my elegant vintage black gown and accidentally shoot the architecture. No, these were after-musings.

Instead, at the time, I had shot the horse that had been the instrument of my husband's death.

And no one else.

Fifty-Six

I spent a lot of time alone in the library, revisiting old friends on the shelves. The books and I were back on solid footing, I felt, since the dinner party when I'd asked for their help and they had acquiesced. And I had brought Poe back down from the attic and reshelved him, with apologies. Even though I'd said I wasn't going to apologize anymore, I felt he deserved an exception.

It was likely that the books had agreed. The soft background of whispers was back again. I still couldn't discern any specific words—the conversations in and among them were not meant for my ears—but they let me know I wasn't alone.

I felt so much more comfortable in the library than in the large, empty expanse of the bed I'd shared with August. Despite my resolve at his funeral, I wasn't ready to replay the events of that day and the weeks leading up to it, to conduct my own version of an autopsy to settle in my mind whether my husband was dead because of a heart attack or a stroke or some antic of that demon horse causing him to fall or . . . something else. Gloria believed her husband, August's father, had staged the accident that had taken his life. Had committed suicide to ensure there was money to keep the estate going rather than face the humiliation of having to sell. August had told me about it that day in the stable. Had also said that, in a way, he understood his father's actions. But we weren't in dire financial straits—just a business deal gone awry—so my thoughts veered

away from the possibility of repeated history that skulked in
the corners of my consciousness. Still, these worries came out
more boldly when I slept.

My usual leather chair was wide and deep, with rounded
arms and a high, cushioned back. I'd sling my legs over one side
then the other or slouch down with them splayed out in front of
me and my body curved into the position Mother had always
threatened would lead to horrible posture. More than once I fell
asleep in that chair, waking to sunlight streaming in through the
wavy glass of the windowpanes, reaching to tickle my face until
I opened my eyes.

I lost myself in the pages of my books. I kept a stack of
favorites next to my chair. August's chair I kept empty. Even
though the books didn't speak to me, I felt their presence; lives
all around me. They were, after all, made of paper and leather
and cloth—the raw materials had once been alive as either plant
or animal. Characters came to life through the authors who created them, sometimes springing from the head fully formed and
dressed for battle, like Athena out of the head of Zeus; sometimes
maturing as the story progressed, much as a child grows up and
discovers its identity.

Not that I'd ever be a mother.

These were my companions.

There really wasn't anyone I wanted to see—except maybe
Grant, who was pretty much running the estate for me while
I buried myself in books. I also didn't mind Leah, who continued to come several times a week to clean, cook, and run
errands for Gloria with calm, quiet efficiency, just as she
had been doing since before August and I had been married.
Anyone who wanted to see me could come to my library to do
it—there weren't many—and I would listen to what my books
told me about my visitor and respond accordingly. I didn't
need to go anywhere.

Jacqui came by about a week after the funeral. We had coffee in the library—despite Georgia's exhortations, I'd never cared for tea and didn't care enough about anything at the time to ask Leah to provide it for my guest. Jacqui didn't stay long but did invite me to join her at the next planning session for the Junior League Benefit. It would do me good to get out of the house, to get involved, she said, looking pointedly at my unkempt clothes, unwashed hair, and face devoid of makeup. I thanked her and told her I would think about it. Apparently I didn't need to apologize to get back into her good graces. I just needed to become a widow.

Two books spoke to me while Jacqui was there. The meaning of the first was pretty plain.

"Reserving judgments is a matter of infinite hope," said Fitzgerald's *The Great Gatsby. "Whenever you feel like criticizing anyone, just remember that all the people in this world haven't had the advantages that you've had."*

Jacqui had grown up with every advantage a wealthy southern family of good name could provide. She had a kind heart, a blind eye when it came to her husband, and an intolerance for anything outside the norms of southern gentility. I'd flouted those norms more than once, and most flagrantly at Gloria's dinner party the month before. Despite this, *The Great Gatsby* indicated Jacqui thought there was still a chance of redemption for me. At the very least, I was a charity case.

But it was what *Sense and Sensibility* said of Jacqui that puzzled me.

"I will be calm. I will be mistress of myself."

Wasn't she already?

Fifty-Seven

It was early. As the landscape lightened with the coming day, I could see through the wavy glass of the windows that fog hugged the ground, shrouded the tree line at the far end of the pasture. I imagined the nocturnal animals finding their beds, the first stirrings in the stable. The swallows would be darting out of their nests in the eaves, caring for their broods. The night had been mild; hours before, I'd pushed the library windows open a hand's breadth, and through them I'd seen the gleaming smear of the Milky Way and had smelled freshly turned earth and the distinct scent of moisture on new growth that has always defined spring for me.

I was in my leather chair, *The Complete Works of Shakespeare* and a cinnamon-colored chenille throw on my lap. Sleep had been elusive as I had waited for May to replace April, and I felt as though I were half in one place and half in another—fully aware in neither. The sound of a wooden drawer slapping shut broke through my reverie. I glanced at the clock on the fireplace mantel. It was too early for Leah to arrive. Grant, a creature of habit, would be at the diner in the village, working on his second cup of coffee and reviewing notes in his moleskin notebook about what needed his attention today, here and at Brodigan.

I got up and carried Shakespeare with me, cradled against my chest—it was a heavy leather-bound edition and I figured I could throw it at an intruder's head, should the need arise—and padded in bare feet the short distance to August's study.

When I saw who it was, I stood in the doorway for a moment to collect the random bits of myself from where they had wandered in the night.

"What in the hell are you doing here," I said.

I took two steps into my dead husband's study. One step could be easily undone; two was emphatic.

Trey looked up from where he stood behind August's desk. He had an open file folder in his hands, the kind with metal clasps to hold pages in place, and a stack of paperwork in front of him. He was dressed for the office in a smoke gray suit, a crisp white shirt with monogramed French cuffs, and a thin, ruby-colored tie crafted into an impeccable Windsor knot.

"Hello, Margaux," he said conversationally. He flipped through a few pages without looking up, then closed the folder and set it on the pile in front of him. He took another from an open drawer. He lifted his head, cast his gaze at me, up and down. "Wow. You look like hell."

"I guess I need to start locking the doors. I asked you what the hell you're doing here."

"Just picking up some Trident paperwork." Trey smiled the disarming smile I'd seen him use at restaurants when he didn't have a reservation. He always got a table. He resumed leafing through the file in his hands.

"One may smile, and smile, and be a villain," said *Hamlet.*

I appreciate the heads-up, I thought in reply, but I twigged on that one myself.

"Funny, I didn't hear you ring the bell. Or knock. Or any of the other methods people use to announce themselves before walking into someone's house," I said. I stepped farther into the room. I couldn't remember the last time I'd showered. I hoped I smelled to high heaven.

Trey tossed aside the file in his hand. He lifted a sheaf of folders from the drawer and sifted quickly through them, adding some to the pile in front of him while tossing aside others. August's desk was littered with castoffs. "I knew it was early. Didn't want to wake you. Besides, I'm practically family. Just ask Gloria."

"This isn't Gloria's house. It's mine. And you're not family."

He looked up at me, and the smile shifted from practiced to something genuine, as though he were a lawyer in the privacy of his office receiving the last tidbit of information that would ensure he won his case. "Packed her off already, have you? Don't blame you a bit." He closed the folder in his hands, added it to the pile, and opened another drawer of August's desk. "Mind you, I had a bit of a crush on her when I was a teenager. But after a woman turns forty . . . " He let the sentence dangle, then shrugged. "Well, hell. It just becomes harder for her to keep a man's attention. Even a woman like Gloria. And then there was the incident with August's father. Gloria just wasn't the same after that. And who would be?" He looked me in the eye. "What wife wants to think her husband committed suicide?"

"Get out," I said in a flat monotone, feeling a small globe of anger and resolve ignite in my belly, searing away the cobwebs of indifference and distance I'd woven since August's death.

Trey just continued to smile. He leaned down to sort through the drawer he'd opened. I swung the book down to my side, gripping it in one hand, fingers clenched to maintain control of the weight of it. Cross the few steps, swing it up, and slam it against his head? I thought, or just trust my aim and fling it at him from here?

"I am very proud, revengeful, ambitious, with more offences at my beck than I have thoughts to put them in, imagination to give them shape, or time to act them in."

At *Hamlet*'s words, I released the tension in my arm. I didn't swing, didn't throw. What good would it do? Help me, I thought, appealing to wherever my husband's soul had gone. "This is where Gloria lives," I said. "And will be as long as she wants it to be."

"How noble of you." Trey didn't even look up. He added another file to the stack in front of him.

I strode over to the desk, slammed the book down, and raised my arm to sweep his stack of selected files to the floor. Trey grabbed my wrist, and I was surprised at the strength of his grip as he twisted, forcing me at an angle against the top of my husband's desk.

"These violent delights have violent ends."

I understood the book's meaning, but I refused to succumb to a scream for help that no one would hear.

"Get. Out. Now." I leaned across the desk as far as I was able and spat the words into his face. I hoped he found my breath repulsive.

Instead, he leaned into me, tightened his grip on my wrist. Pain shot up my arm and into my hand. "Careful," he said, his face inches from mine. His voice was nearly a whisper and the smile was gone. He had the same steel blue eyes, the same strong jawline I'd noticed the night we'd met. There were new lines around his eyes, a few creases around his mouth not attributable to smiles, but the man had hardly aged since the first time I'd met him and lied. "If we're not family, then the alternative is that this is business. And business is all about balance and negotiation."

"We have nothing to balance or negotiate. You don't have anything I need."

"Don't be so sure." Trey relaxed his grip, let go of my wrist, and picked up the stack of folders and a box of computer discs. "Spent any time going over your books lately?" He nodded at the weeks of mail I'd had Leah collect in and around one of August's leather trays. There were envelopes slit open that had been closed the prior afternoon when I'd stood in the doorway and put off, again, stepping into this room and going through them. "You've got quite a pile of invoices there. You might want to take some time out of your busy schedule to give them some attention." He reached over, picked up one of the envelopes. "The farrier's bill, in particular, seems a little high. Do you want me to talk to him? No? Suit yourself." He tossed it back on the pile. "You know, Margaux, when you put your mind to it, you're still a beautiful woman." He looked me up and down again. "When you put your mind to it," he repeated. He raised his brows in invitation. "You could use that to your advantage, you know."

My arm throbbed, but I focused on keeping my voice cold. "I've heard that three's the charm. So maybe if you hear it for the third time, it will have an effect. Get out of my house."

"Such spirit." Trey came around August's desk and stopped beside me.

Touch me again and I will claw that smug expression right off your face, I thought.

He must have read something of that thought in my face. He smiled. It was the indulgent smile of someone who knows he has power and would be delighted to use it.

"The paperwork for August's life insurance claim is sitting on my desk for signature," Trey said, in a different tone of voice. "August was my best friend. We watched out for each other since the second grade. Believe me, I feel a debt to take care of his widow." He patted the stack of files he held crooked in one arm. "To do that, I need to protect the business. If you and I work together, it's a win-win." He turned from me toward the door.

"God hath given you one face, and you make yourself another."

I stepped in front of him.

"I appreciate that, Trey, I do," I said. "But I really don't see how you looking after the widow of your childhood friend correlates with skulking around his house to ransack his office."

"Then let me explain it to you," Trey said softly.

To this very day, there is nothing, absolutely nothing, that gets under my skin so quickly or thoroughly as a condescending tone. I felt the searing away of the last vestiges of indifference, of distance, that I'd worn like a thick, comfortable sweater since the funeral.

"If you interfere or create any complications," continued Trey, "I won't sign the paperwork affirming that everything is on file and in order for August's life insurance payment to be processed. I'll stall the paperwork for buying out August's partner shares. He's not drawing a paycheck from six feet under. Without my help, you won't get a penny for months and precious little even then. And I don't think whatever they pay you to fix up buildings that should have been bull-dozed long ago is going to keep this place running. So be a good girl and I'll see that you're set for life." He leaned in but didn't touch me, his breath close but not stirring the weight of my stringy, unwashed hair. "But then again, maybe I'm misjudging you. Maybe you have a different plan and it doesn't include Lockeswood. After all, Margaux, you're young enough—you still have options. And despite your lofty words, everyone knows there's no love lost between you and Gloria. If you lose Lockeswood, you don't have to worry about her at all, do you? You have the perfect defense—no alternative, really, except to send her off to a home, let the state worry about her. And maybe that's your endgame. Maybe you're more clever than even I've given you credit for."

"Get out." My wrist ached where he had twisted it, and I wished I had the revolver that I'd cleaned and placed back into the nightstand drawer, this time on my side of the bed.

Trey smiled. He stepped around me. "On my way. Gotta say, I admire your spirit. But you really do need a shower."

I stepped in front of him again, more closely this time. We were less than a foot apart. I didn't like how far I had to tilt my head to look him in the eye, but I wasn't about to take a step back in order to get a more comfortable perspective.

"Not with those," I said, nodding at the folders and computer discs he cradled. "They don't belong to you. Put them back on the desk."

"Oh, but you're wrong. These files should never have left Trident. So while they may not belong to me, they certainly don't belong to August's estate, either. They don't belong to you. And as a partner at Trident, I'm acting as the duly appointed representative to collect them."

"Then ask for them and I'll go through my husband's office and box up anything with a Trident logo. I'll call your office when they're ready to be picked up. You don't sneak into my house unannounced and start rifling through the place like you own it."

Trey paused a moment. I saw his jaw tighten. "You're making a mistake, Margaux," he said. "Play your cards right, and I could be the greatest ally you've ever had. Why don't you step aside, pretend I was never here, and go up and take a long, hot bath. It'll do you good."

I didn't budge.

I should have expected his next move. My books had given me plenty of warning. But I wasn't prepared when he shoved against me and swept his arm wide to throw me to floor. My head grazed the desk as I fell. I don't think I lost consciousness, but I saw a bright flash as the world tipped to one side. It took me a moment, maybe two, but I gained my feet and my balance and grabbed the long, steel letter opener on the desk.

But he was gone.

I went out to the front porch to be sure. I saw taillights at the far end of the driveway. Trey's car turned onto the road and was gone. I stood there a moment, tried to slow my breathing. I put my hand up to my head, felt the welt that was already swelling just above my hairline.

I went back into the house and shut the door behind me. I locked it. Like most everyone in the village, we didn't usually lock our doors if someone was home—and sometimes not even when no one was home. I wasn't sure if Leah had a key, but she always came in through the side door in the kitchen anyway. Then again, I didn't know for sure through which door Trey had come. I went to lock the side door and was surprised to find Leah in the kitchen, unpacking a paper sack of groceries. She looked up at me and murmured a good morning but didn't show any sign that she'd been aware of our visitor. I decided to leave the side door alone. I went to the French doors that led from the living and dining rooms onto the terrace and made sure those were locked.

My steps slowed as I went back to August's study. The desk was a mess, discarded files strewn across it, several drawers hanging open, as though aghast at the assault it had suffered. I set the letter opener down within arm's reach, gathered up the folders, shoved them into one of the drawers, and then shut them all.

I thought of Trey's words and looked at the top of the credenza where Leah had faithfully sorted all the mail. Bills arriving by post and invoices received with deliveries were neatly stacked in August's leather-sided in-box. To the left of the box were condolence cards and letters. To the right, mail Leah thought I might want to review—apparently the country club, the hunt club, August's alma mater, and myriad other organizations were grief-stricken but nonetheless ready, willing, and able to set up a memorial scholarship or other charity, should I be inclined to provide the necessary seed money.

I picked up the in-box of bills and sat down in August's chair. I hadn't sat in it since August had died, but since seeing Trey's ass in it, I no longer considered it akin to consecrated ground. I felt a spark of myself re-ignite at this somewhat blasphemous thought, and I looked at *The Complete Works of Shakespeare* still sitting on the desk.

"And what do you have to say to that?" I said aloud, knowing it wouldn't answer, but feeling I had a kindred soul in the room with me.

I picked up the letter opener again. I tested its metal tip against my palm, specifically the section below my thumb known by fortunetellers as the Mount of Venus, indicator of love, passion, and sensuality. August had often kissed me there. I pushed until I saw a welling of deep red. I watched it a moment, then sucked on my palm until the blood no longer flowed.

I shook my head. Enough. I stropped the tip of the letter opener against my shirt to clean it.

I slit open the envelopes that Trey had left sealed. I went through the entire pile. I used a piece of August's stationery, the Lockeswood crest expensively embossed at the top, and a ballpoint pen emblazoned with the logo of the local feed store to write down a column of numbers.

It was a fairly long column. Quite a few of the numbers included a comma. I went to the credenza and located the ledger. August had never hired an accountant; he'd prided himself on keeping his own books, and I had always been content to let him handle all the finances. It was, after all, what he did for a living. Had done for a living, I corrected myself. The sharp pang of loss hit me again, but this time I was ready for it.

I flipped through pages of the ledger, ran my fingers down the columns of debits and credits. August had not been cryptic; notations in his careful script were detailed. I bit my lip as I scanned the entries going back six months. *"Maintaining first-class chicken coops isn't cheap, you know,"* August had once said to me. Indeed not.

I closed the ledger and sorted through the credenza cabinet where I'd found it. The ledger didn't encompass the sum total of assets. There had to be more. I remembered the box of computer discs Trey had taken with him. We didn't have a computer at home—August had said there wasn't a need and they were "boxy, ugly things"—which was undoubtedly why Trey had latched onto the discs. They almost certainly stored documents related to Trident. But might August have kept our household records on them, as well?

I found an accordion folder of bank statements and another of statements from Trident. My heart sank as I leafed through them. Our investments and most of our savings had been held through the company, of course. We kept a checking account with the local bank, but that apparently was maintained just to cover what was needed to run the estate. With Trey as gatekeeper, the funds I needed likely would be held as collateral to ensure my good behavior, just as he'd said the partner shares and life insurance would be.

I set aside the ledger and statements. For a few moments I just sat there. I could hear birdsong through the windows. Sunlight streamed in, glinting off the silver platters and loving cups that represented Lockeswood's equine conquests. They were silver plate; I wondered what I could get selling them as scrap. My eyes continued to scan the room. August was everywhere here. The room was redolent of him. It was why I hadn't wanted to enter; hadn't entered until this morning. I would stand at the threshold and just look. While my head knew others had walked in here since August's death—Leah to sort mail into various piles; Gloria in the random, silent meanderings she'd started since August's death—my heart still pretended that the last person to breathe the air in this room had been my husband. I hadn't wanted to break the spell.

But now the spell *was* broken.

I picked up a baseball from one of the shelves. It had a scrawled signature on it. I couldn't read the name and didn't remember whose it was. August had told me; it was signed by a minor-leaguer who'd gone on to pitch in a World Series. August had planned to give that ball to our son one day.

The mythical son.

I thought of the day August had first shown me the stable, all its dilapidated potential. The story he'd told, leaning on a doorframe, looking out onto all the land his family had once owned but didn't anymore. A legacy that went back to before the Revolutionary War.

Lockeswood is down to fifty acres . . . I would, of course, be required to maintain her at Lockeswood . . . My father could be such as ass . . . My mother doesn't believe it was an accident . . .

There would be no more Lockes. At least not in Drakes Forge. At Lockeswood.

I had failed August in not giving him a child.

He had failed me in dying before we could try again.

I could walk away. I was a Locke by marriage, not by birth. I didn't have to assume the burden of his family legacy, what August had seen as his duty. August was dead.

I looked around the office again. The bills piled high. The ledger with its sorry tale. I decided that the heavy *The Complete Works of Shakespeare* didn't look out of place at all on the corner of my husband's desk. The sunlight streamed in, and I thought of the library. Of what I'd seen happen during and after an estate sale.

I put the baseball back on the shelf.

I took a deep breath.

I needed to call the bank. I needed to hire an accountant. At least I knew where to find a good lawyer.

Before any of that, I needed a shower.

Fifty-Eight

I wiped the condensation off the large bathroom mirror with my hand and dropped the towel I had wrapped around my body to the floor.

The woman looking back at me was thinner than I remembered. Her collarbones strained high against pale skin and her cheeks had a hollow look. She didn't smile and I didn't do anything to try to make her. There were deep, dark circles that accentuated her blue-gray eyes. Her wet hair hung in thick ropes past her shoulders, partially hiding her breasts, and I wondered if, when it was dry, there would be strands of gray among the brunette. It seemed so long since I had looked, even longer since I'd cared.

What did she want, this woman looking back at me? Husband and home, the thrill of a child on the way, loving evenings in front of a fire in a library with enough books to last a lifetime.

That possibility, that future, was gone, because the first on that list—her husband—was gone.

So what else? Was there anything else to seek? To work for? I leaned forward, looked closely at the woman looking back at me. My breath clouded the glass. I wiped it away with a swipe of my hand.

"Stop acting like some star-crossed heroine, grab the pen, and write your own damn story," I said.

I turned away from her and left the bathroom to get dressed, leaving the towel on the floor.

Fifty-Nine

I called the bank. When I identified myself, I was immediately connected with the branch manager. Mr. Norwood offered his condolences. I thanked him but moved directly to the reason for my call. Nothing he told me contradicted what I'd seen in the bank statements. Did I want to make arrangements for a deposit of funds? he asked delicately.

Not at this time, I replied in my most confident tone. I would be in touch shortly. I thanked him and hung up.

I wandered around the house for a while to clear my mind, hoping some inspiration would come to me. I had some money left in the trust fund from Aunt Vieve. It should cover the bills that were waiting to be paid, but that would pretty much tap it out. The property taxes would be due soon, I knew—last month I'd heard someone down at the post office grumbling about the most recent assessments. And Trey was right—my paycheck wasn't nearly enough to keep Lockeswood running, based on what I had seen in the ledger.

As I walked, I took notice of the house's furnishings—expensive rugs, oil paintings, bronze figurines. I eyed a round claw-foot table with gilt along its fluted edges. Circa 1870s, I guessed—maybe an original furnishing from when the house had first been rebuilt after the fire. It was just the kind of piece I often sourced for one of my restoration projects—the right look, the right pedigree. I climbed the stairs to the second floor, passed by Gloria's rooms where strains of Wagner's *Parsifal* seeped out from under the door. We hadn't seen each other in days, and that was fine with me. At the end of the hall was the staircase that led to the attic. I made a mental note to spend some time up there to determine if there was anything I could sell.

The biggest expense was, of course, the horses. I grabbed *The Sun Also Rises* from the shelf of books in my bedroom. Hemingway's novel was the only one that had ever spoken to me about taciturn Grant, and that had been years before, but maybe it would speak again. Another book caught my eye—one I hadn't read in quite a while—but I took it as a sign and brought Kipling's *Captains Courageous* with me to the stable, as well.

Walking to the stable, I looked out over the expanse of acreage that belonged to the estate. It was beautiful. Rolling pasture, stands of hardwood, a meandering line of sycamores and willows that marked the course of a stream. Beyond the property, the gentle spine of the Blue Ridge Mountains created an idyllic backdrop. All that land, but it didn't really produce anything. We didn't farm, didn't raise livestock for any purpose other than pleasure, didn't have so much as a chicken on the property. I thought of my mother's garden, started decades before as Great Aunt Trudy's World War II Victory Garden, the vegetables and fruit my mother had gleaned from it every year. In the butler's pantry had been shelves and shelves of tightly sealed Mason jars; food my mother had canned, pickled, and preserved, ensuring there would always be something to put on the table. And all produced on less than an acre of land.

I thought of Georgia, raising a family in an apartment above the store that had been in her family for generations.

The horses were in the pasture just outside the paddock, tails swishing, noses to the turf, enjoying the mild spring breeze and sunshine. I went to the fence and whistled for Isolde. She ambled over and lipped my palm for the apple I pulled out of my barn coat pocket. I stroked her neck as she ate it. It seemed a little odd not to see Rockefeller tossing his head and stomping at the sight of me. Five. Lockeswood had five horses. I did the cost-per-month multiplication in my head.

Grant was sitting outside the stable on an old cane chair near an open doorway, repairing a piece of tack. I told him about my impromptu and unwelcome visitor. I left out the details of the conversation. And of Trey knocking me down. Before I'd left my room, I'd made sure my hair covered the welt where I'd hit the desk.

"So if you see his car or him around, could you let me know? Or better yet, just run him off the property?"

Grant had set aside the harness in his hands as I'd spoken, the corners of his eyes creased against the sun as he looked up at me from where he sat. "I'm happy to do that, Margaux," he said. "More than happy to do that."

I waited for him to say more. As the silence lengthened, I shifted the books from one hand to the other. "I also wanted to talk to you about expenses," I said.

"I took care of payroll."

Payroll. Damn. I'd forgotten all about payroll. We had Joe and Joe, who split a full-time job to muck the stalls, take care of the horses, and assist Grant with training and exercising. There was Leah. And then there was Grant, of course.

"There was enough in the petty cash box?" I already knew the answer, of course. I felt a flush creep up my neck.

Grant picked up the piece of tack again and a punch tool. "No. But payroll is taken care of. Not due again until mid-month."

"*Never be daunted. Secret of my success. Never been daunted. Never been daunted in public,*" said *The Sun Also Rises.*

"Thank you," I said to both of them. I couldn't think of anything else. My prepared speech about possibly selling the horses to Brodigan had fled my head. What could I say? You covered my payroll; want to buy my horses, too? You could still keep them here, if you want . . . "I'll get things settled by the middle of the month."

"There's time," he said. He focused on the harness in his hand.

I nodded. The silence stretched. I looked toward the house. There was a call I needed to make.

"About Janus," Grant said. He looked up at me. "It would give me great pleasure to run that man off the property if he shows up again. But I'm not always around. You know what you need here?"

My husband, I thought, but I didn't say it out loud.

"A dog," said Grant. "A young dog with big paws that'll imprint on you and doesn't have a history with Janus or any of that crowd. A dog that won't be taken in by stories of old hijinks and a custom-made suit. I could get you one. I know a guy whose bitch just had a litter two weeks ago. August gave him hunting privileges here the last ten years or so. He'd let me have one for you, if I asked."

I thought of Aunt Vieve's dog, the Colonel Brandon I'd come to know and love and that had lived with us when she'd died. He'd died, too, a few months later. Papa had said it was because he'd been old. I believed he'd gotten old when Aunt Vieve had died. We'd buried him in the backyard near the beech tree, wrapped in the Fair Isle sweater Papa had brought back from Aunt Vieve's Quebec City flat.

"I can't handle a dog," I said. "The last thing I need right now is something else depending on me to take care of it." I pressed the books against my empty womb.

Grant seemed to consider that, then stood up, the tack and tool in his hand. "Just think about it," he said. He waited for my nod of assent and then gave me a brief smile and disappeared into the stable.

I went back to the house, grateful he was there.

Sixty

I flipped through the spiral-bound notebook where I kept the phone numbers I didn't call frequently enough to know by heart, then dialed the personnel department at Trident Investment Group. The woman who answered offered her condolences when I identified myself, then asked me to wait a moment while she checked on the status of Mr. Locke's paperwork. I was on hold for several minutes before she came back, during which time I was reminded of my dislike for Barry Manilow.

"I'm sorry, Mrs. Locke, but we haven't received the necessary signatures from upstairs yet. I'm going to transfer you to the secretary there."

There were a number of secretaries at Trident, but only Cole Dempsey, as senior partner, had one all to himself. August, Trey, and Colin had all shared Danielle, a young woman with a small waist and a penchant for skyscraper heels. Danielle's dual aspirations appeared to be remaining Trident's preeminent source of gossip and getting a Missus in front of her name. So far, the first was well in hand.

The woman from the personnel department connected me with Danielle, explaining the request to her before hanging up. Danielle put me on hold, leaving me once again with Mr. Manilow. We were halfway through "Copacabana" before I heard her voice again.

"I'm sorry, Mrs. Locke. The paperwork is still on Mr. Janus's desk for his signature. I just asked him if he could sign it now and he said to tell you that he needs to discuss it with Mr. Dempsey and he'll get back to you soon." She paused. "Do you have a message you'd like me to relay?"

I could picture her leaning into the phone, hoping for a tidbit that would easily lend itself to elaboration. I remembered the Givenchy scarf that August and I had given her for Christmas, and I had a strong desire to see it tighten around Trey's throat, my hands holding either end.

"No, I'm sure he'll take care of it," I said airily. "I was just going through some paperwork and it came to mind." I hung up the phone.

After a moment, I picked up the receiver again and dialed.

"Danielle? Actually there is one other thing. Could you connect me with Colin?"

I HAD ASKED Leah if she would answer the door when Colin Dempsey arrived and show him into the library. It was a bit of an odd request for me to make—I almost always answered the door myself if I wanted it answered at all—but I didn't want to take a chance that he'd just drop off the box I'd requested and make a quick exit.

Hopefully Gloria would be elsewhere when he arrived. I found I missed the days when I could count on her routine; when her mood could be derived from the music emanating from her suite of rooms on the second floor. Her recent roaming had her popping up in unexpected places, often seeming distracted. I wondered if I should be concerned about it. But Leah would let me know if something were really wrong. Wouldn't she?

I heard the doorbell ring and looked around the shelves of the library, as though reassuring myself that all the actors in my play were in the wings and ready for their cues. "Ready? We're ready, right?" I said to them.

A few minutes later, Colin came into the room carrying a fairly large cardboard box.

"I left the framed pieces in the foyer," he said. "I hope that's okay."

I nodded, my eyes fixed on the box, my throat suddenly tight. He motioned with the box at a corner of the room, and I nodded again. I sat down in one of the wooden chairs around the library table where we kept some of the large photography and travel books, pointedly drawing my guest away from the two leather chairs by the fireplace. I looked out the window at the familiar landscape. I could see the dry-stack stone wall had fallen in several places and needed repair. Beyond it was open pasture, the tree line in new leaf on its far side. The colors blurred, making the view look like a Monet painting. I closed my eyes and focused on not thinking about the box in the corner. After a moment, I heard Colin pull out a chair and sit down.

"Thank you for bringing August's things from the office," I said, stuffing my emotions in a box of their own and sitting on the lid.

"No trouble at all. Danielle already had everything packed and ready to go." He faltered a bit. Shook his head ruefully. "That didn't sound right. Margaux, I was happy to drive everything out here for you. I know you likely don't have any desire to visit the office."

I turned to look at him.

"You're absolutely right about that," I said. "Which is another reason I'm so glad you're here. I was hoping you could help me with something."

"You're going to ask about August's paperwork." He grimaced at my look. "Danielle," he said, in explanation.

I fantasized again about the Givenchy scarf, but this time around a different neck.

"I read over the partnership agreement," I said. "It says that if a partner dies, the surviving partners will buy out his shares, with the proceeds going to his estate. It's pretty clear."

"It is. But that kind of transaction can take time."

"How much time? And what about the life insurance? Does that take time, too?"

Colin looked uncomfortable. "Not normally, no. But sometimes there are complications."

"Be bad, but at least don't be a liar, a deceiver!" I heard Tolstoy's *Anna Karenina* say. The book seemed to almost spit the words.

"Complications," I said flatly.

"There has been some . . . discussion . . . that maybe August's death wasn't an accident."

"The coroner ruled it an accident. What would it be if not an accident?" But my heart pounded in my chest. I remembered the conversation with August in the stable before we'd renovated it. The belief Gloria held about her own husband's riding "accident." A suicide, I knew, would invalidate the life insurance policy.

"Is there scotch in that decanter?" Colin looked over at the sideboard near the window.

"Of course," I said. "I'm being a terrible hostess. Please, help yourself."

Colin went to the sideboard and poured, remained by the window and looked out. I noticed his auburn hair still curled around his ears but was thinning in a tonsure at the top of his head.

"I can't get into a lot of detail, Margaux, but things are a bit up in the air at Trident right now. We've got some legal issues." He took a healthy sip.

"I gathered as much. What's going on with that company you bought in New Orleans?"

"I really can't get into it."

"The forceps of our minds are clumsy forceps, and crush the truth a little in taking hold of it." said *The Time Machine.*

"Well somebody better get into it. I need answers. And I want the life insurance money. And the partner shares money. I want access to August's investment account. This place doesn't run on pipe dreams, you know," I said, gesturing at my surroundings.

"I measured love by the extent of my jealousy."

The voice from Greene's *The End of the Affair* made me catch myself. I needed to use what the books were telling me. Looking at Colin's back, I realized sharp words wouldn't get me anywhere with him. I needed to take a different tack.

"I don't know what I should do next, Colin," I said, softening my tone. "I was hoping you could help. I'm so grateful you're here."

I let the silence lengthen. So did my books. He tilted up the glass to his mouth again, then turned and came back and sat down. "How are you getting along with Trey?"

"He stops by from time to time."

Colin nodded. "August's life insurance is part of his partnership agreement. So to get the insurance payment released requires a signature from Trident. There's a lot of . . . red tape . . . right now around anything involving the transfer of money. Particularly for partners. Although I'm surprised it's affecting the investment account. Have you mentioned this to Trey? Your best bet is to get him to sign the paperwork. Ask him to hand-deliver it to accounting with a word that it needs to go through right away. That should move things along. Maybe he'd do it as a personal favor. He and August were close."

I stifled the obvious retort. "Can you sign it for me? You're an executive of the company, right? Aren't you next in line?" I said instead.

Colin took another drink. I saw his neck flush. "By Trident's bylaws, only three people at any given time have this level of signature authority. Trey and my dad can sign. August could. I expect I'll be given signing authority, but it's part of the paperwork that's tied up. And nobody is willing to sign much of anything while Trident is embroiled in this legal mess."

I closed my eyes. "So everything is tied up with Trident. August's piece of the company, the life insurance, his investment account—and I can't get at any of it until the legal issue is resolved. Unless I can get Trey to use his influence." Of which you apparently have none, even with your dad a senior partner, I thought to myself.

"I'm sorry."

The silence stretched again. Colin set down his nearly empty glass. He looked at me across the table.

Breaking the silence for me, I heard Fitzgerald's *The Beautiful and Damned.*

"He had been futile in longing to drift and dream, no one drifted except to maelstroms, no one dreamed, without his dreams becoming fantastic nightmares of indecision and regret."

I let the silence between us linger, sorting through what I was hearing, determining what my next gambit should be. Maybe I could leverage Colin's indecision and regret. But I wasn't going to go to bed with him, even in the unlikely event that he got up the gumption to actually make a pass.

"I want to reassure you, Margaux, that whatever is happening at Trident, August was a good man. He was tough—I would never have wanted to be on the other side of a negotiation from him—but he was a good man."

"Thank you."

"I think his . . . flaw . . . was that he was very protective of those close to him."

"You think that's a flaw?" I said.

Colin leaned forward, his forearms resting on his spread knees, his hands folded together. He seemed to choose his words carefully. "I think it can be. What was your reaction when you found out August had fired your father's law firm?"

"Trident fired my father's law firm."

"Is that what August told you?"

I didn't reply.

Colin nodded. "August fired your father's law firm to protect your father and, by extension, protect you." He paused. "Your dad is amazing—knows corporate law inside and out, very thorough—but this situation we're in now . . . It's messy. And anyone involved is likely to get splashed."

I thought of the evening of Gloria's March dinner party when I had met August at the door, demanding he call Colin's father and "fix" the situation of Papa's firing.

"How messy?" I asked.

Colin dropped his head, looked between his knees at the carpet for a moment. "I've heard all the stories about August and Trey growing up."

"We've all heard the stories about August and Trey growing up." I was starting to feel a cold lump in my stomach.

"I know they were close friends since childhood," Colin continued, as though I hadn't interrupted.

I pressed my lips together, holding in any additional retort. I wanted to hear this. I hoped, when he was done talking, I would still want to have heard it.

"Not all pranks are harmless. And not everything can be categorized as a prank and swept aside. Sometimes people get hurt. Sometimes there are consequences."

"You think my husband died because of a prank? A Trey-and-August prank?" I heard my voice shake a little, and I drew my arms close to me, holding my elbows, as though that would help still my center, keep me calm.

Colin raised his head. "I don't know why August died. It was an accident, right?" He waited for my nod. "I'm talking more about Trey. Remember the story about how in tenth grade he picked the lock to the principal's office, got into the file cabinets, and changed a couple of his grades?"

"He was just shy of what he needed to get into the National Honor Society."

"Right. Ironic, huh? Cheating to get membership into an honor society?"

I tried to smile, but my mouth didn't fully cooperate. "I've heard the story," I said.

"Then you can help me finish it. Where was August while Trey was busy in the principal's office with Wite-Out and a pen?"

I held my elbows tighter. I'd never liked this story. I much preferred the one where the outcome was Trey wearing a cast on his arm, not an NHS cord on his high school graduation gown. "He was in the school parking lot with the hood of his car up, pretending it wouldn't start."

Colin looked at me, waited.

"He was distracting the school night guard, Mr. Clemens, to give Trey time," I added reluctantly. I saw where this was going. I didn't like it.

Colin nodded, seeing that I understood. "And Trey got into the National Honor Society, which helped him get into the college he wanted, which led to the internships he secured, which led to a strong start for his career, which helped him land a rich, well-connected Southern belle for a wife, and so on, and so on."

I didn't say anything.

"It's a bit of a non sequitur, but you know Trey was married that night the three of us met you at your parents' house, right?"

I nodded. "But I didn't know it then," I added. "Trey wasn't wearing a wedding ring."

"No, he wasn't. It's always been an accessory for him."

I thought of the New Year's Eve party. "Speaking of non sequiturs, how's Caroline?" I asked.

Colin smiled ruefully. "I wasn't her type." He picked up and drained his glass. He went to the sideboard and refilled it, though not as full as the first time. "What I want to say about that night at your parents', though—that was the first time I ever saw August step in and purposely thwart Trey. They usually worked hand-in-glove; once one set his eye on a goal, the other did what-ever he could to support it. This usually involved August having Trey's back, of course, rather than the other way around." A shy look crossed his face. "That's why I . . . stepped back. I'd known August long enough, and had enough respect for him, that I figured if three minutes in a room with you was long enough for him to decide to step in front of Trey, well—I likely didn't stand a chance."

Probably not, but we'll never know, will we, Colin? I thought. I smiled but didn't say anything.

After a moment Colin gave a sharp nod, as though to break his train of thought. He drained his glass again. "Well, I should be going," he said. "Thanks for the drink. And I'm glad we got to talk."

"Ah, lips that say one thing, while the heart thinks another," said *The Count of Monte Cristo.*

As I walked Colin down the hallway, past August's study and to the foyer, my mind tumbled over everything I'd heard from my books: regret definitely, and more than a bit of guilt. Desire? Still? Attraction, at least.

I could use these.

"Thank you, Colin," I said as he opened the front door. The fresh spring air drifted in, replete with the scent of the lilacs that flanked the walkway. I saw the framed artwork from August's office leaned against one wall, only the backing and hanging wire to witness whatever I put into play.

Colin hesitated a moment, then leaned in and gave me a quick kiss on the cheek. "My pleasure," he said. "I wish I could do more to help."

I put my hand on his arm, let it linger there, a light touch. "Me, too," I said. I kept my eyes steady on his.

He held my gaze, and I saw his neck flush again.

"But break, my heart, for I must hold my tongue," said a muffled voice, and I remembered the paperback copy of *Hamlet*

I'd stashed in the hall closet when I'd been hiding books from flea markets and garage sales all over the house.

"I'll see what I can do," Colin said, after a long pause. "I'm afraid my hands are pretty tied, though."

"I'll lend you a book on Houdini."

He laughed. He placed his free hand over mine. It was warm. "Dad comes back from New York on Thursday night. I'll talk to him. Try to convince him to sign the paperwork. For the life insurance, at least, and maybe to free up the investment fund, although that's less likely. And nothing is going to move about August's partner shares until the legal issues are resolved."

I knew both Colin and his father well enough to be able to predict the outcome of that conversation. Dempsey senior and Trey were cut of the same cloth. I tilted my head and looked at Colin with speculation. "How good is your forgery?" I asked. How deep is your regret and guilt? is what I really wanted to know.

Colin barked another laugh, this one without humor.

"Conscience doth make cowards of us all."

"You plan to have car trouble in the parking lot while I pick the lock to the principal's office?"

"If that's what it takes." I didn't laugh, didn't smile. I gave him my best damsel-in-distress-but-by-God-I'll-do-it-on-my-own-if-I-have-to look.

Colin's flush deepened, crept up his cheeks. He patted my hand, then pulled away and stepped through the doorway onto the front porch.

"I'll do what I can," he said again.

"Be all my sins remember'd!" Hamlet called after him.

I watched Colin walk to his car, returned his wave as he drove away. Then I went to the phone to call Grant.

Grant knew all the trainers from Pennsylvania to North Carolina. I needed to sell the horses, fast, to raise some cash.

Sixty-One

That night, I picked out a bottle of Châteauneuf-du-Pape that August and I had been saving for a special occasion. I selected a long-stemmed glass and poured, then turned to leave the rest of the wine in the open bottle on the kitchen counter to sour overnight. As I left the kitchen and turned out the light, I rethought that and retraced my steps to instead hook a finger around the neck of the bottle and take it with me.

Upstairs, I put on a negligee of black lace. It was a floor-length gossamer thing that left nothing and everything to the imagination. It had been a gift from August, although it had been as much for him as for me, he'd said when he'd first seen me in it. I stood now in front of the floor-length mirror, remembering the look in his eyes when he'd said that. A part of me expected to see him in the mirror's reflection, coming up behind me to put his arms around my waist. To lower his head to kiss my neck. I leaned my head back and closed my eyes, imagining it.

I went to our bed and lay there, sipping the wine. I let my mind meander as I thought about firsts and lasts. The first time we'd met. The last time we'd spoken. The first time he'd made me laugh. The last. Our first kiss. Our last. The first time we'd made love. The last.

I thought about how I easily remembered the firsts—had known when they'd happened that they were noteworthy—but had to work to recall the lasts.

At the time, I hadn't recognized them for what they were.

Sixty-Two

On Friday, Colin called to say he hadn't had any luck in his conversation with his father. I wasn't surprised. I thanked him for his efforts.

I'd taken the call in August's study and now looked at the pile of condolence cards and letters. I picked up the stack and brought it to the desk, started sorting through them. Many were business-related, people for whom August had been a colleague, client, or customer. A number were from those who had known us as a couple: people from the country club, the hunt club. There were some from people who had known me better than they'd known August, including a letter from the general manager of the St. Christopher Hotel, who offered me a long weekend's stay and services in their spa at no charge when I was ready for a change of scenery. I smiled, reading it, and set it aside. A spa weekend sounded wonderful. Later.

There was a card from Georgia, which surprised me a little, but maybe it shouldn't have. I knew Papa's routine still involved a visit nearly every day to Pillard's Sundry Shop for the morning newspaper. They would have heard the news.

Few people in Drakes Forge had sent cards; instead they'd sent food. Leah had frozen most of the casseroles and breads. I'd had her take home the dishes that didn't lend themselves to freezing; neither Gloria nor I had had much of an appetite those first days after the funeral.

Jacqui had sent a handwritten note, of course. It reminded me of the terse comeuppance card she had included in her thank-you note in March. I still had that card tucked away in my bedroom; had considered it almost a badge of honor at the time.

A note folded into quarters caught my eye, stuck between a condolence card from the landscaping company and one from the farrier. It didn't have an envelope with it and was written on simple typewriter paper. The cursive writing had a masculine look, long and slanted.

August,

You know I count you as my closest friend. What the hell are you doing? I can't get involved with this mess, and I can't believe you're risking everything to cover up what's been going on in New Orleans. Come clean, August. You've got me worried. Let's talk. I don't want you to get to the point that you do something stupid and irreversible.

Trey

My hands shook.

"*. . . something stupid and irreversible.*"

Leah had been placing cards and notes in this pile as they had arrived. This would not have been one of them. Trey hadn't come that morning just to take things away; he'd left something behind, too. For what purpose, I had no idea, unless it was just to rattle me. If it were for someone other than me to find, he would have left it in August's office at Trident. Then again, I couldn't rule that out. There was no saying this was the only note he'd planted.

I ripped the paper into small pieces and sent them down the commode to join the April calendar bits.

I seethed.

Then I remembered the card from Jacqui. Two can play that game, I thought.

I went up to my bedroom, took Jacqui's card out of the drawer of my writing desk where I'd kept it, the smaller envelope tucked into the larger one that had held the innocuous thank-you note—a Trojan horse for Jacqui's reprimand. I reread the card that had *Jacqueline Evelyn Halloway Janus* engraved on the front in royal blue ink.

It pains me to write this, but I am unwilling to remain silent any longer. I don't know all the details behind your actions, but I find them deplorable. You must be made to realize there are repercussions. Sometimes they can be a while in coming, but they do come. I take no satisfaction in being the agent of this, but feel it is necessary. Perhaps one day you'll agree I took the right steps.

J

Blue ink, I noted. I looked through the assorted pens and pencils I kept in the pewter tankard from my eighth-grade field trip to Colonial Williamsburg. A few tests on a scrap piece of paper told me which pen had the same color of ink. I pulled out the dinner party thank-you note from the larger envelope.

Dear Margaux,

Thank you for opening your home to Trey and me the other night. It is always a pleasure to spend time with friends.

Best regards, Jacqui

I practiced on scrap paper until I was sure I could do it. It was only four letters, after all, and Jacqui's handwriting was round and schoolbook perfect, not a scrawl.

I picked up the small envelope that perfectly fitted Jacqui's personal stationery and wrote her husband's first name on the front. I compared it to the thank-you note. I smiled, tucked the card back in the envelope, and set it on the desk.

Now to figure out how to get it to Trey. If it caused him some heartburn at home, I would be delighted. Even if Jacqui simply pointed out that the message had never been intended for him, at least he'd know that I knew the note he'd left for me to find was a fraud, too.

Satisfied for the moment, I changed into the clothes I wore for warehouse scavenger hunts. Time to tackle the attic.

Sixty-Three

I prowled around the house, looking for a few more items to round out my planned trip to Philadelphia. It felt a little odd—very mercenary—to look at paintings, rugs, and furnishings in my own home the way I did when I was at an estate sale or warehouse, but I needed money and no one was going to miss whatever I took. And it was all mine, anyway. I could do with it what I liked.

It still felt mercenary, though.

I paused in front of a half-open door. The nursery. It had been August's nursery, of course, and his father's before that. We'd had such hopes for this room, August and I. We'd even waltzed in here once, our bodies close, feet moving in three-quarter time to the sound and vibration of August's hummed lullaby tune, his head leaned against the top of mine. I hadn't entered this room since I'd lost the baby, but now I placed my hand against the wooden door. I needed to confront my ghosts, my regrets. Set them aside. They could—likely would—still be with me, ever present in some fashion, but I couldn't let them control me. I took a breath, pushed the door open, and stepped into the nursery.

Dust motes danced in the light streaming in through three long casement windows. The curtain rods were bare; I'd taken down the curtains for cleaning two months before. Hadn't put them back yet. The large oval rug in the room had been sent out, too, and the heels of my shoes on the wide, chestnut floorboards sounded loud in my ears. I cast my eyes around: a squat chest of drawers, a changing table, a rocking chair where I'd spent dreamy afternoons rocking, imagining a babe in my arms, the crib August and I had agreed would need to be replaced with a more modern version.

The crib.

Gloria stood at the head of the crib, one hand on the oak frame.

"Gloria," I said, "My goodness, I didn't see you there."

"What are you doing here?" she said quietly, flatly. She stood erect, regal, wearing a dress more suited to the 1930s than the 1980s.

"Well, I was just walking by and . . . "

"You and your noisy shoes. You would wake the baby."

Wake the baby?

"Gloria?"

"Get out."

"Gloria . . . "

"You have no place here, Margaux," said Gloria. She lifted her chin. "Do you?"

I took a breath. "I presume you mean in this nursery and not in the house."

"Well of course I mean the nursery. You have no child here. Will never have a child here. Isn't that true?"

I kept my hands at my side. There was nothing in my womb to cover, to protect. I didn't answer her.

"Go along, then. I'd like to spend some time with my memories. Alone."

I turned and left. I didn't hurry. I kept my steps rhythmic and steady. I don't know why it mattered to me; I'm sure my presence left Gloria's mind as soon as I was gone from the nursery.

I made it all the way to my bedroom before the tears came.

Sixty-Four

I was away the good part of the weekend.

I had loaded the bed of the pickup and driven to Philadelphia. My foray into the attic had uncovered mostly odds and ends that hadn't had much immediate sales value, but I'd found a set of four chairs under a drape, a console table with detailed inlay, and a tapestry that would be welcomed at a high-end consignment shop where I'd previously bought items for various restoration projects. I'd also included a painting of some unnamed ancestor or other with a judgmental expression I'd decided I just didn't want watching me anymore. Getting the furniture down two flights of stairs and into the pickup by myself had been an adventure, and driving all the way to Philly had been a hike, but I hadn't wanted word getting around that Margaux Locke was peddling the family heirlooms to keep a roof over her head. That would bring the vultures.

Grant had driven this point home to me. Try to sell more than a couple horses at a time, especially right after August's death, and word would spread like wildfire that we were in dire straits, he'd said. We might as well give the horses away.

Always an option, I had thought. Surely cheaper than maintaining them.

"You know I don't begrudge a bit what you did," Grant had told me as we'd stood outside the stable after Colin's visit, "but I could have sold Rockefeller in a heartbeat. I know the offers August had for him. And people would have completely understood why you'd want to sell him."

My eyes had narrowed. I had not been in the mood to be reprimanded for putting a bullet in the head of the horse that had killed my husband.

Grant had held up his hands. "Margaux, don't get your back up. I'm on your side. I told you once I thought you and Gloria were more alike than different. She came out here with a gun after her husband died in a riding accident, too." The corner of his mouth had twitched, and with a hitchhiker's thumb, he had indicated the copper weathervane on top of the stable. "But she put the bullets through that horse up there. Not Tristan. Him she sold, for the price of Asa's casket and the signed contractual promise that the horse would never again be within one hundred and one miles of Lockeswood Manor." He looked at the weathervane I'd had patched, admiration on his face. "She always was a helluva shot."

I hadn't told him that she had been roaming the house at random hours since August's death.

I got back late Sunday night to a dark house, nothing but the sound of tree frogs and crickets to welcome me home. I played a scenario in my head where a dog with a big blocky head and very large paws was there to welcome me. He would greet me with a sizable scrap of torn, charcoal-colored suit fabric in his mouth. I would praise him effusively.

I planned to take the artwork that had hung in August's Trident office to DC in the morning. I had an appointment with a gallery on K Street. No one would think it odd if I sold those pieces. They'd been appraised several years ago; I was confident that I could get enough for them to cover a few payrolls.

I got up a little later than usual, showered, and dressed. Remembering my trip to the Carlton with Aunt Vieve all those years ago and the reaction of the businessmen as she'd walked by, I put on a pencil skirt and a silky chiffon blouse and took the extra time to weave my hair into what I hoped looked like an elegant knot that left the nape of my neck exposed. Makeup helped with the dark circles that lingered under my eyes.

The hall phone rang as I was coming down the stairs.

"Margaux, it's Colin." The voice on the line was terse. "Call your father. Get him over to your house. The FBI is here packing up every file and computer they can get their hands on. They'll likely be paying you a visit."

I hung up the phone and dialed Papa. My hands shook, but I felt a tinge of elation at the thought of Trey standing by help-lessly as his office was packed up and hauled off. As I listened to the phone ring on the other end, I fantasized about him trying to push aside an FBI agent the way he had me. But the agent wouldn't fall to the floor. He'd stand his ground and deliver an effective right hook. In my imagination, fist connected with jaw with a satisfying thunk. Trey would fall to the floor and lie there, motionless. My fantasy was interrupted by Papa answering the phone. His voice quickly went from fatherly to businesslike.

"I'm on my way. If they get there before I do, ask to see iden-tification. If they are who they say they are, let them in and then just stand out of the way. Don't talk to them about anything other than the weather. Don't talk about August or business or what's going on at Lockeswood."

My heart was beating fast as I heard the click on the other end, but not because I was worried about what the police might or might not find in August's office. I trusted him. He wouldn't have anything in the house that could hurt me. And I'd found the note Trey had tried to plant as a seed of doubt.

I stood in the hallway, gripping the phone receiver. While I had a personal interest in Trident coming through this quickly and cleanly, I fervently desired Trey to go down in flames.

Which did I want more?

I thought of the card from Jacqui I had planned to get into Trey's hands to plant a seed of doubt of my own. What if the FBI had it instead? Would a wife's words to her husband help point a finger at Trey specifically, rather than Trident as a whole?

Probably not.

But what the hell.

If it led to even one uncomfortable conversation between Trey and the FBI, if it made him sweat a little bit more than he surely was sweating now, I'd count it as a victory.

I hung up the phone and ran up the stairs, debating where in August's office to leave the envelope so that it was likely to be scooped up by the FBI. I would put it with a couple of the condolence notes, I decided, and bury those in a stack of mail and invoices. Surely the agents would be gathering financial information. And it would look like Jacqui had accidentally included the envelope for her husband with the hand-delivered condolence note she'd sent.

At least that was what I hoped the FBI would think.

I rummaged around my writing desk. The paperwork from Philadelphia was where I'd set it the night before. Copies of the artwork appraisal documents were in a separate stack. I found Jacqui's dinner party thank-you note. I found the scrap paper on which I'd practiced her looping cursive.

But the envelope I was looking for, on which I'd so painstakingly forged Trey's name in Jacqui's handwriting, was gone, along with the ambiguous, damning note tucked inside it.

Sixty-Five

My father arrived mid-morning, dressed in his lawyerly best and carrying his briefcase. He kissed me on the cheek, patted my arm, and then sat me down at the kitchen table and poured coffee for both of us.

I told him about my concerns dating back to before Thanksgiving, August's frequent business trips to New Orleans, his assurances that everything was fine—that I just needed to trust him. I told him about the conversation I'd overheard between August and Trey when Trey had referred to Papa's law firm as the Boy Scouts. His face got tight at that, but he didn't interrupt me. I told him about Trey's unexpected raid. After a bit of an internal debate, I told him about Trey's assault on me. I told him about the freeze on our Trident assets and the life insurance policy. I waved off his inquiries about my finances as not an issue.

I told him what my books had said, all the way back to the evening with August and Poe.

I didn't tell him about the baby.

THE FBI NEVER came.

Sixty-Six

At least I just killed a horse.

Sixty-Seven

I first got word of Trey's death from Colin the next morning. He sounded stunned on the phone. So was I. Colin didn't have any details; just that Trey had died at home the evening before. He'd call me if he learned more.

I set the receiver back on the phone cradle and stood there in the hallway, my hand still on the phone as though to hold it in place. Or maybe to steady myself.

Trey was dead.

I waited for the elation, the satisfaction, but it didn't come. I imagined I felt a brush along the underside of my arm, the same touch I'd felt from Trey the evening we'd first met at my parents' house, the sexual electricity of it. I shuddered and rubbed my arm, dispelling the notion. The first coherent thought to cross my mind was that maybe now Colin would sign the life insurance paperwork for me. If the FBI hadn't scooped it up in their sweep of the Trident offices, of course.

I looked up to see Leah standing in the archway that led from the hall to the kitchen. She had a dishcloth in her hand, was wiping dry a cooking pot. Leah never put cookware in the dishwasher.

"Miss Jacqui killed him," she said. Unlike Colin, Leah didn't sound stunned. "It was self-defense. They got in an argument. He was yelling at her, wanting to know who she'd talked to about what, and she was yelling back that the FBI better not show up at her door, she'd had enough, and what would the Junior League and the neighbors think. My friend Becca is the housekeeper there and peeked in the living room just in time to see Mister Trey hit Miss Jacqui so hard across the face it spun her around against that side table by the windows. Do you know the one I mean?"

I think Leah wanted to make sure I was listening, not just standing there in a stupor. I nodded.

"Well, Miss Jacqui grabbed that bronze Remington statue of a cowboy that sits there. That one Mister Trey showed off to everyone and anyone who come over. He even showed it to me one time when I drove Miss Gloria there for a Junior League meeting. Becca said Miss Jacqui grabbed that cowboy around the neck with her hand all bloody from broken glass and come up swinging. Clocked Mister Trey upside the head, and he went down and didn't get up again." Leah paused, a satisfied look on her face. "The police came, along with an ambulance. Becca gave her statement, but they could see the marks on Miss Jacqui's face for themselves. She's real fair-skinned, so it was plain as day that he'd hit her, and hit her hard. And her hands was all cut up from the glass in that big framed wedding photograph she kept on that table." Leah finished wiping the pot, pushed back her bottle-red hair from her face. "Any man who'd hit a woman deserves whatever retribution he gets. Me, I'd like to have one of those bronze cowboys to keep on my nightstand."

She went back into the kitchen, then leaned her head out. "Miss Gloria asked that I make a casserole to take over tomorrow. She thought I should make a King Ranch, but I don't think Miss Jacqui would appreciate the cowboy joke. I'm sure Miss Gloria wouldn't mind if you came with us."

"Thanks, Leah, but I think I'll stop by on my own."

Leah considered me a moment, then nodded. Her head disappeared back into the kitchen.

I picked up the phone and dialed the Januses' number. I let it ring a dozen times, then a few more, before I set the receiver back in the cradle.

Sixty-Eight

It was mid-afternoon two days later that I rang the bell at Jacqui's front door. I heard it chime deep within the house. The neighborhood had always been quiet—upscale homes of brick and stone with expansive, manicured lawns and few children playing outside—but it seemed more hushed than usual.

Or maybe it was just my imagination.

I heard the rhythmic click of Jacqui's heels and the door opened. She was wearing tailored, camel-colored slacks and a crisp white shirt with a patterned scarf artfully tied around her neck. Her blond hair was pulled to the side in a half-braid that let the ends drape, unfettered, across one shoulder. She looked ready for a Ralph Lauren photo shoot, as long as she turned her face so that the camera wouldn't see the bloom of a dark bruise along her left cheekbone that makeup couldn't fully hide. Her right hand was wrapped in a bandage as pristine as her shirt.

"Margaux, please come in."

I recognized the smile of practiced hospitality. "Thank you so much for having me," I said. "I thought you might have had enough of casseroles, so I brought you these." I held out a bottle of Riesling and a book I'd picked up in DC when I'd taken August's office art to the gallery.

This time the smile reached Jacqui's eyes as she took the gifts. "Chilled," she said, looking at the bottle. "How perfect." She glanced at the book, around which I'd tied a green satin ribbon. "*Sense and Sensibility*. You know, I haven't read this since I was a girl. I was skimming through a copy at the club a couple of months ago and was just thinking the other day how I'd like to sit down and read it through again."

We made our way to the kitchen, pointedly avoiding the living room. I brought my purse with me, my favorite Virginia Woolf novel tucked inside. It was *To the Lighthouse* that had first spoken to me about Jacqui, her longing for intimacy. But it was *Sense and Sensibility* that had spoken the last time I'd seen her. *"I will be calm. I will be mistress of myself,"* it had said. I wanted to continue to think of her that way. I suppose it was a dare, of sorts, to the books. I hoped the one in Jacqui's hands would speak and the one in my purse would be silent, no longer identifying with her.

I watched her precise, economical movements as she opened the wine, selected two long-stemmed glasses from a glass-front cabinet, and then led us out onto the large sun porch on the side of the house. She settled in one of the overstuffed chairs and motioned me to take another. I saw a heavy afghan blanket draped over the back of her chair, the ottoman pulled up close. I recognized the signs of a woman avoiding her bed.

"Leah asked me to let you know she's more than happy to help Becca if you're planning to have everyone here after the memorial service," I said.

Jacqui used her left hand to raise her glass to her lips. "I appreciate the offer, but as I told Leah when she came over with Gloria yesterday, there isn't going to be a memorial service." She took another long sip of wine, her eyebrows raised over the rim of the glass. "It would be a little awkward, don't you think?"

"Pray, pray be composed, and do not betray what you feel to every body present," said *Sense & Sensibility* from where Jacqui had set it on a side table.

"I see your point. Just don't shoot the messenger," I said, keeping my tone light. "I promised Leah I'd extend the offer."

"No, I wouldn't do that. Shooting is more your style than mine."

"Touché." I took another sip but didn't put any effort into keeping up with Jacqui. I didn't particularly care for sweet wine, but I'd known Riesling was her favorite. "How are you doing?" I asked in a more serious tone.

She didn't say anything for a moment. *To the Lighthouse* filled the space.

"What is the meaning of life? That was all—a simple question; one that tended to close in on one with years, the great revelation had never come. The great revelation perhaps never did come."

"I could ask you the same question. It's been what, a month?"

"Thirty-four days."

"Thirty-four days," Jacqui repeated. She picked up the wine bottle and topped off her glass, then reached over to add a bit more to mine. "But you're doing better now than when I last saw you."

"Well, I've showered at least."

She smiled and looked off into the middle distance.

"Jacqui, do you want to come stay at Lockeswood for a while? Maybe you should give yourself some time away from this house."

"You two were really in love," she said, as though I hadn't spoken. It was a statement, not a question.

"Yes. We were." I still am, I thought.

"I could see it. The way he would watch you across the room. The little things he'd do, like how he would always pull out your chair for you, or help you on with your coat. You two had a snowball fight one time—do you remember? Trey and I were coming over for something or another and there you two were, laughing and covered in snow."

"I remember." A few volleys back and forth had led to a chase around the yard and ended with the two of us lying in the snow and August's hands working their way through layers of my clothing. It was probably for the best that we'd heard the crunch of tires in the driveway when we had.

"I wanted that," said Jacqui, and she lifted her glass to her lips again.

I recalled the look of sardonic amusement on Trey's face when we'd met them in the driveway. I hadn't been able to place it at the time, but now I thought I knew what the look on Jacqui's face had been.

"You just want someone to look at you and think you're beautiful and important and to love you," said Jacqui. "To believe that there's nothing better than spending time with you—just you."

"Intimacy," I said, remembering what *To the Lighthouse* had said about Jacqui. "Intimacy even in a crowded room."

She smiled and nodded. "Exactly. And you think it's there, or it's almost there, or it will be there—it's just going to take a little more time, a little more effort. So you put in the time. And the effort. But then you find out he never thought that, never felt that way at all. And you don't have a response." She poured more Riesling into her glass—turned to look at me. "Until, one day . . . you do."

"When so many hours have been spent convincing myself I am right, is there not some reason to fear I may be wrong?"

Jacqui's face betrayed nothing, but the wine bottle was less than a quarter full. I topped off my glass again.

"Leah told me what happened, Jacqui. She heard it from Becca. You had every right to defend yourself."

She smiled, but there was no humor in it. She held up her bandaged hand. "The stitches come out next week. Likely some physical therapy after that, although it's too early to know if there's nerve damage. We had a lot of framed photos on that table. I'm having the carpeting pulled up once I get word from my lawyer that everything is settled. Who knew hands and heads bled so much?"

"Your lawyer?" I wondered whether Jacqui was having the same trouble with Trident that I was—or maybe it was a different kind of trouble.

"To finalize everything that it was self-defense."

"Ah. Well, I imagine that will be settled pretty quickly." I paused. "Have you heard anything from Trident?"

She made a face, poured the rest of the wine bottle into her glass. "The FBI came the next morning and cleaned out Trey's office. Dempsey called, but I told Becca to tell him I was indisposed. That place can take a fast train to hell for all I care. It has nothing to do with me."

I hoped she was right about that last. "What about Trey's assets in the company? The life insurance and partner shares?"

Jacqui set her glass down in a deliberate motion. "Don't talk about money, Margaux, it's gauche." She looked at the empty bottle. "I have more wine in the fridge. Shall I open another?"

"I would love to, Jacqui, but I'm meeting Grant at five."

"I hear you're selling a couple of horses."

I shrugged, hoping it came off as casual. "I really don't have an interest in continuing the steeplechase circuit, so Lockeswood doesn't need that many horses."

She nodded. "Makes sense."

I got up to leave. "Think about what I said about coming to Lockeswood for a while. You know you're always welcome."

She took another sip from her glass, then stood to walk me to the door. "I'll think about it."

"For now she need not think of anybody. She could be herself, by herself," I heard *To the Lighthouse* say, and I knew that Jacqui wouldn't accept my invitation.

I decided I needed to read that book again.

"Let me know if you need anything," I said.

"Actually," said Jacqui, as we reached the front door. "There is something. I'm chairing the Junior League Benefit again this year—Leah drove Gloria over for one of our planning meetings while you were away this past weekend. I need help writing all the thank-you notes to the people and companies that give silent auction items. We already have a couple dozen donations."

"Of course," I said, fixing a smile on my face as I stepped out onto front porch. Thank-you notes. Lovely.

"That would be wonderful. I'll let you know the date and time of the next meeting. I can't trust just anyone with this, you know, since I insist they be hand written. And you have very nice handwriting, Margaux." She paused. "It's almost like mine."

Sixty-Nine

The whispers became murmurs, though still unintelligible. I
knew it was either Gloria or Leah entering the library.

The books of Lockeswood, I'd learned, spoke often among
themselves about the two of them but very rarely included me
in the conversation. Perhaps it was because Gloria had lived
here, been mistress here, for so long and with so much passion
and emotion. Books fed off passion and emotion, I'd decided,
adding that to the list of books' proclivities Aunt Vieve had told
me so many years before. Many of these books had been here
when Gloria had arrived as a bride. As to why they murmured
about Leah—well, I honestly didn't know a lot about Leah. She
kept largely to herself, but Gloria liked and trusted her, and so
apparently the books did, too. And Leah's family was Welsh.
Her mother had come to the United States in her early twenties,
after marrying an American soldier who'd won her heart. The
Welsh had a long history of connection with a world not everyone
could see or hear.

I could have tried to figure out from which position on which
shelf each voice came—by now I knew this library very well—
and then make hypotheses about who was saying what. But books
had been my ally and kept my secrets for years—why shouldn't
they have a few of their own?

I turned my head from where I sat in my usual leather chair
and saw Gloria perusing the shelves. She had her cane at her
side but wasn't leaning on it the way she had in the first weeks

following August's death. I closed and set *The Little Prince* in my lap and gazed at the windows. Raindrops trailed down the panes of glass, leaving paths of artistry, grays and more grays behind them as the day departed.

"It's a good evening for a cozy chair and a book," Gloria said, leaving the shelves to come toward me, no book in her hand. "Rainy days always are." She set aside the cane and sat down in August's chair, smoothing a thick chenille throw over her lap.

I bit my lip and reminded myself that the chair wasn't hallowed ground. August's spirit wasn't sitting in it, his eyes smiling at me over the rim of a book or newspaper. It was just a chair.

"You're not too chilly?" I said. "I can close the windows." The weather was blustery, but I'd opened them anyway. I liked the sound of the rain on the new leaves outside, the scent of the turned earth of the flowerbeds.

Gloria waved a hand. "Not necessary," she said. "I'm not so frail as all that. And Leah will bring in some tea for me shortly. I know you prefer coffee; I asked her to bring that, as well."

"Thank you." I waited, curious. Gloria looked very different than she had since August's death, and different from the stern and forbidding figure I'd encountered in the nursery last week. The deep lines around her mouth were softened, the dark circles under her eyes lessened. I hadn't heard music coming out from under her door this evening as I'd come down the hall, which meant she was wandering again. I was glad this was one of the days that Leah stayed late. Tea was coming, Gloria had said. I wondered if it truly was. If Gloria had truly remembered to ask for it, or perhaps if Leah just knew to bring some around this time, here or upstairs, just in case.

Gloria stroked her hands along the leather arms of the chair. "I bought this chair for Asa, you know," she said. "We used to spend most of our evenings in this room. Asa would be in this chair, usually with some dusty biography or history or some such thing. I would sit where you are now with a novel, and August would sit at the table over there and leaf through the big travel books. We had one on Africa and he would spend hours with it and others from the shelves, jotting down notes, planning the safari trip he'd take one day."

"I think that book is still there on the table," I said. I remembered flipping through the pages, admiring the stunning photography taken in a place I doubted I'd ever visit. "Did he ever make the trip?" I didn't think August had ever told me about a safari.

"No, I think he was still planning it when Asa died." She paused. "A lot of things changed then."

A silence stretched. Gloria put her hands in her lap and looked at the flames. It was late in the season for a fire, but May evenings could still be chilly and I liked the ambiance. After a while I opened my book again, nonchalantly seeking where I'd left off in the story. It didn't really matter. I was just reading paragraphs here and there anyway. My typical evening visit with another old friend.

"I understand you went to visit Jacqui today," Gloria said, in an abrupt change of subject.

"I did. It's a shame about Trey," I added, remembering Gloria's fondness for him.

She snorted. "Don't lie, Margaux. You're not good at it."

I felt a surge of annoyance. Détente hadn't lasted long. "Fine. You're right. I don't think it's a shame at all." I pushed aside the other feelings I'd been battling since leaving Jacqui's house that afternoon.

I kept my eyes mostly on the book in my lap but saw a satisfied smile flit across Gloria's seamed face. She stood again and picked up her cane, walked to another of the bookshelves, and ran her long index finger along the spines as though seeking a specific volume. I turned a page, pretending to be intent on *The Little Prince* as he traveled from planet to planet.

We watched one another covertly, she and I. We both knew it but maintained the charade of literary distractedness.

Gloria selected a book and took it off the shelf. Opened it and turned a few of the pages. "Were the reporters still there?"

Reporters? Well, I guess Trey's death would have been a bit of a sensation.

"No, no reporters. The street was quiet." I remembered Jacqui's pristine outfit when she'd met me at the door.

"Ah, that's good. They were there when Leah and I went over. I guess Grace was right."

I turned another page. Grace? I was curious, now. But I wasn't ready to give Gloria the satisfaction. I let the silence stretch.

And stretch.

Gloria broke it first. Her voice was low, conversational, almost as though she were talking to herself—almost.

"Grace made me swear never to let anyone know Horace was hitting her—and she never, ever fought back—exactly because of what just happened with Jacqui. Grace never wanted to risk a scene. Well, and it's understandable. She *was* president of the Junior League." Gloria shook her head. "Reporters," she said, her voice dripping distaste.

My head came up. The hell with sparring with Gloria. If a woman was out there being beaten by her husband while others knew and stayed silent... I ran through the Rolodex in my head—Grace? Horace?—I came up empty. I didn't think this was anyone in the village. And Jacqui was president of the Junior League . . .

"Who is Grace? And Horace?"

Gloria took her time. Answered my previous silence with a measure of her own. She closed the book in her hands and put it back on the shelf. Moved farther down, out of my line of sight. "Jacqui's parents, of course. Didn't you know? You really should pay more attention to family lines and connections, Margaux."

Gloria came out from behind the shelf and made her way into the next row, her eyes seemingly intent on book spines. She again moved out of my line of sight. "Grace and I grew up together. Best friends. Were in one another's weddings, as a matter of fact."

I took a breath. Then reached over for the glass of pinot noir I had on the side table and took a healthy swallow. I remembered Papa telling me about his father taking the belt to him and his brother when they'd been boys. That had been a different time, I reminded myself. Things were not the same now. Jacqui was proof of that.

"So Jacqui's dad was beating up her mom, and you were Jacqui's mom's best friend and knew about it, but neither you nor anybody else said anything because she was president of the Junior League and reporters might show up?" I said finally, carefully.

"Oh, don't make it sound so cut and dried, Margaux," said Gloria with exasperation. She leaned her cane against the book-shelves and took down two books, held one in each hand. "Why on earth do we have two copies of *The Postman Always Rings Twice*, for heaven's sake? I doubt we'd ever have two people in the house wanting to read it at the same time. Oh, I see. One is a first edition. Fine, then. The other should go in the rubbish bin." She put them both back on the shelf.

I made a mental note to check on the value of that particular first edition while my brain sorted through Gloria's other remark.

I was still framing a response when Gloria continued.

"I tried to warn her, you understand. I knew what Horace was by the way he treated his horses. You can always tell from that. But Grace was willing to overlook a great deal. We'd lost so many gallant men in the First World War, you know. That was just a bit before our time—we'd been in grade school—but Grace's mother instilled in her a real fear of being a spinster. It was silly, and I told her so many times, but fear can drive a lot of actions."

"Jacqui wasn't afraid," I said. I don't know why I felt the need to defend her—it wasn't like she and I were close friends—but I'd heard what *Sense and Sensibility* had said about Jacqui's internal struggle to be mistress of herself and what she'd said when I'd visited—her wish to have with Trey what August and I had had. She'd fought for it. A losing battle, as Orwell's *1984* had noted at their New Year's Eve party: *If you loved someone, you loved him, and when you had nothing else to give, you still gave him love.*

"Oh, I think she was afraid," said Gloria.

That brought me up short.

"Trey hit her, and her response was to clock him upside the head with his own goddammed statue," I said. "That doesn't sound like fear, to me."

Gloria came out from the stack and looked me in the eye. "Doesn't it?"

I paused. Remembered yet again Leah relating what had happened at the Janus house that evening through the eyes of Becca, their housekeeper. Jacqui aghast at the thought of the FBI pulling up in front of their home in multiple vehicles, uniformed officers striding purposefully toward the front door. *What would the Junior League and the neighbors think?* Why hadn't she done what she always did? Gone somewhere else—in her head or physically—and pretended nothing was happening? That everything was just fine?

Because they'd been in an argument, I answered myself.

He was yelling at her, wanting to know who she'd talked to about what, and she was yelling back that the FBI better not show up at her door, she'd had enough, and what would the Junior League and the neighbors think.

Why would Trey believe his wife had talked to the police or the FBI?

Could it be because of a note? A note in Jacqui's handwriting that I'd intended to plant for the FBI to find in my house if they raided August's home office?

Which they never had.

And the note had disappeared, in any case. Along with the envelope on which I'd forged Trey's name in Jacqui's handwriting. Both gone from the desk in my bedroom.

I heard a rattle of cups and turned my head to see Leah enter the library, a tea tray in her hands. Her eyes met mine and she winked.

"Miss Gloria, I'm heading out soon, but I thought you might like some tea here in the library before you go up."

"Thank you, Leah. Did you bring the coffee for Margaux?"

"I've got just what she likes in the evening, Miss Gloria." She raised her eyebrows at me and tilted her head at the sideboard that had scotch, bourbon, Madeira, and port, but I smiled and gave a quick shake of my head, indicating my half-full wine glass. I really liked Leah. She had a firm head on her shoulders and had been around Lockeswood for more than twenty years. If things were going sideways with Gloria, I'd need her help. I just had to figure out a way to be able to keep paying her.

I picked up my glass. I took a deep breath, thinking about the missing note from my room. About the source of the argument between Trey and Jacqui.

Maybe my mother-in-law's wanderings weren't as random as they appeared.

"Gloria," I said, "Did you take an envelope off the desk in my bedroom and take it to Trey and Jacqui's house?"

Leah stiffened midway through her pour.

Gloria turned to look at me, her hand poised to pick up her teacup. She raised her eyebrows, then nodded at Leah to continue. Once the cup was filled, she added a careful dribble of sugar from a teaspoon, stirred, and then picked up the cup and raised it to her lips. She sipped, sat back in August's chair, and sighed in contentment.

"Well, of course I did," she said. "You'd addressed the envelope to Trey, practiced his name over and over again to get it just right, as I recall. I thought you'd consider it a kindness, since I was going there anyway, to make sure it got into the right hands. You were away for the weekend, remember? Philadelphia, was it? Did the chairs fetch much?"

I glanced at Leah, who didn't look at me as she set the teapot down on the tray. Loyalties, I reminded myself. Leah had been with Gloria a long time. Well, I still liked her. I'd just have to remember there were eyes in the house.

"Enough," I said casually. "What did Trey say when you gave him the envelope?"

Gloria frowned. "Well of course I didn't actually hand it to him, Margaux. I'm not your servant or some Western Union person. And Trey wasn't anywhere near the house that afternoon, anyway. He's a hound dog, but he knows better than to sniff around at a Junior League meeting. I found a moment to go to his office and tuck it into a corner of the leather blotter on his desk where I was sure he'd find it. By the way, you really should lend a hand with the Benefit, you know."

"Jacqui already asked me," I said. "I told her I would."

Gloria nodded, satisfied. "Good."

Leah puttered around another moment or so, still avoiding my gaze, then finally said her goodbyes for the evening and left.

I got up and poked at the fire, added another couple of split logs. Waited for Gloria to say more. Had she read the note? Of course she had. She said she'd seen the scrap paper with my attempts at writing Trey's name in Jacqui's round and looping script. What had she made of it all? Had that note really set in motion the argument that had led to Jacqui delivering a killing blow? Well, Trey *had* hit her first. Jacqui had said the police agreed it was self-defense. So I couldn't be complicit, right? Or maybe it was just her lawyer who'd said it was self-defense. Could someone be a conspirator in a self-defense murder?

Criminy, where was my wine glass? I needed to sit down and think.

I set down the poker and found my glass. Went in search of the open pinot noir bottle and poured. Came back to my chair and sat down.

All the while, Gloria sipped her tea.

I could read her body language; I suspected she could read mine.

We both knew who was going to break the silence first.

"You read the note," I said. It wasn't a question.

Gloria gazed at the stoked fire and sipped from her cup.

"What did you hope to accomplish by taking it there?" I asked.

She turned to look at me.

"What did *you* hope to accomplish by making Trey think Jacqui's note was written for him?"

I slid my eyes from her gaze to look at the fire. I sipped my wine. Felt a gust of wind come in through the open window. It was raining in earnest now. I considered my answer.

"Maybe a little mayhem," I finally admitted. "Some discomfort. Something to rattle him a bit." I turned back to see Gloria watching me intently.

"A little mayhem," she repeated. "Trey was good at that. Of course, August was typically around to defuse the situation before it got too out of hand. But not this time. August wasn't there this time." Gloria turned her head and looked again at the flames. I saw her jawline tighten and her fingers grip the edge of the chair's leather armrest.

"We all have our time machines, don't we. Those that take us back are memories...And those that carry us forward, are dreams."

The first spoken words I'd heard from this library about Gloria in a long time. I turned my head and placed it, the book that felt so much emotion in the room that it must speak loudly enough for me to hear. It was H.G. Wells's *The Time Machine.*

"I didn't expect it to get so out of hand," I said. "I didn't know the FBI would raid the Trident offices on Monday."

"No, you couldn't have known that. Would it have mattered? Would you have changed anything?"

There was a hint of softness, perhaps even kindness, in her tone. I took a breath. Considered her question. We were alone. It was just the two of us. No one else in the house to hear. I voiced what I'd been thinking the whole evening, what I'd been thinking since my conversation with Jacqui that afternoon. What I needed to say out loud to somebody.

"I think Trey read that card and thought Jacqui had talked to the police. About whatever the hell is going on at Trident and that company in New Orleans they acquired. And then the FBI raid at Trident upped the ante. Trey just wasn't thinking clearly and, like you said, August wasn't around to help. To do—I don't know—whatever it was he'd been trying to do. And so then it all spun out of control. The argument, Trey hitting Jacqui, the broken glass, the . . . the everything."

I took another breath. Took another drink from my glass.

"I didn't mean to kill him."

There. I'd said it. I'd taken responsibility. Well, in this room, anyway. In the hearing of Gloria. And the books.

I looked up from my hands clutching my wine glass to see Gloria watching me, her head at a slight tilt.

"Why ever not?" she said softly, after a moment. "A life for a life."

I realized my mouth was slightly open, waiting to say words I just couldn't seem to conjure following such a statement. I closed it.

The books were silent, as well.

Gloria dropped her eyes to where I'd set *The Little Prince* on the side table. "Trey killed my grandchild. Leah found the bloody towels you tried to hide."

My hand went to my belly and my jaw tightened. "I miscarried," I said. I'd never said the words out loud, and I felt them sting my eyes as they left my mouth.

"And if you hadn't been spending every waking moment worried and agitated about what was going on at Trident and what August might be doing to yet again protect Trey? If August had been here, taking care of family, instead of flying all over hell and gone trying to untangle whatever Gordian knot Trey had himself in this time?"

"I might have still miscarried."

I had a lot of crimes to lay at the door of Trey Janus, but I had never considered this to be one of them. But Gloria did.

Gloria stood, took up her cane. She came over and touched my arm.

"For after the Battle comes quiet," said *The Time Machine* as she left the room.

Seventy

Y ou should always generously tip the waitstaff.
This is particularly true if the waitstaff is providing tips
to you.

I don't know if it was Trey specifically who insulted the waitress and made her decide to cooperate with the authorities who
had, apparently, been hovering for a number of months. It fits
my fantasy to think it was his actions that led to Trident's spec-
tacular downfall, but I rather doubt it. From what I had heard
and seen over the years, Trey was always ready to be charming
and generous when the cleavage was.

And, judging from the newspaper articles and tabloid photos,
Celia Connor, the New Orleans waitress/business owner who
allegedly had been providing insider-trading tips and other information to Trident executives, definitely had the cleavage to
get Trey's attention.

New Orleans hosted a number of business conferences each
year. And the more the businessmen drank, the less guarded
they tended to become in their conversations, with each other
and, occasionally, with the attractive waitress who truly appre-
ciated their perspectives on business, both during and after
her shift.

Celia was savvy and ambitious. And waitressing was just a
side gig, as it turned out. A means to an end. She was leverag-
ing the information she gleaned to finance a very comfortable
lifestyle, with considerable success. Her biggest client was

Crescent Investments, a small financial firm that seemed to have a magic touch in predicting the real estate and other markets.

After building the business over the span of a dozen years or so, Crescent Investments's founders had considered several acquisition offers. All but one had been withdrawn after the company hadn't adequately addressed some due diligence concerns. But a merger-and-acquisition team from the reputable firm of Trident Investments, led by a charismatic and up-and-coming partner, the late Trey Janus, had recommended to the Trident Board of Directors that an acquisition move forward. With the endorsement of senior and founding partner Cole Dempsey, it had.

Acquisition complete, Trident had also continued to retain the services of Connor Consulting.

This had gone on for a couple of years but, apparently, had come to a swift end the previous October, according to one newspaper article. A personal relationship and disagreement between Celia Connor and a Trident senior executive were more than inferred in a torrid tabloid headline that featured a photo of Celia serving drinks over the shoulders of a group of businessmen. I peered at the black-and-white photo, but the lighting in the New Orleans locale had been dim and the photo was grainy. I couldn't see the face of the man whose hand was touching the underside of the waitress's forearm, but the gesture was familiar.

I was relieved that Trey's name wasn't in that tabloid article, for Jacqui's sake. There had been a piece in the Richmond newspaper about his "accidental" death at home and several references in various financial pieces on the sudden death of a senior Trident executive, but nothing Jacqui couldn't weather. I was grateful to Becca, her housekeeper—both that she had been there as an eyewitness to corroborate self-defense and that she'd not shared the more lurid details with the press.

Celia Connor was cooperating with the authorities, who were still investigating the scope of the insider-trading scheme. It was conjectured she might receive immunity in exchange for testimony. Indictments were expected.

I wasn't really interested in the financial and legal details of who did what to which company and why it mattered—although I suppose I should have been. I was mostly looking for August's name. It wasn't there, it never appeared, and I was glad. Whatever he'd been hiding when "The Tell-Tale Heart" had spoken to me had likely been about his efforts to help Trey while not getting himself entangled in the legal morass. There had ended up being financial repercussions for us, but that wasn't his fault. August had tried to take care of me, protect me, while living up to his own code of loyalty and integrity.

I thought about the stress he must have been under, no doubt trying to fix what was broken at Trident while protecting his oldest friend. I recalled him flexing his left fist the day of the race. It had been weeks since he'd ridden Rockefeller. I remembered Grant storming out of our house days before. "Cranky," he'd said, when August had asked him how the horse was. Grant hadn't wanted August to ride in that race.

I suspect it was my husband's pride, his need to demonstrate control over something when things had clearly been spinning out of control at Trident, that had made him get on the horse anyway.

Another name that didn't appear in any of the newspapers was Papa's. August had protected him, too. Papa took great satisfaction in declining the request to represent Cole Dempsey.

Seventy-One

Within three months, Jacqui had Trey's study gutted and completely redone, making it her own. She started an interior design business. No one can bully with such charm and grace as a southern belle, and it wasn't long before she had quite a few families associated with the Junior League, the country club, and the hunt club on her list of clientele. I wasn't one of them—I couldn't afford it—but I did help out at the Junior League Benefit. I became quite skilled at writing eloquent and effusive thank-you notes.

It took a while, but I was able to get the life insurance money. Copies of the paperwork arrived by registered mail, Colin's signature at the bottom. He didn't include a note. It was all very official.

I didn't expect to ever see much from the investment account we'd held at Trident, nor from August's partner shares. I didn't follow the court case. I made a few more visits to the attic, thinned some clutter from hallways, walls, and rooms, and drove to Philadelphia a few more times. These strategies yielded far better returns.

Seventy-Two

1985

I came down the stairs, my shoulders squared and ready. This had been harder, more energy-draining, than I had expected. I carried with me a half dozen books. For the first time in a long time, the novels in the library had been of no help at all. I hoped the ones I'd brought down with me from the hide-away collection in my bedroom might be more forthcoming. I was out of my element.

My guests were no longer in the library. Nor were they in the living or dining rooms. The doors to August's study were still shut tight.

No one knows more about what goes on in a house than the help.

I made my way to the kitchen.

"They went out to the stable," Leah told me. "They said to me you knew they were going there." At the look on my face, she turned to peer into the oven, her eyebrows raised and her lips pressed tight.

The doorbell rang.

I muttered a curse word, eliciting a lowering of Leah's brow.

THE MAN STANDING on my front porch was exceptionally tall, very slim, and neatly dressed in a cambric blue button-down shirt and khakis. He carried a large black case. He looked at me expectantly.

I returned the same look.

"Hi," he said. "I'm Tom Jayson."

I waited for more.

"Can I help you?" I finally said.

The friendly smile didn't waver. "I'm here to tune the piano."

"The piano?"

We did have a piano. It was a beautiful baby grand that resided in the living room, positioned for maximum effect opposite the French doors that led to the terrace. The only time I'd ever heard it had been at a party several years ago before when Jacqui had sat down, lifted the black lacquered cover that protected the ivory keys, and played several bars of a complicated melody I hadn't recognized. No sooner had people turned to see who was playing than she had closed the cover and abandoned the upholstered bench.

Maybe it did need tuning.

"Are you Mrs. Locke?"

"Yes, but I don't recall making an appointment to have the piano tuned."

The smile slipped a bit, and Tom Jayson set down his case and reached into his shirt pocket to pull out a small piece of paper. "Mrs. Gloria Locke," he read. "Urgent request. Ten a.m. on Monday. Please be prompt." He glanced up from the note and I saw a trace of a blush. "My wife makes the appointments," he explained. He looked at his watch. "It's ten now."

"Ah. Gloria Locke," I said. "That's my mother-in-law. It's her piano. Please, do come in."

The fact that it was Gloria's piano was the only reason it was still in the house. I could have saved a few trips to Philadelphia with what I could have gotten selling that piano. But it had been a wedding gift to her from Asa. Early arthritis had robbed her ability to play at the level she felt sufficient, and so I'd never heard her, but August had told me of fond memories coming home from school or an afternoon riding to hear the strains of Rachmaninoff, Mozart, and Vivaldi.

I led Tom Jayson to the piano, made sure he was settled in with his black case of tools, and let Leah know of our additional guest.

Then I left the house for the stable, suppressing the urge to run.

The brisk autumn air felt good on my face. We hadn't had a hard freeze yet, so most of the hardy annuals and late perennials were still in bloom in the terrace borders, accented by the colorful hues of leaves fallen and blown from neighboring maples, oaks, and hickories.

I had had no interest in planting anything following August's death, and less in paying the landscaping crew to do it for me. I had been content to see it all barren or taken over by weeds.

Mother, however, had not been content. Two days after August's funeral, she had disappeared early in the morning, coming back after lunch with the car laden. She'd spent the rest of the afternoon and the next morning digging and planting and watering.

I knew I'd never get Gloria to admit it, but the border looked far lovelier after Mother's makeover of perennial flowers and herbs mixed with annuals than it ever had with the usual uninspired beds of impatiens and marigolds the landscaping crew installed each year. Mother had planted it so the perennials would continue to fill in until, in a few years, I wouldn't need to replenish the annuals at all. Even with Papa's success, she had never abandoned her frugal streak.

Perennials, she'd reminded Papa and me that April evening over tea and bourbon in the library—tea for her, bourbon for Papa and me—come back year after year. They may look like all life has left them, but give them time to rejuvenate, and then sunshine and spring rains, and they're back more beautiful than ever.

I'd declined to explain to Mother that I wasn't a perennial. I'd known she'd meant well.

What I did love about the border was that it had come from home. The flowers and herbs she'd brought to me were plants divided from those in her own garden.

Gloria, thankfully, had refrained from further comments about getting my mother a job with the landscaping crew. Our relationship was different now. We never spoke again about the conversation on a rainy afternoon in the library. She'd gone back to playing Vivaldi records, rather than Wagner, and I always offered her a silent toast in the evening as I made my way down the hallway past her rooms and her music to my own bedroom, a full wine glass in my hands. I'd meant what I'd said to Trey: this was Gloria's home, and would be for as long as she wanted. As for her part, she had defended me—in her own way. We still observed our separate boundaries, but it was a different kind of détente now. One I thought would last.

I hopped over the asters, creating a shortcut to the stable while leaving two deep footprints in the garden soil.

THE STABLE SEEMED empty with only two horses and a donkey named Mauzy that we were fostering from the local rescue society, but it would be emptier yet, soon. The mare I'd bought the November before August's death would foal in a few months, and Grant said he had a buyer interested in both of them, if the foal was born healthy—and particularly if it were a colt. I'd be sorry to see them go; it felt like severing yet another tie to the life August and I had had. Between Jacqui's renewed good graces and my own outreach, I had a steady stream of restoration work. I was meeting expenses and had most of the life insurance money tucked away against a rainy day. Still, I didn't feel completely at ease. I wanted to be sure I didn't overextend.

If I started stocking a butler's pantry with home-canned goods, then I truly could say I'd become my mother.

I heard them before I saw them. I walked around to the paddock.

Georgia's girls, Mila and Trees, were working in tandem, as I'd seen them do so many times over the last few days. Mila was holding Isolde's bridle and stroking her nose while Trees stood on the paddock fence, one long, slim leg reached out to slide across the horse's broad, bare back. Isolde, for her part, was obviously aware of the distraction subterfuge underway. But the years had made her mellow, and she seemed to like the attention. I relaxed.

I stayed by the fence, watching. I heard Isolde whicker and knew she was aware I was there. It was the girls I didn't want to spook. Mauzy wandered over to me, and I scratched the donkey behind her long ears. She had a wonderful temperament and would be company for Isolde once November and her foal were gone. But Mauzy was a rescue, and rescues always come with a history. She'd been keeping clear of the children.

The girls had the same long blond waterfalls of hair as Georgia. They and their younger brother were spending a few days with me while Georgia and Stuart enjoyed a much-deserved getaway. It had been Mother's idea. I wondered now if there had been an ulterior motive. Three days down, three to go, and I was positively exhausted.

THE GIRLS HAD first been introduced to me as Pamela and Patrice. Born minutes apart, they resembled one another but were fraternal twins, not identical. Along with the blond hair, they had inherited their mother's ability to make everything around them seem a mere satellite. Georgia and Stuart's car had been barely out of the driveway before the girls had corrected me.

Pamela went by Mila.

"Spelled with an 'i' instead of an 'e' because otherwise everyone pronounces it wrong," she said with the lofty air I remembered in Georgia when we, like the twins, had been ten years old. "It's pronounced 'Meela'—that's how Daddy says they say it in French-Canada."

I had looked expectantly at Patrice, knowing that if one had customized her name, the other would have, too.

She had held out her hand for me to shake. "Please call me Trees," she said. "Spelled with two 'e's but with a soft 's,' not like what's growing outside with trunks and leaves."

I had shaken her hand, then her sister's, repeating the names to confirm that I was pronouncing them correctly.

It was likely I was being bamboozled, but that was okay.

Maurice was just Maurice. I was grateful. He had looked at me with eyes that had seemed too solemn for a seven-year-old and asked where the bathroom was.

I WAITED UNTIL Trees was settled on Isolde's bare back and the reins were firmly in her hands before I spoke.

"I have a saddle in the barn," I called. "Do you want it?"

"No," said Mila, at the same time Trees said "Yes."

It wasn't Mila trying her best not to slide off the mare's broad back.

"Ride over to the far door," I called to Trees. "I'll come around and meet you."

The barn swallows had left weeks before, and I missed them. I trusted that they'd be back in the spring, but without them, the mud dauber nests in the eaves seemed like halves of drab, misshapen clay pots attached to the wood. There wasn't any song in the stable to accompany the faded majesty of champion ribbons and framed news clippings going back nearly a century and the homey scent of hay, straw, leather, and horse. As I walked by, I nodded to the framed photo of Asa as he clenched his cigar in his teeth, mid-leap.

If I ever had to leave Lockeswood, I'd take that photograph with me.

I stroked November's nose as I walked down the line of empty stalls to the tack room. It had been my name for her since she'd come to us, and both August and Grant had indulged me. She was mild-tempered and hadn't seemed to care what we called her so long as the Joes provided clean straw in her stall and oats on a regular schedule, and I always had a carrot or apple in my pocket when I came to visit. I'd renamed her November because it was the month I'd bought her, a month of celebrating bounty, and nothing bad had ever happened to me in November.

I sure as hell would never name anything April.

I met the girls at the paddock door and Mila immediately put her arms out for the saddle I carried.

"Do you know how?" I asked.

She gave me a withering look. I raised my brow. I'd grown up with her mother and so had survived withering looks from a master. Mila's had a ways to go. I didn't relinquish the saddle to her tug.

"Of course," Mila said. "We went to horse camp this summer. I've done this lots of times."

I gave her the saddle. I watched as she turned to the horse.

"It'll be easier, Trees, if you get down," I said.

Trees slid off the horse and came to her sister's side. I handed her the blanket. They looked at the saddle, at Isolde, and then at me.

"It's a weird saddle. Where's the thing where you hang on?"

"It's an English saddle. It doesn't have a horn on the pommel. Western saddles have a horn."

"Why do you use an English saddle?"

"Because you use English saddles for hunt riding and point-to-point races, and that's the history of Lockeswood, so Lockeswood only uses English saddles."

They looked skeptical.

"Why would you ride with an English saddle if we're not in England?" said Mila. "This is America," she said.

I smiled, recognizing her mother's tone—and logic.

"But it's not western America," said Trees to her sister. "There are no cowboys in Virginia. Daddy likes Clint Eastwood cowboy movies," she explained to me.

"There are a lot of different kinds of saddles to fit a lot of different purposes. At Lockeswood we have English saddles."

"What's a point-to-point?"

Criminy. I glanced at the tack room, but no voices came drifting around the corner from the books shelved there. I thought longingly of the stack I'd brought downstairs but had inadvertently left in the living room with Tom Jayson and the piano.

"Where's your brother?" I was looking for a distraction, but I felt a stab of guilt realizing I had no idea where one-third of my charges were at the moment.

"He's with the old lady."

Oh God.

"He is?" I hesitated, but these were Georgia's daughters. "Why?"

Mila shrugged. "He really likes her music. Yesterday he was humming while we had breakfast and then Trees saw the old lady. She was just standing there by the doorway listening to him, and when he saw Trees looking, then he looked, and then he stopped humming. And then she got kind of mad."

"Mrs. Locke got mad?"

They looked at each other, then at me.

"The other Mrs. Locke," I said. "I'm Mrs. Locke, but so is she." I hesitated. "She's like a Grandma Locke. But I don't think she'd want you to call her that. So just call her Mrs. Locke."

Mila looked skeptical. "You're both Mrs. Locke?"

"It's like the men who make the deliveries call Mom Mrs. Peche," said Trees, "but when Grandmamma comes to visit, they call her Mrs. Peche, too."

Mila seemed to consider this. "It would be easier to call her 'Old Mrs. Locke' and you 'Young Mrs. Locke.' It would avoid confusion," she added.

Maybe just once. I could thrive for a long time on even once seeing Gloria's reaction.

Trees rolled her eyes. "The delivery guys don't call Grandmamma 'Old Mrs. Peche.'"

"I doubt the other Mrs. Locke and I will be in the same room at the same time very often, so I don't think there will be any confusion. Why don't we just stick to Mrs. Locke for both of us." I felt a sudden, intense urge to invite them to call me Aunt Margaux. I squashed it. Maybe someday. "So the other Mrs. Locke got mad. And then what happened?"

The girls looked at each other again.

"She pointed a finger at Maurice and said 'You—what is that you're humming?'" Mila recited this in full thespian splendor: imperious, shoulders back, arm raised, and index finger extended. It was quite a good imitation, actually. "And Maurice just set down his spoon and said 'Bach.' And then the old lady said, 'You, boy, come with me.' And we all looked at Miss Leah, and she nodded, and so he went."

Trees nodded in corroboration, then threw the saddle blanket over Isolde's back and smoothed it. She looked at her sister expectantly. The two of them worked together to put the saddle in place. Isolde was patient. I made a mental note to bring her another apple. Or two.

I'd have my own reward later: my evening glass of wine. Or two.

"And this was yesterday?" I tried to remember what the kids had done all day. I had been busy with correspondence and bills in the morning, and a call in the early afternoon that had lasted longer than expected, but I'd taken them to the diner in Drakes Forge for lunch in between, and we'd gone to a neighboring farm in the late afternoon to pick out a pumpkin they could take home for Halloween, which was coming up in a few weeks.

"He's back with her today," Trees said. "She said they're listening to some records first and then she's going to teach him piano."

MILA WAS CLEARLY annoyed that I kept this first foray on Isolde to the paddock, but Trees nodded and rubbed Isolde's nose when I explained that the mare was pretty old for a horse and we needed to take it easy on her. The girls took turns riding around and around the paddock for more than an hour. I did feel a bit of guilt for lying when, after twenty minutes of this, Isolde had stopped at the paddock gate, tossed her head twice, and given me a look. I knew that look. It was the why-the-hell-aren't-we-out-there look. But I didn't feel guilty enough to change my mind and open the gate.

"An extra apple, I promise," I murmured to the horse when we finally led her into the stable.

"YOU HAVE A lot of stalls," Mila said as she and her sister brushed Isolde in tandem, one on each side.

I remembered making a similar observation to August the afternoon he'd given me the stable for renovation.

"I do," I said. "I used to have more horses, but keeping horses is expensive. So after my husband died, I decided I didn't need so many."

"It's really hard to do what you want when it's expensive," agreed Mila. She stroked Isolde's neck, and the horse turned her head and whoofled softly into her hair. She giggled.

"Mama told us that your husband died," said Trees. "I'm really sorry. She said that he was so handsome and you two were so in love." Her brush slowed. Something must have shown on my face, because she turned her attention back to Isolde. "Is that his picture in the frame by the tack room?"

Georgia had never even met August. But I could imagine the story she would have spun for her daughters. I wished I had been there to hear it. I managed a smile. "No, it's of my husband's father. He rode horses in point-to-point races, too."

"And that's how he died? Mama said it was a riding accident."

"Actually, that's how they both died—my husband and his father. In riding accidents." I kept my voice calm and even as I said it. "That's why I'm so concerned about safety around horses," I added.

Criminy, now I sounded like a television public service announcement.

"*That* explains a lot," I heard from Mila on the other side of the horse. I saw Trees duck under the horse's neck, and there were a few moments of intense whispers.

"All done," said Trees brightly, popping back up on my side of Isolde.

I wondered what they'd whispered. I made a commitment to myself to find a photograph of August on horseback to hang near the one of Asa.

November, ever curious, was watching us from her stall as we prepared to go back to the house. Trees stopped to stroke her nose. "When will the baby horse be born?"

"A few months. Sometime in January."

"Could we maybe come back then and see it?"

"Of course," I said. "But November and her foal will go to a new home in the spring, so we'll have to work out with your mom the best time for you to come."

"You're selling them?"

"Yes," I said. I pulled a sugar cube out of my pocket and gave it to Trees. She offered it to November on an open palm, as she'd been taught. I gave another to Mila and motioned for her to offer it to Isolde. I walked over to Mauzy with the last cube in my pocket. Farewell sugar cubes had been my routine for years.

I could hear the girls behind me conferring in low tones as we walked back to the house.

"Could you change your mind, if you wanted to?" asked Trees. "November is so sweet, and if you kept the baby horse, I could come on weekends to help you take care of it and maybe even for school vacations. Joe said he would teach me how to muck a stall."

I nodded contemplatively, as though I were seriously considering this option. Hell, maybe I was. It was nice having the kids around. Exhausting, but nice. I wondered what Georgia might think about regular visits. I looked toward the house. I'd left my third charge on his own for quite a while. Hopefully Tom had finished his ministrations to the piano and Maurice was getting along with the "old lady."

"And maybe if I got a horse for Christmas, I could keep it here," said Mila in what I knew she thought was a very reasonable tone. "There's lots of room in the stable. And I heard Mama tell Papa, 'What's one more? Throw another potato in the pot!' So having just one more horse here would be okay, right? I'll bet if I ask Joe and Joe, they'll say they won't even charge more."

"Your mom said that about one more?"

The girls exchanged a glance. Mila smiled, convinced her reasoning had me on the brink of capitulation. "Last week," she said. Trees nodded.

I returned the smile, but for a different reason. I hoped Maurice would get a brother, to even the odds.

Seventy-Three

On Thursday, Georgia and Stuart arrived shortly after supper to pick up the children. There was the chatter of reunion as the girls told Georgia about English saddles and how well they could now ride, Mila no doubt setting the stage for her Christmas request. Maurice took Stuart by the hand and led him into the house, and Georgia raised her head when she heard the notes of an elementary version of Bach's "Jesu, Joy of Man's Desiring" wafting through the open door. It drew her in, the rest of us in her wake. I watched from the periphery, the boy's small head bent in concentration, the nascent dexterity of his young fingers on the black and white keys. Gloria didn't come downstairs, but I imagined the notes sliding up the bannister, down the hall, and slipping through the small space between the bottom of her door and the chestnut plank floors to reach her.

Georgia deferred the invitation by the girls to visit the stables with a "next time," and we walked out to the car. The girls piled into the back seat, chattering, while Stuart loaded suitcases and the Halloween pumpkin into the trunk. I saw Maurice looking up at the second-floor windows. I didn't see Gloria, but that didn't mean she wasn't there, watching. Maurice lifted his hand in a small wave, but he didn't smile. I wondered if he saw something I didn't. He started to climb into the car, but then came back to stand quite close in front of me. He tilted his head back to look up at me.

"Can I come visit again?"

He was so solemn in his request that I resisted the urge to tousle his hair, convinced it would impinge on his dignity.

"Of course, Maurice. You are welcome any time. Please consider the doors of Lockeswood open to you."

It was a very formal response, and apparently exactly the correct one. He nodded vigorously and smiled as I hadn't seen him do the entire time of his stay. It was quite enchanting, and I caught a hint in the son of what in the father must have captured Georgia's heart. He climbed into the car and was instantly relegated by his sisters to the middle seat.

"And you," said Georgia, grasping me by the shoulders. "I can't thank you enough. They weren't too much, I hope?"

"Of course not," I said. I was absolutely drained after only just shy of a week. "I'd love to have them back again—and you and Stuart, too."

Georgia hugged me, hard. It startled me, but then I returned the hug with equal fervor. "Congratulations," I whispered.

She pulled back and looked me in the eye. "Spooky," she said. And she smiled.

Over my friend's shoulder, I saw Maurice watching us. He lifted his hand in a small wave.

Stuart kissed me three times, alternating cheeks, before climbing behind the wheel.

I watched the car as it turned from the driveway onto the road, all the windows down and hands waving, heading back to the crowded, love-filled apartment over Pillard's Sundry Shop.

I went into the house and, on my way to the library, scooped up the books I'd left in a pile by the piano. They hadn't spoken while Maurice had been playing. Even without my books, I thought I had Mila and Trees pretty much nailed. But their brother was a puzzle. An interesting puzzle.

Seventy-Four

I stayed with her.

The doctor had left. He hadn't forced the issue when Gloria had refused medication to "make her comfortable." He had placed a hand on my shoulder as he'd exited the room. "I know my way out," he'd said. It had been late. I'd sent Leah home hours before.

It was the way he'd said it. The squeeze on my shoulder. This was different from the times before. All the times before.

I moved from my usual post standing by the door to the chair at Gloria's bedside. I heard her labored breathing. It was almost in rhythm with the cirrus of the wind in the trees outside. She'd insisted, weeks earlier, that the windows never be closed. Under any circumstances. Leah had put towels on the floor when it had rained. Changed them if they had become drenched. There were extra covers on the bed and a cozy throw on the chair to thwart the late autumn chill. The windows had not been closed.

I set my hand on the bed next to hers. Not touching.

Never presuming to touch.

I looked to the corner where a turntable perched on an art deco stand. The turntable was one of the newer models, a gift from August and me a few Christmases before. I didn't know the origins of the stand. I'd asked, admiring the art deco lines. My inquiry had been deftly deflected. There was a story there, I suspected. A story I'd never know.

"Do you want me to put on a record?" I asked.

For as long as I'd lived in this house, music had emanated from this room, slipping under the closed door and seeping down the hallway like a fog, a barometer of the mood of its occupant.

But not recently. Not since she'd decreed the windows be left open.

Gloria moved her head slowly to one side of the pillow, then the other, her eyes closed.

I nodded. Remembered that her eyes were closed and she couldn't see me. Resolved that I would stay, regardless of my welcome—or lack of it.

She patted the mattress next to her, not far from where my hand rested.

"Sit by me," Gloria rasped.

I got up and perched on the edge of the bed. Gloria patted the mattress again. Taking a breath and half-expecting a caustic remark, I settled more firmly next to her.

We listened to the wind in the trees for a while, the occasional lowing of a cow in a distant field. It was a kind of music.

"I heard you, that night," Gloria said without looking at me. Her voice this time was stronger. Was more than a rasp. Had a hint of its prior command. "I recognized your voice." She opened her eyes and looked at me. They were clear. She'd refused the medicine that might have clouded them, shrouded her thinking, her memories.

I knew which night she meant. A night the year before when I'd stood on the lawn where we'd said our wedding vows and howled my anguish up into star-spangled night sky. August.

August.

"That wouldn't have been hard," I said lightly. "It was just you and me in the house. No one else around. Who else could it have been?"

"That isn't what I mean." She turned her head on the pillow and closed her eyes. Her hand twitched. Her fingers opened. It was an invitation.

Her first. Here at the end.

I took her hand. Her skin felt dry and thin. She was a book of brittle onion-skin pages and faded ink. To read her would be to destroy her in the process.

"I recognized you," my mother-in-law said in a whisper, her eyes still closed.

She didn't say anything more. Neither did I. I held her hand. I listened to her labored breathing and the music of the trees through the windows she'd insisted be left open.

A little before the sky began to lighten, I heard only the trees.

Seventy-Five

I rode Isolde out to the creek and left her to graze. I swung my small satchel to rest against my back and climbed up onto the lowest of the thick, spreading branches of a sycamore that leaned over the burbling water. I was finally sleeping again, but I'd been up most of the previous night—this time by choice—noticing as I'd finished the last page of *Fahrenheit 451* that the sky was beginning to lighten.

Settled on the tree branch, the music of the creek splashing over smooth rocks rising up to me, I gave my attention to the question that had been insinuating itself into my consciousness for days, like a previously unnoticed character in an often-read book.

It's really hard to do what you want when it's expensive, Mila had said.

Well, yes, but the bigger question for me was what did I want? August was gone and, with him, all the plans we'd made over wine and after making love and during long horseback rides and on winter evenings watching the flames dance in the library fireplace.

There would be no children.

I was young enough yet, Mother had told me, after the traditional year of mourning had passed.

But I knew myself.

August was gone.

There would be no children.

But there was still me. I had my life, with lots of it left—God willing and the creek don't rise, as the saying went.

So what did I want?

Sense and Sensibility was happily-ever-after. A place where women on the edge of destitution were rescued by men who, despite their faults, were good and solid at their core and loved with fervor; who recognized the worth of a good woman and spent the time and energy necessary to woo and win her. Where joy sprang from the ashes of sorrow. It had been Aunt Vieve's touchstone, as she'd danced through the world when others had chosen to walk.

Fahrenheit 451, on the other hand, was a dystopia. A place where, amid so many things going wrong, people found peace and hope and companionship by carrying books in their heads. By, in essence, becoming books. There wasn't a happy ending, but it wasn't really unhappy either. Things hadn't turned out the way the main character, Guy Montag, had wanted or expected. The world had been smashed. But, in some ways, it had then been ready to be remade. It could be what you made it to be.

And then there was *The Secret Garden*—the book Aunt Vieve had said was my touchstone. A place where magic was recognized in what so many others took for granted.

I balanced myself to stretch out my legs on the branch, crossed my ankles, and looked out over the late-autumn landscape: the rolling fields, the lines of blackboard fence and dry-stack stone walls, the sycamores and brush along the creek. Not too far in the distance, mostly hidden by a fold in the hills, I could see the stable cupola and its weathervane of a rider, the horse mid-leap, its two patched bullet holes invisible at this distance. Not everything I could see was mine—only the smallest part of it—but the view, the peace I derived from it, was all mine to enjoy from the sanctuary of this tree.

Mine so long as I could hold on to it.

What did I want?

I should feel lonely, I supposed. Georgia's children had left and I had none of my own. August was gone, and there was a hollow in me that I wasn't sure I ever wanted to fill. Gloria was gone—my nemesis and my champion—and with her, a promise made by August to his father was fulfilled. Lockeswood had been Gloria's home until the day she'd died.

I pulled *The Secret Garden* out of my satchel and smoothed my hand over the cover of the book Aunt Vieve had sent me all those years before. I turned the pages, reading paragraphs and lines at random. I practically knew the words by heart. Knew these characters by heart, just as I did those in *Sense and Sensibility* and *Fahrenheit 451*. These books were thoughts, emotions, and ideas born in someone's imagination, translated into ink on paper. Read, again and again, by one, by many, over years, perhaps decades, until the characters had become real in the collective consciousness, achieved life, as much flesh and blood as those who had once walked the earth but were now dust beneath it.

Paper and ink.

Flesh and blood.

No, I wasn't crazy.

What did I want?

I let my gaze drift from my perch to where Isolde contently cropped, enjoying the sunshine that filtered through the trees. I thought about November and the foal that would arrive just before the spring. The swallows would come back soon after. It'd be a shame to have them return to so many empty stalls. Maybe Grant knew of someone looking to board a horse or two. It would help meet expenses. Jacqui had offered to recommend me to someone who was looking to transform an old house into an epicurean destination.

I turned the pages back to the beginning of the book and settled in to spend time with an old friend.

Seventy-Six

2019

I awake to sun streaming through the windows, almost a glare. From this I know without looking that the snow is likely nearly to the windowsill, creating a blanket of light-reflecting white. I stretch, easing muscles and joints that protest, then relax at finally being relieved from the confines of my chair. I gather up the chenille throw around me and walk to the window, setting my fingertips against a pane of cold glass.

On a whim, I open the window and lean out to scoop up a handful of snow. It's a numbing powder in my hands and, despite the windbreak of trees around the house, a gust carries most of it away. I draw my arm back in and shut the window, then sip the melting snow from my cupped palm. It tastes like lavender, which reminds me of the hand lotion I slathered on last night.

At the sideboard, I pour a finger of tawny port. I sip it, letting it coat my lips and tongue, savoring the mellow heat in my mouth, the feel of it going down my throat. I'm not usually an advocate of port this early in the day, but it's the nearest thing to hand and far better than the taste of hand lotion in my mouth. Glass empty, I pour another finger.

I carry the glass with me to the far window to look out again, touching as I do the mid-pirouette figure in the small, still-unframed painting of a blustery day in Quebec City. I hope this is all the snow we'll get for a few days and that the plow will make it out to me before too long.

I've a flight to catch on Thursday.

My cousin Bobby, one of Uncle Matthew's twin sons, has invited me to spend some time with him and his family. He and his wife have two children, a boy and a girl. He sent me a photo of them.

I won't tell Bobby, but the first thing I noticed in the photo was my creepy monkey lamp sitting on an end table in the background. I retrieved my reading glasses and peered closely at the photo, wishing I could shoo the two children in the foreground out of the way for a moment so I could better see my old friend.

Chester looks just as he did the last time I saw him, all those years ago in Quebec City. He's still holding up the magic of illumination, but I don't know that he considers a sofa end table "a position of trust." Then again, it's definitely a very prominent location. I look forward to meeting Bobby's wife. The woman who would agree to have that lamp in her living room is the kind of woman I'd like to get to know.

The children look much like any other children. They clearly have been asked to stand still for this photograph, interrupted from whatever they would rather be doing. The boy, who Bobby says is nine years old, has crusts of mud on his sneakers and looks like he could use a haircut and to be thrown, clothes and all, into a bathtub of warm, soapy water.

I take this to be a very good sign.

The girl recently turned eleven. She is holding her arms behind her back, but I can see the corner of a book peeking out from behind the embroidered peasant shirt she wears over a pair of jeans. I dearly wish she were holding the book in front of her so I could see what she is reading. But, then again, I'm not surprised she has it behind her back. According to Bobby's letter, she's a voracious reader and has quite an imagination. It's creating some problems at school.

I suspect she and I will hit it off.

Book Club Discussion Guide

1. As a young girl, Margaux was bullied for being different and felt she had to hide who she was—even from her family. Do you think she was right to hide it? Or would things have been easier for her if she had trusted her parents with her "secret"?

2. In what ways do you think Aunt Vieve shaped the woman Margaux became?

3. Both Aunt Vieve and Margaux were drawn to particular novels and the characters in them. Are there any novels or characters in literature that have been of particular importance to you?

4. Do you think Margaux's reaction to her husband's death was appropriate? Why or why not?

5. On her deathbed, Gloria tells Margaux, "I recognized you." What do you think she meant?

6. Are there any characters in *Paper & Ink, Flesh & Blood* with whom you particularly identify? If so, why?

7. How would you use Margaux's "ability" if you had it? Would you see it as a blessing or a curse?

Acknowledgments

Paper & Ink, Flesh & Blood has been my labor of love and a work in progress for a long time. I am so delighted and grateful to see it come to life but could never have done it without the help and encouragement of a number of people.

I want to thank those in the MFA Program at Queens University in Charlotte, North Carolina, for seeing in me a diamond in the rough and giving of their time and talent to make it shine. Thank you, Fred Leebron, Melissa Bashor, and Michael Kobre for building and nurturing a dynamic MFA program that let me pursue my dream while still working a demanding full-time job. The Queens MFA faculty is made up of amazing and dedicated professors, but I would be remiss if I didn't particularly mention Pinckney Benedict. I requested him as my professor for my last semester because I'd been told by several trusted fellow students that he would be the toughest critic I'd likely ever encounter and, while I might emerge from his workshops a bit scathed, I would cheat myself if I didn't take advantage of Pinckney's experience, perspectives, and mentorship. Wow, were they right. Thank you to those ladies— Gisele Firmino, Nikki Melton Shaw, and Carrie Neil—as well as to Jenn Goddu, Ellen Birkett Morris, Steve McCondichie, and Jim Button for your friendship, your critiques, and for sharing your writing with me. An extra thanks and a hug to Nikki for one particular late-night conversation during my first MFA residency that encouraged me to write about the demons that had haunted me for decades. I didn't believe you at the time that it would help banish them, Nikki, but you were right.

I'm so grateful to my husband and best friend, Tim, for supporting my decision to go back to school to earn my MFA in Creative Writing. It was after reading a short-story assignment I'd written about the background of a minor character in the novel I was attempting that Tim said, "Forget the other story. This character is your novel. She's really interesting. I want to know more about her." And Margaux Locke became the centerpiece of my debut novel. I'm grateful to my son Quentin for long hours spent talking about books and authors and stories and aspirations. And to my son Zach for cheering me on as I juggled earning a master's degree while climbing the corporate ladder at my full-time job.

I want to thank my dear friend Martha McGrath for being my reader and advocate and not letting me give up when sometimes the obstacles to publishing this novel seemed too much.

Thank you to the late, great Brett Phillips, who was my first editor and then my boss when I joined *Loudoun Magazine* in the early 2000s to write regional lifestyle pieces. It was Brett who wrote the letter of recommendation that helped me get accepted into the Queens MFA program. He touched so many lives with his acerbic wit and keen observations. Rest assured, Libby, that Brett will live on in the shared memories of those of us lucky enough to have known him.

Thank you to the publishers who gave me permission to quote passages from some of literature's best-loved and best-known works.

Perhaps most of all, I want to thank Steve McCondichie, fellow Queens alumnus and founder of Hearthstone Press, for taking a chance on me and Margaux. I'm so blessed that you are my publisher, Steve. I hope this debut novel is just the beginning.

All of you have been a great blessing to me, and I thank the Lord God for bringing each of you into my life at just the right time.

And Another Set of Acknowledgments

I am greatly indebted to the work of the authors and publishers of the novels and plays quoted in my novel. Among them:

About Rita Mace Walston

Rita Mace Walston is a first-generation American, born and raised in Michigan. After moving four times in five years without staying in the same time zone, she and her family settled in rural northern Virginia. She lives there with her husband, three dogs, one cat, and eighteen chickens. Rita was the writer of the About.com website *Germany for Visitors*, a contributor to regional lifestyle and business publications, and managing editor of *Loudoun Magazine*. She is a graduate of the Queens University MFA program in Charlotte, North Carolina. *Paper & Ink, Flesh & Blood* is her debut novel.

RitaMaceWalston.com
Facebook.com/RitaMaceWalstonBooks
Instagram: RitaMaceWalston
Twitter: RitaMaceWalston

Rita is available for speaking engagements, readings, and book club visits. Please send inquiries to Rita@RitaMaceWalston.com.

Photograph by Molly Steele, msteelephotography.com

Share Your Thoughts

Want to help make *Paper & Ink, Flesh & Blood* a bestselling novel? Consider leaving an honest review of this book on Goodreads, on your personal author website or blog, and anywhere else readers go for recommendations. It's our priority at Hearthstone Press to publish books for readers to enjoy, and our authors appreciate and value your feedback.

Our Southern Fried Guarantee

If you wouldn't enthusiastically recommend one of our books with a 4- or 5-star rating to a friend, then the next story is on us. We believe that much in the stories we're telling. Simply email us at southernfriedkarma@gmail.com.

Do You Know About Our Bi-Monthly Zine?

Would you like your unpublished prose, poetry, or visual art featured in *The New Southern Fugitives*? A bi-monthly zine that's free to readers and subscribers *and* pays contributors:

$100 for essays and short stories
$50 for book reviews
$40 for flash/micro fiction
$40 for poetry
$40 for photography & visual art

Visit **NewSouthernFugitives.com/Submit** for more information.

Also by Hearthstone Press

Sanctuary: A Legacy of Memories, T. M. Brown
Testament: An Unexpected Return, T. M. Brown
Purgatory: A Progeny's Quest, T. M. Brown
Ariel's Island, Pat McKee

CPSIA information can be obtained
at www.ICGtesting.com
Printed in the USA
FSHW020301010720
71675FS